# Becoming
# Madame Mao

BOOKS BY ANCHEE MIN

RED AZALEA

KATHERINE

BECOMING MADAME MAO

# Becoming
# Madame Mao

## Anchee Min

Houghton Mifflin Company
*Boston · New York*
2000

For information about permission to reproduce selections from
this book, write to Permissions, Houghton Mifflin Company,
215 Park Avenue South, New York, New York 10003.

*Library of Congress Cataloging-in-Publication Data*

Min, Anchee, date.
Becoming Madame Mao / Anchee Min.
p.    cm.
ISBN 0-618-00407-6
1. Chiang, Ch'ing, 1910 — Fiction.  2. Spouses of heads of
state — China — Fiction.  3. China — History — 20th
century — Fiction.  4. Married women — China — Fiction.
5. Statesmen — China — Fiction.  I. Title.
PS3563.I4614 B43 2000
813'.54 — dc21    99-058520

Printed in the United States of America

Book design by Robert Overholtzer

QUM 10 9 8 7 6 5 4 3 2 1

*To Lloyd with all my love*

You are what your deep, driving desire is.
As your desire is, so is your will.
As your will is, so is your deed.
As your deed is, so is your destiny.

— *Brihadaranyaka Upanishads* IV.4.5

## Madame Mao

as Yunhe (1919–1933)
as Lan Ping (1934–1937)
and as Jiang Ching (1938–1991)

*Author's Note:* I have tried my best to mirror the facts of history. Every character in this book existed in real life. The letters, poems, and extended quotations have been translated from original documents.

# Prologue

*What does history recognize? A dish made of a hundred spar-*
*rows — a plate of mouths.*

*Fourteen years since her arrest. 1991. Madame Mao Jiang*
*Ching is seventy-seven years old. She is on the death seat. The only*
*reason the authorities keep postponing the execution is their hope*
*of her repentance.*

*Well, I won't surrender. When I was a child my mother used to tell*
*me that I should think of myself as grass — born to be stepped on.*
*But I think of myself as a peacock among hens. I am not being*
*judged fairly. Side by side Mao Tse-tung and I stood, yet he is con-*
*sidered a god while I am a demon. Mao Tse-tung and I were mar-*
*ried for thirty-eight years. The number is thirty-eight.*

*I speak to my daughter Nah. I ask her to be my biographer.*
*She is allowed to visit me once a month. She wears a peasant*
*woman's hairstyle — a wok-lid-cut around the ears — and she is*
*in a man's suit. She looks unbearably silly. She does that to hurt*
*my eyes. She was divorced and remarried and now lives in Beijing.*
*She has a son to whom my identity has been a secret.*

*No, Mother. The tone is firm and stubborn.*

*I can't describe my disappointment. I have expectations of*
*Nah. Too many perhaps. Maybe that's what killed her spirit. Am I*
*different from my mother who wanted the best for me by binding*

*my feet? Nah picks what I dislike and drops what I like. It's been
that way since she saw how her father treated me. How can one
not wet one's shoes when walking along the seashore all the time?
Nah doesn't see the whole picture. She doesn't know how her father once worshiped me. She can't imagine that I was Mao's sunshine. I don't blame her. There was no trace of that passion left
on Mao's face after he entered the Forbidden City and became
a modern emperor. No trace that Mao and I were once lovers
unto death.*

*The mother tells the daughter that both her father and she hate
cowards. The words have no effect. Nah is too beaten. The
mother thinks of her as a rotten piece of wood that can never be
made into a beautiful piece of furniture. She is so afraid that her
voice trembles when she speaks. The mother can't recognize any
part of herself in the daughter.*

*The mother repeats the ancient story of Cima-Qinhua, the
brave girl who saved her mother from a bloody riot. The model of
piety. Nah listens but makes no response. Then she cries and says
that she is not the mother. Can't do the things she does. And
should not be requested to perform an impossible task.*

*Can't you lift a finger? the mother yells. It's my last wish, for
heaven's sake!*

*Save me, Nah. Any day a bullet will be put into my head. Can you
picture it? Don't you see that there has been a conspiracy against
me? Do you remember the morning when Deng Xiao-ping came
to your father's funeral and what he did? He just brushed fingers
with me — didn't even bother to shake my hand. It was as if he
questioned that I was Mao's widow. He was aware of the cameras
— he purposely let the journalists catch the scene. And the other
one, Marshal Ye Jian-ying. He walked past me wearing an expression as if I had murdered the Chairman myself!*

*Your father warned me about his comrades. But he didn't do* anything to protect me. He could be heartless. His face had a vindictive glow when he made that prediction. He was jealous that I got to go on living. He would have liked to see me buried with him, like the old emperors did with their concubines. One should never have delusions about your father. It took me thirty-eight years to figure out that sly fox. He could never keep his hands away from deception. He couldn't survive a day without trickery. I had seen ghosts in his eyes stretching out their claws. A living god. The omniscient Mao. Full-of-mice-shit.

You are a historian, Nah. You should document my role in the revolution. I want you to demonstrate my sacrifices and contributions. Yes, you can do it. Forget about what your father will think about you. He is dead. I wonder what's happened to his ghost. I wonder if it rests in its grave. Watch out for his shadow.

The hands to strangle me are creeping up fast. I can feel them at my throat. That's why I am telling you this. I am not afraid of death if I know my spirit will live through the tip of your fountain pen to the lips of the people, generations to come. Tell the world the story of a heroine. If you can't print your manuscript in China, take it outside. Don't let me down. Please.

You are not a heroine, Mother! I hear my daughter fire back. You are a miserable, mad and sick woman. You can't stop spreading your disease. Like Father said, you have dug so many graves that you don't have enough bodies to lay in them!

Their dinner has turned cold. Nah stands up and kicks away her chair. Her elbow accidentally hits the table. A dish falls. Breaks. Pieces of ceramics scatter on the floor. Grease splatters on the mother's shoe. You have killed me, Nah. Madame Mao suddenly feels short of breath. Her hand grips the edge of the table to prevent herself from falling.

Pretend that you never had me, Mother.

You can't disown your mother!

*

*Well, all my hope is gone. I am exhausted and ready to exit the stage for good. The last curtain time will be tomorrow morning at five-thirty when the guards change shift. They are usually dull at that time. The old guard will be yawning his way out while the new guard yawns his way in.*

*It's dark outside. A beautiful black night without stars. The prison officials have put me on a suicide watch. But they cannot beat my will. I have saved enough handkerchiefs and socks to make a rope.*

*The rubber walls emit a terrible smell. But all is fine with me now. Tomorrow you will read about me in the news: Madame Mao Jiang Ching committed suicide by hanging. The day to mark is May 14, 1991. Am I sad? Not really. I have lived an extraordinary life. The great moments . . . Now as I think about them for the last time, they still make my heart hammer with excitement . . .*

# 1

SHE LEARNS PAIN EARLY. When she is four, her mother comes to bind her feet. The mother tells the child that she cannot afford to wait any longer. She promises that afterwards, after the pain, the girl will be beautiful. She will get to marry into a rich family where she doesn't have to walk but will be carried around in a sedan chair. The three-inch lotus feet are a symbol of prestige and class.

The girl is curious. She sits on a stool barefoot. She plays with the pile of cloth with her toes, picks up a strip, then drops it. Mother is stirring a jar of sticky rice porridge. The girl learns that the porridge will be used as glue. Good glue, strong, won't tear, Mother says. It seals out the air. The ancient mummies were preserved in the same way. The mother is in her late twenties. She is a pretty woman, long slanting almond-shaped eyes, which the girl inherited. The mother hardly smiles. She describes herself as a radish pickled in the sauce of misery. The girl is used to her mother's sadness, to her silence during family meals. And she is used to her own position — the last concubine's daughter, the most distant relative the family considers. Her father was sixty years old when she was born. He has been a stranger to her.

The mother's hair is lacquer black, wrapped in a bun and fixed with a bamboo pin. She asks the girl to sit still as she begins. She looks solemn as if she is in front of an altar. She takes the girl's right foot, washes it and wipes it dry with her blouse. She doesn't tell the girl that this is the last time she will see her feet as she knows them. The mother doesn't tell her that by the time her feet are released they will look like triangle-shaped rice cakes with toenails curled under the sole. The mother tries to concentrate on the girl's future. A future that will be better than her own.

The mother begins wrapping. The girl watches with interest. The mother applies the paste in between each layer of cloth. It is a summer noon. Outside the window are climbing little bell flowers, small and red like dripping blood. The girl sees herself, her feet being bound, in her mother's dressing mirror. Also in the frame, a delicately carved ancient vase on the table with a bunch of fresh jasmine in it. The scent is strong. The pendulum of an old clock on the wall swings with a rustic sound. The house is quiet. The other concubines are napping and the servants are sitting in the kitchen quietly peeling beans.

Sweat gathers on her mother's forehead and begins to drip like broken beads down her cheeks. The girl asks if her mother should take a break. The woman shakes her head and says that she is finishing the task. The girl looks at her feet. They are as thick as elephant legs. The girl finds it amusing. She moves her toes inside the cocoon. Is that it? she asks. When her mother moves away the jar, the girl jumps on the floor and plays.

Stay in bed from now on, her mother says, the pain will take a while.

The girl has no trouble until the third week. She is already tired with her elephant legs and now comes the pain. Her toes scream for space. Her mother is near her. She is there to prevent the girl from tearing off the strips. She guards the elephant legs as if guarding the girl's future. She keeps explaining to the crying girl why she has to endure the pain. Then it becomes too much. The girl's feet are infected. The mother's tears pour. No, no, no, don't touch them. She insists, cries, curses. Herself. Men. She asks why she didn't have a son. Again and again she tells the girl that females are like grass, born to be stepped on.

The year is 1919. Shan-dong Province, China. The town is the birthplace of Confucius. It is called Zhu. The ancient walls and gates stand high. From the girl's window the hills are like giant turtles crawling along the edge of the earth. The Yellow River runs through the town and its murky waters make their way lazily to the sea. The coast cities and provinces have been occupied by foreign forces — first the Germans and now the Japanese — since China lost the Opium War in 1858. China is collapsing and no one pays attention to the girl's cries.

The girl is never able to forget the pain, even when she becomes Madame Mao, the most powerful woman in China during the late 1960s and '70s. She recalls the pain as "evidence of the crimes of feudalism" and she expresses her outrage in a series of operas and ballets, *The Women of the Red Detachment* and *The White-Haired Girl,* among many others. She makes the billion population share her pain.

To understand the pain is to understand what the proletariat went through during the old society, she cries at a public rally. It is to understand the necessity of Communism! She believes the pain she suffered gives her the right to lead the nation. It's the kind of pain that shoots through your core, she tells the actress who plays the lead in her opera. You can't land on your toes and you can't fly either. You are trapped, chained down. There is an invisible saw. You are toeless. Your breath dies out. The whole house hears you but there is no rescue.

She remembers her fight with the pain vividly. A heroine of the real-life stage. Ripping the foot-binding cloths is her debut.

If there is no rebellion, there is no survival! she shouts at rallies during the Cultural Revolution.

My mother is shocked the moment I throw the smelly binding strips in front of her and show her my feet. They are blue and yellow, swelling and dripping with pus. A couple of flies land on the strips. The pile looks like a dead hundred-footed-octopus monster. I say to my mother, If you try to put my feet back in the wrap I shall kill myself. I mean it. I have already found a place for myself to lie. It will be in Confucius's temple. I like the couplet on its gate:

> The temple has no monk
> So the floor will be swept by the wind
> The temple has no candles
> So the light will be lit by the moon

You need to have the lotus feet, my mother cries. You are not made to labor.

Afterwards my mother quits. I wonder if she already knows that she will need me to run with her one day.

The girl's memory of her father is that he lives on liquor and is violent. Both her mother and she fear him. He hits them. There is no way to predict when his temper will rise. Each time it shocks the soul out of the girl.

He is not a poor man. Madame Mao doesn't tell the truth later when she wants to impress her fellow countrymen. She describes him as a proletarian. In fact he is a well-to-do businessman, the town carpenter and owner of a wood shop. He has four full-time workers. Two of them are blind. He uses them to sand wood. The family has food on the table and the girl goes to school.

I never understand why my father beats my mother. There never really is a reason. Nobody in the house interferes. All the wives hear the beating. All my stepbrothers and -sisters witness the act. Yet no one utters a word. If my father is not pleased with my mother, he comes to her room, takes off his shoe and starts hitting her. Concubines are bought slaves and bedmaids, but I wonder if my father's true anger is because my mother didn't produce a son for him.

This is how her father plants the seed of worthlessness in her. It is something she lives with. The moment she begins remembering how she was brought up, she experiences a rage that bursts at its own time and pace. Like the flood of the Yellow River, it comes and crashes in big waves. Its violence changes the landscape of her being. The rage gets worse as she ages. It becomes a kept beast. It breathes and grows underground while consuming her. Its constant presence makes her feel worthless. Her desire to fight it, to prove that it does not exist, lies behind her every action.

It is my nature to rebel against oppressors. When my mother tells me to learn to "eat a meatball made of your own tongue," and "hide your broken arm inside your sleeve," I fight without ever considering the consequences.

In frustration Mother hits me. She hits me with a broom. She is scared of my nature. She thinks that I will be killed like the young revolutionaries whose heads are hung on flagpoles on top of the town gate. They were slaughtered by the authorities.

Mother scolds me, calls me a *mu-yu* — a monk's chanting tool — made to be hit all the time. But I can't be set right. It is always afterwards, after she has exhausted herself from hitting me, that she breaks down and sobs. She calls herself an unfit mother and is sure that she will end up being punished in her next life. She will be made into a most unfortunate animal, a cow who when alive bears heavy burdens and when dies is eaten, its skin made into jackets and its horns into medicine.

Every time I see Mother's tear-stained face I age. I feel white hair sprouting out of my head. I am sick of seeing Mother tortured. I often wish that she were dead so she would be released from having to take care of me.

But the mother goes on living, for her, the daughter she wishes were a son. This is how misery permeates the girl's soul. Most of her life she can't be satisfied with who she is. The irony is that she truly wishes to satisfy her mother's wish. This is how she begins her acting career. Very young. In her own house. She slips into roles. When she thinks that she is not who she is, she becomes relaxed and fear free. She is in a safe place where her father's terror can no longer reach and her mother's tears can no longer wash her away.

Later on it becomes clear that Madame Mao doesn't forgive. She believes that one must collect the debts owed to one. She has little desire to understand forgiveness. Revenge, on the other hand, she understands. She understands it in the most savage way. In her life, she never hesitates to order her enemies' complete elimination. She does it naturally. It is a practice she started as a young girl.

I see my father hit Mother with a shovel. It happened suddenly. Without warning. I can hardly believe my eyes. He is mad. He calls Mother a slut. Mother's body curls up. My chest swells. He hits her back, front, shouting that he will break her bones. Mother is in shock, unable to move. Father drags her, kicks and steps on her as if to flatten her into a piece of paper.

I feel horror turning my stomach upside down. I jump. I get in between them. You are no longer my father, I announce, my body trembling all over. I will never forgive you! One of these days you will find yourself dead because I put mice poison in your liquor!

The man turns and raises the shovel over his head.

My lips burn. My front tooth is in my mouth.

*

During the production of her operas and ballets in the 1970s, Madame Mao describes the wound to the actresses, actors, artists and the nation. Madame Mao says, Our heroines must be covered with wounds. Blood-dripping wounds. Wounds that have been torn, punctured or broken by weapons like shovels, whips, glass, wooden sticks, bullets or explosions. Study the wounds, pay attention to the degree of the burn, the layers of the infected tissue. The color transitions in the flesh. And the shapes that remind you of a worm-infested body.

Eight years old and she is already determined. It is not clear whether her father kicked her mother out of his house or her mother ran away herself. At any rate the girl no longer has a home. The mother takes the daughter with her. They walk from street to street and town to town. The mother works as a maid. A washmaid, lower in rank than a kitchenmaid. The mother works where she and the girl will be given a corner to sleep at night. At night the mother often leaves mysteriously. When she returns it is usually dawn. The mother never tells the girl where she goes. One day when the girl insists, she says that she visits different houses. She either peels potatoes or serves as a foot warmer for the master's children. She never tells the girl that she is a foot warmer for the master himself. The mother withers quickly. Her skin wrinkles up like ripples in a lake and her hair dries like a winter stalk.

Some nights the girl gets bored waiting for her mother. She can't sleep yet she is afraid to go out. She lies in bed quietly. After midnight she hears bullets being fired. She counts the shots so she will know how many people have been killed.

My number always matches the number of heads that hang on the gate of the town the next day. My schoolmates talk to each other like this: I'll slaughter you and hang your head on a hook and then I'll stick an opium pipe between your teeth.

I hate school. I am an object of attack because I have no father and have a mother who works at jobs that arouse suspicion. I beg my mother to transfer me to a different school. But the situation doesn't change. It gets so bad that one day a classmate unleashes a dog.

Madame Mao later uses the incident in both a ballet and opera of the same title, *The Women of the Red Detachment*. The villains come with vicious-looking dogs to chase the slave girl. A close-up of the dog teeth and a closeup of the wound. The bleeding body parts.

My mother's face becomes unrecognizable. Her pretty cheek-bones start to protrude and her eyes have deep pockets. She is so sick that she can't walk far. Yet we are still on the run. She has been fired from her job. She can't talk, she whispers in between breaths. She writes a letter and begs her parents for shelter and food. I wonder why she hasn't done that earlier. She won't ex-plain. I sense that she wasn't her parents' favorite. There are prob-ably bad memories of the past. But now she has no choice.

My grandparents live in Jinan. It is the capital of Shan-dong Prov-ince. Compared to the town of Zhu, it is a fancy city. It is on the south side of the Yellow River, about nine miles away. The city is a center of business and politics. It is very old. The names of the streets reflect its past glory: Court Street, Financial Street, Mili-tary Street. There are magnificent temples and dazzling opera houses. I don't know until later that many of the opera houses are in fact whorehouses.

*

My grandparents and I have never met and our meeting changes my life. My dependence on my mother begins to shift dramatically as my grandfather takes charge in caring for me. He is a kind fellow, a meek man actually, knowledgeable but powerless in handling reality. He teaches me opera. He asks me to recite after him. Phrase by phrase and tone by tone we get through the most famous arias. I don't like it, but I want to please him.

Every morning, sitting on a rattan chair with a cup of tea, my grandfather begins. He tells me what the story is about first, the situation and the character, and then out his voice comes. He is a terrible singer, which makes him quite funny. I follow him, not remembering exactly what I am singing. I purposely imitate his poor tone. He tries to correct me. After a few efforts, he discovers that I have been naughty and threatens to be upset and then I behave. I hit the notes in a perfect voice. He claps and laughs. With his mouth wide open I see a hollow with all the teeth gone.

We move on. Soon I am able to do passages from *The Romance of the Three Kingdoms,* especially *The Empty City.* My grandfather is pleased. He lets me know that I count. A boy or a girl, to him it makes no difference. There is only one condition: as long as I follow him and learn. He lets me do whatever I want around the house. My grandmother is a quiet little lady and a Buddhist. She echoes her husband and never seems to have an opinion of her own. She always covers up for me. For example, when I accidentally break Grandfather's favorite ink bottle, she uses her own savings and hurries to the town on her lotus feet and buys a new bottle to replace the broken one. She does it quietly and I adore her.

My grandfather continues his cultivation. His head swings in circles. I do the same. When he is in a good mood, he takes me to operas. Not the good ones — he can't afford the tickets — but the imitations presented in the whorehouses. During the performances fights often break out among the drunkards.

It is my grandfather's wish that I complete elementary school. You are a peacock living among hens, he says. He is fixing the arm of his rattan chair when he says this to me. His head is on the floor and his rear end points toward the ceiling. The phrase has an enormous effect on me.

My grandfather enrolls me in a local school a block away. He gives me a formal name, Yunhe — Crane in the Clouds. The image is picked from his favorite opera, *The Golden Pavilion.* The crane is the symbol of hope.

The new school is a terrible place. The rich kids beat the poor whenever they like. Yunhe endures as much as she can until one day she is hit by a boy and a group of girls applaud. It enrages her. For days afterwards she is chewed by an incredible pain. I would have endured as usual if it were just the boys taking advantage of the girls, Madame Mao says later. I wouldn't have felt so alone and betrayed. I wouldn't have taken it so personally because mistreating women was considered a tradition. But it was the girls, the women, the grass, the worthless creatures themselves, laughing at their own kind that hurt, that opened and dipped my wounds in salt water.

# 2

SLOWLY MY MOTHER FADES from my life. It is said that she is married. To whom? She never introduces us to the new husband. She just disappears. Gone. The door is shut. I don't hear from her. She is done with parenting. I don't know what to do, only that I don't want to end up like her.

I watch operas and copy the arias. *The Legend of Huoxiao Yu* and *Story of the West Chamber.* I dream about the characters in the ancient tales, the rebellious heroines, women who fight fiercely for their happiness and get it. I decide that I shall be an opera actress so I will get to live a heroine's life on stage. But my grandfather opposes the idea. To him, actresses and prostitutes are the same. I don't give in. My grandfather regrets that he ever introduced me to opera. He threatens to disown me. But it is too late.

The girl is not sold to the opera troupe as she later claims. She runs away from home and delivers herself to a local troupe. She begs to be accepted. She is pretty, already a full-size young woman, already attractive. She claims to be an orphan. She runs away before her grandparents get a chance to disown her. This becomes a pattern in her life. With her husbands and lovers, she takes the initiative. She abandons before being abandoned.

The girl becomes an apprentice. While learning her craft she washes the floors, cleans makeup drawers, fills water jars and takes care of the leading actress's wardrobe. She gets to sit by the curtain during performances. Like a spring field in the season's first rain, she absorbs. During the New Year's Eve performance she gets to play her first one-line role. The line is: *Tea, Madame.*

For the role she dresses up in full costume. Her hair is up, pinned with pearls and glittering ornaments. In the mirror, in the painted face, in the red lips, the girl sees herself in the world she has been imagining.

Yet the place shows its ugly face. At night, after the performances, the girl hears sobbing. After her mistress takes off the makeup and costume, the girl sees a withered face. A young woman of twenty but who looks forty. A face of wood, carved heavily with wrinkles. There must be a ghost's hand working on this face, the girl thinks to herself.

When the girl goes out to fetch duck-blood soup on her mistress's order, she sees men waiting. Each night, a different man. They are the troupe owner's friends. Most of them are old, and a couple of them have a mouthful of gold teeth. The mistress is told to entertain them, to help them realize their fantasies. It doesn't matter that she is exhausted, doesn't matter that she wants to spend time with the young man of her heart.

The girl is waiting. She waits for a bigger role. For that she works hard, does everything she is told, endures an occasional beating. She tells herself to be patient, to perfect her skills. She is aware of the changes in her body. Aware that it is blooming. In the mirror she sees her eyes become brighter, her features ripening. Her waist grows smaller while her chest blossoms. She believes that her chance is coming her way. At night she dreams of the spotlight tracing her, only her.

I follow my grandfather and we head home. I am not giving up acting. I was not given the role I wanted to play. I was bored.

The wait was too long. I became sick of cleaning backstage. Sick of my rubber-faced mistress, her complaining, long and smelly words, like foot-binding cloths. My grandfather has paid a large sum to get me out of the troupe.

But when the moon buries itself in the deep drifts of cloud, my thoughts get busy again. I thought I had caught a glance, heard a tone, seized my dream, but . . . I stay wide awake in my old bed trying to figure out where to go and what to do next.

The sticky-rice-pasted wrapping cloths. The swelling toes. The inflammation. The prickling pain at the ankles. The girl remembers how she saved herself.

My grandparents are busy traveling from town to town and from matchmaker to matchmaker. They are trying get rid of me. I am sixteen years old, already beyond ruling. Because of my size, I am often mistaken as eighteen. They should have my feet bound. Now I can walk and run on this pair of — what my grandmother calls — liberation feet. My feet feel strong, as if they are on wings.

I run to free myself. I find another opera troupe. It is called the Experimental Theater Troupe of Shan-dong Province. It's bigger and better known, headed by a Confucius-looking man named Mr. Zhao Taimo.

Although Mr. Zhao Taimo has the look of Confucius, he is not a man of tradition by any means. He is a man of Western education. He is the torch that lights Yunhe's early life. Later on Madame Mao refuses to credit him for his guidance. Madame Mao takes all the credit for herself. It is because she is expected to prove that she was a born proletarian. But in 1929 it is Mr. Zhao Taimo who grants the girl admission even though she lacks important qualifications. Her Mandarin is poor and she has no acrobatic skills. Mr. Zhao is attracted instantly by the rebellious spirit in the girl.

The bright almond eyes. The burning passion behind them. From the way the girl marches into the room, Mr. Zhao discovers a tremendous potential.

The circle of literature and arts in Shan-dong regards Mr. Zhao as a man of inspiration. His wife, the elegant opera actress Yu Shan, is popular and adored. Yu Shan is from a prestigious family and is well connected. The girl Yunhe comes to worship the couple. She becomes a guest at the Zhaos' open house every Sunday afternoon. Sometimes she even comes early in the morning, skipping her breakfast, just to watch Yu Shan go through her opera drills. Yunhe's modesty and curiosity impress Yu Shan and the two become good friends.

At parties, Yunhe is usually quiet. She sits in the corner chewing sunflower seeds and listens. She observes the visitors. Most of them are students, professors, musicians and playwrights. There are mysterious visitors too. They are the left-wingers — the underground Communists.

My first encounters with the revolutionaries take place at Mr. Zhao Taimo's parties. I find them young, handsome and passionate. I look at them with respect. I can never forget those bloody heads hung on the poles. What is it that makes them risk their lives?

In Mr. Zhao Taimo's house I find the answer. It is their love for the country. And I think that there is nothing in life more honorable than what they do.

The girl suddenly has the urge to join the discussion. It takes her a while to finally gather her courage and project her voice.

I was never told that the foreign occupation was the result of our nation's defeat, the girl says. In my schoolbook China is as glorious as it has always been. But why are foreigners the masters of factories, owners of railways and private mansions in our country? I remember once my grandfather sighed deeply and said that it was useless to learn to read — the more one was educated, the deeper one felt humiliation. I now understand why my grandfather loves opera. It is to numb himself. In opera he relives China's past splendor. People are fooling themselves.

At the school Yunhe proves herself to be an ardent student. Her shirt is constantly wet with sweat. Bruises are visible on her knees and elbows from practicing martial arts. During voice class she spends hours studying one aria and won't quit until it is perfect. The teachers are pleased by the high expectations she sets for herself and she is adored. After classes one can hear Yunhe's laughter. It sounds like bells. The male students find it extremely pleasant. They find themselves unable to take their eyes off the girl. There is something about her that is utterly irresistible. It catches their attention and has a mysterious effect on them.

Not only does the girl love drama, she creates drama in her daily life. It becomes her interest first, then it extends itself to become a need, an obsession and an addiction. Finally her entire existence is based on it, her fantasy — she has to feel dramatic, has to play a role, or she gets restless, stressed and sick. She doesn't get well until she assigns herself another role.

It is midnight. The Temple of Confucius is said to be a visiting place of abandoned ghosts — the ghosts who had disobeyed tradition during their breathing time and have been punished. No temple will collect them. It is said that if the long grass sways in the empty courtyard after dark, bricks will drop from corners of the eaves. The statues of Confucius and his seventy-two disciples will come to life. They will lecture the ghosts and help them find their way back. The statue of Confucius is the tallest figure and is located in the deep end of the temple. It is covered with thick dust and spider webs, all the way from his feet up to his head scarf.

The boys of the opera school are afraid to go into the temple at night. One night they invent a game and set up a reward for anyone who dares to enter the temple after midnight to fetch the scarf from Confucius's head.

All week long, no one answers the challenge. The fifth night, someone grabs the scarf.

To everyone's surprise, it is Yunhe.

With two thin pigtails and a naughty grin on her face, the girl smiles toward the clapping audience.

The girl has a feeling that Mr. Zhao and his wife will do her good — for example, introduce her to someone or provide an opportunity. She relies on her instinct. Later in her life, on many occasions, she does the same.

She continues to practice her trade. She is taught *Qingyi*, traditionally a beautiful tragic female character. The girl's good looks earn her the role. Her movements are expected to be filled with elegance.

There are already rivals. Yunhe realizes that she has to fight to get chances. There is a part in a new play by a well-known Shanghai playwright, Tien Han. It is entitled *The Incident on the Lake*. Yunhe participates in the audition but is unlucky. The part goes to her roommate, a thin-haired girl whose brother is an instructor at the school.

Yunhe feels depressed during the opera's opening. She is unable to deal with her jealousy. Her discomfort is written all over her face. During the performance she forgets her job — to pop out of a tree. Inside she is tortured. She thinks of herself as a much better performer.

Some evil hands are always there trying to bind my feet, Madame Mao will say.

Even when winds buffet me from all directions, I never give up hope. This is my biggest virtue. Someone said that it was by accident that I sprouted. No. It was no accident. I created my own opportunity. Raining or snowing, I never missed one show. I was always there and always made myself available. I was never late or gave myself an excuse to retire early. I didn't waste time on gossiping or knitting sweaters by the stage curtain. I watched the leading lady.

Yes, I was bored to tears, but I made myself stay. I memorized the character's every aria and every word. It is not that I am so wise that I can predict what will happen next. What I do know is that if one wants to get a boat ride, one must be near the river.

The leading lady has the flu. Sick as she is, she doesn't want to leave the show. For days she drags herself through the play. It is Monday evening and it is rainy and wet. The actress is on the verge of collapsing. After peeping through the curtain at the small crowd she asks for the night off. The stage manager is furious with such short notice. The actress calls up a rickshaw and leaves the theater. It is seven o'clock. Fifteen minutes to curtain time. In the makeup room the stage manager paces in circles like a dog chasing its own tail. When the curtain bell rings he punches his fist into the makeup room mirror.

In the broken mirror Yunhe's face appears. Fully made up and dressed for the role.

I am ready to carry on the show, the girl says. I have been ready. Please, sir, give me a chance.

*Thy white face doth powder spurn . . .* The manager recites an aria from the middle of the play.

*Vermilion must yet from thy lips learn.* Yunhe opens her mouth with a full voice. *Flesh of snow, bones of jade, dream thy dreams, peerless one, not for this world thou art made.*

When the curtain ascends I am my role. Oh, how fantastic I feel! My cheeks are hot and I move about the stage at ease. I am born for this. I let myself flow, be led by the spirit of the character. The audience is mine. A shout comes when my character is about to end her life for love. *Take me with you!* I hear. *Take me with you!* The rest of the audience follows. And then there is the sob, the whole theater. It sounds like an incredible tide. Wave after wave. Sky high. Vast, wrapping my ears.

The performance is a success. It turns out to be the best opportunity I could ever hope for — Mr. Zhao Taimo and a group of critics he had invited to review the show are among the audience. He didn't call in advance to make reservations because he was aware that the show had been slow and that seats would not be a problem.

Yunhe's tears pour uncontrollably. The heroine finally wins her lover's affection. But her tears are not for her character. They are for herself, her victory, that she had outshone her rival, that she can no longer be ignored. And that she had single-handedly made all this happen herself.

Backstage, as she is being helped to remove her makeup and costume, she breaks down again. The sob comes so suddenly, with such an overwhelming impact, that she grabs the door and dashes out.

The year is 1930. Right after her first appearance on the stage, the theater is shut down. And then the troupe and the school. The reasons are lack of funds and political instability. Unable to pay its debts, China submits itself to deeper and wider foreign penetration. The infighting between warlords has exhausted the peasants and months of drought have devastated the landscape. By the time Yunhe decides to pack up, everybody else has already left. It is like a forest on fire where all the animals run for their lives.

The girl has no money to flee and she doesn't want to go back to her grandparents. Her mother has never tried to find her. She doesn't let herself miss her, especially in these moments, moments when she needs a place to go and a familiar face to turn to. She despises herself when she feels weak and helpless. She pinches the little-girl-crying-for-help voice inside her, pinches it as if it were her worst enemy. She keeps pinching until the pitiful voice turns into ice drops and forms a hard crystal. A crystal that never melts.

I sell all my belongings and buy a train ticket to Beijing. I look for acting jobs. I have to try. But the city is cold to me. Wherever I go, my Shan-dong–accented Mandarin brings laughs. None of my auditions ring back. Two months later, I am completely broke. No one wants to lend me money. No one believes that I will ever have a future as an actress. It doesn't bother me at the beginning. But when I am cold and hungry, I begin to doubt myself.

The girl comes back from Beijing and consents to her grand-parents' wish — she will marry. She is seventeen. The husband's name is Fei, a fan of hers when she played *The Incident on the Lake*. He is a small-business man. Later on in her life, she never mentions her marriage to Mr. Fei. She refuses to recall the face of the man. To her, he happened to be a rock in the middle of the river in which she was drowning. She reached for the rock and pulled herself up.

But at the wedding ceremony she is obedient. She is carried on a sedan chair and wrapped in red silk like a New Year's present. It is to satisfy her parents-in-law. They are not smiling. Yunhe suspects that her grandfather has paid money to have Mr. Fei propose.

Now she is on her own as a wife and a daughter-in-law. She feels strange and unprepared for the role. The first night is awful. The man claims his territory. She thinks of herself as an animal on a slaughtering table. His expression reminds her of a goat after a satisfying chew of grass. His jaw moves from side to side. Blood seeps from between her legs. She is resentful and disgusted.

I had dreamed of falling in love as in the operas. I expected my new husband to be intelligent and caring. I expected that we would court like butterflies in spring. I expected to feel for him. But my chances are taken away unasked. Mr. Fei is on my face every night ripping away every thread of my beautifully embroidered dream.

I weep in the middle of his act. How different am I from the prostitutes on the streets? It makes me think that. I have wronged my mother. I have always thought that she had done something wrong to mess up her life. Now I understand that a girl can do everything right and her life will still be a mess.

Now the girl has a place to stay and a man to pay her bills. Her energy resumes. She is ready to take charge of her life again. She doesn't consult her husband. She thinks of him as a prop in her real-life show.

The in-laws' complaint becomes her excuse. I am not going to stay where your mother wants to have my feet bound again, she says. The husband comes in between the women and tries to negotiate. No deal. His wife can't wait to be divorced. He can't outsmart her. Nothing will satisfy her until she is released.

Mr. Fei sits down and takes out his abacus. He calculates and decides that he doesn't want to invest more in a business of no profit.

With some money in her pocket the girl is on the run again. She never mentions the husband to anyone. Later in life she denies that the marriage ever existed. As the woman who will lead China after Mao, she must be a goddess. Having too many husbands on record will impede her path to power.

In 1930 she thinks herself a peacock among hens. Her life is the proof. She tells herself, sometimes one has to be put in a henhouse in order to be measured, compared and recognized.

I run away from my marriage. A girl of eighteen. Not very well educated and all alone in the world. I can't remember how many days I wander from place to place. I have lice in my hair and my underwear smells. I think about giving up. I almost do.

Finally I manage to locate Zhao Taimo, who is now the new president of Shan-dong University. I am sure that he remembers me and I assume that he will find a way to lend me a hand. But I am disappointed. Mr. Zhao says that he is too busy. If I want to be a student, I have to apply through the admissions office. How can I? I have no diplomas. I haven't even completed elementary school. But I try not to feel discouraged. I make myself go to Mr. Zhao's wife, Yu Shan, to beg.

She plays her role passionately. Stories of her struggle, shows lice in her hair, blisters on her feet. She moves the audience. Don't cry, says Yu Shan. Don't worry. There is hope. I know someone who might be helpful. Let me work on it and I'll get back to you in a few days.

Yu Shan finds the girl a job working in the school library as an assistant, which allows her to be a part-time student. The girl feels excited and nervous at the same time. She attends classes, walks around the campus and meets new people. She speaks humbly and carefully. She is eager to impress and eager to make friends. One day, Yu Shan brings a handsome young man to meet her. It is her brother, Yu Qiwei. Yu Shan introduces him. The student leader, the secretary of the underground Communist Party on campus.

Neither Yu Shan nor Yunhe could know that this man will become the girl's next husband — and more dramatically, one of the power-managers of Mao Tse-tung, the girl's fourth husband.

My first impression of Yu Qiwei is that he is extremely good-looking and calm like a summer lake. His smile relaxes me. He is in a navy blue Chinese two-piece suit. A pair of black cotton sandals. He sits opposite me, drinking tea. His sister has been trying to explain the meaning of his name — *Qi* as enlightenment and *Wei* as power and prestige.

It is a beautiful autumn day. We sit outside the teahouse near the campus under a large maple tree. The ground is carpeted by the red and yellow maple leaves. The colors are pure and bright. When the breeze stirs, leaves rain down. A couple land on Yu Qiwei's shoulders. He picks up a leaf and admires it. Yu Shan finishes her introduction and makes an excuse to leave.

The girl is interested but doesn't show it. She nods politely, sips her tea. Yu Qiwei asks what kind of classes interest her the most. Literature and theater, she answers. How interesting, he responds, and tells her that he has been involved with artists who put on political plays. She says that she doesn't know the group but admires them. Maybe you would like to work with them someday, suggests Yu Qiwei. Maybe, she smiles.

He then asks whether she enjoys campus life. She answers his questions. She doesn't ask any. There is no need. She knows all there is to know about him through Yu Shan. Finally he asks, Don't you have any questions regarding me? They both laugh. Your sister told me that you were a talent in the biology department. Oh that, he laughs. Yes, but that was before I became a full-time Communist. I see politics as a much more effective way to save the country.

Looking into the young man's eyes, Yunhe discovers something extraordinary. When he begins to talk about his country and his belief in Communism his expression is exalted. She is instantly attracted. But she is not sure whether he is attracted to her. It doesn't stop her. She pursues. She lets him know that she would like to meet people, his friends. He is glad. He finds her beautiful and pleasant.

The next day he takes her to see a street play. He introduces her to his friends. She is impressed and discovers that he is adored by almost everyone, especially women. His charisma and ability to communicate and lead make him a natural magnet.

She sits in front of a checkout desk expecting him without knowing whether he will come. He usually steps into the library right before she gets off work. She sees him now. She turns away, pretending that she is writing. She doesn't want him to know her feelings. Yu Shan has told her that he has many female admirers.

She sees him approaching. He comes near, smiles, and tells her that he is here to deliver a message from his sister. Yu Shan and Mr. Zhao have invited us both for a private dinner. Would you please come?

We begin to meet. We take long strolls around the campus as the sun is setting. The campus was originally a German military base. The library was built on the waist of a hill facing the sea. Its roof is made of red glass tile and its windows have delicate wooden frames. The views from the hill are breathtaking. Our other favorite spot is the port of Qing-dao. Its beauty lies in the mingling of traditional and modern architecture. At the end of the long seashore is a pavilion which, when the sun sets, brings one onto the stage of the ancient poet Ci Yin's poem "On Farewell." Sometimes we recite the lines together.

> *And so, dear friend, at Brown Crane Tower*
> *You bid the west adieu*

*Mid April mists and blossoms go*
*Till in the vast blue-green*
*Your lonely sail's far shade no more is seen*
*Only on the sky's verge the river flow*

Every morning, when the sea awakens the city, the young woman Yunhe and young man Yu Qiwei appear shoulder to shoulder at the shore. There is the faint smell of rotten fish and salt water. Blown by the wind Yunhe's hair brushes softly over Yu Qiwei's cheek. They come again in the evenings to watch the moon. To watch how the ocean puts on its silver nightgown and dances. In the distance are blinking lights of passing ships. The night stretches in front of them endlessly.

In the beginning, the conversation is about banned books and plays — *A Doll's House, The Dream of the Red Chamber* — and then the future of the nation, the inevitable foreign invasion, freedom, socialism, Communism and feminism. She listens to him and gradually feels herself falling in love. She doesn't tell him about Mr. Fei, her ex-husband. But a couple of times she makes odd remarks: The true poverty is having no choice in life. No choice but getting married, for example. No choice but to be a prostitute or a concubine, to sell one's body. She is in tears when she says that.

Yu Qiwei pulls her closer and holds her. He finds himself becoming inseparable from her. The girl from Jinan. The bright almond eyes. He feels the sweet-stir inside him. Suddenly he tears himself away from her and runs toward the night waves. He dives into the water, swims, splashes his arms. Under the white moonlight, the silver water streams down from the tips of his fingers.

She watches him, wiping her tears happily.

Through him she learns to be comfortable with herself. She learns that her own judgment counts, that she can trust herself. She is no longer restless. Yu Qiwei makes her happy, content and inspired. They court seriously. She is his everywoman. Each night, she is different. She loves to perform. Last night she was Nora and to-night she is Lady Yuji. She does this genuinely and effortlessly. She likes the idea that he is popular among women. It gives her the chance to prove herself, to prove that there is no way a hen can outshine a peacock. In his arms she realizes that she is capable of playing any role.

She thinks of him as a hero of the time. It stimulates her to think that she nurtures a powerful man, that thus she is the source of the power, strong and worthy. Each night when she opens her-self she feels this way. She likes to witness how she is desired, how he becomes helpless without her. She likes to prolong the moment of sweet torture, to make him want her so much that he begs and cries. Sometimes she is quiet from beginning to end. The only sound in the room is the sound of their breathing, its rising and falling like a distant sea, the ocean, the water that wraps the earth.

Yu Qiwei is daring and shy at the same time. He is a respected public figure, a wise man, almost fatherlike, yet with me he is a young boy in a fruit shop. I love it when he wants me in his sleep. This is often the case. He comes home late. He has been promoted as the provincial Party secretary. His meetings take place in dark-ness, in disguise and secrecy. Each night I wait for him.

It is the late autumn of 1931. Through Yu Qiwei I learn that the Japanese invasion has deepened. China's three northern provinces are occupied. The workers and students put on demonstrations. Day and night, my lover is there to call the public's consciousness. We decide to get married. There is no time for the wedding cere-mony. We have more important things to do. Moving into a small two-room place we settle down. Our friends and relatives are notified of our union. In fact I have been respected as Yu Qiwei's wife from the moment we started dating. Everyone thinks of us as a perfect couple.

I volunteer to work for the Communist group under Yu Qiwei's leadership. He has convinced his theater friends to take advantage of my talent. I become a leading actress for a small left-wing troupe. I help create anti-Japanese plays and take them to the streets. The first play is called *Put Down Your Whip*. I play a girl who finally stands up to her abusive father. It feels like I am playing my life. I act out what I couldn't back home. Yu Qiwei is my most faithful fan. It always makes me happy when I see his face in the crowd. He hugs and kisses me as he congratulates the other cast members. He leads the crowd, shouting *Down with the Japanese invaders!*

I am part of my lover, part of his work and part of China's future.

In his bed, I am tame, settled. He is exhausted. He falls right to sleep when his head hits the pillow. He hasn't been able to sleep for days. I get up and cook noodles and vegetables. I know that he will want to eat when he wakes. He eats a lot. Three bowls. It makes me laugh to think about the way he eats. He apologizes for his manners but continues to eat. He calls himself a toilet that flushes the food down.

I cross my legs on the floor and watch him sleep. His sweet, boylike face. Sometimes he drools. He is so tired he sleeps in his coat; he hasn't the energy to take it off. I don't wake him. I take off his shoes, slowly and gently. There is a truck passing by outside on the street. I am afraid that he will wake. But he is fine, keeps dreaming.

I lie down next to him and fall asleep myself. Once in a while the noise outside keeps me up. I feel that I haven't seen him for so long that I still miss him. I am afraid that he will wake and tell me that he has to move on.

I take off his coat, shirt and pants. I push him toward the wall side of the bed. He doesn't wake up. Maybe he just knows that it is me and knows what I am going to do.

He has told her that he loves it, loves what she does when he is dreaming. He says that she always knows when he has a steaming dream. He is too busy to feed his body, and the desire comes in his dreams. She knows the timing — when, exactly, he needs her.

It usually begins with a towel. For he is covered with dust and sweat. She rubs him with the cloth. A few strokes, the towel turns brown. She moves around, tosses the towel in hot water. Sometimes he turns around, in half sleep, as if to help her out. A born pleasure seeker, he used to describe himself. It has to do with his background, a bourgeois family spoiled with comforts. What makes him a revolutionary? She has no idea. There are such people in the Communist Party. What do they risk their heads for? It isn't food, she is sure. The power to control? The love of country? Or just following an instinct — to be a bigger man than the rest?

The smooth body, the golden flesh. He is a naked god who doesn't know shame. I can't stop myself from tasting him. I taste him alongside the dishes I have prepared for him, next to his dirty clothes. I unbutton my blouse. I have the urge to feed him.

He opens his mouth, like an infant. Smiles, sweetly. I touch him gently as I take off my underwear. It is at this moment I feel his hands coming.

In his desire I hear the singing of a storm as it breaks across a river.

The time-mountain will be there, left there, years later. It remembers the passion of the storm and the river.

❀

We are walking in the dark. Three of us. A friend of Yu Qiwei walks a half block behind us. This is going to be our ceremony, he says, a spirit union. I smile, nervous but excited. I thank him for the guidance. We slow down to allow the friend to catch up. Yu Qiwei then passes me to the friend — a secret Communist agent. He talks to the friend again about safety, instructs him to take the alley behind the silk factory on Yizhou Road, not the cross street, Xin-ming Road. Be careful of the spies. The man nods. Congratulations, Yu Qiwei whispers to me.

I follow the man, my heart a rabbit in a bag. We walk quickly toward a small park where the bushes are thick. The man takes the alley. Before we make a turn the man looks back. There is no tail.

A half-hour later, I am pronounced a member of the Communist Party. I have just completed my oath and registration.

As Yunhe raises her right fist above her head, facing a cigarette-pack-size red flag with a crossed sickle and hammer, she thinks of Yu Qiwei. She thinks that they are now soulmates and she is his partner. She will be entitled to have access to all his activities. She will get to go out with him, to secret meetings and places. They will risk their lives for China together. She still doesn't know enough of Communism itself. This doesn't bother her. She believes in Yu Qiwei, and that is enough. She believes in the Communist Party the same way she believes in love. In Yu Qiwei she finds her own identity. If Yu Qiwei represents the conscience of China, so does she. That is how she looks at herself in 1931. It matches her image of herself, the heroine, the leading lady. Later on, the same pattern repeats itself. When she becomes Mao's wife, she thinks, logically, that if Mao is the soul of China, so is she.

# 3

IT HAPPENS ONLY A FEW MONTHS after we have been together. One week Yu Qiwei is out traveling from place to
place and then he disappears. No one is able to locate him.
The next thing I learn is that he has been arrested, jailed, said to
be killed. Yu Shan comes to me and tells me the news.

I am afraid to open the door. The way Yu Shan knocks tells me
that something terrible has happened. I stare at Yu Shan's tear-
washed face. My mind goes blank — it can't comprehend.

I want to do something but Yu Shan says there is nothing I can
do but wait. I say what about the Communist Party? Can the
Party save him? She shakes her head, says that the Party is in terrible shape itself. The members have gone underground and have
cut off communication for reasons of safety. The warlord-turned-
head-of-state, Chiang Kai-shek, has betrayed his commitment to
unite Communists. He has ordered a military raid to arrest the
Communists. He has proclaimed the Communists his biggest enemy. His order says, *If we have to kill a thousand innocents in order to catch one Communist, so be it.*

Didn't Yu Qiwei know when the raids would begin? I ask.

Yes, Yu Shan replies. He knew he was on the wanted list. There
were signs. For example, the university was forced to dismiss students who were known members of the Communist Party. But my
brother had to carry on his work. When the arrests began he tried

to move people out of the city into the countryside. He was conducting a secret meeting on a public bus where he was spotted and taken away.

In her early years Yunhe flirted with danger. To her, danger fueled excitement. She enjoyed the moment when she went into the abandoned temple and grabbed the head scarf from Confucius's statue. She enjoyed singing *Put Down Your Whip* on the streets where she confronted the policemen. She felt that life was filled with meaning when she questioned the policeman in front of the crowd, Are you Chinese? How can you bear it when your mother and sister have been raped and your father and brother have been murdered by the Japanese?

Danger has given her chances to show her character. You are too weak, she later says to her third husband, Tang Na. You hide yourself from reality, you live in fantasy and are ruled by fear. You have never faced danger.

However, in 1931, after Yu Qiwei is arrested, there is a moment when she breaks away from her role as a heroine. Suddenly she is terrified beyond measure. She visits Yu Shan every day to inquire about Yu Qiwei. She waits impatiently. Every day her hope fades a bit. Finally she convinces herself that Yu Qiwei is dead. She begins to tell friends about her despair. Her hot tears pour. She wears a white dress. A white daisy in her hair. She moans. Then she stops going to Yu Shan.

She washes her face, takes her white dress and daisy off. She continues to take classes. She signs up for a course in eighteenth-century tragedies. She takes a new job working in the school cafeteria. After classes and after work she is bored. She goes to the seashore herself. She sits by the ocean under the bright moon. First she looks away and then she returns men's smiles. Then she is busy again.

Months pass before Yu Shan comes to tell her the news: Yu Qiwei has been released with the help of their uncle, David Yu, an influential figure in Chiang Kai-shek's congress. Yu Shan's visit is unannounced. She thought that the news would make Yunhe happy. But she is more than disappointed. Yunhe cracks the door a slit, looks awkward and embarrassed like a kid caught in the act of stealing. She is in her pajamas, her hair messy and lipstick smeared.

Won't you open the door? asks Yu Shan.

It's a mess inside. Still blocking the door, Yunhe suggests, Can I meet you in the teahouse in an hour?

But Yu Shan already sees.

Behind the door there is a young man, Yunhe's new boyfriend, Chao.

Madame Mao doesn't remember Chao. She has erased him from her memory. She remembers that she was lonely without Yu Qiwei, unable to sleep. She was depressed. She didn't expect Yu Qiwei's return. She told herself to move beyond the pain. A heroine's character is to move on. She can't explain Chao.

Yu Qiwei doesn't question her, doesn't confront Chao either. Yunhe never gets a chance to know how Yu Qiwei felt. One day Yu Shan comes with word from her brother.

My brother has left Qingdao for Beijing. The Party needs him to work there.

There is no mention of how Yu Qiwei feels about leaving, about their relationship or future. No words.

For the first time the actress is confused by the role she is playing — a heroine who betrays like a slut.

She goes on with Chao, but in the meantime writes to Yu Qiwei. When hearing nothing back she leaves the city, wanders, comes back and leaves again. A year passes. Then a point comes when she can no longer bear it; she sells her belongings and puts herself on the train to Beijing.

*

I sob like a widow on the train. Passengers bring me hot towels trying to calm me down. After I arrived in Beijing I suddenly lose my courage. I have no face to see Yu Qiwei. I am ashamed of myself.

But I am compelled to move forward, to see him again. Before I left I found out from Yu Shan that Yu Qiwei is the head secretary of the Communist Party of northern China. I manage to locate his headquarters in the library of Beijing University where he holds meetings frequently. I wait for days and finally I "run into" him.

He is with his comrades and I can tell that he is not pleased to see me. I ask if we can schedule a meeting. He makes a date reluctantly.

It is cold and raining. I have been wearing the same pair of wet sandals for days. My feet are soaked and my ankles are covered with mud. We meet in a park. The river is magnificent but frozen. There are no visitors. When I see the familiar figure approaching I try not to cry.

He is still handsome and wears my favorite two-piece blue suit. But the moment he sees me he turns his eyes away. It is awkward but I am determined to try. I force myself to speak, to apologize. I say, there was a mistake. I waited for you.

He doesn't want to hear. He asks what I am doing here.

I don't know myself, I say. What else can I say? It's not my nature to check the water's depth. I believe that I will float somehow. I am nineteen years old. I have been working to support myself. I teach Chinese at an adult night school, I baby-sit and sell theater tickets. I take care of all these things, I figure them out myself and I survive. But I can't figure out what happened to us . . .

You should not have come to Beijing, he says.

I need to see you, Yu Qiwei. I don't know, I am living with your ghost.

Yunhe, he calls me, calls my name. It makes me weep uncontrollably.

*

She stands in front of Yu Qiwei. Her eyes are filled with tears. The wind blows and messes her hair. She doesn't touch it, doesn't fix the mess. She looks at him. Take me back.

It is a night she will never forget. They make love as if the world is coming to an end. Both of them try to overcome the blank stare between them. She repeats the familiar ritual. His body tells her that she has been missed. She weeps, takes control of his desire. She explores every trick she knows to please him. The memory comes back. She thinks that she has won. He tells her that he loves her, no one can replace her, that he will always be there when she needs him.

But the truth is always in the shadows. Things are not the same. In the next few days the struggle begins to show. It is seen and heard when she speaks, moves and makes love. It is even in the words she uses: I am strong. Nothing puts me down.

By projecting these words, she deals with the inevitable parting. By yelling those phrases aloud, she survives and prevents herself from being crushed.

Yu Qiwei places her in the university dormitory. No money, no visit. She waits, days, weeks and months. He makes promises but doesn't show up. He is polite but distant and unmoved. She goes out and seeks him. She follows him and finds out that he will not be coming back to her arms — he is seeing another woman.

She spends the whole winter in a cold dorm room. She feels like a homeless dog. She tells herself to wait until spring. Maybe by then Yu Qiwei's ice-cold heart will melt. Maybe he will invite her out, maybe the blossoms of the spring will arouse him, and time will make him realize that he has tortured her enough.

I have tried but I am unable to let go of this feeling. Not after we separate, not after he is remarried, not even after I have married Mao. I can't make peace with him and myself although I accept that this is my fate. Emotionally I can't let go. I can't stand him being possessed by another woman. The burn lasts all my life. It doesn't end after his death, of heart failure at the age of forty-five, in 1958. I don't hide my dislike of his wife, Fan Qing.

When she looks back, she can almost see the reason. The passionate pain of abandonment. Yu Qiwei didn't let her finish her role. He left her to wonder why she didn't play it successfully. He walked out of her show before the curtain was down. It was not her character to accept humiliation. Maybe that's why he let himself slip out, die before she became the ruler of China. Maybe he knew that she wouldn't know how to live with his rejection, that she would make him pay for what he did. And he didn't want to pay what he didn't consider his debt. He was right. She spent her life cashing in the deposits of her disappointments.

# 4

I HAVE NEVER SAILED, never imagined that sailing could be this awful. I am seasick and have been throwing up. Ten days ago I boarded the *Pellet,* a cheap cargo ship going down the coast from Shan-dong to Shanghai. I have never been to Shang-hai. I felt that I had to do something to escape my situation. What do I have to lose? When I am not retching over the side I watch the sea. I forbid myself to think of Yu Qiwei. At night I sleep on the cargo floor among hundreds of low-class passengers and their animals. One night I wake up with duck shit all over me.

Leaving seemed to be my only choice. After I got back to Shan-dong from Beijing Yu Shan came to see me. She tried to be a good friend. But her brother was between us. Yu Shan came again the day I left for Shanghai. I had asked her and Mr. Zhao for contacts in Shanghai. They were kind enough to provide me with a name, a man called Shi, a film-maker originally from Shan-dong. Yu Shan wished me good luck. She seemed relieved to see me go. She didn't tell me that her brother was about to get married.

Yu Qiwei never wrote after he left me. Not a word. It was as if we had never been lovers. He didn't care to know where I was or how I felt. He didn't know I once wanted to quit living because of him.

The girl is determined to leave the pain behind. Toward the fu-ture she stares hard at the horizon. In her weakest moment, she still believes that she has the power to bring life to a new role. She feels this with every fiber of her being. She has decided to return to acting — it is what she does the best. If she can't fulfill her dream of being a leading lady in life, she can realize it on stage.

It is early morning and the fog is thick. The ship finally makes its way into the East China Sea and heads toward the Huangpu River. The ship's wake is a sweeping arc of white in the dark water. When the girl turns around and faces the bow of the ship Shanghai is there, its skyline touching the clouds. The ship slips clumsily into its berth. The gangplank is lowered. The crowds rush and press. Halfway down the walkway a foreign dialect strikes her ears. Everything will be different here, she thinks to herself. Above her neon signs blink like dragon's eyes. BRITISH SOAPS, JOHNSON TOOTHBRUSHES, FRENCH VELVET ROSE LIPSTICK. She is fascinated.

Mr. Shi is a man in his early thirties. He has the features of a typical Shan-dong man, tall and broad shouldered. His laughter sounds like thunder. He welcomes me warmly and lunges for my luggage. Before we have walked two steps he tells me that he is a producer in theater and film. Yu Shan has told me as much, but I have not heard of his work myself. By the way he talks I gather that he is at least well connected. He seems pleased to see me. He calls to a pedicab.

Mr. Shi keeps talking as we pile into the cab. I can hear the faint traces of his old Shan-dong accent. Shanghai is Asia's Paris, he says. It is heaven for adventurers. It can excite as well as break people. As I listen to Mr. Shi I notice the fashion in Shanghai. Women are stylish. They dress in rather short skirts and pointed shoes with high heels. The designs are creative and bold. Our pedicab wheels though the crowd. I hold tightly to the bar to prevent myself from falling out. The buildings on each side of the streets are much taller than any I have ever seen. I get the sense that Mr. Shi plans to show me the entire city right now, but I am not in the mood. I am tired and filthy.

As kindly as I can, I ask Mr. Shi to tell the driver to take the shortest route to the apartment he has secured for me. Mr. Shi seems a little disappointed but leans forward to speak to the driver. Leaning back, he offers me a cigarette. He is surprised when I decline. Everyone smokes in Shanghai, he says. You have much to learn, and I shall be honored to be your guide.

We enter a poor neighborhood, turn onto a shabby street and come to a stop before a two-story house. The building seems to lean in on itself and is encrusted with dark soot. Mr. Shi pays the cab and collects my luggage. We make our way into the building. There is no light. The stairs are steep and some are missing. Finally we stand in the second-floor hallway. Mr. Shi struggles with the key in the lock. Turning the key back and forth, he apologizes for the condition of the apartment. For your budget this is the best I could get. I tell him that it is all right. I had expected worse. He is relieved. Finally he gets the door open. A bad smell hits my face. In the dark I can feel the cockroaches skitter across my feet.

The girl sits on the floor in the middle of the small room. Outside, daylight fades. A strange kind of peace descends. She feels as if she has found a new home. It's not going to be easy but right now she feels calmer and considers it a good sign. Even the sounds coming from beyond her walls seem soothing. The family to her right has a brood of noisy children, a father that screams to shush them. On her left, there is an out-of-tune piano, a player who is just beginning. Across the hall is the public kitchen, with its noise and smells. The clanking of pans and the aromas of garlic and soy sauce. She feels as if she has awakened from one dream and is about to enter another.

❀

Mr. Shi doesn't quite know how to handle the girl. Every time he comes to visit she is out. A few times he catches her and convinces her to have tea with him. She reports her latest activity — she has already checked out all the contacts he had given her. Her mind seems to race constantly in every direction. One moment she asks him about how the buses work, how to get from one point to another by the most economical route; the next moment she wants to know where Tien Han, the playwright of *The Incident on the Lake,* lives and if she could visit him soon.

After only a week, Mr. Shi has lost his ability to track the girl. He is surprised to learn that she has already made a visit to Tien Han and is calling from his house. Not only is she staying at his house for the week, she has also gotten herself a job selling tickets at a left-wing theater. She also mentions that she has enrolled in classes at Shanghai University.

I rush from one side of town to the other. I am moving so fast that I barely have time to remember where I have been. I believe that if I meet as many people as possible something will come of it. I shoot for the top, arrive unannounced in the offices of producers and directors — I can't be rejected. I would like to star in both film and theater, I tell anyone who will listen. Some are annoyed by me. They are taken aback by my presumption. She is pretty, yes, but who is she? Others, like Mr. Tien, whose play I starred in in Shan-dong, find me attractive, and are charmed by my daring. Mr. Tien is flattered by my admiration for his work and takes an interest in me. When he learns where I am living he offers his home to me. He feeds me, gives me more contacts, and off I go again clutching my bus map.

A number of producers are encouraging. They promise to keep her in mind for their next projects. Through clouds of smoke, they describe their projects in detail and renew her hope. Attractive men with attractive ideas. There are hints of ways to "secure" her place in line. She sees it in their eyes. But she will not sleep with them. She is cautious, still nursing her lost love. She doesn't want to get involved in a relationship that will end in her being nothing better than a concubine. She sees no harm in a little flirting, though, and accepts as many invitations as come her way.

After a few months without any real offers, she gets anxious. She is back in her apartment. The noises from beyond the walls irritate her now. She is tired of being nobody and tired of being poor. She is sick of people telling her that her look is not bankable. She sits on the floor and examines her face in a palm-size mirror. She hates to confront her imperfections: her lower jaw is too protruding and her lips are thin; the distance between her nose and upper lip is a few millimeters too long.

She calculates her chances and looks for alternatives. She has heard stories of stars whose careers have soared because of their participation in small-budget political films. The idea appeals to her. She is ready to combine her acting interest with her background as a Communist. She doesn't tell people that she is a Communist, not yet. She trusts no one. At the moment she simply feels the need to separate herself from the pretty girls who are known as rich men's pets and layabout starlets.

I have little money, but I would starve myself in order to buy good theater tickets. I watch movies and operas so I can learn from the finest actresses. I can't do without going to a performance for too long. Every time I walk out of an opera I feel magically charged and all my frustrations disappear. I tell myself that lack of willpower has led to more failures than lack of intelligence or ability. I push myself to meet more people so I can advertise myself. My audience must know that I have a soul and that I live with a sense of purpose.

*

The girl is disappointed in her contacts. She doesn't want to see Mr. Shi anymore. She finds herself wasting her time running from place to place and meeting one useless person after another. The part-time job she has at the theater only makes her more hungry for acting. But nothing is working. She can't make herself stand out.

I was a one hundred percent Communist when I was young. I risked myself, Madame Mao recalls. I spread anti-Japanese leaflets throughout the city for the Party. I was in Shanghai to reconnect myself with the Party. We took patriotic plays to the streets. I taught at night school where I preached Marxism. I encouraged workers when they put on a strike. Working at the grass-roots level has always been my interest. Just like Yu Qiwei, I stuck my neck out for China. I very well might have been a martyr. I might have died.

The truth is that she ceased her membership after Yu Qiwei's arrest. The truth is that she hides her identity as an ex-Communist. Mr. Shi and Tien Han think that she is merely sympathetic toward Communism. When she has no luck getting roles in the theater she assigns herself a role: a patriot. It makes her feel less fearful about her inability to make things work.

She plays her real-life role with the same passion she brings to the stage. She catches attention and develops an audience. She does her job creatively, with flair. She puts leaflets on men's backs and makes them walking posters. In the Chinese class she teaches she asks her students, What makes the word "heaven"? She writes the character on the board and explains: It's the combination of two words, "slave" and "man." If we treat ourselves like men, and insist that others treat ourselves as such, not like slaves, we become heaven itself. She illustrates and animates. Soon her class becomes the most popular class in the school. In the meantime, she attracts unwanted attention: she is now on the list of the police as a suspected Communist.

She is not aware of what's coming. She is at peace with her life: looking for a role on stage during the day and playing a patriot at night. She sees her name mentioned in left-wing papers. It's better than nothing, she comforts herself. She keeps praying, hoping the paper will catch the attention of the studio heads. Why not? She is different. A true-life heroine, like those the studios have begun to portray in their new movies. For a movie to be successful it now has to be political. China is under invasion. The public is sick of ancient romance and is ready for inspiring roles from real life.

She is waiting, making herself available.

The night is windless. The air is moist. She is wearing a navy blue dress, walking out after the Chinese class. She is happy. The students, especially the women textile workers, have developed a close relationship with her. They trust and depend on her. They make her feel that she is a star in their lives. They have brought homemade rice cakes for her. The pieces are still warm in her bag. She will not have to make dinner tonight. Maybe she can use the time to catch the second half of her favorite opera at the Grand Theater on the way.

When she makes a turn onto a dark street she suddenly notices that she is being followed by two men. She becomes nervous and walks faster. But the men follow her like shadows. Before she is able to make a sound, she is handcuffed and pushed into a car parked down the street.

At the detention house she is dragged out of the police car and thrown into a cell with a crowd of women. The inmates are waiting to be interrogated. One cellmate explains the situation to her. Until there is a confession, we won't be released. The women cough raggedly. The cell is cold and damp. Yunhe observes that every fifteen minutes one person is thrown back into the room and another person taken away. People gather around them trying to get information. Lying naked on the ground, the women are beaten and bruised. Water drips from their hair. In choking gasps they describe the interrogation. Head dunked in hot-pepper water. Blows to the back. I don't know any Communists, one woman sobs. I wish I did so I could go home.

Yunhe is scared. Yu Qiwei had a rich uncle to bail him out and she doesn't. She feels sick. She is sure that the woman who keeps coughing has tuberculosis. The blood-streaked spit is everywhere.

Two weeks pass. Two weeks of terrible sleep. Two weeks of living in terror, knowing that her head might be removed from her shoulders at any given moment. Where is the Party? There has been no sign of rescue.

Finally it is her turn. The interrogator is a man whose face is a mask of scars. He has a massive upper body and tiny legs. Before questioning he soaks her head in a bucket of hot-pepper water.

Yunhe shuts her eyes and endures. She confesses nothing. Back in her cell she witnesses the death of a cellmate. The body is dragged out to be fed to wild dogs.

At her next interrogation, Yunhe seems to be having a nervous breakdown. She laughs hysterically and lets saliva drip from the corner of her mouth.

It's my fifteenth day in prison. I am very sick, running a high fever. I pick up my trade and begin to play the convincing role of an innocent. I sing classic operas. The entire opera from beginning to end. It is for the guards.

> The autumn moon is half round above Omei Mountain
> Its pale light falls in and flows with the water of the
>     Pingchang River
> In the night I leave Chingchi of the limpid stream for the
>     three canyons

*And glide down past Yuchow, thinking of you whom*
  *I cannot see*

The guards feel sorry for me. They begin to respond. One suggests to his supervisor that I seem to have nothing to do with the Communists.

Yes, sir, I reply at the interrogation. I am lured by evil people.

The girl is told that she can be released under a condition: she must sign a piece of paper denouncing Communism. She hesitates but convinces herself to proceed. I'm just playing a trick with the enemy.

I have never lowered my head to an enemy, Madame Mao later says. I have never dishonored the Communist Party. The truth is that she never admits she signed the paper. Her claim is consistent for the rest of her life. People who doubt her words are put in prison.

# 5

To her comrades Yunhe says that her release from prison was pure luck. She claims that because she had left no evidence, she was merely considered a suspect from the beginning to the end of the case. It had to do with my strong will — I could have confessed under torture, but my commitment to Communism won me victory.

In truth she knows that she has betrayed the oath. She justifies this by thinking that she is more useful to Communism alive than as a martyr.

After signing the paper, she is released. The first couple of days back in her apartment she tosses all night. She sees images of dogs attacking her cellmates. The screams from the torture chamber haunt her thoughts. After midnight she gets up and gathers together her books and magazines. She walks downstairs and throws them in the dump. During the day she avoids streets where Communist leaflets are posted. She no longer communicates with Communist friends. She finds the house noises endearing again. The sound of the husband and wife fighting next door keeps her nightmares at bay. The neighbor boy's piano becomes music from heaven. She doesn't mind the smell of burnt soy sauce from the kitchen. She lies in bed all day and she still misses Yu Qiwei.

I decide to change my name. A new name symbolizes new life. I want the name to ring my character too. Besides, changing one's name is fashionable in Shanghai. It helps one to get noticed. Some people cut out their last name so that there are two syllables instead of the traditional three. This is considered an act of rebellion. The sounds stand out by themselves. There are names that have inspired me, especially those of established writers and actresses. They are Bing-xing for Ice Heart, Xiao-yue for Smiling Moon, and Hu-dee for Butterfly.

I name myself Lan Ping. *Lan* means Blue, my favorite color, and *Ping* means Apple and sweetness. Blue associates with the images of sky, ink and myth, while Apple evokes the idea of harvest, ripeness, fruitful future and also my hometown Shan-dong, where apples are the trademark export product.

After my recuperation from prison, I start to branch out. I reconnect myself with old friends for acting opportunities. I tell people that I am committed to helping the country. A good play promotes the nation's conscience and this is what's important.

I put my will to the test. I wear my biggest smile. To take care of my blue dress I wear an old jacket. That way I feel free to push my way through crowded buses. I take the blue dress with me and change before my meetings. I change back to my old jacket after the meeting. Because my empty stomach often growls in the middle of meetings I drink a lot of water. I have to hide my feet, because they swell from walking too much.

But still there are more rejections. Everyone tells me that I am good yet I receive no offers. Many girls in the same situation give in. They go to bed with the leering men who call themselves directors or producers. I tell myself over and over that I cannot give up.

In June the girl discovers that there is an audition for an interpretive rendition of Ibsen's *Doll's House*. The director is Mr. Zhang Min, a Russian-trained theater master. She is excited the moment she hears the news. She had read Ibsen's play so many times back in school and has already memorized most of Nora's lines. Although she is aware that she has very little chance to win the role, she tells herself to try. If nothing else comes out of it, she will make an impression. She will get to meet director Zhang Min.

She registers for the audition and begins to prepare the part. She invites her neighbors to come and hear her while their soups are on the stove. She gets the ladies little stools to sit on so that they can listen to her while cutting beans and carrots.

The day of the audition she gets up early and puts on light makeup. She feels confident and comfortable. The first to arrive at the Arts Club where the audition is to take place, she chats with the doorman and finds out that there have already been three days of auditions.

The good news is that Mr. Zhang Min is still looking. The doorman winks and puts his palms together to wish the girl luck.

By nine o'clock the room is packed with young women. The director's assistants come in and begin to set up tables and chairs. After the stage is set Zhang Min appears. He already seems bored. He orders the audition to begin immediately.

While waiting for her turn, Lan Ping takes a close look at the director. He is a soft-spoken man who wears a black cotton jacket and a black French beret. He smokes a cigarette and holds a tea mug in his hand. His assistant calls the contestants by their numbers. He looks at them without expression.

The young women do everything to overcome their stage fright. One girl takes deep breaths while the others massage their throats. Lan Ping waits with her heart beating fast. She is not as nervous as she thought she would be. She reflects on her time in jail. What can be more frightening? She smiles.

Mr. Zhang Min notices the difference. With his thumb supporting his chin he leans forward and begins to watch the girl. He keeps the same pose from the beginning to the end of Lan Ping's performance. He doesn't say anything afterwards. From the way he looks at her Lan Ping knows that she has made an impression. Before she leaves the room Zhang Min gets up and waves. I want to see you do that part again.

She does the part again.

He watches. He stops her and demands, Chisel the phrase this way. How about softening the tone a bit? *Oh, Torvald, I'm not your child.* Don't bang your chest. It's too cartoonish. Let yourself miss a beat. Hold the tension. Pivot your head toward the window, then the door, now speak.

She follows the direction, improvising at the same time. She is in a plain blue blouse, her body tall and slender. She is full of desire yet vulnerable. The assistants whisper to each other. Zhang Min doesn't smile, doesn't say anything more. After Lan Ping finishes, the director sends an assistant to tell her to wait in the greenroom. Mr. Zhang Min would like to talk with you after he is done. He is wrapping up. He won't be seeing anyone else today.

They meet and have tea. It goes well. Her senses tell her that he appreciates not only her acting skill but also her personality. She is flattered. You understand Nora, he remarks. Strangely, in the back of her mind, there is a recurring, seemingly irrelevant thought: he is a married man.

Later, much later, after the play, after the role, after her heart is broken over her next husband, she will listen to that thought and go to Zhang Min for shelter. She will move into his place and become his mistress. But at this point, she is a professional. And she is going to play Nora.

Nora is a traditional Western housewife, the mother of three children, Zhang Min says. Her husband and her friends think that she lives a good life — well fed and clothed. She gets expensive gifts at her birthdays.

But she is like my mother, the girl interrupts. Her man doesn't regard her as an equal but a bedmaid.

Go on, Miss Lan Ping! Go on.

She is not allowed to make decisions about the house, her children or her own activity. She is a wing-clipped bird, kept in an invisible cage. She is a concubine, a foot warmer and a slave. She is a prisoner. I was a prisoner. I know what it's like to be a prisoner.

The director encourages her. Describe your background, he orders. She enters her role. She describes her father, his drinking and his violence, and then her mother, the slave. She describes herself, how she ran away and grew up in hardship. The director listens attentively, forgets to drink his tea. Later on he tells her that her interpretation was exactly what he had been looking for. He falls in love and could have kissed her right on the spot. You are my perfect Nora. The play is going to fly because of you.

Then she meets her costar, Mr. Zhao Dan, her lifetime curse, the king of Chinese stage and screen. Dan plays her stage husband, Torvald. Lan Ping can hardly believe her luck. She remembers the sensation of being introduced to Dan for the first time. Awestruck. The handshake that makes her tremble. She is unable to hide her nervousness.

He is a tall and handsome man with a pair of penetrating eyes. He nods, acknowledging her.

Miss Lan Ping is a member of the left wing. When Zhang Min says this to the actor, the girl feels belittled.

I am new but I don't lack talent, she says, as if to nobody.

Would you like some candy? the actor yells. Who would like to have some candy?

They work fourteen hours a day and make the theater their home. Sometimes they sleep behind the stage. They are a good pair when they are acting. But there is already tension between them. What annoys Dan is Lan Ping's boldness, her assumption that she is his equal. The way she uses her new status and her association with him to show off to others. He can't stand her elation.

She begins to set herself up to be burned. She can't help being attracted to him, first toward his genius, as a mentor, a teacher, and then to him as a man. Later she says that it was simply her nature to conquer the unconquerable — she was attracted to the challenge, not the man.

She is Dan's partner and fan. He makes her focus on her character. But she becomes confused, she mistakes her stage relationship with him for the real thing. It is all new and exciting. She loses herself.

It eventually becomes clear that he doesn't appreciate her as much as she appreciates him. He pays no attention to her although they act in intimate scenes together. He is his own inspiration and she is a prop, an off-camera object, which he takes as a lover, to which he speaks love. He regards her as a provincial actress, miscast for the role.

Dan wants to have nothing to do with me after working hours. He doesn't want to discuss the role with me. Instead he offers suggestions regarding my part to Zhang Min. Besides what's on the script he has no interest in hearing what I have to say. He has many friends who are influential. They come by after the show and usually go for tea or snacks. I make myself available but am never invited. It tells me that Dan thinks of me as a poor choice for Nora. I see this in his arrogance, and from the way he begins to miss rehearsals. He doesn't want to be my Torvald. I am not sure whether he has ever spoken to Zhang Min about a possible replacement. I am sure that if it wasn't for Zhang Min, I would have already been replaced.

Dan is flirtatious. He likes to play with Lan Ping using the lines of Torvald. He squeezes her hands, presses her body against him during acting. He makes excuses to get her into his makeup room, pins himself against her. Come on, it is a perfect day in spring, he says.

Dan's lightness torments her. It hurts her more than anything when he makes jokes about the moments on stage where her intense effort has made her awkward.

It is in her relationship with Dan that she learns her fate. Learns that she can't escape Dan and men like him. Later she watches him as he moves on, to abandon her as a stage partner, and to pair with her rival, Miss Bai Yang.

Yet she can't forget Dan, who has not said one worthy word about her. The childish grin on his face every time he greets her. For that, in the future, Dan will pay with his life.

Madame Mao believes that one must collect one's debts.

I rebuff Dan. I demand his seriousness. Although nothing seems wrong on the surface, there is this undercurrent, an unspoken resentment. One day, the day after I had pushed him off of my chest, he mentions a girl. I am in love, he says. Her name is Lucy. Lucy Ye. She is the one I intend to marry. She is an actress too. A tender creature unlike you.

He brings Lucy in between us, too often, as if mentioning her will protect him from being attracted to me.

Maybe the truth is there, speaking its own voice for Lan Ping and she doesn't know it. She wants to swallow Dan up. She has not had a man since arriving in Shanghai. Her longing for affection is dreadful, and she cannot escape her feelings.

When Dan is asked to comment on Lan Ping as a stage partner, he says, No, no comment. Truly. He says this to every journalist, critic and friend. A shrug of the shoulders. Truly, no comment. It hurts Lan Ping beyond healing.

Yet, underneath all of this, in the midst of her resentment and tension, there is never a sense of finished business — never an end to wanting Dan.

In the weeks leading up to opening night, I pour myself heart and soul into the role. I feel the character, feel the rightness of the story for our times. Although Dan won't take me out, I go out with others, lesser cast members. I tell them how I feel about what we are involved with. I find myself getting emotional, my voice loud. Let's toast the show!

One night, there is a playwright in the group. He says that I should consider myself very lucky. He points out that if it were not for Dan, no one would come — no one is interested in watching me. I am terribly offended. I bounce off my chair. Who are you to say this to me?

I make enemies. I can't avoid them. After the fight some friends advise me that I should have just ignored the stupid playwright. But I am hurt by his words! My friends say, You're too serious. Those were the utterances of a drunkard. It doesn't mean anything. But I disagree. I believe that it was his true view. He is influenced by Dan.

On stage she lives out her eternal despair. Nora's lines fall from her lips like words of her own. *I've lived by performing tricks, Torvald, and I can bear it no more.*

On opening night the theater is jammed. Five-foot-tall flower baskets sent by friends and associates pile over the terrace. The seats are packed. The add-up seats — seats that have no backs — are sold at full price. Dan and Lan Ping's pictures are painted on wall-size posters on each side of the theater. Both their eyes are shadowed with dark blue paint. Lan Ping is in a black satin dress. The characters are in a dramatic pose, standing chest to chest and lips an inch apart.

The crowd is spellbound. Although most of them are Dan-fans,

Miss Lan Ping takes them by surprise. As she catches her breath in the makeup room during intermission, Zhang Min rushes in. He gives her an affectionate hug without saying a word. She knows that he is proud of her, knows that she has succeeded.

*This Nora has a Communist's mouth,* one paper raves. *It attacks and bites into our government's flesh. Miss Lan Ping's Nora speaks the voice of the people. The audience identifies with her. What we hear in Nora's voice is a political message. The people of China are sick of the role they are forced to play. They are sick of their incompetent government, the head of state Chiang Kai-shek, and themselves as the obedient, discreet and child-rearing Nora.*

This is what she has always wanted in life — being able to inspire others. It is what the operas did to her when she was a young girl. Now she has finally arrived. The novelty of fame brews on. She is thrilled to be recognized when walking on the streets.

She likes the interviews although the big papers are still not interested in her. They do stories on Dan. She doesn't give up. She is determined to make herself Dan's equal in every respect. She offers her stories to the smallest papers and accepts invitations to talk at schools. She loves to pose for photos. She adores the lights, the clicking sound of the cameras.

On stage they are lovers. She sits on his lap. He returns her affection. She tries her best to hide her feelings for him. She leaves the theater in a hurry, pretending to run to the next engagement. She tries to run away from her loneliness. Just looking at Dan makes her heart ache. Since the play's opening Lucy Ye has come to see Dan every evening. They steal kisses in between scenes. Dan's dressing room door is always closed.

She tries to handle herself, tries to get over Dan. She invites Dan and Lucy to tea, to discuss improving their performances. It is to make her heart learn reality. To go through a funeral. Eat yourself. She sits across from the couple and speaks seriously. She focuses on the roles, voices her opinions. She bends down to sip tea while feeling her tears coming.

*I am walking out of this house that suffocates me and I will survive. You will see, Torvald!* she cries on stage.

It is at this moment that her fate answers. It is then that he, a man named Tang Nah, appears in her view. He makes her see him. Nothing extraordinary at the beginning. He pushes himself like a photo-print in a darkroom. The texture gets richer by the second. Now it is clear.

He is among the critics attending the show on opening night. Fashionably dressed, he is in an elegant white Western suit and white leather shoes with a matching hat. He comes to meet his destiny, the woman for whom in the near future, he will twice try to kill himself.

Tang Nah is a liberal. A typical Shanghai bourgeois. A stylish-looking man, above average in height, a pair of single-lid eyes, long straight nose and sensuous mouth. He is well educated and an expert in Western literature. Among his favorite novels is *Lady Chatterley's Lover*. He drinks tea and speaks English at parties in front of pretty women. On opening night his face is neatly shaved and his hair smoothly combed to the back. He is in an excellent mood. He enters the theater and walks to his seat, into the web of passion. Later on he is criticized for having an unrealistic mind, for his need to live in a fantasy world, and for being a weak man who lets emotion drive his life. But he is already in it when he enters the dark space where she is to appear, to present herself as an illusion.

It is right here, on this night, the first sight, already nothing is real. Her makeup, her hair, her costume, the little picture house. The fantasy itself. She is his Lady Chatterley.

*

Each night, she relies on her role to carry her up high.

Lan Ping–Nora leans herself against Dan's chest, against the man who twenty-five years later she will throw into prison for having rejected her. But now she feels his heartbeat, his body heat. She feels strangely in love, touched by her own passion. The characters speak their lines. She tears herself away from Dan. He grabs her. She struggles, pushes him, giving him a chance to tame her. He comes back, locking her arms behind her, bending her toward the floor. They strike a final pose. Her hair falls back, her breasts pressing against Dan. She sees his sweat melt his makeup and feels his breath hit her lips.

*A Doll's House* becomes the talk of Shanghai. The talk of 1935. Lan Ping rides her fame and begins her move toward the movie industry. Yet she finds herself unwelcome. It is another circle and another gang. To break in she realizes that she has to start from square one. During the day, she looks for opportunities in film, at night she continues to play Nora. Her audience grows, and the government feels threatened by the play's political impact. One month later, Zhang Min is ordered by the Department of the Censorship to remove the political element from the show. When he leads the troupe in protest, the government shuts down the play.

A public letter is issued by the troupe criticizing the government. Lan Ping's signature is on the top. With the same passion, with the same tone and voice which she uses on stage, she speaks on radio and at rallies. She passionately calls the government "Torvald."

It is a fateful evening that Tang Nah and I meet. It is the course we both are meant to be served.

I am on my way to the Shanghai Film Studio. Not too long ago the studio took a chance and signed me up. It is a small contract, and in business terms I am still on my own, but I feel better being under the studio's wing. The tiny roles I get I must earn. I am not sleeping around. In this business actresses are for sale. It's a tradition that certain men in town "take care of" the new girl on the block. These are powerful men. The money guys of the industry. They approach me for coffee and tea. You definitely have star potential, they say. Their breath stinks. Why don't you come with me to my place so that I can introduce you to . . .

She has tea and coffee with powerful men. She puts on makeup for them. She always manages to walk out at the last minute. She knows many girls who didn't. They get shut behind the door and lose their souls for good. Lan Ping believes that she can ride the momentum of *A Doll's House*. But underneath her smile she is lonely and depressed. Her sweet voice is often out of place. It carries an edge of fear. She has nightmares about the ground splitting and silently swallowing her.

It is in fear she meets Tang Nah. He walks toward her on a noisy street at dusk. He smiles, stops, takes his cigarette from his lips and introduces himself.

The sun has just set. The sky is covered with red clouds. I am in a lousy mood. But the man in front of me is a well-known journalist. A staff member of a major newspaper, *Dagongbao*. I can't afford to be rude. I offer him my hand.

Sorry I can't quite recall . . . Have we met?

Dan introduced us, remember?

Oh yes, that's right, now I remember. Mr. Tang Nah. I have read your reviews. They are excellent.

He nods. I miss Nora.

Thank you. For some reason my nose begins to tickle. I quickly look down at the pavement and say, It is very nice of you to say that.

No, please, he responds. I don't mean to just pay you a compliment. You are a very good actress.

He tells me that he has seen the show at least eight times. He mimics my stage moves, turns around and walks a couple of steps — it is my entrance scene.

He lifts my mood. I can't help laughing. He is funny.

Once your satin dress got caught on a prop, he says, hands animated. Remember? No? Anyway I got nervous for you. But you turned the accident into part of the plot. Oh, I was completely impressed. I have seen a lot of shows in my life and I have never seen anyone like you.

I find myself listening to him. I miss Nora too, I answer.

I've longed to meet you personally, he goes on. More than once I went to the backstage gate hoping to get a glimpse of you after the show.

Many years later Madame Mao visits the moment in her dreams. The lovers stand on a small street lit up by a line of food stands. Tofu soup, sweet and sour cabbage, water chestnuts, duck-blood soup with rice noodles. She remembers clearly that there was a boy selling gingko nuts at the corner. He roasts the nuts in a wok on top of a little portable stove. The flame is reflected on his chest. It looks like the boy is holding an armful of light.

This is how they begin. Just for a walk first. He picks her up and takes her to places she has never been. A cigarette held between his fingers, he displays his knowledge. On one hand, he is gentle, enthusiastic and modest, on the other hand, he is arrogant and opinionated — this is how he makes his name as a critic.

They are different, almost opposite in character. She finds Tang Nah stimulating. His English fascinates her. He is a new world she can't wait to discover. She is charmed by his liberal attitude. He is a very different man from Yu Qiwei. If Yu Qiwei brought her a sense of adventure, Tang Nah cultivates a sense of culture. If Yu Qiwei opened her character and shaped it, Tang Nah embraces her and loses himself in her role. If Yu Qiwei is a man of calm and determination, Tang Nah is a man of sensitivity and pure passion. To Yu Qiwei she was a star in his universe, to Tang Nah she *is* the universe.

Tang Nah is like an old horse who knows his way around Shanghai. In Tang Nah's circle everyone admires the West and everyone hates the Japanese. Often singing breaks out in the middle of one of Tang Nah's parties. People compete to sing the loudest. The composers write notes on napkins and musicians strike up the tune. The playwrights construct their scenes in between toasts and the actors play them out on the floor. A few days later the song will be on the radio or the scene in a movie.

I am getting to know Tang Nah's close friends, film director Junli and his wife Cheng, a writer. Junli is the most talented among his friends. He is in his late twenties and is becoming popular with his new movies. He is a peculiar-looking man with thin hair. He calls Tang Nah a pure romantic. Tang Nah's way of living gives me ideas for movies, he says. If I had known I wouldn't have taken Junli's words as a compliment. Tang Nah lives for drama and this gears him to disaster.

At the moment what friends say about Tang Nah impresses me. I never consider that Tang Nah's passion could be negative, or even harmful. Tang Nah's friends won't ever have to live with him so they don't know. I will discover that Tang Nah can't tell movies from reality and that he doesn't want to. But he is extraordinarily kind to his friends. He has done reviews for Junli's films and volunteers to be Junli's publicist.

I am not certain what Tang Nah tells Junli about me. Tang Nah says that it's a secret. Man to man. I am sure he tells Junli his opinion of me. And I am sure Junli has seen *A Doll's House*. But Junli never voices his impression of me. It seems that he is not sure about me or about Tang Nah's relationship with me. He observes and studies us like characters in his films. He probably thinks that I come on too strong with Tang Nah. He might have doubts about Tang Nah too. As a best friend he must know Tang Nah's way with women. He must have sensed that we will end up badly. But Junli never gives me any advice or warning. He cares about Tang Nah too much to betray him.

However, I sense it. The way things clicked between me and Zhang Min does not happen between me and Junli. It is a great pity. I can't force a director's affection. If I weren't Tang Nah's girlfriend, Junli might be able to look at me in a different light. But Tang Nah didn't make that possible. I couldn't meet Junli as anything else but Tang Nah's latest woman — the damage was already done.

Still, I continue to hope that with Tang Nah's help Junli will offer me a role in one of his movies. Or he can refer me as a talented actress to his colleagues. I am anxious to get my career going again. I am twenty-one years old already.

Tang Nah says, I am twenty-five years old. And I think enjoying life is more important than anything else.

But my question is, How can one enjoy life at its fullest when one is not doing what one wants to do?

Tang Nah believes that Lan Ping can be better than she is. He is confident about transforming her. He thinks that she can be a goddess.

Tang Nah tells Lan Ping the meaning of being a modern woman. It is her pursuit of culture. This is the difference between Shanghainese and other Chinese in general. This is where the Shanghai women's self-confidence and elegance come from.

Compared to the inlanders, Shanghainese have a much more bal-
anced attitude toward life. For example, they admire the foreigners' culture but never fawn on them. Tang Nah points out to Lan
Ping and asks her to observe that even the rickshawmen, the lowest class in Shanghai, are able to toss phrases of English into their
dialect. It is the smoke that makes the ham tasty. See what I mean,
Miss Lan Ping?

He leads and she follows. He teaches Lan Ping to read the English
version of *A Doll's House*. Since she already knows the transla-
tion he thinks that this will make it easier and more interesting for
her. She repeats after him. But she can't get rid of her accent. She
has this Shan-dong tongue. Stiff. Tang Nah tries his best but she
still pronounces X as *ai-co-sih* and V as *wei*. Tang Nah gets frustrated. He tries every way. She thinks he is very cute. He begs her
to be serious. She tells him that he is teaching a dog to catch a
mouse.

Every night she goes to his place to study English. He lives in a
two-room apartment in a nice neighborhood. He is a neat fellow
and grows plants by his windows. There is calligraphy in his
room, all gifts from well-known masters. She is bored after a few
lines and he kisses her and begs her to endure a little longer. She
plays with him like a naughty girl. He loses his focus and quits.
He gives her a spelling test. It always begins with L-O-V-E. And
she always says L-O-Wei-E. He laughs and bites his lower lip to
demonstrate the V sound. She bites her lower lip. But when the
test begins, it is still L-O-Wei-E. He scratches his head, lies on top
of her, puts his mouth between her lips and asks her to bite it
when sounding V.

He is a good lover, not always in a hurry to possess her. He takes
her out and tries to relax her. He takes her to galleries, antique
shops, bookstores, concerts and poetry readings. They look at

their reflections when passing the street windows. They are a handsome couple. Both tall and slim.

She appreciates it that he never makes fun of her mistakes. She knows that sometimes she overplays her cleverness. She appreciates it when he goes out of his way to ignore it when she lies out of embarrassment. Tang Nah is critical of others but never of Lan Ping. He never says, How terrible you don't even know who Su Dong-po is. He explains patiently that Su is a famous ancient poet and then reads her the work. Then he buys tickets to visit Su Dong-po's birthplace and gives her a lecture on the way.

The white-colored cliffs shoot out of the horizon while the Yangzi River rushes toward the east at its bottom. Around the cliffs there is a narrow path for climbing. The view steals my breath away. At the bottom, there is a little wooden boat and a fisherman for hiring. As we sit in the boat looking up, the cliffs seem to be pressing air back into my lungs. The sky is magnificently clear and blue. At noon we are on top of the cliff. As we look down from a bird's perspective, the boat is smaller than an ant. The comparison between greatness and smallness gives me a sense of life's range and depth.

This is how I fall in love with Tang Nah. I begin to see everything through his eyes. A new world that begins with the story of Su Dong-po. Tang Nah is comparing Su's encounter with the ancient court with our current government. The way *A Doll's House* was forced to shut down. The way my role was taken away from me.

A group of court officials made their dislike of the poet known to the emperor, Tang Nah explains. They reported that they had discovered in Su's verses disrespect and provocation. Playing on the emperor's doubts, Su was sentenced to a lifetime in exile. The poet must take leave of his family forever. He is dragged through his hometown to enter upon a long bitter journey toward the western desert. Imagine facing the endless interrogation and torture by local executioners. Imagine all his friends turning away from him in fear of the government.

No pain could ever be greater than the isolation and loneliness of the heart, Tang Nah continues. Yet, alone the poet was alive with his own spirit. It was then that the idea of the great verse *Writing on the Red Wall* was conceived. It was born in despair. It burst out in the middle of suicidal thoughts.

The girl looks up at Tang Nah in awe as he explains maturity.

It is like the radiance of the sun but not as bright and hurtful to the eyes. It is a sound that is pleasant and resonant but not sugar-filled. It is a kind of ease. It doesn't demand attention. There is no longer a need to please. It is the point at which one no longer begs for another's understanding. It is a smile that forgives all. It is one's peacefulness, one's remoteness toward the world of materials. It is a height that one doesn't have to climb to achieve. It is when the passion-dough is ready for steam, when the shrill sound of a mountain wind gives way to a gentle moan and the streams gather into a lake.

One evening we are strolling after dinner at a local restaurant. Suddenly there is noise. A block away, on the side street, someone is calling for help. As we get near we see a big-shouldered Russian hitting a thin rickshawman. The Russian complains that the man has asked for too much fare. There is a crowd but no one speaks for the rickshawman.

We watch for a while. Tang Nah becomes upset. Why don't you two talk and come up with a reasonable price? Tang Nah goes up to the Russian. He demands that he stop hitting the rickshawman.

The Russian says, Get out of my face!

No, replies Tang Nah. No paying no leaving.

I worry that the Russian will turn around and hit Tang Nah. It is what he will obviously do next. But Tang Nah stands firm. At that very moment I feel my love for him. A perfect hero.

The rickshawman is unable to speak clearly. His mouth is bleeding. The Russian speaks English. He insists on leaving without paying.

How about five yuan? Tang Nah pitches his voice. I know the area. The distance where the ride began and ended would cost at least eight yuan. Let's be fair.

One dime, the Russian offers insultingly. He throws a dime on the ground.

Suddenly the rickshawman rises and jumps on the Russian. With the help of the crowd, Tang Nah and I push both men to the nearest police station.

We assume that the rickshawman will get justice at the police station. But we are disappointed. Who gives you the right to violate a foreigner? the police chief yells at Tang Nah. He might be an investor and we can't do enough to make him feel at home.

Are you a Chinese? Tang Nah yells. It's your obligation to help another Chinese when he is mistreated! Tang Nah's whole frame shakes when the police chief frees the Russian and fines the rickshawman.

For a long time Tang Nah is unable to speak.

We continue our stroll. But our mood has changed completely. The smell of the gardenias is no longer sweet and the night scene is no longer soothing.

There has to be a revolution, Tang Nah mutters finally. Chiang Kai-shek's government is completely corrupt. It has to be brought down or China has no hope. I shall write about this incident in a play and you will perform it.

Suddenly we stop walking. We embrace and kiss passionately

in the middle of the street, in the middle of the night and in the middle of the pain.

I think I am ready. I am over with Yu Qiwei and the rest of the mess. I am beginning a new relationship with the man I totally adore. Yet I am afraid. I can't proceed. There is this little voice speaking in the back of my head, in a panicky tone. It tells me that I am about to hurt myself.

I am in Tang Nah's arms. I ask him to hold me tight, tighter. I ask him to convince me.

What are you afraid of? He is in tears, he can't stand my pain. You will never be hurt again, I promise.

I am a revolutionary! The strange phrase pops out of my mouth. My voice is blunt, as if it were a statement of caution.

Tang Nah makes no response, he is confused.

I too. It is odd. I have no explanation. There must be a reason. There must be tension building already. Tension that will break us apart even as it pulls us together. I speak in order not to be tempted, in order to refuse. I am sure this is it. My senses try to tell me that there is a mismatch. A gap between us that is impossible to fill. It happens right then, right in the middle of novelty. But it is no use. No one can escape fate. We must come together to share this path, to share the view of the gingko-nut boy and his armful of light.

A few days after the Russian incident we sign a lease on a small apartment on the north side of Shanghai. We move in and begin to live together.

# 6

SHE DOESN'T REMEMBER how the trouble started. It began slowly, crept up on them and then there it was. She assumes that there is too much heat in both of their personalities and that this has begun to melt their relationship down. They battle over what seems to be nothing yet everything. Bills, jobs, habits, differences in opinions. She knows another reason — she is not getting any offers from the studio and Tang Nah's connections are not helping. She is frustrated that he not only doesn't help to fix her trouble, he doesn't take her trouble seriously.

You can always survive by doing something else, he suggests. Be a secretary or a nurse, for example.

She feels like a peacock being forced into a hen cage. She tries not to argue back. She tries to make herself understand that Tang Nah has troubles of his own and needs support. Because of his radical views his paper recently became the target of the government. As a result Tang Nah was fired as the paper's key writer. At first he felt proud that he had stood up for his beliefs. But lately his job hunting hasn't been successful. She has tried to be supportive. He pretends to be unconcerned and shrugs her off.

Before my eyes Tang Nah slips into misery. No one will hire him and he is becoming short on money. He shouts at himself. And yet he still goes to restaurants. He can't live without style. He borrows money to buy me gifts. He has to feel rich and capable. He continues to throw big parties to entertain his friends.

I am scared of going into debt, scared of Tang Nah's desire to keep spending. I pull money out of our joint account and hide my savings. One day I am caught and he accuses me of betraying our love.

We haven't spoken to each other for two days. I feel guilty and try to make up by cooking dinner. I prepare his favorite food, pot-stickers. I do it carefully, making sure each pot-sticker turns a perfect golden brown.

He lies on the bed, staring at the ceiling and smoking.

Dinner is ready, I call.

He gets off the bed and comes to the table.

I serve him, putting a pair of chopsticks, a napkin and a little bowl of vinegar in front of him.

He pushes away the plates and begins to speak in a strange voice. Craving for fame is the enemy of happiness. There is nothing worse. You are losing your best qualities. You are influenced by the worst of Shanghai. You have bought its superficiality. I am worried about you. You are destroying yourself. You can't see it because of your poor education. I feel sad and sorry for you. You play smart at small situations but you lose the big battles. You are losing. It is like covering your ears while stealing a bell — you think no one is going to hear you. You know what you are turning into? A philistine. Yes, you are.

She tries to ignore him. She stuffs her mouth with pot-stickers and chews viciously. She tries to think that he is taking his frustration out on her and doesn't mean harm. He has nowhere else to deposit his anger. She has to be there for him. It's time to prove her love. He needs her to hold his trash. That is what she should do for him.

She endures until she reaches her limit.

He continues. I am beginning to believe what my friends say about you. You have come from a small place. I am trying to grow a flower out of a cooked seed.

At this point her rage rises. The impact chokes her. You are my lover, she says, pointing her finger at him, her tears pouring. I can bear nasty rumor, insulting gossip and mean criticism. I can hold up a falling sky, but not your words.

It hurts her too much to go on. She picks up the pot-sticker plate, carries it into the bathroom. She dumps the pot-stickers into the toilet and flushes. She shuts herself in and sobs.

He comes, knocks and begs her to open it. It's all because of my frustration. I apologize. I am afraid. I fear that you will be disappointed and you will leave me.

At midnight, she opens the bathroom door and comes out. She tells him that she can't stay with him anymore. She is unable to erase what he has said from her head.

He looks at her as she starts packing. She takes out her jackets, pants and shoes, her toothbrush and towels. She has a small suitcase and she doesn't have much to pack.

Is this the way you punish me? he says bitterly. You know I have no strength to resist you. All my friends predicted that. But no one can talk me out of loving you. I thought you cared, but . . . You don't give our love a second chance. You don't. He breaks down.

She has never seen a man sob like this. His whole frame shakes like cucumber frames beaten down by a storm. She quits packing.

After a long while he stops sobbing. He gets up, goes to the door and opens it widely. Don't bother with me. Just go.

The room is quiet. The water pipe in the toilet tank has stopped filling.

She gets up and walks to the door and closes it. After that she looks at him and waits.

Ping, he calls.

She stretches out her arms.

It is a night of tears and promises. We swear to never let anything get in the way of our love. The next day he is confident again. He goes out job hunting and comes back with flowers in his hand. No good news, darling, but love is the best news, isn't it?

I smile and hug him. I tell him about my news — no roles but I got myself a part-time job, a production assistant.

The days go on. Weeks and months. Still no good news for Tang Nah. To avoid embarrassment he hangs out late. He comes home drunk and doesn't get up until noon. He parties with friends endlessly.

The world stinks, he says to me. It absolutely stinks.

Dan and Junli continue to embrace Tang Nah. They listen to him with pleasure. They put no pressure on him and he leans on their support. He even talks enthusiastically about Dan's new role and Junli's new movie. He makes it sound like his own success.

What about you? I ask. My tone is sharp and I don't intend to hide my disappointment.

His parties and friends become irritating to me. I can't stand them. Tang Nah has run out of tricks to solve the trouble building between us. To avoid conflict I start to close myself. We withdraw affection and rarely make love. When we do, it is a way to stop a fight, a way to escape reality. But it is losing its magic.

Her own frustration comes to bite her now. None of her auditions are picked up. One day her temper bursts. They are attending the opening of a play, *Empress Wu*. She and Tang Nah have come with friends. She is fashionably dressed in an indigo-blue full-length silk gown with a thin scarf around her neck of the same fabric. Tang Nah is in a white Western suit. They look handsome together. At the beginning she seems to be having a good time.

*Empress Wu* is an experimental play. It is the first time Chinese actors recite prose instead of poetry. Empress Wu is depicted as a woman of greatness. The audience cheers loudly when the curtain descends.

It is at the reception that Lan Ping loses control. She speaks harshly. The performance is much too dull in my opinion. It lacks energy. The actress is unfit. There is no sincerity. She is not acting, she is a young monk chanting — with her mouth, not her heart.

People are shocked. But Lan Ping keeps going. In her animation her scarf falls off the shoulders. She keeps picking it up but the scarf keeps falling. Finally she leaves it off. She continues to criticize, her voice gets louder and louder. She wraps her fingers with the scarf nervously. Tang Nah comes. He pulls her gently to the side. Come on, you are tired.

Let me finish!

Listen, I am a critic. And it's my job to comment and I think it is a good show.

Oh, Tang Nah, you are a lousy critic and that's why you are not hired.

At this point Tang Nah shoots back. He says what hits a nerve, says the words that split them forever. You know what, Lan Ping? The only reason you are angry is because you didn't get to play Empress Wu!

For Lan Ping the winter of 1936 starts with slammed doors and tears. The couple has decided to separate and each is renting a different place. Although they try to come back together again, there is a wall between them. Mentally she tells herself that she is finished with Tang Nah, but physically she is unable to break the habit — their bodies depend on each other. After every fight she goes back to him only to run away the next day.

One night he comes to see her with roses to congratulate her on a new stage role she has been offered. It is a small role, but it gives the two a reason to meet. After the door has been closed only a few minutes, an upstairs neighbor hears Lan Ping's cry, followed by sounds of furniture being smashed. Fearing for Lan Ping's life the neighbor rushes down and breaks in. The lovers are at each other's throats.

On stage, I play a working-class girl who is at a turning point in her life. A girl very much like me, from a small town, confused by big city living. During the performance I take the opportunity to weep for myself. I am ill. My headache is severe, but I can't leave the stage. I have no other place to go.

I can't close my eyes. If I do, there is Tang Nah.

The night of March 8 I suffer from the desire to see him again. I am risking my health. My fever is getting worse. Maybe this is why I want to see him. My sense that I might be dying. Maybe I will be relieved — my body is doing the job on behalf of my heart.

I deliver myself to his apartment even as my head keeps telling me no. He lives on Nan-yang Boulevard in Chingan District. It is a cultured, upscale neighborhood. A place that suits his fashionable tastes. What am I doing here? I am out of myself. He has given me the keys, but doesn't expect me — I have declined his invitations. I have told him that it is not in my character to look back.

I break my own promise this time. I want to let go, to speak with him for the last time, to love him for the last time. On stage it would be the farewell scene. A heartbreaking but liberating act.

Her body is shivering, sweating from fever. She longs for his arms. She turns the key and enters. He is not in. The room is neat, as she had imagined. Everything is in its place. Shoes lined up behind the door, dishes piled up in baskets. Magazines and books stacked up, dust-free. A window is left open slightly. The white curtain moves with the breeze. She has only been in this room once before. It was two months ago.

There is a book on his desk. Something sticks out from its pages. Letters. She can't help her curiosity and decides to take a look. Two letters. One is a stranger's handwriting. A female-fan letter admiring one of his past columns. At the end she flirts. It is sweet but stupid. The writer says that she can't wait, has been dreaming about him. Says he is meant for her. She begs for a chance to meet him. The signature is like a dragon-dance, shows that she is not well educated. The paper smells fragrant with the scent of wild lilacs.

The other is Tang Nah's. It is sealed, waiting to be mailed. She feels the burn inside her. She can't think further. She has to open the letter and she does. She tears the seal, her hands trembling. I am greatly interested, she reads, for love like this is unusual and rare. His charm, again lavishing his knowledge and wisdom. He gives compliments to the girl using phrases he once used on Lan Ping. The words Lan Ping once held in her heart, depended on for strength and took as a weapon against her mother's ghost. Now as her eyes hit Tang Nah's elegant handwriting her breath stops.

I force myself to sit still and breathe. I leave him a note. I thank him for the opportunity to read the letters. I say things seem to be going very well. Now there is nothing to worry about anymore. Everything is falling into the right place. I couldn't be happier for him. I wish that I didn't so appreciate his handwriting, but unfortunately I do. It is beautiful.

Without telling a soul I go to the train station. I buy a ticket to Jinan. I don't know why I am running off to Jinan. My grandparents have died and I have long ago lost contact with my mother. But Jinan is my hometown and there is comfort in the idea. After I get off the train I head toward my grandparents' old house where I find a distant relative occupying the place, who doesn't recognize me. I decide to call her Aunt and I ask if I can stay for a while. She welcomes me.

I can't believe it when I receive a message from the manager of the town's only hotel. It is the third day. Tang Nah is waiting in the Railway Inn for me. I am surprised that he has found me. But I refuse to see him. He keeps begging, comes to the neighborhood, walks up and down the street and stands in front of the house. Finally my aunt invites him in.

He looks pale as if his blood has drained out of him. He says he needs to clarify something.

What's the point? We're finished. We can't change ourselves.

He yells loudly, almost screaming, I knew I would not be able to fight fate the moment I met you!

I fail to help myself. It is impossible to gather my thoughts. My will retreats but I manage to say, I won't go back.

He says fine, never mind. It is no problem.

The next morning, the hotel manager runs gasping up to our house. He looks like a man who has lost his soul. We can hardly make sense out of his words. Finally he gets me to understand that Tang Nah has overdosed himself with sleeping pills and is in the hospital.

I rush to his bedside. I call his name. He opens his eyes, tries to force a smile and passes out again. I don't know what to say. After Tang Nah gets out of the hospital I bid my aunt good-bye and go back to Shanghai with him.

Lan Ping moves into Tang Nah's place. They make themselves believe that love will conquer all. While they put on their best behavior they are still on guard. When his body recovers and he wants to make love, she is unable to. He feels her rejection. Her body's coldness, its stiffness. He feels its dying. He weeps. He knows that they can't go on. He gets up and asks if she has forgiven him.

For what? The letters?

It was terrible, he repeats over and over. I was frustrated and drunk. It doesn't mean anything. I don't even know the girl. She could be a prostitute. I don't remember her at all.

He says he is destroying himself — that is who he is without her affection. She says, It is not up to me. My heart has its own way. You see how hard I try. You see I am forcing myself. But my body remembers the hurt. Again it is not up to me. One reaps what one sows.

He gets up and passes into the drawing room, which they share with other tenants. She lies in bed. She is not aware that he is leaving her a note.

She doesn't recall how long it took her to find the note. She followed him as one sleepwalker might follow another, tracing his steps along on the edge of a high roof. The shadow of their past, the ghost of their love must have dragged her. She discovers his note. It says that he is going to kill himself again. There is no other way, the note says. He has to go. That way he will free her from his trouble.

Show my note to the police, so they'll know that it is my own choice to end my life. You may pity me for I am unable to give up this love. Now, finally, you know the truth about me, you know that I am not strong enough for you.

She looks into the crowd, trying to locate him. Finally she sees him, running away from her. She races.

They are face to face. He is stared at by death. Yes, this is the look in his eyes. Stared at by death. She shakes him. He doesn't respond. The buses, bicycles, crowds pass by them. Scenes seem unreal. People, objects move, pull in and out. The suffocation. Slowly everything begins to freeze. The way death stills. She hears her heart's cry.

We will talk, she says.

They are coming down from the peak of their crisis. In Lan Ping it takes the form of fever. She lies in bed in his arms, shivering, collapsing. One moment she cries hysterically, sits up, punches the mattress with her fist. The next moment she passes out, unconscious. He tends her, in repentance. He feeds her porridge the way a mother would her infant. He is at her bedside every time she wakes. Sometimes it is at midnight. Three o'clock in the morning. She opens her eyes, sees him sleep, head over his folded arms, on a stool. In front of him, a bowl of porridge, still warm.

She weeps, doesn't know what to do with him and herself. She feels for him but cannot love a man who has lost his way. The image of the letters haunts her. She pities him, wants to love him back but can't break through the wall. It is impossible to see him in a new light. She can't erase what happened — can't even decide what troubles her most: his infidelity or his attempts to take his own life.

Yet another part of her fights this logic. There are reasons to revive their love. She is attracted to his stubbornness, his doglike loyalty. His willingness to die for her. The way he bluntly said that if love doesn't conquer, then it is not love. She is moved by his faith in love and his promise that he will never abandon her. She is sure there is no other man on earth who would do what Tang Nah does for her. She remembers the unhappiness of living without love. She is not sure which is worse.

They bury themselves in work. He becomes a freelance writer and she still hunts for roles in theater and film, but their loneliness grows. She doesn't want to find out about the girl who wrote the

letter, and yet she can't let go. The girl preoccupies her thoughts
— the ghost opens a kitchen in her mind and cooks. She can taste
her in him sometimes. She is suspicious. She can't stand him
touching her. She has lost her desire for him completely.

He goes out, spends evenings with his friends, doesn't stop
drinking until he's drunk. In Dan and Junli he finds comfort and
understanding. They have been trying to help him locate a staff
position on a paper or magazine, but the editors reject him — his
suicide attempt is now a household story. In their eyes Tang Nah
has sacrificed his dignity.

Interestingly enough, on Lan Ping's part the story increases her
popularity and helps her find work. She becomes involved in political low-budget movies produced by independent film-makers.
She has had no luck getting roles in mainstream romantic-themed
movies. She can't beat those moon-face and vase-body creatures.
But the political films serve her well. There is less competition.
The producers are unable to get the famous actresses so they turn
to the starlets and even unknowns.

China, my country, matters more to me than my personal misfortune. The news of Japan's preparation for further invasion has
filled the papers. To my distaste, the Shanghainese are not terribly
affected. Seeking pleasure is forever the city's priority. Theaters
are still packed for romantic movies. The audience's lives seem to
require sucking on illusions. I resent those who play conscience-
numbing doctors, those who offer opium-feeding tubes to the
masses' brains. Many of them are Tang Nah's friends. Tang Nah
hangs out with them to escape his own frustration. He has become a layabout.

Tang Nah no longer answers her challenge. He avoids her. Soon
she discovers that he is having an affair again.

She finds herself too hurt to weep. She goes out and walks in the shadows of the streetlights. One night she stops at the door of Zhang Min, the director of *A Doll's House*. She knocks. He is home and is surprised at her visit. She asks if she can come in. He opens the door, offers a chair, puts out drinks, tells her that his wife and daughter are away. She breaks down, sobbing, tells him her story. He has all the time and attention in the world for her. He has always adored her.

They drink, she feels better. She says she doesn't want to go home, says that there is no reason. He offers his arms. It is what she wanted. She is here for this. To be cared for.

She thought she would feel better afterwards. But it is not the case. She can't speak of it to herself. She gets up to go. Says it's time. He understands and goes to open the door. He helps her into the coat and hugs her good-bye. Ping, I want you to know that I will always be here for you.

# 7

WE ARE HEADING TO a group wedding ceremony. We are joined by two other couples, Dan and Lucy, Eryi and Lulu. Junli will act as our host. The witness is Tang Nah's lawyer friend, Mr. Sheng. Both Tang Nah and I hope that the ceremony will rescue our love. We are vegetables after a heavy frost. We need the warmth of the sun. The journey seems perfect. It is a soothing spring day. We ride a train from Shanghai to Hang-zhou. The place has been described by poets and travelers throughout history as the face of heaven.

They can't see the trouble-mountain because they are on it. The truth is that there is nothing left in their love. She has doubts, but chooses to believe in love, plus the bonus — Tang Nah has promised to convince Junli to cast her in his films. That is how she decides to go forward, on to the wedding ceremony.

Here is Junli. She presents herself to him again, performing her tricks. But in the end there are no results to her effort. She tries as hard as she can, so does Tang Nah. But Junli is not only unmoved but disgusted. If it weren't for Tang Nah, he wouldn't even look at Lan Ping. She takes it so personally that she feels a sense of disgrace. Her resentment is so great that thirty years later, during the Cultural Revolution, she orders the Red Guards to destroy Junli. Put him away so he won't spread rumors about her. Junli is beaten to death by the Red Guards and Madame Mao won't admit that it has anything to do with a personal grudge.

Junli's sympathy toward Tang Nah has spoiled everything. He disregards my expectations for Tang Nah. If it weren't for his lazy attitude, Tang Nah could be a much greater man than he is now. Junli and Dan would have come to beg me for Tang Nah's favor. I think it is selfish for Tang Nah to accept himself as a loser. His friends are selfish to stand by while his talent slides down the drain. They buy him drinks when he is depressed. Junli even holds special parties to cheer him up. He invites Tang Nah to stay at his house so that he can avoid me. Tang Nah calls Junli his soulmate. Once Tang Nah confessed things that Junli and Dan had said about me. It made me furious. They believe that Tang Nah is too good for me. They give him permission to forget his responsibility to our love. They have ruined Tang Nah's future along with mine.

The truth is deeper. They are star-crossed. There is betrayal. And then comes her disappointment. She had expected Junli to cast her. She thought he was Tang Nah's best friend. But he did the opposite. He cast her rival, Bai Yang, a pancake-faced actress, in his film *The Spring River Runs East* and made her a superstar. How foolish she was. How can she possibly be liked while the man thinks that she is the source of his best friend's misery? The one who drove Tang Nah to attempt suicide? Junli is too smart. He has always seen Tang Nah and Lan Ping as a mismatch. He disliked her before she even introduced herself.

We are posing for photos. The Pagoda of Six Harmonies is a perfect background. Junli is trying to direct us in his frame. The stars of China. The most handsome men and women. I am aware that the photos will generate attention and career opportunities. But my intention is not just to be in this shot. My intention is to show Tang Nah how much I care for and love him. I am making a lifetime commitment to a man whom it is hard to keep loving. It is a sacrifice. But for love I am willing to do anything. I am shaking inside. I am rolling the dice.

Why am I nervous? You must have faith first to let it work for you, a Buddhist preacher once said to me. I must establish faith in Tang Nah, I must establish faith that our relationship will work. This is what I am thinking when the picture is being taken. I offer myself no alternatives. I burn all bridges. I cut my backings in order to be fully engaged in the battle.

Standing in the middle toward the back I am trying to smile but I am unconfident. I am afraid that my face will be compared to those of the other two obviously love-struck couples. I try to hide myself from the truth.

Junli is holding the camera. It is he who has suggested the Pagoda of Six Harmonies. A symbolic place. We have six in our group. The lucky number. Always stand up tall like the pagoda, Junli says. He is a good director who knows how to inspire actors.

Dan is by Lucy on my right. They can't stay off each other. I am jealous of Lucy. In Dan's look God teaches the beauty of men. Dan could have anyone he wanted, but he chooses Lucy. Dan can't wait to belong to her. Surely they know happiness. Eryi and Lulu too. I am sad.

I can't tell what's on Tang Nah's mind. He seems nervous too. His beret is pressed low, almost covering his eyes. He places himself behind me as if he wants to be out of focus.

Thirty years later Madame Mao desperately wants to destroy this picture. She wants to erase every face shown here. It is 1967 and she is on her way to becoming the ruler of China. The aging Mao is her ticket. She has to prove to the nation that she had been

Mao's love since her birth. She has to prove that there had been no one between her and Mao.

It is then Junli and Dan become the men-who-know-too-much. Madame Mao feels that she has no choice but to let them go.

Cut! Junli calls as he would on the set. The actors exhale. The group heads back to Shanghai the same night. Three days later they all attend a big reception. As expected, it catches the media's attention.

Tang Nah and Lan Ping are back home. But the marriage seems to be dead. They pretend that it is not bothering them. Both try to bury themselves in work. Yet there are no calls, no offers of roles for her. No business for Tang Nah either. Bills pile up. Money demons keep visiting from hell. But he still smiles, says that she is the biggest prize he has ever won. The rest he couldn't care less about. Broke or jobless, it doesn't bother me. I am a complete man as long as I have love.

She is in despair. You are not keeping your promises, she yells at Tang Nah. They are out of each other's bed. Can't be together yet can't be apart either. The bad pattern repeats.

Then they go out again to seek air and comfort in friends. They end up sleeping in other people's beds. He goes to the girl who wrote the letter, and she to Zhang Min, who is now working on a new play, *The Storm,* by the Russian playwright Ostrovsky. They deny their acts. It is becoming her new role in life. With Tang Nah it is a perfect scene.

In this scene she develops her own plot. When there is tension she makes the protagonist leave. She pulls out, disappears from the stage. Yet she is not able to turn her table around. Like her country she keeps falling apart. The Japanese troops enter in full force. The studios downsize. The box offices close. 1936. Absolutely no sign of luck.

Make up your mind and do it, I tell myself. I am packing and will be gone tonight. I will stay in a friend's place and will keep my address a secret. When I write the letter I imagine how Tang Nah will receive it. I give the letter to Junli. I ask Junli to pass the letter to Tang Nah when they are alone together. It is not that I trust Junli, or his wife Cheng. It is just that they will be the ones to sustain Tang Nah's anger. Junli will be the one to stop him from killing himself right on the spot — making me a true criminal. I will not be manipulated this time. I won't give Tang Nah another chance to control me.

*I am sure you have been waiting for this letter. Well, this is the last time you will hear from me. I believe that you understand perfectly what kind of pain I must undertake in order to write this way. You have no idea how I suffered in order to save both of us. I need to leave in order to live. That is what I am telling myself. Banging my head, for I am numb, deaf, blind, and dead inside.*

I'm trying to explain the contradiction of my feelings. How hard it is to tear myself away from this relationship. Our love operates in a very strange way. The darkness that didn't end until I met him. I explain what the departure means to me. Moments during which my nerves almost break down. Moments in which it is clear to me that life was not worth living.

*You know how I tried. I lived to please you. I can't believe that this is the way I am supposed to feel happiness. To please you. I can't forget how we fought. The nastiness of it. Our selfishness. The moment that comes to me as an ending.*

*I break down every time I recall how you used to love me. The words you said when we walked along Nan-yang Boulevard in the evenings. It pulls me back, tells me to go on, to stick with you until the end of time. It tells me not to allow this pain to spoil my future. The pain is like a fish bone stuck in my throat — can't take it out yet can't swallow it. This is where I am. A fish bone stuck in the throat.*

She feels the passion. The passion of speaking in a familiar voice, Nora's voice. The sensation of being on a real-life stage keeps her going. She is her role again. Like Nora she is struggling to break away. She tells Tang Nah–Torvald that she must depart.

*I live to be recognized, to leave a trace, to be someone, mean something. I had expected to see the same effort from you, for you are a talented man. You ought not to waste your life. You ought to perform to your highest capacity. To show the world who you are. I hate it when I see you opiumed by those who you call friends. You claim to be an artist only to excuse yourself from obligations. It gives you a reason to be lazy.*

*Isn't it true even when writing that you are a last-minute person? You never turn your papers in before the printer begins to roll. To me it is a sign of weakness. I am shown here a man of no action, no goal. Worse, a man who, instead of confronting his shortcomings, hides them. You love to say that you're misunderstood, mistreated by society — you don't hesitate to make yourself a victim of fate. But you forget that I am in the same boat. By acting weak you are drowning me.*

*At any rate, I have suffered enough. You have made your problem mine. Don't think I am strong. It is just that I don't allow myself to be fragile, for I know I will break. I am sorry that I must leave. It's time for you to learn to walk on your own legs, learn to fix problems with your own hands. Or else it would be a shame to even mention that you and I were once lovers.*

At last she mentions Aixia — she has finally found out the name of the girl in a poem he wrote inspired by her.

*Although you have denied the affair and the poem, you have forgotten that I have learned my lesson. I am twenty-three, not thirteen. I know what love is, for I have loved and been loved. I know what it is like. You can't fool me. I can easily imagine the lines you two speak. The lines that you used to lure me. Believe me I know. Nevertheless I will always remember you as a man of warmth and kindness. Your feelings of love, even toward your enemy. Sometimes you are kind beyond reason. It always amazes me, because I am not at all like that. I don't put up with my enemy.*

In a twist of fate, as if to compensate her, after dissolving her relationship with Tang Nah Lan Ping's career takes off. The hatred for the Japanese suddenly means that anti-Japanese movies are getting financed and produced and are becoming hits. Roles start to come her way. First the movie *Blood on Wolf Mountain*. She is cast as the wife of a soldier. Alone she fights a pack of wolves on screen. The vulnerable yet brave woman who fights without knowing whether she will ever win. Fights, knowing that she might be eaten before she gets to her next strike. A story about a simple woman, it is also about China's struggle under Japan's invasion. The acting is heartfelt and passionate.

Then the next movie, *Old Bachelor Wang*. Again she plays a heroic leading lady, Wang's wife. Again it is about a Chinese family that lives in poverty under the invasion of Japan. Again survival is the only theme. And she is extraordinary. At the end of the film, she carries her husband's dead body and swears to the camera: You can slice or shred me to a thousand pieces, but my spirit will never quit fighting!

My good luck ran out quickly. In the summer of 1937 Shanghai is under occupation. The flag of Japan flutters on top of the city's tallest building. The city is paralyzed. The last studio shuts down. I am totally broke and have moved in with Zhang Min. We have developed a great affection for each other. His wife has walked

out because of me. But I wouldn't remarry. My relationship with
Zhang Min is not that kind. Zhang Min is a harbor to and from
which I come and go. I am here to rest but not to stay.

I was told the other day that Tang Nah had attempted another
suicide. It was after receiving my letter from Junli. Apparently
Junli couldn't stop him. He jumped into the Huangpu River. It
was during the day and he was rescued. He should have done it at
night if he didn't mean it to be a show. I knew his purpose. It was
his way to get back at me, to blame me, to have all our friends,
critics and the public alike, point their fingers at me. And they did.
It was in the evening paper. My name meant selfishness — the opposite of the heroines I portray. The rumors damage my chance to
play leading roles in the future. Once a villain, always a villain.
My face lost its credibility overnight.

Tang Nah moved to Hong Kong right after the Communist liberation in 1949. He was wise. If he had stayed Madame Mao
wouldn't have known what to do with him. Would he have ended
up like Junli or Dan? Maybe Tang Nah knew that there would be
trouble. He is a man of good vision.

The Pagoda of Six Harmonies stands like a silent man in deep
thought against the velvet indigo sky. How many loves sworn and
broken has it witnessed? I still taste my tears. I counted on it the
moment we were pronounced husband and wife. God knows
how much I wanted to be cured. I gave him everything. The man
from Suzhou.

Now that I am finally leaving him all the good times come back
to me. The memories, so vivid. He takes me in my dreams unin-
vited. I wake up screaming his name. It was after he explained to
me his delirious notion of women. The way he worships the female body. He was not comfortable with his own body, especially
not particularly proud of his member. He always left his shirt on

when coming over me, like an eagle with its wings fully spread. His face hung upon my face. It was a rather funny picture.

He loved to keep the light on, low and dim. Each night he moved the light to a different angle, so he could see my body in different shades. He would put the light on a chair or on top of a closet, or under the bed. He watched me and would say that I had the body of a goddess. He worshiped my skin. Its ivory color. Strangely my skin doesn't age, Madame Mao said later. I have gone to places that are terrible for anyone's skin, but my skin stays unchanged.

I remember him lighting a cigarette, taking a drag and then puffing the smoke around my breasts. Like a dirty old man, he then lay back to watch the smoke make circles around my breasts. Aha, he would say. Aha, he would wink.

Aha, I would laugh, and get up to bring his tea. I took the opportunity to display myself, knowing this would please him. Stop, he would say, extinguishing his cigarette in the ashtray. Come here.

It could be anywhere, on a chair, or on a sofa, on the floor, or by the window, in a hallway, or sometimes just standing in the middle of the room, as if we were on stage.

# 8

JULY 1937. A TRAIN WAILS through the night like an angry dragon. It heads toward Shanxi Province in the northwest of the country. This is guerrilla territory — the heartland of the Communist Party and its Red Army. Lan Ping is twenty-three years old. She rides the train. The track condition is poor. Outside the window the scene is desolate. There are no mountains, no rivers, no trees or crops. Barren hills extend mile after mile. The train has crossed the provinces of Jiangsu, Anhui and Henan.

An elderly man sitting next to Lan Ping asks if she had seen anything interesting. Without waiting for a reply he points out that they are passing through ancient battlefields. The sun is beginning to rise. Dark-skinned men and women are plowing in the fields. The women carry their infants on their backs. The man tells Lan Ping that in 1928 and 1929 three million people died of starvation in the area.

At first *Yenan* is a strange word to her. A place in the middle of nowhere. It is the opposite of Shanghai. Lan Ping feels like a blind woman in an alley — finding her way by touching walls. After Shanghai she tried other places. She tried the cities of Nanking, Wu Han and Chong-qin. She spoke to friends and acquaintances and asked for help and recommendations. Nothing worked. People had either never heard of her or they had heard too much. She knocked on doors, announced her name to strangers. She kept going, pushing herself, and kept a picture of hope in her head.

She began to hear more and more the name Mao Tse-tung. A guerrilla hero. A folk legend in the making. He represents the inland Chinese, the majority, the ninety-five percent of the peasants who are concerned about their homeland being taken over by the Japanese. There is no money for school, arts or entertainment, but the peasants send their sons to join the Red Army, to be Communists and be led by Mao Tse-tung.

She has the eyes of a pioneer. It is with this vision that she finds her next stage. Yenan is territory available for her to claim.

Before her departure she wrote an article which was published in the *Shanghai Performing Arts Weekly*. The title was "A View of Our Lives." In the article she criticized "pale art," the art that promotes bourgeois sentimentality. The plays in which women are praised for their sacrifices. The plays that embrace the foot-binding tradition. The art that turns a blind eye on the country's fatal condition. She called it "the selfish art." "To me art is a weapon. A weapon to fight injustice, Japanese, Imperialists and enemies alike."

"A View of Our Lives" was a loud cry. This performance, it was said, had legs and walked its way to Yenan, to Mao's cave, his bed.

The old truck she is on groans like a dying animal. Coated with red dust the girl from Shanghai is in good spirits. After three weeks on the journey she has just passed Xian, the gate of the red territory. They enter Luo-chuan, the last stop before Yenan.

August 1937. She has made friends with a woman named Xu who comes to join her husband Wang. Wang is the secretary of the Communist organization called United Front Against Japan's Invasion. He is here attending an important meeting.

That night Lan Ping and Xu stay in a peasant's cabin. Their beds are made of straw. They plan to fetch Wang the next day from the meeting and continue their journey together to Yenan. Lan Ping is tired and goes to bed early. She doesn't know that tomorrow morning will go down in history as an unsolved mystery of modern China.

At breakfast Xu tells Lan Ping that the place of her husband's meeting is a few houses down the path. The meeting has already ended by dawn. Xu suggests that they pack buns for the trip. It is fifty-some miles from Luo-chuan to Yenan.

The morning is cool. The color of the rising sun dyes the hills golden. Lan Ping is neatly dressed in her new gray cotton Red Army uniform. A belt fastens at the waist. Her slender body is willowlike. Two long braids are tied up with blue ribbons. Carrying bags she and Xu walk toward their truck. Just beyond sit three other weather-beaten vehicles. One of the cars has characters written on it: *Emergency Medicare — Life Support. The New York Chinese Workers' Association*. It is Mao Tse-tung's car.

In the future the next moment is discussed as a moment of historical significance. Different views and interpretations have been adopted. Some say Mao walked out of the little meeting house and got into his car while Lan Ping was climbing into her truck — they missed each other. Some say that Lan Ping watched the leaders walk out one by one and thought the ink pen they each carried in their chest pockets was funny — she didn't recognize Mao. Some say that Mao bent his head as he exited the house because of his height and when he raised his eyes again, he was caught by her beauty — love at first sight. In Madame Mao's own story everyone comes to greet her with warm hellos.

The truth is no one comes. No one says hello to anyone. The girl from Shanghai gets in the truck, settles herself in a comfortable spot and waits for the truck to take off. She sees the men exiting the house. She knows that they are men of importance but she doesn't know which one is Mao nor does she expect to meet him.

It is not until the truck begins to move — not until she over-hears Wang whispering to his wife, Look, that's him! That's Mao! — that she pays attention. She had crossed his path but missed him. The biggest big shot in Yenan. He is already in the car. *Emergency . . . Life Support.* She didn't catch him, only the smoke his car puffed. She remembers the car shaking, hopping like a patient with heart failure.

If people in modern China barely know the name Yu Qiwei, they are all familiar with the name Kang Sheng. Comrade Kang Sheng, Mao's most trusted man, the head of China's national security and intelligence. Educated in Russia by Stalin's people, Kang Sheng is a man of mystery and conspiracy. No one can tell any-thing from reading his facial expressions. No one knows how he relates to Mao or how the two work together. All his life, Kang Sheng keeps himself in the background, out of focus. One doesn't feel his presence until one is suddenly caught by his shadow. And then it is too late. You have sprung his trap. You are seized by a nightmare. You are swallowed and dismembered by a mysterious creature. No one so far has been able to get out and tell the world what happened. No one can tell the story of Kang Sheng. Only a few have described the invisible black hand, its fingers stretching across China.

I had a long relationship with Kang Sheng, Madame Mao later says. A very special relationship. Fifty-two years. He played an important role in her life. He was her best friend and worst enemy at the same time. He helped her and betrayed her. Once upon a time he was her mentor and confidant. During the Cultural Revolution they became comrades in arms. They worked hand in glove. Have you ever heard the legend in which different kinds of wolves join forces to prey on cattle?

Kang Sheng and the girl are from the same Shan-dong province. Not only that, as they discover with amazement, they are from the same town. The girl can't clearly recall how they first met. He tells her that she was too young, about eleven. He was the principal of the Zhu-Town Elementary School. She must have known him through the townspeople, possibly her grandfather. Her impression was that he was a man of silence. He had a frozen expression. He gave only two words, yes or no. Once in a while he nodded at children and spoke a few words in a dry voice. He was respected by the townfolk because he got things done.

His skin is almost too fine for a man. Goat beard. He wears a pair of thick glasses with painted gold frames. Behind the glasses is a pair of fish eyes. The pupils protrude so much they are ball-like. He is thin and moves elegantly. In old times he wore an ankle-length long gray gown. During the war he wears a Red Army uniform with extra pockets and after the liberation he will wear a Mao jacket.

When I hear that my fellow townsman Kang Sheng is the Communist security's chief in Yenan I am thrilled. I have been in Yenan three months and have been desperately trying to find my way. Feeling lucky I decide to visit Kang Sheng. One day during a break I slip away from my work team and make my way to his office. I walk straight through his door and beg him to take me under his wing. He is busy, leafing through a document, and glances at me through the side of his glasses. He doesn't recognize me at first. Then he looks at me again. I see the recognition but still he says nothing. He continues to stare at me. It is an analytical look. Bold, even rude. Like an antiques dealer checking on a piece — he spends time. It makes me uneasy. Then he says he'll do his best. You'll do fine in Yenan. He lies back and smiles suddenly.

He invites me to sit and asks about my life in Shanghai. I tell him a bit of my struggle and my career as an actress. He doesn't seem to be interested. But I don't have anything else to tell. He then interrupts me and asks about my relationships. Are you married or involved?

I say I am not prepared to talk about my personal life.

I understand, he says. But if you need my help I've got to know these things. You see, in Yenan, as a Communist, all your secrets belong to the Party. Besides, I intend to help you succeed. Not many people will have your opportunities.

I pause for a moment and then begin telling him about Yu Qiwei and Tang Nah. I skip my marriage with Mr. Fei. Kang Sheng asks me the details of my divorces. Are there any ongoing attachments?

I am through, I report.

Very good. He nods and glances at me through the side of his glasses again.

Kang Sheng makes me understand that in Yenan, background is more important than one's present performance. The Party believes in what you have done not what you promise to do. The Party puts everyone in constant check. The trick to getting ahead is to prove your loyalty to the Party.

I tell Kang Sheng that I have come to Yenan to renew my Party membership.

Well, good then, you will need to draw up a history sheet. We need names of witnesses.

I have no friends in Shanghai who can be my witnesses.

Are you still in touch with Yu Qiwei?

Before I reply, he tells me that Yu Qiwei has recently arrived in Yenan from Beijing.

I am suddenly stirred. It takes me a moment to ask if Kang Sheng knows how Yu Qiwei has been doing.

He is doing fine, Kang Sheng replies. He has changed his name from Yu Qiwei to Huang Jing and is the Party's general secretary in charge of the entire northwest area. In fact, Comrade Lan Ping, Yu Qiwei can be a good person to help you build your history. Seeing me a bit confused and lost in a moment of memory he advises, Come on, let the past be past. He takes off his glasses and looks right into me. Did you pay attention when I said the word "build"?

So I understand.

I am grateful, Kang Sheng *Ge*. I call him "big brother" in Shandong dialect.

No trouble, he replies. Keep me posted. And forget Yu Qiwei.

From that moment on Kang Sheng and I become friends. The friendship quickly turns into a partnership. He is probably the only person in my life I have trusted completely. Decades later my secret-keeper decides to make a ring for my neck — when I become his boss and am about to step onto the throne, he fires a fatal bullet behind my back.

He is on his deathbed then. Colon cancer in its last stage. And he wants to drag me down with him. He wants to punish me for not putting him in the big-brother position which he expects and thinks he deserves. I refuse to make Comrade Kang Sheng the chairman of the Communist Party because I intend to take the position myself. I have earned my right.

I don't think I owe Kang Sheng. We have been each other's steppingstones when crossing Mao's river. We are even.

As history reveals itself in the official documents Kang Sheng wrote nothing in his will but eight characters. They read, *Madame Mao Jiang Ching is a traitor. I suggest: Immediate elimination.*

But in Yenan as the partnership begins to form he looks at the beauty with a pimp's eye — he is in it for a good-deal profit.

I am aware of my feelings toward Yu Qiwei. Although I have long stopped pursuing him, I would be lying to say that I don't care anymore. I write him. I keep him posted of my whereabouts. It is something I can't help. A ghost hand writes for me. In those moments I am scared of myself.

For the rest of his life Yu Qiwei never demonstrates his feelings toward me. He never utters a word about our past. He avoids me by being extremely polite. He lets me feel his wall. The distance he places between us. I have to admire him. He is a man of determination. He makes up his mind and carries it out. He doesn't answer my letters. Not once.

He is doing well and has become powerful. I am not surprised at his achievement. He is unlike Tang Nah. Tang Nah makes me appreciate Yu Qiwei, makes me regret what I did to him. I should have endured the loneliness. But how could I know that he would come out alive while others of his status were killed?

I am curious about Yu Qiwei's feelings. I want to know if he ever misses me. We were part of each other's youth. It can't be erased.

I locate Yu Qiwei. He is in Yenan's hotel for outer-state officers. I am sure he is aware of the effort I made to see him. Yet he is cold when receiving me. He makes me feel that I am bothering him. He keeps his official smile. Sit down, Comrade Lan Ping. Tea? Towel? He asks what he can do for me.

He is a mature-looking man now. Very sure of himself. His confidence makes me crazy. I am in pain to see him. He makes me feel like I am a prostitute trying to make a sale. I remember who he was. I remember the way he liked to be made love to.

We are so close, sitting inches away yet oceans apart. I don't see myself in his eyes. A mosquito's eyelash maybe. He doesn't want me there. He gives me a tired look to show me that his fire has long since died. He tells me without words that I should stop embarrassing myself.

It makes me angry. Makes me want to win. Win hard, win big, win to prove that he was wrong to give me up.

But I know not to show my rage in his office. I say that I come for business. I need a witness on my record as a Communist. Can you help? You were my boss in Qingdao. He understands and says that he will fill out the forms for me. Tell the investigator to contact me if he has any questions.

Thanks, I say. Thanks for taking the trouble.

Then I leave. I leave him alone for the rest of his life. I don't see him for the next thirty years. But I make sure my husband sees him. I make sure Mao gives him a job, and orders him around. He worked for Mao as his regional Party secretary. He was made the mayor of Qingdao. I don't know anything about why he died in his prime. I have no idea of his happiness or unhappiness. I know his wife, Fan Qing, hates me. The feeling is mutual. Whatever happens in the end is no longer my concern. Losers give me a bad taste.

The young woman is getting to know midland China, the rising swell of the Shan-Bei plain. It is a bleak landscape. Next to a snakelike little river is a gray town where houses are made of mud with paper windows. There are roosters, hens and chickens on the side of the street that break the silence of the otherwise dead town. Here donkeys are the only means of transportation, and wild grain is the main source of food. On top of a hill is the Yenan Pagoda, built in the Sung dynasty around A.D. 1100.

This is where China's future ruler Mao Tse-tung lives, in a cave like a prehistoric man. He sleeps on a bed laid with half-baked bricks, broken ceramic pots and mud. It is called *kang*. Although the brown-skinned soldiers are wood-stick thin, they are tough minded. They live for the dream Mao created for them. They have never known cities like Shanghai. Each morning, on the grounds of a local school, they practice combat. They might only have primitive weapons but they are led by a god.

A few weeks later, the girl will appear on the grassless hill. At sunset by the river, she will sit by a rock and watch the ripples spread in the water. She will wet her lacquer-black hair and sing operas. Although she is twenty-three she looks seventeen in the eyes of the locals. The girl has the finest skin and brightest eyes men here have ever seen. She will come and catch the heart of their god.

# 9

CAVES, FLEAS, HARSH WINDS, rough food, faces with rotten teeth, gray uniforms, red-star caps are my first impression of Yenan. My new life begins with a form of torture. In order to survive I forbid myself from thinking that this is a place where three million died of starvation in a year. I forbid myself from acknowledging that the locals here have never seen a toilet in their lives and have never taken a bath except at birth, wedding and death. Very few people know the date of their birth or where the capital of China is. In Yenan people call themselves Communists. To them it is a religion. The pursuit of spiritual purity gives them gratification.

I am assigned to a squad with seven female comrades. Five are from the countryside and two including me are from the cities. When I ask the peasant girls their reasons for joining the army, Sesame, the boldest one, says that it was to avoid a prearranged marriage. Her husband was a seven-year-old boy. The rest of the girls nod. They came in order to escape being sold or starved to death. I congratulate them. We spend the morning learning an army drill.

The other city woman has odd features. Her eyes are on the side of her face near the ears, like a goat's. She is arrogant and speaks imperial Mandarin. Her voice is manlike, syllables sliding into each other. The Red Army is not a salvation army, she remarks. It's a school for education. We are Communists, not a bunch of beggars. It's terrible that you have never heard of Marxism and Leninism. We are in the army to change the world, not just to fill our stomachs.

She irritates me. The peasant girls look at each other — don't know how to respond to her. She intimidates. I ask the woman her name. Fairlynn, she responds. I was named after the ancient woman-poet Li, Pure Reflection. Have you heard of her works? Gorgeous verses!

What are you? the peasant girls ask Fairlynn.

A poet.

What is a poet? What is a poem? Sesame still can't get it after an explanation is given.

Fairlynn throws her a book. Why don't you help yourself and find it out?

I don't read, Sesame says apologetically.

Why did you join the Red Army? I ask Fairlynn.

To continue my study with Chairman Mao. He is a poet too.

Fairlynn is a spiritual athlete. She needs a rival to exercise her mind. She calls me Miss Bourgeois and says Yenan is going to toughen me up. In the morning she leaves the door open and lets the wind bang it about. She gets a kick out of it. I hear her man-like laugh. The harsh wind will resculpt your bones and nerves! She is happy that she has made me speechless. Thank Buddha she is ugly, I think to myself. With such a chunky figure, I am sure she has plenty of loneliness to deal with. Her hairstyle, according to her, is inspired by Shakespeare. It looks like an open umbrella. Her long face has sharp lines. A chain-smoker's yellow skin. When she talks her hands are on your face.

I play *Qu* and *Pai* verse games with poems, Fairlynn says. I can't wait to play with Chairman Mao. I have heard he loves to be challenged. I am strong in Tang's and I hear he is strong in Song's.

His specialty is *Fu*. Among the Song's, he prefers "Late North" and I "Early South." My specialty is in Zu Hei-Niang's four-tone-eight-line verses and the Chairman's is two-tone-five-line verses. The *pin-pin-zhe-zhe* stuff.

That will be a surprise if the Chairman receives her, I tell myself. Men must look for different kinds of stimulation in different women.

The place where I live for the next few months is called Qi Family Slope. The cave village has over thirty families and everyone's last name is Qi. Because of the valleys the wind blows harshly. My skin has already begun aching. I have been put in the new soldiers' training program. The village has only one street, which extends and connects to an open field. At the east end is a barn. At the west end stands a public well. The well has no bars and is covered with ice in winter.

My squad passes the street heading toward the training base. I see a young boy with applelike cheeks by the well. He is pulling up a rope with a bucket of water. The weight makes him bend dangerously over the well's mouth. He could slip and fall at any second. I shut my eyes while passing him. There is a blind man selling yams in the street. His yams look ages old. Next to him is a coal shop. A pregnant woman sits in front of a heap of coal washing clothes. Her two young children wear open-rear pants and are playing with the coal. Their butts are coated black. Next is a wood shop. A carpenter is making giant buckets. His young children help sand the surface of the wood.

Fairlynn and I are assigned to live with a peasant family. I have developed a crick in my neck from sleeping on the ground. When the master of the house comes to say good morning one day I mention my pain. The next day the master brings in two straw mats.

My hope for a good night's sleep is ruined by Fairlynn. It's our job to overcome bourgeois weakness, she says, and picks up the straw mats and sends them back to the master.

After a week of poor sleep I begin to feel sick. Fairlynn tosses all night long too. One morning after breakfast, the house master comes with a neighboring woman, who is a tailor. The master explains that he has asked the tailor to lend out her sewing room. It has beds, the tailor says. The city comrades who have fragile bones may prefer beds more than the ground.

This time Fairlynn accepts the offer without a word. We pack up and follow the tailor to her room. We are presented with two beds. One is a single bed made of bamboo and the other hangs down from the ceiling. It is actually a board. Fabrics and miscellaneous rags are laid over it. It is about four feet wide and eight feet long. And it is about seven feet up from the floor, nearly at the ceiling.

Fairlynn suggests that I take the board and she the bed. I'm not like you, light as a bird, she says. The board won't hold my weight — I will crush your bones if it falls.

When I look at the board, I immediately develop a headache. To reach it, I have to step on her bed first, then part my legs to climb onto a wooden stud. Then I have to reach out one foot as a support and lift the other onto the board. Once I lie down I will not be able to sit up, for my head will hit the ceiling if I do.

At night she rests her body against the wall and is afraid to turn. There are no railings to prevent her from falling. Many times she dreams of rolling toward the edge and falling. It takes her weeks to get used to the fear. In order to avoid getting down at night she dares not drink water after three o'clock in the afternoon.

After the dry corn is collected, the squad is sent to transport the field stalks with a single-wheeled cart. It takes Lan Ping a while to learn to use the cart. Once she figures out the tricks she holds the handles steady with both arms bent inward to gain control. She walks on her heels. When going downhill, she pulls the handles and squats down. The weight of her body serves as a brake. Sometimes she squats all the way and her rear end drags on the ground. Unlike her, Fairlynn tumbles over when making sharp turns going down the hill.

Lan Ping begins to feel the distance. The distance between her and the role she wants to play. She is not grasping it. She wonders when she will meet people of significance.

If you are a soldier, act like one. Fairlynn's tone is serious. You don't pop out with questions like a civilian. You don't ask to see Mao, for example . . . Suddenly Fairlynn farts. It is a loud fart. Comes in the middle of her sentence. The smell is strong.

Too many yams, observes Sesame.

Gas pills? Lan Ping offers.

Fairlynn is straight-faced as if someone else had farted. Then she starts to fart again. The girls begin to laugh. One of the farts is so long that it lasts a minute. The group bursts with joy when the fart modulates down a couple of notes before it finally dies out.

When I have to go to the bathroom I must squat over a manure pit. It is about three feet in diameter. There is only a wooden board across the pit. On rainy days the surface becomes extremely slippery. Even thinking about it makes me more depressed than I already feel. I have learned to operate guns, throw grenades, roll through bushes, over rocks. I fight and I labor. Communism to me is a moon-in-the-pond and a flower-in-the-mirror. Everything else tells me that I am in the wrong place.

It is midnight and I again have diarrhea. I don't want to climb down in the cold and wake up Fairlynn. But after an hour of tossing I can no longer bear it. I put on my clothes and begin to climb down. Fairlynn is sound asleep. The darkness wraps me as I get out. I have a hard time imagining myself balancing on the wooden board. I think about waking Fairlynn. But I change my mind. I don't want to be called Miss Bourgeois again.

I walk, my hands touching the wall. When I reach the gate, the discomfort in my stomach increases. I push the gate but it won't open. The rings won't budge. In a hurry I make a turn and finally manage to open the door.

I am lost. In front of me is a deserted courtyard. I can't remember where the manure pit is, I only know that it is not far.

It is not like what she later told people, that she never doubted the path she had taken. She doubted seriously, as now.

In tears she visits Kang Sheng. It is on a clear afternoon that she comes to his cave office.

Comrade Lan Ping! How have you been? he welcomes her. How are you getting along with life in Yenan? Come on. Have you eaten? Join me for lunch, please.

She hasn't seen meat for months.

They talk over the meal. She is humble, begs for advice.

Well, my knowledge of things is no better than yours, he replies. It is only that I am older and have tasted more salt. Have you tried the opera troupe here? Yenan has a lot of opera fans. The Party bosses are opera fans.

I want to try, but my squad head wouldn't allow me a day off. How would I explain the reason?

Well, let me see. I can transfer you in the name of the personnel department. I'll tell your squad head that the revolution needs you.

She almost wants to stand up and give him a kowtow. Holding herself back she asks for the names of the persons in charge of the Yenan opera troupe.

The people you will work with might be politically advanced, he says, as he tears off a piece of paper and quickly writes a list of names. But they can't sing, can't play roles. You will stand out. So put your mind to it. Would I bring people to see your show? If you are good I'll bring Chairman Mao.

The subtle hint in the words. He reminds me that time doesn't allow me to wait. Youth counts. How easily city girls' fine skin fades into sandpaper here. The harsh wind doesn't argue. It whispers ancient wisdom. While many receive advice, only the wise profit by it. Use your head. Put it this way. There is a different garden of love in Yenan. A woman loves a man for what he can do for China.

A local woman comes in with a teapot. She pours Kang Sheng and me tea. She is young but she has heavy wind-carved wrinkles. Kang Sheng adds, In Yenan, a woman's height is her husband's rank. He laughs as if joking. I am sure a girl of your quality attracts admirers. You should save yourself. Of course this is not our subject today. Here, take it. He pulls out a file from his drawer. Advance yourself with knowledge of the Party — read Mao's works. Remember, only when one's life intertwines with history will one be truly great.

She begins to read what Kang Sheng recommends. Books and papers. The stories fascinate her. They are about the history of the Communist Party, but more about one man's success. One man who single-handedly established and led the Party. One man who three times fell out of the Party's favor and three times made his way back to a role of leadership.

It is the story of Mao Tse-tung.

He is a self-taught man, a son of a Hunan peasant. He established the Hunan Communist group when he was a student in 1923. His mentor was the chief of the Communist Party, Mr. Chen Duxiu. In 1927 after Chiang Kai-shek massacred the Communists, the teacher-student relationship soured. They developed opposing views. Mao believed in the power of force, while Chen believed in the negotiating table. Chen had the say at the time. Yet history proved Mao right. After Chen's negotiations failed he furthered his mistake by ordering positional warfare — building body-walls to block Chiang Kai-shek's bullets. The result: the Red Army lost ninety percent of its force.

Frustrated, Mao took a small peasant force and moved to the remote Jing-gang Mountain to hide. Mao was determined to develop and train his men into an iron force. For his action Mao was accused as a traitor and an opportunist. He was fired.

But Chen had no luck and the Red Army was on the verge of being completely wiped out. Mao was offered back his job, for he had already developed his force into thirty thousand well-equipped men. Taking the new job, Mao battled with Chiang Kai-shek's force, ten times his number. Mao played cat and mouse with his enemy. Then he faced another internal blow. The central Communist Party Politburo believed that the Red Army was so strong that it was time to claim Chiang Kai-shek's main cities. Mao pleaded to withhold action. Again he was labeled a narrow-minded bumpkin and again he was fired.

Mao fell ill but he didn't give up. By the time the bad news came — the Red Army sent to attack the city was destroyed — Mao was ready to sit back in his commander's chair. Like an ancient strategist he applied his art to war and magically turned the situation around. The Red Army not only survived but also began to win again.

Yet Mao's problems were far from over. The Russian-trained army experts expressed their doubts about his guerrilla style. They convinced the Politburo that Mao's conservative tactics were ruining the Party's reputation. The Politburo was convinced that it was necessary to launch a second attack on Chiang Kai-shek's stronghold. When Mao fought again he was criticized as losing confidence in the revolution and was named a coward. This time Mao was not only fired from his job, he was ordered to leave the base. In 1932, as a form of exile, he was instructed to establish a Party branch in a remote province.

Mao didn't wait for his turn. He actively lobbied, talked to his friends and connections. His prediction was proven right every step of the way. The Red Army lost key battles and finally was blocked by Chiang Kai-shek's force, unable to break out.

Mao was called back the third time. Yet he didn't want to be a dispensable bridge just to save the army from its troubled waters. He wanted a permanent position in the power-house — he wanted complete control over the Communist Party's leadership including removing his political enemies.

He was satisfied.

In 1934 the god led his followers and performed a miracle. It was called the Long March.

The girl sits in front of a stack of paper. She can see her thoughts forming. The syllables pop in the air, the sense falls into place. It's overwhelming. The birth of a sudden vision. Its vital energy. The combination of forbidden intimacy and illicit understanding.

I want to be a place on his map! the girl cries.

Kang Sheng tells her that there are women who have invited themselves to Mao's cave. Domestic and exotic alike.

I am not going to turn into a rock because of that, the girl replies.

By the hill the sun begins to set. Companies of soldiers arrive and line up. They sit down in rows in front of a makeshift stage, built with bamboo sticks against the deepening blue sky. The orchestra is adjusting its instruments. The girl from Shanghai has made herself the leading lady of the Yenan Opera Troupe. She is about to play a solo called "Story of a Fisherman's Daughter."

The girl prepares herself in a tent. She wraps her head with a bright yellow scarf. She is in her costume, red vest with green skirt-pants. She picks up an "oar," pretends to be on a boat and starts to warm up, stepping in a pattern of one step forward, one step back and one step across. She rocks, swinging her arms from side to side.

The sound of clapping tells her that the leaders and their cabinet members have arrived. The stagehands rush the performers to the curtain. The beat of drums thickens moment by moment. The actors' faces are masked with powder. The eyes and eyebrows are drawn like flying geese.

Looking into the mirror the girl recalls her life in Shanghai. She thinks of Dan, Tang Nah and Zhang Min. The men who traveled over her body but never found the jewel inside. She thinks of her mother. Her misfortune. Suddenly she misses her. Only after the daughter had experienced her own struggle was she able to comprehend the meaning of her mother's wrinkles and the sadness sealed under her skin.

The cartwheels fly across the stage. The actors crack their voices on the high notes. The enthusiastic audience screams excitedly. The sound breaks the night. The actress is told by the stagehand that Mao has arrived. He is sitting in the middle of the crowd. The girl imagines the way the Chairman sits. Like the Buddha on a lotus flower.

She enters the stage in *sui-bu*, sailing-sliding steps, and then *liu-quan*, willow-arms. She picks up the "oar" and makes graceful strokes in the imaginary water. Up and down she bends, then straightens her knees to depict the movement on a boat. The beats of the drum complement her motion. She toe-heels from the left side of the stage to the right showing her "water-walking" skills. She makes *liang-xiang* — flashing a pose — and then opens her mouth to sing the famous aria.

Mao's face appears solemn, but inside his mind wind rises and blows through the trunks of his nerves — the girl's voice is like a strong arrow shooting straight toward his mind's estate. His world turns. Seaweed grows in the sky and clouds begin to swim in the ocean.

> I would ride with thee on the Nine Streams
> With winds dashing and waves heaving free
> In water cars with lotus covers . . .

His mind is now a shackled horse running against the gale, whipped, kicked, winding up toward a mountaintop draped in thick fog.

> I mount Quen-Rung cliffs to look about
> My heart feels flighty and unsound
> Dusk falling
> I feel lost and lorn
> Thinking on faraway shores
> I come round . . .

He smells damp air. The air that carries the weight of the water. He hears the rhythm of his own breathing. He blinks his eyes and wipes the sweat from his forehead.

After the curtain descends Kang Sheng guides Mao onto the stage and introduces him to the actress. Handshake. The grace of an ancient sage. He is taller. He has thick black hair, longer than anyone else's in the crowd. It is combed to the sides from the middle — a typical Yenan peasant style with the touch of a modern artist. He has a pair of double-lid almond eyes, gentle but focused. His mouth is naturally red with great fullness. His skin smooth. A middle-aged man, confident and strong. His uniform has many pockets. There are patches neatly sewn on both elbows and knees. His shoes are made of straw.

She feels the pulse of her role.

❀

Winter is leaving and spring has yet to arrive. Overnight the grass on the hill is blanketed with frost. Not until noon does the white crust start to melt. After four o'clock the ice begins to form again. The whole hill, the yet-to-turn-green grass, looks like it is under the cover of a crystal film.

It is at this time that Fairlynn becomes the editor-in-chief of Mao's newspaper, *The Red Base*. It is said that Mao has personally appointed Fairlynn to the position. The paper cheers the recent victories and calls Mao "the soul of China."

Miss Lan Ping is in her uniform. She wraps her neck with an orange scarf. It's the look she cultivates — a soldier with a hint of romantic goddess. It is the effect of a tiny rose among a mass of green foliage. She knows the way men's eyes seek and register. The camera of her future lover's heart. Her comrades, including the wives of the high-ranking officers, are gossiping. The subject is Madame Chiang Kai-shek Song Meilin. It is about her ability to speak a foreign language and more important her ability to control her man. They say she has brought attention to her husband's campaign. She spoke at the League of Nations and obtained funds for her husband's war. The girl is greatly interested.

For the next few weeks, the snow comes down with rain. One moment, the universe of Yenan is soaked, the rain turning the earth into a marsh. The packed ground becomes muddy paste. The pots and cups in the room flood like little boats. The next day, the sun is out. It dries the path and turns the wheel tracks hard as knives. When the rain comes again, the road is a slippery board. On the mile-long path she must carry yams along, Lan Ping falls like a circus clown.

The cafeteria is a large cave with leaking walls. Half of it is used to store carriages and tools. My comrades and I hold our rice bowls and squeeze toward one side where the ground is less paste-

like. The rain drips into my bowl. To avoid the drips, I have to eat
and move around at the same time.

My boots are heavy with mud. They drag as if trying to get
away from my feet. I try hard not to miss Shanghai. The pavement, the pruned trees, the warm restaurants and the toilet.

The rain mixed with snow keeps pouring. The sky and the
earth are wrapped in one giant gray curtain.

A crowd fills up the hall of Yenan's LuXiun Art College. Mao
is expected to lecture here. The girl from Shanghai is sitting in
the front row on a wooden stool. She has come early to ensure
the best seat, the spot where she can see and be seen. Now she
waits patiently. The air is exuberant. The soldiers sing songs with
strong northern accents. The songs are composed from Mao's
teaching with a folk melody.

> We believe in great Communism
> We are the soldiers of the Red Army
> We punish looting and stealing
> We live to serve the people
> And to fight the Japanese invaders and
>   Chiang Kai-shek nationalists

The girl likes the straightforwardness of the lyric. By the third
time the song is repeated, Lan Ping picks it up and sings with her
full voice. She arouses immediate attention. She goes on, carrying
the highest note to its place effortlessly. The soldiers pay her
glances of admiration. She sings louder, smiling.

> The highest building starts with a brick
> The deepest river starts with a drop of water
> The revolution starts here in Yenan
> In the red territory led by the great Mao Tse-tung

She is moved by the atmosphere, by the action she is taking to
achieve her dream, by the fact that she might become a casualty of

this dream. A perfect tragic heroine. She could weep, she thinks, smiling.

Amid thunderous clapping Mao appears. The crowd cheers at the top of its voice: *Chairman Mao!*

He begins with a stylish folk joke very few understand.

The girl is star-struck. It feels as if she has met Buddha himself.

The man on stage talks about the relationship between art and philosophy, between the roles of an artist and a revolutionary.

*Comrades! How are we doing with the weeds that have been growing in our stomachs?*

His movement is scholarly and relaxed. His voice has a heavy nasal sound, mixed with a vibrating Hunan accent.

*I have been cleaning up mine. A lot of pulling and scaling. The thing is that Chiang Kai-shek and the Japanese are easy to identify as enemies. We know they are there to get us. But dogmatism is like weeds. It wears a mask of rice shoots. Can you tell the difference? To be a good artist one has to be a Marxist first. One has to be able to distinguish dogmatism from Communism.*

She detects metal in his frame. She suddenly wonders if there is any truth in Kang Sheng's advice: what counts in Yenan is the proof of one's background as a Communist. Her instinct is telling her a different truth, telling her what nature tells men and women. There isn't anything to prove. Everything is in the bodies, in the catching of the eyes of the human animals.

The man on the stage continues. Words, phrases and concepts flow.

*The dogmatists pretend to be true revolutionaries. They sit on important seats of our congress. They do nothing but mouth Joseph Stalin. The revolt and attack has started from within, inside our Party's body. They are invisible but fatal. They call themselves one hundred percent Soviets, but they are spiders with rotten spinners — they can no longer produce threads, they are useless to the revolution. They speak in Karl Marx's tune, but they help Chiang Kai-shek. We have been mocked. We have been given glasses with scratched lenses — so we can't see clearly. We have believed in Stalin and trusted the people sent by him. But what do they do here except make social experiments at our cost?*

Mao elaborates on Chinese history in light of the current situation, applies theories with military design and invention. Then his expression changes, withdraws, sinks into solemnity, as if the crowd has disappeared in front of him.

The girl can't help but begin measuring. She measures the man's future with a fortuneteller's eye. She zooms in. On his face, through a glittering, she sees an imprint of a lion's claw. She hears its roar. A howling out of time. It is at that moment she hears a click between herself and her role.

His bodyguard comes with a mug of tea. The boy has a caterpillar-like scar between his eyebrows. He places the tea on the ground in front of his master's feet. This amazes the girl. In Yenan it seems natural for people to pick up a mug from the ground instead of a table.

The voice on the stage grows louder. *The truth is, comrades, we have been losing — our men, horses and family members. Because of the wrong direction we have been forced to follow, our map has shrunk again. Haven't we learned enough lessons? We didn't lose the battles to Chiang Kai-shek or the Japanese, but to the enemy within. Our brothers' heads roll like rocks . . . About preserving political innocence, yes, we want to preserve it, not out of ignorance, but out of knowledge and wisdom. Our leadership is so weak that bad luck has been glued to us. Our teeth fall out when we drink cold water, and we stumble over our own fart! We must stop taking the road to our own graves! Comrades! I want you all to understand that dogmatism is about making sausages with donkey's shit!*

He bends, picks up the mug and takes a sip.

She hears the sound of pencils scratching paper.

The crowd, including Fairlynn, writes down Mao's speech.

The girl doesn't write. She memorizes Mao's lines, the spoken and unspoken. It is where she puts her talent to work.

He paces, sips the tea and waits for the crowd to raise their heads from the notepads. He has no printing machine, no newspapers. He relies on the mouths of his crowd. His eyes brush through the hall. Suddenly there is an unexpected sight. His focus is interrupted. He recognizes her, the girl who doesn't take notes like the rest. The actress with her makeup off. The impact is like dawn-light lunging through darkness. Its sensation shoots through him.

A sleeping-seed sprouts.

She looks away, knowing that she has altered his focus. His attention is now on her, and on her alone. It happens in complete silence. A wild chrysanthemum secretly and fervently opens and embraces the sunbeams. The girl feels strangely calm and experienced. She is her role. She takes the moment and tries to make it shine. She is pleased with herself, an actress who has never failed to cast a spell over her audience. Her heart misses no beat. In silence she introduces herself to him. Every part of her body speaks, delivers and reaches. She has him watching her, freely and boldly. Her neatly combed hair, her ivory skin. She sits still, on the ground of Yenan. She lets him find her.

And he smiles. She turns toward him. Her eyes then pass and go beyond him. She doesn't allow him to make contact. Not yet. She crosses him in order to light the fire, to grasp him, to have him begin the pursuit.

The arias of opera flow in her head. The butterfly wings are heavy with golden flower-powders . . . She then hears Fairlynn. Her shout. Marvelous! I love the lecture! I love the man!

*

Mao signs autographs and answers questions. The girl raises her
arm. He nods her a yes. She projects, asks a question on women's
liberation. Suddenly she notices that there is an absent look in his
smile. He is looking at her but his eyes don't register.

She drops her question. She feels unsure of herself as she sinks
back into the sea of the crowd. Mao raises his eyes. She hopes that
he is looking for her. She can't tell. He discontinues the search.
She stands up and walks out. She tells herself that she would
rather disappear than be unrecognized.

Later on he explains to her the problem. Although he has been living alone the obstacle is that he is still married. The wife's name is
Zi-zhen, a heroine as popular and respected as he is. When he was
a bandit Zi-zhen rebelled against her landlord family to follow
him. She was seventeen then. She was known for her beauty and
bravery. She had bullets beneath her ribs from the Long March in
1934. She had borne him six children, but only one, a girl, is alive.

Their separation began when she became terrified of another
pregnancy. She refused to sleep with him and he started to sniff
around. Zi-zhen found out. Then give it to me, he demanded. She
punched him in the face and then went straight to the Politburo.
Make him behave like Mao Tse-tung the Savior! she demanded.

Mao wished that he could gun down the marriage certificate
that hung between him and Zi-zhen. He moved out of the cave
and told Zi-zhen that the marriage was over. Zi-zhen took out her
pistol and shot every ceramic pot in the room. He imagined that it
was his head that she smashed. He ran away. She broke down but
was determined to get him back, determined to make herself suit
him. He avoided her. Gradually she learned his will.

Teach me how to suit you! She moved back, he left the room.
She insisted that he had to give a reason. He made one up: You
know too little of Marxism and Leninism.

She marked his words in her notebook and put herself on a

train to Russia. I'll be one hundred percent Marxist and Leninist when I come back.

Agnes Smedley, an American journalist visiting Yenan at that time, recalled her effort to teach Mao to dance. She made a prediction in a letter to a friend: If Mao ever picks up dance he will abandon his wife Zi-zhen. Mao asked Agnes whether romance really existed. I certainly have never experienced one, he said.

When the girl from Shanghai enters his cave, she becomes the representation of what Mao has been looking for.

The time when Zi-zhen leaves Yenan is the time Lan Ping arrives. In the recorded history it is a windy afternoon. Cold and chilly. Zi-zhen is with her small daughter. She looks exhausted and is full of resentment. She talks to a fellow traveler about her life with Mao. Talks about the time when she was eighteen and had a pair of eyes described as jewels. I met him on the mountain of Yong-xin, at a Communist gathering. After days of meetings we chatted, had meals together. Liquors and roasted chickens. He asked me to share his tea cup. Zi-zhen remembers vividly the way Mao made an announcement to his friends: "I am in love." She remembers his dream to build an army of his own. Now he has his army, now she has lost her health and gayness. She is twenty-eight years old and is sick and straw-thin. She sits on a stool in a cheap hotel and is frozen with her thoughts.

The goat-beard man can't help but admire the actress.

Although I have found Chairman Mao's lecture enlightening, I have difficulty comprehending certain points, she says. Is there any way I can ask the Chairman questions in person?

Kang Sheng has never met a girl like her. Sweet but aggressive. He finds her a good partner already. So he says, Of course, the Chairman is a teacher who likes students who challenge themselves. But because of his status, it is not easy to arrange a visit with him. His place is heavily guarded. Kang Sheng pauses, looks at the girl and frowns. Let me see what I can do.

After three days Kang Sheng sends a message to the girl that a private meeting with Mao is scheduled.

As if getting a stage call, Miss Lan Ping comes to the curtain. In the mirror she checks herself for the last time. She has put nothing on her face. In fact she has washed her face twice. She has decided to show her down-to-earthness, her reliability. She is in her uniform, her full costume. Her waist is tightened by a belt.

She marches to his cave. The guard with the caterpillar scar between his eyebrows blocks her. She announces her name. The guard looks her up and down suspiciously. The Chairman has invited me. Wait here, the guard says and goes inside the cave. A few minutes later he comes back. The Chairman is expecting you.

Sit. He grabs a chair for her. Tea?

She sits down and looks around. Sorry to bother you, Chairman. I understand you are a busy man. I . . . She stops as if too shy to go on.

It's my job to listen to what people have to say, he says, smiling. Sometimes a little bit of relaxation makes me work more effectively.

She smiles, finds herself relaxed.

He clears his desk and comes to sit opposite her.

She sips her tea and looks at him. She knows what her eyes can do to a man. She had been told by Yu Qiwei, Tang Nah and Zhang Min. She bathes him with her sunshine.

He breaks the silence. I have heard from Comrade Kang Sheng that you have difficulty comprehending points in my lecture.

Yes, she answers, again sorry to bother you.

My pleasure. He gets up and adds hot water to her cup. As

Confucius has said, one ought to take delight in teaching. My door opens to you. Any time when you have questions, just come.

There is formality as they play the teacher and student. Then he asks about her story. Who she is and where she is from. She enjoys the telling. The lines she has rehearsed well. Once in a while she pauses, observes him. He is attentive. She continues the story, adding, changing and skipping certain details. When she mentions the immensity of Shanghai he joins in.

I was there in 1923. It was for the Party's convention, he says, playing with his pencil and drawing circles on a telegram. Our Party only had a handful of members at that time and we were constantly tailed by Chiang Kai-shek's agents.

Where did you stay? she asks curiously.

District of Luwan by Cima Road.

The street that has red-brick black-arch-door houses?

That's right.

The tea-eggs are excellent on that street.

Well, I was too poor to afford a taste.

Which province did you represent at the convention?

Hunan.

Did you have side jobs besides working for the Party?

I was a laundryman at Fu-xing's.

A laundryman? she laughs. How interesting!

The difficult part of my job was not washing but delivery, he adds, as most of my earnings from washing had to be spent on tram tickets, which were so expensive.

Why didn't you stay in Shanghai?

Let's put it this way. I had a hard time swimming in a bathtub.

She gets up to leave. It is dinner time.

Please, stay for dinner.

I am afraid I've been bothering you too much.

Stay. The voice comes from behind as she moves toward the door. Please honor my invitation.

The guards set up the table. Four dishes. A plate of stir-fried pork with soy sauce, a plate of radishes, a plate of greens and a plate of spicy tofu. She wolfs the food down, apologizing for her manners. Life in Yenan is much harder than Shanghai, isn't it? he says. Like a father, he watches her eat. She nods, continues stuffing her mouth.

He picks up a piece of meat and drops it into her bowl. He then comments, I consider the food delicious in comparison to what we ate during the Long March. I have eaten tree bark, grass and rats.

She stops eating and asks to be told more of what it was like to go through the exile.

It was after Tatu, he begins. Our army turned north. In the snow mountains we found comparative safety, yet the prodigious heights weakened everyone. Many perished and pack animals and supplies were abandoned. We were in swampy regions of the grasslands. It was a picture of horror. Near Tibet, my men had been attacked and now we were passing again through a region of hostile tribes. No food was available. Our kitchen heads dug up what seemed to be turnips, which later proved to be poisonous. The water made us ill. The winds buffeted us and hailstorms were followed by snow. Ropes were laid down to guide us across the marshlands, but the ropes vanished in the quicksand. We lost our few remaining pack animals.

She notices that he tries to make light of his words but cannot do so.

He takes a deep breath and continues. A small column was seen walking across a sea of thick foggy grasses, and then . . . the whole column disappeared.

She stares at him.

*

When the guard lights the second candle she gets up to say good-bye. It might sound funny to you but I thought you would be arrogant, she says, walking out of his door.

What reason do I have to be arrogant? I am Mao Tse-tung not Chiang Kai-shek.

She nods, laughing, and says she must get going.

The path is not smooth and it is moonless tonight. Little Dragon! Walk Comrade Lan Ping home, will you?

It is the third time they meet privately. The stars look like voyeurs' eyes opening and closing. Mao Tse-tung and Lan Ping stand in the descending darkness, shoulder to shoulder. The day has begun to cool. Weeds bend lazily over the riverbank. The reflection of the moon trembles in the water.

I was born in the village of Shao Shan in 1893, Mao says. He describes the landscape of his hometown. It is a land of hibiscus, orchards, serfs and rice fields. My father was a poor peasant. While young he joined the warlords' army because of heavy debts. He was a soldier for many years. Later on he returned to the village and managed to buy back his land. He saved carefully and operated a small trading business. He was petty. He sent me to a local primary school when I was eight but he wanted me to work on the farm in the early morning and at night. My father hated to see me idle. He often yelled, "Make use of yourself!" I can still hear his voice today. He was a hot-tempered man and frequently beat both me and my brothers.

It is at this point the girl inserts her comments. She describes her own father. Says she understands perfectly how he must have felt as a young boy terrified by his father. She looks up at him in tears.

He nods, takes her hands, holds them and continues. My father gave us no money whatsoever. He fed us the most meager food. On the fifteenth of every month he made a concession to his laborers and gave them eggs to go with rice, but never meat. To me he gave neither eggs nor meat. His budget was tight and he counted by pennies.

What about your mother? the girl asks. His face lights. My mother was a kind woman, generous and sympathetic, who was always ready to share what she had. She pitied the poor and often gave them food. My mother didn't get along with my father.

Again the girl responds that she shares the feeling. What could a woman do but weep and endure under such circumstances? The comment let Mao speak of rebelling against his father, of his once threatening to leap into a pond and drown himself. The beating must stop or you will never see me again. He demonstrates the way he yelled at his old man. They laugh.

He describes his turbulent years as a student. He left home at sixteen and graduated from the First Normal School of Hunan. I was an omnivorous reader and I inhabited the Hunan Provincial Library.

To her embarrassment, none of the titles he mentioned has she heard of. Adam Smith's *Wealth of Nations,* Darwin's *Origin of Species* and books on ethics by John Stuart Mill. Later on she would be required to read these books but she would never be able to go beyond page ten.

He seems to enjoy talking to her tremendously. The girl is grateful that he doesn't ask whether she has ever come across one of his beloved books. She doesn't want to go into poetry. She has no sense of it. She is afraid, of a name, Fairlynn. She decides to quickly change the subject.

Sounds like you skipped a lot of meals, she interrupts gently. You didn't take care of your health.

He laughs loudly. You might not believe this, but I was more than fit. In those days I gathered a group of students around me and founded an organization called the New Citizen Society. Besides discussing the great issues, we were energetic physical culturists. In winter we tramped through the fields, up and down mountains, along city walls. We also swam across rivers. We took rain baths, sun baths and wind baths. We camped in the snows.

She says that she would like to hear more.

It's late, I should not keep you from sleep.

Her eyes are bright like morning stars.

Well, I'll tell you one last detail of my story. He takes off his coat and wraps her shoulders with it. No more after this, all right?

She nods.

It was one over-rained summer when all the plants outgrew their sizes. A giant honeycomb constructed by horse bees was discovered on a tree in front of my house. The object was like a mine hung in the air. In the morning the tree was bent over because of the comb's weight — it had absorbed the moisture of the previous night and gotten heavier. After noon, the tree straightened itself back up.

This was a very strange honeycomb. Instead of being filled with honey and wax, it was filled with fiber of all sorts: dead leaves, seeds, feathers, animal bones, straw and rags. It was why the honeycomb smelled rotten at night. The smell attracted bugs. Especially lightning bugs. They swarmed in and covered the comb. By this time the horse bees had gone to sleep. The light of the bugs turned the comb into a glowing blue lantern.

Did you know that when lightning bugs get together they turn on and off their lights in unison?

Every night, the girl goes to sleep with the same fairy tale in which she always sees the blue lantern described by Mao.

The desire to meet in the dark increases. Mao begins to send the guard away. One evening Lan Ping is determined not to be the one to invite affection. She bids good-bye right after dinner. Taking his horse he offers to walk her a mile.

They are silent. She is upset. There are rumors about my spending time with you alone, she tells him. I am afraid I can come no more.

His smile disappears.

She starts to walk away.

I have been trying to use a sword to cut the flow of water, he murmurs behind her.

She turns around and sees him setting a foot in the stirrup.

Suddenly he hears her giggle.

What's funny?

Your pants.

What about them?

Your rear is about to show in a day or two — the fabric has melted.

Damn.

I'll fix it for you if you like.

His smile returns.

# 10

THE VILLAGE TAILOR IS GLAD to have Lan Ping as her sewing companion. Lan Ping is working on Mao's pants, which have been brought to her by Little Dragon. She doesn't know where the sewing is going to take her. She is aware that he is lonely and is fascinated by pretty women from big cities, places that rejected him as a student and as a young revolutionary. Later on she finds out that he calls her type of people bourgeois, but he pursues them. He calls Americans imperialists and paper tigers and says they should be put off the face of the earth, but he learns English and prepares himself to one day visit the United States. He tells his nation to learn from Russia, but he hates Stalin.

In 1938 Lan Ping finds herself falling in love with Mao Tse-tung. Falling in love with the poet in him, the poet his heroine wife Zi-zhen tries to kill. Although Mao later on will establish himself as an emperor and take many concubines, in 1938 he is humble. He is a penniless bandit and tries to catch the girl by selling his mind and vision.

One morning his guard comes and leaves me a piece of his scribbling — a new poem he composed the night before. He wants my comment. I unfold the paper and hear my heart singing.

*Mountain*
*I whip my already quick horse and don't dismount*
*When I look back in wonder*
*The sky is three feet away*

*Mountain*
*The sea collapses and the river boils*
*Innumerable horses race*
*Insanely into the battle*

*Mountain*
*Peaks pierce the green sky, unblunted*
*The sky falls*
*Down the clouds my men are home*

She reads his poems over and over. In the next few days the guard will bring more for her. Mao copies the poems in ink in the elegant calligraphy of Chinese ideograms, lucidly arranged.

His scribbles become her nightly treat in which passion speaks between the lines. Gradually a god steps down from the clouds and shares his life with her. He expresses his feelings for his lost love, his sister, brother and his first wife, Kai-hui, slaughtered by Chiang Kai-shek. And his children, whom he was forced to give away between battles and only later found dead or lost. She receives his tears and feels his sadness. What grabs her heart is that she discovers there is no anger in his poems; rather, he praises the way nature shares its secrets with him — he embraces its severity, enormity and beauty.

The tailor gives me a piece of gray rag, which I cut into two large round patches. I stitch them around the rear. The tailor suggests that I thicken the fabric. She says, Make it durable so that it will serve as a carried-around stool.

We sew quietly for a while and then suddenly the tailor asks me what I think about Zi-zhen.

Trying to hide my awkwardness I say that I respect Zi-zhen a great deal. The tailor stops her work and raises her eyes. There is suspicion in the look. Pulling a thread she says slowly but clearly, Mao Tse-tung belongs to the Communist Party and the people. He's no ordinary man to be chased around. He has suffered the loss of his first wife and he is not about to lose his second.

Before I have a chance to respond she goes on. The late Mrs. Mao's name is Kai-hui, for your information. Have you heard of her? I am sure you don't mind me mentioning her, do you?

Please, go ahead.

She was the daughter of his mentor and the beauty of Changsha, her hometown. She was an intellect and a Communist. She lived for Mao. Not only did she support and help organize his activities but also gave him three sons. When Chiang Kai-shek caught her he ordered her murdered. She was given a chance to denounce Mao in exchange for her life but she chose to honor him.

The tailor wipes her tears, blows her nose and continues. Zi-zhen married Mao to fill up the emptiness in his heart. Zi-zhen used to carry around two pistols. She shot with both hands. In one battle she went out and took a dozen enemies. Mao adores her. She is his loyalist. She is the mother of all his children including the ones left by Kai-hui. In order to move on during the Long March they had to give away the children. You have no idea what it felt like to leave your children to strangers, knowing that you might never see them again.

The girl from Shanghai lowers her head and murmurs, I can imagine that.

No, you can't! If you could you wouldn't be doing what you are doing! You wouldn't be stealing other people's husbands!

The angry woman bites off the end of a thread with her teeth. The Chairman and Zi-zhen are separating only temporarily. Temporarily, do you hear me, Lan Ping?

Yes, I hear you.

With a strange light in her eyes the tailor's voice suddenly softens. She will, I am sure . . . Zi-zhen will get better and the couple will unite. No one gives up on Zi-zhen. Chairman Mao is a miracle maker. The victory of the Long March is a good example. The expansion of the red base is another and Zi-zhen will be the next.

The tailor's wrinkled lips fumble like a fish mouth. Words bubble out one after another. The candle begins to flicker. The room is suddenly brightened with a golden-orange ring. And then, a moment later, the candle goes out.

You have a scale and I have a weight, Mao says. There is a match.

Lan Ping nods, studying the face in front of her.

What are you looking at? An ancient skull? Am I a piece of salted dry pork that you are trying to buy?

I come to shake hands with you, she says. I come to wish you health and happiness.

He grabs her hands and tells her that his very soul demands her. It needs to be satisfied, or it will take deadly vengeance on its frame.

She is silent, but leaves her hand in his palm.

I expected you, he whispers.

What have I done?

Come to me.

She hesitates.

He begins to lose ground. His eyes see what they want to see. I have something to add to our talk by the riverbank. Would you care to hear it?

She moves to sit on the edge of his bed.

In the ditches of my hometown grew my favorite plant. It was a red plant called *beema*. Its leaf was larger than a lotus leaf, round in shape. Its fruit was the size of a fist, and its seed the size of a fig. You can crush it — the seed contains quite a large amount of oil.

It's tasty, but you can't eat it. It causes diarrhea. What I liked about it was that I could use it as a light. It's brighter than candles and produces a nice scent. My folks all use it. When I was a kid I spent my afternoons shelling the *beema* seeds. I connected the seeds together with a long string, tied it on one end of my bamboo stick and stuck it in places where I did my reading. Sometimes I took it to the ponds to help me locate fish and turtles . . .

He continues talking and pulls her toward his chest, presses her hands.

She remembers the room had a high ceiling. The wall mud-colored. The floor was packed rock. It looked like the back of a giant turtle.

I like this face, a face with a full forehead. A marvelous head. A head that is worth millions in gold and silver to Chiang Kai-shek. I look into the eyes. The dark brown pupils. The shapes and lines resemble those of the Buddha. It reminds me of a distant land-scape. The surface of a planet with gray rocks, emerald ponds. On this face, I detect an unconquerable will.

I see invisible guards behind the mask. The guards whose duty is to block anyone from entering the path that leads to the master chamber of the mind. The chamber where he is completely naked, vulnerable and defenseless.

He comes to hold me, pressing me against his ribs.

Bolts of silk spread in the air of my mind's picture.

It is in this room, on this bed, that she gives the performance of her life. She feels light filtering through her body.

The sky comes to devour the earth. Her pain from the past es-capes.

Later on when he becomes the modern emperor of China, when she has learned everything there is to learn about him, when all the doors in his universe have been opened, walked through and shut behind, thirty-eight years later, on his deathbed in the Forbidden City, she sees the same pair of eyes and realizes that she had invented them.

He caresses her and whispers in her ear another story of his fatal survival. Tells her how he escaped from the mouth of death. It was September 1927. He was captured by Chiang Kai-shek's agents right after the Autumn Harvest Uprising in Hunan. He was traveling, recruiting members of Communist groups and enlisting soldiers from the workers and peasants. Chiang Kai-shek's terror was at its peak. Hundreds of suspects were killed every day. He was taken to the militia headquarters to be shot.

The listener wears a white cotton shirt she has made herself. Her hair is ear-short. Her slender body is ripe. She feels his massiveness. She feels that he picks her up from the dust. She takes time the way she would on stage.

Borrowing a few yuan from a comrade, I attempted to bribe the escort to free me. The ordinary soldiers were mercenaries, with no special interest in seeing me killed, and they agreed to release me, but the subaltern in charge refused to permit it. I therefore decided to escape. I had no opportunity to do so until I was within about two hundred yards of the militia headquarters. At that point I broke loose and ran into the fields.

Later on when Madame Mao becomes the executive producer of all China's stage productions, she orders an episode dedicated to the scene she hears today. The hero escapes on his way to execution. He breaks loose and runs into the fields, hides in a tiny island in the middle of a lake with tall grass surrounding it. The title is *The Sha Family Pond.*

I reached a high place, above a pond with tall grass covering me. I hid until sunset. The soldiers pursued me. They forced some peasants to help them search. Many times they came near, twice so close that I could have almost touched them. Somehow by fate I escaped discovery. I was almost certain that I would be captured.

Madame Mao's opera singer playing the leader of the guerrillas carries his voice to the highest note and stylishly pitches the final line:

*The victory will fall into your hands*
*If you hold on to your faith*
*Even when the situation seems*
*Utterly out of hope and impossible to reverse*

At last, when it was dusk, they abandoned the search. At once I set off across the mountains. I traveled all night. I had no shoes and my feet were badly bruised. On the road I met a peasant who befriended me, gave me shelter and later guided me to the next district. I had only two yuan with me and I used the money to buy a pair of shoes, an umbrella and six buns. When at last I reached safety, I had only one copper in my pocket.

He makes her see heaven's grace in his valor. In bed he is impatient, like a tomb robber grabbing gold. She presents herself, the gift of seduction. In the future the couple will do the same to the minds of a billion.

At daybreak when he asks her to repeat the pleasure she refuses. She has been awake and has been thinking about Zi-zhen. Her body is caught in the mind's struggle.

You have arms thin like a thirteen-year-old's. He comes to touch her gently. It's amazing that a woman with such thin limbs bears such full breasts.

Her tears well up.

He asks to be given a chance to understand her sadness.

She says that it would be impossible.

No one can take away my right to be educated. He wipes her tears.

It is me who needs education. She turns away. You are a married man with a family. I should not have made a mess of —

You are not leaving me, Lan Ping.

But Zi-zhen is alive!

He looks at her and smiles almost vindictively.

I can't do this to Zi-zhen, she continues. She has never harmed me.

Strangely she realizes that the line is from a forgotten play except that she has replaced the character's name with Zi-zhen. She starts to put on her clothes and moves out of his bed. He has difficulty looking at her ivory skin. It sets his mind burning. Suddenly he believes that she is going to be the bride of one of his young generals or she is going back to Shanghai.

He reaches for her. In silence she lets him fill her.

After a while he gives up. He rolls over, his face toward the ceiling. Desert me now. Be gone.

Buttoning up her clothes her tears flow. I just don't see a way. I don't want to be a concubine.

He watches her and she can hear the sound of his teeth grinding in his jaw.

A mouse appears on the floor near the wall. It advances, cautiously crosses the floor, then scampers around the foot of the bed and stops. Raising its head, the beanlike eyes stare at the couple.

The sun's rays jump over the floor.

If I can survive the Long March, I can survive losing anything, he murmurs. Like any war there will be casualties. Haven't I seen enough blood? . . . Do as you please, but please promise that you'll never come back.

She begins to sob uncontrollably.

Let's get over with this mess. You say that I am a married man, but what you mean is that I am a doomed man. Why don't you fire? He puts a hand on her shoulder. Kill me with your coldness.

The best illusionist is one who can explain to you how the trick works and then still make you believe there is magic . . . She lifts her chin to look at him. This is where I stand at the moment — I still believe that you are meant for me!

Then say you won't leave.

But I must. Oh heaven, I must leave you.

He gets into his shoes and walks away from the bed.

She tries to move but her legs feel heavy.

What's wrong with you? he shouts. Are you a coward? I hate cowards! Don't you hear me? I hate, hate and hate cowards! Go now. Obey my order. Go! Go! Abandon me, abandon Yenan! Out!

She walks toward the door. Her hand feels the knob. She hears him wailing behind her: The war has taken everything away from me, my wives and my children . . . My heart has been shot through and through. So many times, so many holes, it is beyond repair. Lan Ping, why do you offer a man ginseng soup while making him a coffin!

I am back with my unit. The next day I am assigned to a *saomangban* — a team that works to "brush away" Yenan's illiteracy. I teach Chinese and math. My students are from the advanced women's platoon. Among them are the wives of the Party's high-ranking officers. It doesn't take me long to learn that Zi-zhen had been their shooting coach.

An older woman comes and grabs me by the wrist. This is how Zi-zhen likes to practice, she says. By the way, Comrade Lan Ping, Zi-zhen is a crack shot. Zi-zhen used to take me to watch her practice. She loves to do it at night. Especially moonless nights.

She would light ten torches at about a hundred yards away, then shoot with two pistols. Tatatatata, tatatatata . . . Ten bullets out, ten torches down. Then she would have me set up another set of torches, then another set . . . Tatatatata, tatatatata . . .

The students observe the girl from Shanghai as if watching a peasant skin a snake. The girl refuses to be played. What a woman! What a heroine! Lan Ping fills her voice with admiration.

He sends out Little Dragon to invite me for tea. We are awkward. The invisible Zi-zhen stands between us. While I choose to be silent, he begins to mock. Later on I discover that mocking is his style. He mocks, especially when he intends to punish. He chats warmly. One can never know what is coming.

I was thinking about what you told me the other day about your experience in Beijing. He sips his tea. I'd like to share some of mine with you. It also took place in Beijing. 1918, I was twenty-five years old. I was a part-time student at Beijing Normal University. I worked in the mailroom and the library. My position was so low that people avoided me. I knew then that there was something wrong. For hundreds of years the scholars had moved away from the people, and I began to dream of a time when the scholars would teach the coolies, for surely the coolies deserve being educated as much as the rest.

The truth is that Mao failed to gain any attention in Beijing. The country bumpkin felt humiliated. He was unable to forget the disappointing encounter. Later on it becomes one of his reasons to call for a great rebellion — the Cultural Revolution. It is to punish scholars nationwide for his early suffering. But at the moment, the girl from Shanghai lacks understanding. It will take forty years for her to grasp the story's true meaning. Then she will become his battle horse.

She thinks that he has a way to cheer her up. So she listens.

My own living conditions in Beijing were quite miserable, in contrast to the beauty of the old capital. I stayed in a place called Three-Eyes Well. I was sharing a tiny room with seven people. At night we all packed into the large bed made of earth heated from underneath. There was scarcely room for any of us to turn. I had to warn people on each side of me when I needed to do so.

The girl doesn't care if the man in front of her is describing their future home. Her concern is to make the man remove the woman between them.

Yesterday I felt the warmth of the early northern spring, Mao says. His eyes brighten. The white plums bloom while the ice seals over the Pei Lake. It reminds me of the poem by a Tang poet, Tsen Tsan. *Ten thousand peach trees blossoming overnight.*

The girl can't understand the charm of the poem, but she senses his feeling from the lines.

The women squat on their heels eating breakfast. Lan Ping stares at her bowl. Her thoughts are on Mao. She watches the women marching and exercising until class time. The women come and sit in rows in front of her. She tries to be vivid and illustrative. The students pay no attention. They begin to discuss among themselves how to weave fancy-patterned baskets.

Listen, I am here to teach you math! I need some respect.

The students turn to her and begin to complain that her voice is too soft. Our hearing has been damaged by Chiang Kai-shek's air raids. You are from the city, you don't know war . . . One woman suddenly calls the teacher a hypocrite.

This is rude, says Lan Ping.

Rude? The woman spits on the ground. Hypocrite!

The class echoes the woman.

Lan Ping throws the chalk and stops teaching.

The women cheer happily.

Suddenly comes the sound of gunshots.

It's Zi-zhen. The older woman makes a curling gesture with her finger, like pulling a trigger. It's her pistol. Do you know, Miss Lan Ping, that once Zi-zhen almost shot the Chairman?

When? the teacher asks, panicking.

It was when he came to visit her.

Why did she want to shoot him?

Because he was flirting with a lowlife. Zi-zhen always goes after the lowlifes. They make good targets for the crack shot.

I run as fast as I can back to my barracks. I close the door and pour cold water over my face. I know it was not Zi-zhen. Zi-zhen is in Russia. The women, her students, are there to take revenge for her and for themselves. They all would be affected if Mao divorces Zi-zhen. If Mao is allowed to abandon his wife, so are the others.

At night the Yenan Pagoda is a silent sentinel. At dawn there is a sudden explosion. From her window Lan Ping sees half of the sky turn red. A half-hour later, Little Dragon knocks on Lan Ping's door.

What's the matter? She puts on her coat.

The Chairman . . .

What happened?

His cave has been hit.

Is he all right?

He is fine, but the Politburo has to relocate. We are leaving. He sent me to say good-bye.

Good-bye? Is there anything else?

Good-bye and that's it.

Where is he going?

I have no idea.

You must know.

I am sorry. I was told to prepare a month's food for the horses.

*

He is working on a map when the girl comes in. She enters with the night air, hair jelled with sweat and dust. Her eyes are as bright as ever.

He puts down his pencil, pushes away his maps and walks toward her. I didn't expect an iron tree to bloom.

I have nothing to say. You have turned me into a winter. A terrible, terrible winter. She begins to cry.

Shall we visit the spring, then? He grabs a chair for her.

Her body trembles in his nearness.

Sorry I can serve you no tea. He passes her a bowl of water. The bombs have sent all my mugs into the air.

She takes the water and drinks it down in one swallow. She wipes her mouth with her sleeve.

Outside the guards are finishing loading the car. Little Dragon piles up the last documents, stuffing them into bags.

Moonlight shoots through the cracked ceiling. The brick bed is covered with dirt. His hands come to strip her. She pushes them away, but it doesn't stop him.

You debt-seeking demon, she cries.

Their limbs entangle. She feels his leaping and charging.

Like a dry chrysanthemum in a hot tea mug, she feels herself swelling and fattening by seconds.

I am a mythological pillar born to hold up the heavens, he roars. But without you I can only be a chopstick.

Down! Little Dragon shouts. It is followed by an explosion in the near distance.

Mao laughs with his pants at his ankles. Whoever you are, you missed me again! Japanese or Chiang Kai-shek! You smell the fun too? Oh, I love the shake of the earth, Chiang Kai-shek! You don't deserve your reputation! You have promised the world to wipe me out in three months. Look what fun I am having! You are a pregnant woman who screams about contractions but delivers no baby!

Is the Chairman ready yet? Little Dragon calls from outside. For his safety the Chairman has to move on!

Finally the lovers pull themselves out of the bed. Mao lights a cigarette and inhales deeply.

Outside Little Dragon hurries.

Shall we —? Before Lan Ping completes her sentence another bomb explodes. Half of the ceiling falls. Lan Ping screams.

Still like a mountain Mao keeps smoking. Little Dragon! he finally calls.

The bodyguards rush in. They pick up maps and blankets. Little Dragon throws the documents into a burning pan and collects Mao's last few books from the shelf.

Come with me? Mao asks the girl.

In tears she tells him that she can't possibly think straight right now. She needs time to decide.

Come on, the horses are impatient.

I . . . She is unable to make herself say that she first wants a promise.

Are you coming or not? Mao extinguishes his cigarette and stands up.

But Zi-zhen . . . she manages to say.

Mao cries, For heaven's sake! You have looted my heart! Rock by rock you have taken my cities down! Grace me, girl, I promise to make you as happy as you have made me.

In choking smoke Lan Ping watches the last plate of documents burn into ashes. Mao takes off his coat and covers her shoulders. He escorts her into his car while Little Dragon and the guards trash the cave. They tear down all the curtains, smash the furniture and water jars. They shout, We'll leave you nothing, Chiang Kai-shek! Absolutely nothing!

Sitting beside her lover the girl is touched by the operatic quality of her life. Events transform in front of her eyes. On the stage of her mind, Mao becomes the modern King-of-Shang and she his lover, Lady Yuji. She sees herself follow the king. Ever since she was a little girl it has been her dream to play Lady Yuji. She was a devoted fan of the opera *Farewell My Concubine*. She loves the moment when Yuji stabs herself before the king to prove her love. The character is in her beautiful silk gown, wearing a hat encrusted with pearls.

# 11

I T IS IN MAO'S CAVE that the girl learns politics. She learns that Chiang Kai-shek has recently increased the price for Mao's head. It frightens her and at the same time flatters her. She learns that Japan's invasion has deepened and China's provinces have been falling into the enemies' hands one after another. She learns that not long ago one of Chiang's generals, Zhang Xue-liang, initiated a rebellion during which he took Chiang hostage and brought him to the Communists. The Communist Politburo intended to kill him; Mao, however, proposed a negotiation.

It's a good opportunity to show the masses that our benevolence is beyond any personal grudge, Mao says, setting his eyes on pushing the Communist Party toward acceptance as China's major political force. In exchange for his life, Chiang agrees to resist Japan and unite with the Communists.

At home, Mao gains control over the Politburo. He selects his own cabinet members and attacks those who try to adopt the Russian formula over his guerrilla style. Using the Politburo's name he rids himself of his political enemies, the Moscow-trained Wang Ming and Zhang Guotao, by assigning them to remote posts. To his soldiers Mao continues to preach his own interpretation of Marxism and Leninism. His booklet *Eight Laws and*

*Three Disciplines* is printed on a hand press and distributed to every soldier.

Mao makes laws but he doesn't expect himself to be disciplined by them. In mid-1938, stories of his betrayal of Zi-zhen spread widely. Mao's partners, Zhou En-lai and Zhu De, advise him to put a stop to his affair with the Shanghai actress and go back to his wife.

My lover continues to see me regardless of the pressure. I am a monk without hair — I am the law — he says. Our affair is fueled by the force to break us. Mao is a rebel by nature. In me he finds his role. Nevertheless I know what I am risking. I am nobody in Yenan. I could be removed any time in the name of the revolution.

So I run from the trouble. I move back to the barracks. I don't wait to be "assigned" to a remote post. I have already learned the style of punishment within the Communist Party. I take action before the Politburo seizes me. I must make my lover work for his pleasure. Our love has to be put to the test.

The girl leaves Mao a letter saying that his career and reputation are all that matter to her. The Chairman tries to keep his composure, but gradually his strain shows — he has a hard time performing his job. His feet were burned by the foot-warmer stove and his curtains caught the candle flames. He has been losing his temper in Politburo meetings. His decisions are not sound. He often beats the table with his fists. He complains that documents are too messy and telegrams don't make sense — he is not himself anymore.

She doesn't go back. She wants him to go on. She wants him to see her in every corner, in his tea cup, on his maps and telegrams. Later on he tells her that he saw more. He saw her inside his young general's mosquito net. During those days, his chest swelled. The ache was pushing out everything else that was there.

\*

One night when the wind is strong with furious gusts, my lover drops himself at my door. I tell him that I have made up my mind never to see him again.

Please stop coming, I say.

He is quiet. After a while he asks me to take a walk with him.

I refuse.

He starts walking.

I hesitate, then my feet follow him.

The riverbank path leads them into deep reeds. After a half mile she suddenly pivots, says that she can't go on, that she has to leave. Like a lion to a deer he catches her and picks her up from the ground. She struggles to free herself. He becomes intense. His hands tear at her uniform.

You can't do that! She pushes him. Not anymore!

But she opens herself. Leans over him, lies in his arms. She spreads her legs, weeps and melts in his heat. He caresses her, murmurs, groans and wails madly. She lets her body tell him how much she misses him.

Everyone expects me to be a stone Buddha without desire or feelings, he gasps on top of her. My comrades would like me better if I were a eunuch. But I am a tiger who can't be a vegetarian!

1938. Mao is finally acknowledged by Moscow. In September the Communist Party opens its sixth convention with Mao as the chairman. The Russian advisor shows up and announces the abandonment of Stalin's old friend Wang Ming, Mao's rival and the head of the Party's right-wing group. The advisor pronounces Mao Moscow's new partner.

The news hits my friend Kang Sheng as a surprise — he has been a loyal follower of Wang Ming. They were classmates in

Russia. After coming to Yenan Kang Sheng has tried hard to gain Mao's trust, but people haven't forgotten his past. On September 14, in an extended meeting investigating Wang Ming, Kang Sheng's name is repeatedly brought up as Wang's partner in several political crimes. The Politburo is set to have Kang Sheng removed.

The goat-beard man sits in the meeting as if sitting on a carpet of needles.

It is at this moment that Kang Sheng receives a crucial piece of information that turns the danger into a blessing. A telegram from Shanghai is sent by the Party's branch officer Liu Xiao. It is a report of an investigation ordered on Lan Ping during her imprisonment in October 1934. The report states that Lan Ping had denounced Communism and is thus a traitor.

Although she has not caused any harm to the Party, the behavior is serious enough to destroy her chance to marry Mao.

During the contemplation of this telegram, Kang Sheng sees his own future dawning.

Evening dissolves. The cave is filled with smoke. Kang Sheng has been smoking. Lan Ping sits by his desk reading the telegram. Her face is pale.

This is a conspiracy, a setup, she cries. Where is their proof? It's jealousy. They are jealous of my relationship with the Chairman! She gets up but suddenly feels short of breath and she falls heavily back into the chair.

I am not here to discuss whether or not they have proof. I am sure they have. Kang Sheng speaks slowly and looks directly at Lan Ping. The problem is what will happen when the Politburo sees this. You will be suspended — it doesn't matter what the truth is. You will be interrogated and expelled, if lucky, from the Party. If not, shot. The Chairman will be in no position to defend you, neither will I. You know my job. The procedure. You are too big a target.

The sweat begins to seep through the roots of her hair. She wants to argue but her mind has gone blank. She stares at the ceiling and feels her senses paralyzing.

Master Kang, she calls him as if he were still the principal of Zhu-Town Elementary. I love the Chairman more than anything. I beg your help.

Kang Sheng doesn't respond for a long time, then he sighs, expresses his difficulty, describes how he has been attacked at the meetings because of Wang Ming. Only Mao can prove my innocence, he hints.

She grabs the deal. Taking out her handkerchief she wipes her tears. I'll see what I can do about this. I'll talk to the Chairman for you.

She keeps wiping. Her face, neck, shoulders, arms, hands and fingers. And then all over again. I'll say that the boss was Wang Ming. You did what he had ordered, didn't you? It was he who tried to kick Mao out of power. You can produce evidence, can't you? Should I say that you in fact had tried to protect the Chairman? Would it be exaggerating to say that you have suffered a great deal of Wang Ming's resentment? . . . I am sure I can get a word from the Chairman for you.

Kang Sheng is satisfied. Color returns to his face. Comrade Lan Ping, I promise that I won't let this telegram travel an inch farther.

Peace comes out of war, my lover teaches me. Life is paid for by death. There is no middle ground. There are times when we have to make decisions. Doubt is the substitute word for danger. It is better to clear the way than call out a question when unsure who is approaching. You have a lot to learn from Comrade Kang Sheng.

I am learning. He can appear kind, delicate and even vulnerable, but behind the mask it is the face of death. The truth of a bloodsucker. That's how he earns the position as Mao's chief of security. Mao appreciates his quality and style. Mao says that he and Kang Sheng are in the business of goodness. I sense a peculiar side of my lover's nature. It is his ability to deal with suffering. It is what makes Mao. I am learning. The killers with Confucius's appearances. I am learning. The way one wins China.

These are the two brilliant men in my life. Two men who created who I am and I them.

These are the two brilliant men in my life. Two men who created who I am and I them.

The pressure from the Politburo continues. The lovers have gone underground. She has stopped going to the Saturday night high-ranking officials' parties. Dancing as a form of exercise and socializing is the new game in town. The wives are pleased with the disappearance of the actress.

But beyond the public eye and at prearranged times, driven by passion, the actress delivers herself to Mao. She lays herself in his bed on stormy nights and chilly dawns. Afterwards, he asks her to sing from their favorite opera, *Vermilion Pearl Plant*. When she does he becomes lustful again.

> *Like a high-born maiden*
> *In a palace tower*
> *Soothing her love-laden*
> *Like a glowworm golden*
> *In a dell of dew*
> *Scattering unbeholden*
> *Its aerial hue*
> *Soul in secret hour*
> *With wine sweet as love*
> *Which overflows her bower*

Before long Mao brings news to the Politburo: Comrade Lan Ping is pregnant. He demands a divorce and a marriage.

Mao's partners shake their heads in unison. You have promised the Party!

Yes, I have. But things change, like the situation of the war. If you can change yourselves to unite with Chiang Kai-shek, why can't you accept my situation with women? . . . Well, you have pushed me to the limit. Comrade Lan Ping will have no choice but to walk around with her fattening belly to ring her bells. Everyone will know that as Chairman I am imprisoned by my own Party. And that will make all our propaganda a lie. It will be a free advertisement for Chiang Kai-shek — the Communists have no respect for humanity. Chiang Kai-shek will be laughing so hard that his fake teeth will fall out.

Mao goes on. I'm prepared to tell people the truth myself. I am sure they will judge with their own conscience, they will figure out how this Party flatters itself with the emperor's new clothes. They will question. Does anybody care about Mao Tse-tung's personal welfare? Hasn't he worked hard enough? Is he the Party's slave? People will draw their own conclusion and choose whom to follow. By then it will be too late for you to come to your senses — I'll be gone. I will create a new Red Army, a new base where men and women will be free to marry for love, where my children can bear my name, and where the word "liberation" is not a wooden bird!

No one underestimates Mao's capability. All the members of the Politburo clearly remember that it was Mao who saved the Red Army from Chiang Kai-shek's deadly encirclement; it was Mao who turned the devastating exile of the Long March into a journey of victory. After a week of deadlock the men decide to negotiate. The ship can't sail without a helmsman.

Mao is pleased. He promises to place limits on the power of the first lady. Extinguishing his cigarette he says, I am an ordinary Party member. I will unconditionally follow the Politburo's decision.

Rules are drawn up to chain the bride-to-be: she is not allowed to publicize her identity or take part in Mao's business or offer opinions at Mao's pillow. Mao accepts the deal. However, he lets it be known that he would rather not be the one to break the news to Lan Ping. The Party understands.

I walk with Lao Lin, the Party's personal affairs consultant, and my lover, who follows a few steps behind. The afternoon is peaceful and a chatting mood has settled in. We arrive at the riverbank. My lover walks quietly as if contemplating his thoughts. Lao Lin and I have been exchanging words on weather, health and war. Looking toward the sun, which is setting behind the treetrunks, he suggests that we sit in the shade of a tree.

Lao Lin begins by congratulating me. He reports that our marriage application has been approved. I make no reaction. I am waiting for him to drop the bomb. Aren't you pleased? Smiling, he smoothes his bristly beard with long fingers.

I have been preparing myself to fight for my rights, I say frankly.

Lao Lin laughs uneasily.

I glance at my lover, who has been staring at the river.

May I have my marriage certificate? I ask Lao Lin.

Well, I must . . . You see before I am allowed to do that I must have your promise.

Here it comes. The sound of an explosion. Without looking at me Lao Lin lays down the rules.

The impact shakes my core. The pain bites right in. It is more than I had ever imagined. Amidst the quiet of the riverbank I explode: What does it mean not to publicize my identity? Am I a criminal? Doesn't the Party know that the Chairman has lost his first wife? How do you know that he won't lose me in the war? How many times has Mao's cave been bombed? How many assassination attempts have you recorded? Part of marrying Mao is to risk my life! And I am not trusted by the Politburo, supposedly the people I shall depend on? For Marx's sake, what kind of congratulation is this?

She tries to calm her voice but fails. What does it mean, "Do not take part in his business"? Why don't you simply disapprove of the marriage? Say it out loud! Print out the rules and put them on the wall for the public to view! I didn't come to Yenan to be insulted. There are a lot of young women in Yenan who are politically reliable, who are illiterate and won't take part in Mao Tsetung's business. Plenty of them! Why don't you —

Lao Lin interrupts her. The Politburo has sent me as its messenger. I don't have anything personal against you. The same would be required of any woman who marries the Chairman. It's for security reasons. The matter has nothing to do with who you are. Comrade Lan Ping, the Party knows that you are a trusted member. The bottom line is that people want to make sure that their leader Mao will perform without interference.

My lover squats on his heels and continues to gaze at the swirling current. He has not said a word and I have no idea what is on his mind. He is in a difficult position, I understand. After all he can't, and won't, separate himself from his title. Should I ask him to prove his love? He is not Tang Nah. He is not a dramatic type. If I challenge him he will tell me to go my own way. He is used to detaching himself from pain. He would get over me. But would I be able to get over him?

She makes sure that she plays it right this time. She asks herself repeatedly, What is it about her that attracts Mao besides her city-bred wrinkle-free face? Does her brain count? She remembers that he once told her that he liked her character and courage. Was it just a line of flattery? Is she fooling herself? What if it is just her beauty? She can be any man's fantasy in this part of China and if she stays with Mao and he wins China . . . It will be indisputable that she was there, fought with him side by side. She will have earned her right to speak, to take part in his business, even a seat in the Party's convention and maybe the Politburo. Who, by then, will stop her from pillow-talking Mao? To be Madame Mao will be her victory. She will be lower than the man she loves but above the nation.

I can never forget the night when my lover talked to me about the Great Wall. It was after our lovemaking. He wanted to discuss the most exciting project ever built in the history of China. It is not the Great Wall, he said to me. It is the Du-jiang Dike, built ten years before the Great Wall. It was on the plain of Sichuan where drought and flood continually plagued the province. There is no comparison in size, but unlike the wall, the dike has created happiness for thousands of years.

My lover was immersed in his thoughts. His fingers gently fondled my hair. If we say the wall occupies space, the dike occupies time, he continued. The functionality of the Great Wall has long expired while the Du-jiang Dike still holds the life of the province. Because of it, drought and flood are controlled and Sichuan is now known for its harvests. The culture of the Great Wall is like a stiff sculpture, but the culture of the Du-jiang Dike presents the vitality of the universe. The Great Wall acts like an old empress dowager demanding respect while the dike silently provides service like a humble countryside daughter-in-law.

Mao's vision of China is what she expects in a king. She sees what her lover will become to China and its people. If this is not love and respect in its purest form, the girl questions, then what is? How can she not be proud of her passion for Mao?

*

By the time the next moon rises high the actress from Shanghai shakes hands with Lao Lin. She promises to deliver the letter of acceptance of the rules before the wedding day.

The bride-to-be worries that she has made it too easy for Mao. She is afraid that he won't remember her sacrifice. The sacrifice which she intends to hold and claim for credit in the future. It's her investment. But he has not shown her much affection since Lao Lin departed.

Mao has immersed himself in writing his philosophy of war. He writes for days on end without resting, loses all track of time. When he is finished he calls Little Dragon to send the girl. He makes her feel that she is already in his possession. His hands come for her the moment she enters the door. She hears him mumble, telling her in monologue what he has been writing.

Yes, tell me, tell me everything, she responds.

It's suicidal to display a facade when the enemies are massive in numbers. He begins to unbutton her shirt. We have to learn to take advantage of being small — we are capable of flexibility. If we pull the enemy by the nose and lead their horses into the woods, we can confuse them and pin them down. We bite off their legs and then take off quickly before they can guess our numbers or intention. This was my strategy during the Long March and now I establish it as a rule of war.

I want Mao to know that I am interested in what he is doing and want to be part of it. But I try not to follow his thoughts so I can concentrate on the pleasure. I focus my eyes somewhere else, a penholder on his desk. It is made from the joint of a bamboo pole. It is stuffed with brushes and pens, which point toward the ceiling like bunches of dragon-tongue orchids. I am strangely stimulated.

I've created a myth, he goes on. I have told my generals to be playful with Chiang Kai-shek. To take a bite, then run, and take another bite and run again. The key is not to be reluctant to depart after small victories. It's a problem with our soldiers. It's their hometown. They have a hard time letting go. They hate to quit when collecting the heads of those who murdered their family members. But you must quit in order to win more . . . Like right now I mustn't go all the way. I must know when to hold my troops back . . .

I'm no longer amazed that he can make love while sorting out his thoughts. For me, it has become part of our ritual. The moment I detect him losing track of his thoughts my body goes wild.

Was it four times that you crossed back and forth over the Chi River in order to escape Chiang Kai-shek? I ask, teasing him. Did you confuse the enemy?

He is too breathless to answer me.

I heard about your victory in Shanghai, I keep going. You were not known, though — you were an underground myth everybody wanted to unearth. Did I tell you how Chiang Kai-shek's papers described what you looked like? It said that you had teeth six inches long, and a head three feet wide.

He groans and announces his coming.

For the next three weeks he is back to his writing. *A Study on the Jiangxi Peasants' Movement. Revolution Chinese Style. On Establishing the Red Army.* Afterwards he collapses and goes to sleep like a corpse in a coffin. The girl continues to draft the letter she has promised Lao Lin. She sits by Mao's table and plays with brushes and pens. Her mind is empty. She is bored. She counts characters every few lines. She knows that she has to fill up a page for it to be acceptable.

Fart, fart, and fart, she writes, then erases, then writes again. She takes out a tiny mirror and begins to examine her face. The teeth, nose, eyes and eyebrows. She plays with her hair, combs it into different styles. Stretches her skin with her fingers, making different expressions. She likes her face. The way it is reflected in the mirror. It looks prettier in the mirror than on the screen. She wonders why she didn't look as pretty on camera. Her thoughts skip. She wonders what's happening to Tang Nah and Yu Qiwei. And what they will think when they learn that she is Madame Mao.

The thought brings her delight and makes her go back to the draft. She works until Mao wakes. Her heart beats gaily as she hears him reciting a wake-up poem of the Han dynasty:

> *The spring woke my hibernation*
> *The sun is on my buttocks hurrying me up*

She gets up from her chair to pour him tea. She then goes back to the desk and waits. He comes to her. She shows him the draft. He leans toward the light to read. His hands go under her shirt.

Sounds like a letter of protest, he laughs. She says that she doesn't know how to write otherwise. She is unable to bend herself any lower. He comforts her. You shouldn't go to a monk and ask to borrow a comb — you should be kind with my colleagues' shortcomings. After all they are peasants. As for himself, he appreciates her sacrifice. A letter of promise is only a piece of paper. It is up to us to honor it. The truth is that the letter is only going to be used to clamp the lips of those scorpion-mouthed wives.

She is convinced. Laughing in tears. Holding her hand he revises the draft. I want you to pillow-talk me now. I want you to harvest me. Oh, yes. Right here, sign *Sincerely, Lan Ping*.

The wedding day. The wind sculpts clouds into the shapes of giant fruits. It is in Mao's new cave — he has moved from Phoenix Hill to the Yang Family Grove. It is a three-room cave located on the side of the mountain, about fifty feet in depth. The back wall is

made of stone and the front, of wood. The windows are covered
with paper. In front of the cave is a bit of flat ground. There are
stone stools and a vegetable patch.

Mao gets up early and works in the garden. Peppers, garlic, to-
matoes, yams, beans and squash — all are in good spirits. Mao
carries a shoulder pole with two buckets of water on each end. He
walks through the narrow paths watering each plant patiently.
He tilts his shoulders and lifts the string of the bucket to pour.
He looks content and relaxed.

The bride stands in front of the cave and watches her lover. She
watches him nibble off the tips of the cotton plants. She remembers that he once told her that his mind worked best when his
hands got busy with soil and roots. What is on his mind now? She
wonders if he compares her with his ex-wives. You are the girl
who carries your own sunshine, he has told her. Your gaiety is my
soul's health and Zi-zhen's sadness its poison.

To me, he is a father figure. He is all I have ever wanted in a
man. As a father he is wise, loving and formidable. When I asked
why he decided to marry me he replied that I have the ability to
make a rooster produce eggs. I take the remark as a compliment. I
assume that he means that I bring out the best in him. But I am not
sure. Sometimes I feel that he is too great for me to understand.
His mind is forever unattainable. He is a frightening spectacle. To
his comrades, opponents or enemies, he can be intoxicating and
terrifying. I love him but fear for myself. In front of him I give up
comprehension. I surrender. I long for him to want me, the true
me, not the actress. Sometimes I feel that he wants to have my
body near but my soul at a distance. He wants to keep the myth
of me.

Later on, after many years, I discover that he prefers to live
with the counterfeit rather than the human. But as a young
woman I am simple and enthusiastic. I don't need to understand

everything about this god whose essence is out of my reach. I sleep soundly on the question of the unknown. What's the hurry when I shall have the rest of my life to figure him out? I don't compare myself with Zi-zhen. I am not like Zi-zhen, who preserves herself in the bottle of misery and seals the lid with a wrench. If there is such a bottle in front of me I will smash it. I have a passion for stimulation and challenge. I see my future promising *nothing* but that.

But why am I having these doubts on my wedding day?

Eight o'clock. The sunshine bursts out of the clouds. After setting up a table outside I go back to the cave to get dressed. I am a little disappointed that Mao has only invited a small group of people. He has turned down my wish to invite a crowd. His reason was that he didn't want to attract Chiang Kai-shek's attention — he doesn't want to be bombed on his wedding day.

I take out the eyebrow pincers. I fix and paint my eyebrows the way I used to in Shanghai. I powder my sunburned skin. There is no dress. I promised Mao to respect the revolutionary fashion, which is to have no fashion. I wear a faded gray uniform and a belt over it.

When I come out, everyone turns toward me and suddenly the men begin to talk about the sky. Its color. A watermelon with a layer of green in the bottom, yellow in the middle and pink-red on the top.

There is a sudden quietness. Mao tries to hide his elation. He says to his bride, Peanuts! The bride begins to serve around a basket of peanuts. The guests ask the groom to offer tips on romance. Mao sits back down and stretches his arms and shoulders. A tornado blew off my hat — how should I put it? — it landed and caught me a golden bird.

Details! the men cry, passing the boss a cigarette. Smiling, Mao inhales deeply. There are really two tips: One, you have to be a dog and ask to borrow a bone. And two, you have to always be aware that you are holding a dangerous pose, like sticking your head over the stove to dry your hair.

She takes a good look at the guests as Mao introduces them one by one. They are his men. Men she needs to impress. If possible, she begins to think, make them her men in the future. She already knows that the possibility exists in Kang Sheng. She can't forget their first conversation. May I find safety under your wing, Comrade Kang Sheng? If under your wing I may find the same, Miss Lan Ping.

She hears Kang Sheng's false laugh. A disgusting sound. He is flattering his boss. They don't really chat, but there is intimacy. A secret code exists between Kang Sheng and Mao. Somehow she feels that she will never be able break the code. A strange pair of friends, she thinks. Mao once jokingly described Kang Sheng as a small temple that produces witch-wind. Kang Sheng knows exactly what Mao wants and offers it to him. It can be to destroy a political rival or arrange a night with a mistress.

She is satisfied with the moment. For that she honors herself. For it is she who has finally earned the role of the leading lady.

A peacock among hens. She smiles.

I speak Mandarin. I slow down to make his friends understand me. I ask about the guests' health, their family members, animals and the crops. I am learning my husband's business. I discover that his heart is not here for the wedding. Actually he has little interest in the ceremony. He uses the time to gather information. On battles, his colleagues, the white territories.

There is a man Kang Sheng brings to my husband. His name is Old Fish. He has the face of a tamed dog with long ears hanging on the sides. His Western suit shines with grease around the belly, collar and elbows. The sewing stitches are visible. It looks like an army of ants. His pockets bulge with notebooks and papers. The man reports on the white territories. The name Liu Shao-qi is constantly repeated. Old Fish praises Liu as a man of great capability who started out as a striker but doesn't fight just to destroy. He negotiates with factory owners and is able to have the workers' conditions met every time.

Comrade Liu Shao-qi is our Party's treasure, my husband comments. It's terribly important that we win over the workers.

There is not the slightest tone of jealousy in Mao's words, but the seed of Liu Shao-qi as a potential rival is planted in his heart right at this moment. No one in China ever imagined that Mao would be capable of mass destruction simply over his jealousy of someone's talent. No one ever understood Mao's fears. Thirty years later, Mao launches the so-called Great Proletarian Cultural Revolution in which millions of lives are lost in order to pave his way.

There is a trick Madame Mao never manages to learn from Mao: not only does he escape criticism for his responsibility in the crime of the century, he also engages his public, even after his death, to defend, worship and bless his goodness.

The record player is on. The piece is "The Night of Fire in the Capital." The record player was a gift from Mao's foreign admirer, Agnes Smedley. The bride goes and turns down the volume. She then walks around trying to join the conversations. She listens and picks moments to insert her remarks. She asks about the Fascists in Europe. She wants to know when Chiang Kai-shek may attack again. She asks, How long will Chiang Kai-shek's supplies last? How much money are the Westerners willing to pour into Chiang Kai-shek's bottomless pit? Isn't it obvious that Chiang Kai-shek is a dog without a spinal cord? Can we get the Western world on our side? Should Mao launch a media campaign to help tell the world that his action counts? What's going on between the Russians and the Japanese? Shouldn't Stalin be convinced by now of Mao's ability to rule China?

She amazes Mao and the guests with her desire to learn. She is twenty-four years old and the fire in her chest is burning high. Her energy works its charm on some, but others find her naive and presumptuous. She is too excited to notice one way or the other. She witnesses the way Mao plays godfather to his army. She sees what she can achieve through the marriage — she is shown the very best example.

He tells the girl a story on the wedding night. A story that inspires him and teaches him the secret of ruling. During the Dynasty of Spring and Autumn a prince bought soldiers. To prevent their escape he brought in a tattoo man. The prince ordered the man to tattoo his name on both cheeks of every soldier. When the job is done the prince felt their loyalty was secured. He took the soldiers to a distant battle. Before the troops traveled far, the soldiers began to disappear. There was no way to trace them — the soldiers had bribed the tattoo man. The tattoos on their cheeks were so thin that they washed off.

It's the mind you ought to tattoo! my lover concludes when finishing the story.

I feel that my mind was tattooed at that moment. Otherwise how can I explain the reason I answer his every call? He instills himself — the voice of a god — in me and his nation.

*The Book of Chang* itself, she calls him.

By the time the guests leave the couple is exhausted. The floor is covered with peanut shells, sunflower seeds and cigarette butts. Mao doesn't ask his bride's opinion of the guests. He knows she is irritated by their manners. It's obvious that she can't stand it when they spit on the floor, stick their fingers in their mouths to pick out food while talking, and worse, fart shamelessly.

>  *I am a dress made out of a verdict*
>  *— every thread is linked to a bloody crime*

Mao makes his bride give up cleaning and takes her into the bedroom while singing an old opera aria happily.

>  *Like a drought-land clam*
>  *I wouldn't open my mouth . . .*

She is amused and joins his singing.

>  *A mouse is given an assignment*
>  *to guard the grain storage*
>  *And the goat is put to watch the vegetable garden*
>  *— what a pleasurable thing to do . . .*

# 12

JIANG CHING IS MY NEW NAME. It is a thoughtful gift from my husband. I am no longer Lan Ping — Blue Apple. The new characters have straight lines like a boat sailing in full wind — *Jiang* as River and *Ching* as Green. Jiang Ching summarizes a traditional saying: *Green comes out of blue but is richer than blue.*

I have parted from my old role. I come out of blue and enter the richer color green. I am a butterfly out of the cocoon, spring belongs to me. My name has become part of my lover's poetry.

There aren't any photographs hanging on my wall. No books or reviews either. No souvenirs. Not even a poster of me as Nora. It's not that I wouldn't like to be reminded of my old days, my new role simply demands a different setting. I face a different audience.

I need to color my history red. This is what gives one true rights in Yenan. My future enemies hold an invisible mirror. It is said to reflect my political "birth defects." In the mirror they see a demon who has come to steal Mao's essence. They have already begun a war with me by trying to block my marriage.

The rumors and false accusations begin to spread the day Mao and I wed. I have broken many hearts. During and after the ceremony, a number of comrades and our guests of honor, including my husband's ex-brother-in-law Xia Zhen-nong, begin to gossip about Mao's "declining health." It is loud. Look at the Chairman, he has come to depend on liquor to boost his energy.

I am beginning to realize that I don't stand much chance to defend myself here in Yenan. Mao's divorce is considered a betrayal under my influence. What frightens me is that hatred for the actress is in the air before the play opens. It is a show people don't want to see but to which they are forced to come. Every line pricks their ears and every scene burns their eyes.

I am never able to reverse the image of a white-boned demon. Many envisioned my burial the moment I entered Mao's cave. The hatred deepens as the years wear on. So does my anger. The ancient saying goes, *Ten thousand people's spit can make a well deep enough to sink a person.* Well, I am in that well.

I am determined to carry on my show in hope of finding my true audience. Some of my critics say that I make them sick to their stomach. But the truth is that they can't take their eyes off me while giving me bad names. They are doing everything they can to ruin me.

In my costume I am the leading lady. I am described by Mao's visitors as pleasant, sweet and friendly. Yes, I have every reason in the world to be content and grateful, and I am. Inside, however, the sea is never calm. I have to watch myself, to make sure that I appear proper, obedient and tamed. I love Mao enough to leave behind a big part of myself, including my passion for drama and movies. I believe Mao's business is more important and I am trying to make it mine too.

Over the next six months Mao produces the most famous writings of his life. Among them are *Basic Battle Tactics — Thoughts on Guerrilla Warfare* and *On the Protracted War.* Mao's views fascinate and captivate the nation; as a result, the number of Red Army recruits increases dramatically. Enraged, Chiang Kai-shek secretly contacts Adolf Hitler for military advisors and orders the complete elimination of the Communists.

It is at this time that Madame Mao Jiang Ching gives birth to a daughter, Nah. She disappears from the public scene completely. As the new host of the family, she enthusiastically receives the members of Mao's previous families: two sons, Anyin and Anqing, from Mao's marriage to Kai-hui, and a daughter, Ming, from his marriage to Zi-zhen. Jiang Ching spends her days nursing the baby and making clothes and sweaters. Through Kang Sheng she learns that Zi-zhen has secretly returned from Russia with her illness worsened. Mao has arranged for Zi-zhen to live in a private mental hospital in a southern city.

The village tailor comes often to help Jiang Ching with the housework. The tailor brings news and gossip. Jiang Ching learns that her friend Sesame has been killed in a battle near Gan-jiang River. Another name that often surfaces is Fairlynn. Fairlynn has become the star of feminism and liberalism in Yenan. Her novels and essays are widely published and she is idolized by the nation's youth.

Fairlynn is working on a new novel when I knock on her door. I don't know why I've come here. I don't like Fairlynn. I guess I simply have to satisfy my curiosity. She is surprised to see me and greets me delightedly. Holding out her arms, the first thing she says to me is, Look, the mother hen is here!

What's her name? she asks.

Nah. I open my basket to reveal my daughter.

Nah? What do you mean, Nah?

She didn't say, "Don't tell me it's from Tang Nah" but I get the idea.

It is pure coincidence, I explain. My husband doesn't give a damn whom I married in the past. The name comes from Confucius's teaching on behavior. Nah for self-cultivation. It is all Mao's idea.

Welcome to the red base, little soldier! Fairlynn bends to touch Nah, then turns toward me. You look like you are loaded again.

You're nasty, as always, Fairlynn. I smile and sit down. You like to make me feel bad. You know you love to do that to me.

Oh, Lan Ping, you hate me just the same. We already knew that when we met.

Any progress in your personal life, Fairlynn? How old are you anyway?

She lights a cigarette. Thirty-six. I'm too busy.

It's a familiar excuse for those who can't attract. I laugh. Come on, get yourself a husband before it's too late.

A husband? Fairlynn puffs the smoke. I would rather flirt with a chimpanzee!

She throws a half-eaten yam into her mouth. By the way, how does it feel to be Madame Mao?

A dream come true.

Very clever, Miss Lan Ping.

No, Comrade Jiang Ching.

Very well, Comrade Jiang Ching.

The world is yours if you have the talent, Fairlynn. This is what my husband says to me: *The street is filled with gold, but not everyone has eyes to see it.*

Fairlynn smiles. Good. Get more babies and practice sewing.

You can't stop biting, can you? I think the problem is your Shakespeare hairstyle. I am sure it turns men off. I'll be happy to give you a new haircut.

Lan Ping, you can't make me feel unattractive.

Jiang Ching, please — *Jiang* as River and *Ching* as Green. You have no idea how wonderful it is to have children. Look at Nah, she is smiling at you. Come on, girl, go to Aunt Fairlynn.

Oh, it's warm. It's moving like a worm. Look at this fluffy hair. You smell like an overfermented sourdough bread.

Nah starts to lunge at Fairlynn's breast.

Milk time! I laugh.

Fairlynn passes Nah back to me in embarrassment.

Would you like to hear my new novel, Jiang Ching? It's entitled *The New Nora*. It's about how Nora walks out of house number one and enters house number two.

Leaning on the pillow I ask my husband's opinion of Fairlynn.

I don't take those bookworms too seriously, Mao responds. What do Fairlynn types know? Dictionaries? What is a dictionary but pages of dead words anyway? Can she tell the difference between rice shoots and weeds? What could be easier than being a bookworm? It's harder to learn to be a chef or a butcher. A book has no legs, one can open or close it at any time. A pig has legs that can run and a pig has vocal cords that can wail. The butcher has to catch and slaughter it. The chef has to make the stinky meat taste delicious. These are the real talents. What's Fairlynn? She plays in the school of thoughts only because we let her . . .

She cuddles under him. Boss, do you think Fairlynn is attractive?

Why do you ask?

Just curious. She's no beauty, is she?

Huh . . .

Let me tell you a crowd of men are trying to get her attention. They range from generals to soldiers. They fantasize about her as if she were the protagonist in her novel. Little Dragon doesn't even know how to spell, but he recites Fairlynn's poems.

What has been Fairlynn's reaction? Was she interested in our soldiers?

Well, she has said that she doesn't want to enter any house of Torvald's. She calls your men chimpanzees.

That's interesting. Mao's voice is fading.

Have you read her?

I have copies of her books which she sent me. Mao turns over and blows out the candle.

Did you know that Fairlynn hangs out with the local Bol-
sheviks? Jiang Ching suddenly asks in the dark.

I'm tired. I'll look into the matter after . . . after . . . I finish with
the Party's convention.

May I take part in the convention?

No answer.

She asks again.

Mao starts snoring.

Beyond the harsh valley of Yenan, the world lurches toward the
greatest conflagration of the century. The Nazi-Germans begin to
move across Europe. The Japanese fan out over the Pacific. Closer
to home, Mao begins his intense competition with Chiang Kai-
shek for the ruling power of China.

Jiang Ching celebrates her next four birthdays in the small garden at the mouth of their cave. At thirty-one she has become an
expert seamstress and is used to having their living room used as
a war headquarters. Once in a while after an important battle
is won, Mao sends away his comrades. He takes a day off to
spend with the children. More rarely, he escorts his wife to a
local performance to see an opera, an orchestra or a troupe of
folk singers. Sensing his wife's frustration, he makes his horse
available to her.

After only a few lessons from Little Dragon, I am able to ride out
by myself. With a little practice, I soon become quite confident.
The land surrounding Yenan is perfect for riding, open and rolling. I tie my hair up into a bun and speed the animal. I ride over
the hills and along the riverbank. The breeze on my face makes
me feel the spring. Smiling into the wind I think to myself, I am a
bandit girl! I ride until the horse's nostrils are wide with panting

and his sweat has soaked the blanket. And then I dig my heels in for one last gallop.

Madame Mao Jiang Ching is content yet bored at the same time. She is getting tired of her role as a housewife. She realizes that she cannot be satisfied with a house full of children, hens, roosters, goats and vegetables. Her mind needs stimulation. She needs a stage. She begins to exercise her role the way she sees it. She reads documents that pass across Mao's desk. She learns that the United States has entered the war. She learns that Hitler is being pushed out of the Soviet Union and that the Japanese are in retreat. The Chinese Communist Party has expanded and is the largest political group in the world. Her husband has become a household name and a symbol of power and truth.

What has become of me? the actress asks herself. Fairlynn occupies a seat in the Party's convention while she, as Mao's wife, can't even attend its opening.

Fairlynn sits among the delegation in the front row and is voted a speaker for the nation's intellectuals. During a break Fairlynn pays a visit to Madame Mao Jiang Ching. She congratulates her on her husband's rise to power and asks if Madame Mao compares herself to Madame Roosevelt. Fairlynn describes Madame Roosevelt, her achievement in American politics and Western history.

The wife of Mao listens as she washes her husband's and children's clothes in a bucket. The water is freezing. She washes the bowls, woks and scrubs the chamber pot. Her hands are swelling with frostbite. The soap slips through her fingers.

One night I try to discuss Madame Roosevelt with Mao. You are not Madame Roosevelt. He kicks off his shoes and blows out the candle.

Suddenly I am depressed. For the rest of the month I try to read.

But there is no way I can concentrate. An incident almost took place as I neglected my duty — Nah nearly fell into the manure pit — and it makes me put down the books.

The tailor comes to accompany me, but I send her back. I no longer want to hear the news.

Mao holds small meetings at home. He doesn't tell me ahead of time. He doesn't tell me who will be coming either. It's his style. He just sends Little Dragon for them on his terms. It can be three o'clock in the morning or midnight. They are expected to share a meal and discuss battles. I am supposed to put out food and go to war in the kitchen. Sometimes a cook or the guards help me. But it is my job to clean up afterwards.

I am playing a strange role: a queen who is a maid.

At the convention Mao is elected the Party's sole boss. Liu Shao-qi, who has built the Communist network in Chiang Kai-shek's white territories, is voted the second boss. Vice Chairman Liu Shao-qi has praised Mao highly in his acceptance speech. Little Dragon excitedly updates me with the details of the convention. Liu Shao-qi mentioned Mao's name one hundred and five times! The guard expects me to be thrilled, but I can hardly hide my misery.

At bedtime, afterwards, the wife again asks if she can be given a seat at the convention. The husband switches the tone of his voice.

I can't give anybody a seat. One has to earn it.

The wife sits up. You don't think I have earned it?

He doesn't answer but makes a sigh.

She wipes her tears. Well, I need a chance to earn it then.

Mao produces a list of books for me to read. He is giving me the prescription he gave to Zi-zhen. Marx, Engels, Lenin, Stalin, *The Three Kingdoms* and *The Record of History.* But I won't be reading them. Not one of them. I already know what kind of pills are in his bottle. Not only do I refuse to become Zizhen, I am determined not to be a stagehand in his political theater.

As Jiang Ching tries to break onto his stage, Mao launches a movement called Rectify the Style of Work. The year is 1942. At first it is considered a routine political examination, then it turns into terror. All of a sudden "traitors," "reactionaries," and "Chiang Kai-shek's agents" are caught everywhere. What later surprises historians is that the movement is initiated by Mao and conducted by Kang Sheng — two masters of conspiracy who set up an imaginary plot against themselves.

The movement is narrowing. The focus has become the extermination of the enemies within. Panic sweeps through the entire base of Yenan. To make oneself stand out as a hard-core left-winger, a true Communist, one begins to put others down, even to accuse others as right-wingers. In the morning one can be thought of as a revolutionary activist, by noon an anti-Communism suspect, by evening an enemy. One can be seen in a day meeting forcing others to plead guilty, and in an evening meeting be oneself arrested and thrown into a dark confession room.

The drill for the movement is *Ren-ren-guo-guan* — "a critical juncture everyone has to pass." The meetings are like chemical jars — when enemies are dipped, they show disease.

It doesn't matter that she is Madame Mao. To show the Party's fairness she will be checked no differently. She is told that it is her turn to dip herself in the chemical jar.

She is nervous. She worries about her background, in particular, her signature on Chiang Kai-shek's paper denouncing Communism. Although her friend Kang Sheng has instructed her on what to do she is still unsure.

Would you please attend my spot? she begs Kang Sheng.

When her day comes Kang Sheng is among the crowd.

Madame Mao Jiang Ching is put in the center of the room, spotted by the eyes of hundreds. She gives a self-evaluation as the format requests. Taking a deep breath she begins the process of convincing. The description is smoothly prepared and stated in graceful Mandarin. Her background could not be more pure: a child of feudalistic abuse, a young Communist in Qing-dao, her time in Shanghai as a left-wing actress devoted to films against the Japanese invaders, and her final landing in Yenan as a mature revolutionary and wife of Mao.

She believes that her performance is seamless. However, a couple of people in the crowd question the period she had skipped. A witness is demanded to prove her bravery in prison.

Suddenly she panics and turns defensive. Her lines become messy and words disconnected. What's the point? I have to produce a witness! Why? Are you saying that I am making up my story? How can I do this? I have been a revolutionary. And I will not be afraid of you!

For a while there is silence, but it is clear what is on everyone's mind. There is a desire to see the actress fail. To trip over herself, break a prop and fall off the stage. Soon the crowd begins to attack in one voice. What's this attitude, Comrade Jiang Ching? What makes you so nervous if you don't have anything to hide? Why the hysteria? Isn't it healthy for comrades to question when there are doubts? Especially about one's release from the enemy's prison? It is everyone's obligation to cooperate. Nobody is above the Communist Party in Yenan. Not even Mao's wife.

Gradually the nature of the event changes. Doubts grow heavy. The details, dates, hours, minutes are being questioned, compared and analyzed. Demands for an explanation grow more insistent. She is falling into a trap, set by her own previous fabrication. Her story begins to contradict itself. The holes in her lies begin to reveal themselves. She is cornered.

Her face turns red, veins on her neck popping blue. She looks horrified and turns to Kang Sheng, her eyes begging for help.

On cue the master actor breaks into the scene.

The Central Bureau of Security has already investigated the matter, Kang Sheng begins. The conclusion is positive — Comrade Jiang Ching's strength has been tested. It is proven truth that she has been loyal to the Party. She has done tremendous work for the revolution. She has risked her life.

Kang Sheng lights a cigarette. With a straight face he paints a picture of a Communist goddess. Finally he throws the ball to the crowd. How would you explain Comrade Jiang Ching's action in leaving behind the city of luxury and pleasure, Shanghai, for hardships in Yenan? If it is not her faith in Communism, then what is it?

The goat-beard man pauses, looks around and is pleased with his effectiveness — the way he confuses. To tighten the screw, he gives a final twist. Therefore, to trust the result of the Party's investigation is to trust Comrade Jiang Ching. To trust Comrade Jiang Ching is to trust the Party and Communism itself. Any doubts based upon assumptions abuse an individual's rights, which would be a reactionary act and evidence of right-wing activity, implying sympathy with Wang Ming's gang and the ultimate enemy.

The lips are clamped and the voices are silenced. The interrogation stops. I am sure this will get me through this crisis, although not necessarily the next. There are questions hanging on those people's faces. Why is Kang Sheng aggressive and merciless in handling other cases while spoiling this one?

*

Kang Sheng intimidates and never worries about how anyone thinks of him except Mao. And Mao keeps promoting him. In her marriage she discovers that only when she follows Kang Sheng's advice does she succeed. Kang Sheng is her education.

In the future there will be one secret Madame Mao and Kang Sheng never discuss but share knowingly. It is what makes them partners, rivals and enemies at the same time. Count every member of the Communist Party — no one has ever dared to think about surpassing Mao and taking over China but Kang Sheng and Jiang Ching.

Chiang Kai-shek's military equipment is supplied by Americans and is the most advanced in the world. Mao, on the other hand, works with primitive weapons. It is the end of World War II and the beginning of China's civil war. On the international front, Stalin has proposed a negotiation between Mao and Chiang Kai-shek. For Stalin, a united China is more powerful. Stalin sees China as a potential ally with which to oppose the Americans. To show broad-mindedness, my husband takes the risk and accepts Chiang's invitation to Chong-Qin — the capital city of Chiang's government — for a peace talk. Although his colleagues and aides suspect a conspiracy, my husband insists on going.

Midsummer Chong-Qin is a bathhouse. With an American diplomat as a host, Mao Tse-tung and Chiang Kai-shek shake hands in front of the cameras. Next they perform an agreement-signing ceremony. Mao is in his shapeless white cotton uniform while Chiang is in a starched Western-inspired suit with rows of medals glistening over his shoulders and across his chest.

There will not be two suns shining above the sky of China, Mao says to me on our flight back to Yenan. He sees civil war as unavoidable. I tell him that I admire his bravery. He says, Darling, it is the fear, the blindness toward death that drives me to win.

Angry, Chiang Kai-shek begins to drop his bombs over our roof again. Mao orders the famous Yenan evacuation. The Red Army soldiers and peasants are mobilized to move into remote mountain areas. Mao refuses to see anyone who complains about the abandonment of their homeland. To turn people away he invites Fairlynn to the cave for a discussion and chat.

My husband has been meeting with Fairlynn since the early morning. They chat from politics to literature, from ancient bronze to poetry. Bowl to bowl and pack to pack, the two toast in rice wine and smoke cigarettes. The room is a chimney.

After I put Nah to sleep I come out, making my presence a protest against the intruder. I sit next to my husband.

Fairlynn's spirit is fueled by alcohol. Under Mao's encouragement she is argumentative. She scratches her hair with her fingers. Her Shakespeare hairdo is now a bird's-nest. Her eyes are bloody red. She laughs with all her teeth showing.

Inhaling, Mao stretches out his legs, crossing one foot over another.

The history of China is the history of *yin*, he argues loudly as he pushes the ashtray toward Fairlynn. He then pushes his tea mug. He likes to share tea with women. He did it with Kai-hui, Zizhen, Jiang Ching and now Fairlynn. He adds water to the mug, then goes on. Our ancestors invented ammunition to use only for festival decorations. Our fathers smoked opium to avoid thinking. Our nation has been poisoned by Confucius's theories. We have been raped by the nations who are strong in *yang*. "Raped" is the precise word! Mao's fist punches the table. A few peanuts fall on the ground.

Chairman, I don't mean to challenge you. Fairlynn picks up the dropped peanuts. In your writings there is a sense of praising the war itself. I found that extremely interesting, or may I say disturbing? You praised violence itself. You believe in martial law. Your true purpose is to kill the *yin* element in the Chinese, am I right?

Mao nods.

So you kill, Fairlynn presses.

I kill to heal.

Fairlynn shakes her head. Chairman, you are making us the prisoners of your thinking house. You make us bite and chew on each other's flesh in order to exercise your ideal *yang*. Am I allowed to say that you're crazy to give our minds no pleasure to wonder and experience? . . . Sir, you're stir-frying an overnight dish — you are nothing original — you're copying Hitler!

If this wakes up the nation, I'll bear the shame! Mao pitches his voice like an opera character.

Mao! You are the most outrageous individualist I have ever met. You are fascinated by yourself! But what about the rest? What about their right to be as individualistic as you are? The great thinkers, journalists, novelists, artists, poets and actors?

Comrade Fairlynn, you have been poisoned. Mao laughs confidently. The westerners think that the authors and artists are supermen, but they are only men with animal instincts. The best of them are men with mental illnesses. Their nature is to sell tricks! How can you regard them so religiously? You must have spent a lot for this pair of artificial frog-eyes. Poor thing, you have been robbed!

Two o'clock in the morning and I see no end to the discussion. Mao and Fairlynn are on their third jar of wine. The subject has turned to beauty.

You are not unlike any other male creature on this earth. Look at Comrade Jiang Ching! Beauty of the red base! Mao, I thought you were not one of the Shakespearean characters. But look at what you are doing! You are stuffing Marxism into a flashlight — using it only to examine the others. Don't embarrass me with your so-called knowledge of Western literature. You remind me of the frog who lives in the bottom of a well who thinks the sky is only as big as the ring. You're selling your hot-pepper tricks to illiterate peasants. You are making yourself a fool in front of me. Yes, yes, yes. Sometimes I do think your writings on morality are a joke. After I read them, they lie on the floor of my mind in complete disarray and disorder!

What a pleasure to hear this! How daring that you come to my cave to burn my grains! Water! Hot water! Jiang Ching!

I get up, pick up the teapot and go to the kitchen.

In the kitchen I hear them continue. They laugh and sometimes whisper.

You're irresistible, Fairlynn. If . . .

Imagine that! The hoarse voice rises, laughing.

You're right, Fairlynn. Beauty does arouse me. It makes me sympathetic toward deformity. However, the drive to save this country makes me a true man. I have only one understanding of politics — it is violence. Revolution is not a tea party, it is violence in its purest form. I worship ancient politics, the politics of simple dictatorship.

Standing in front of the boiling teapot my mind travels to exile. When I return to the living room I find myself empty-handed. I have left the teapot behind. Politely I interrupt the conversation. I mention that I am tired. My husband suggests that I go ahead to bed.

It's the middle of the night, I insist, showing no intention of leaving the room — I am determined to kick Fairlynn out.

I know. He waves a hand.

You must be exhausted, I say to my husband, so must Comrade Fairlynn.

Don't you worry about me! Fairlynn stretches her arms upward. Leaning to the side she places her elbows on the table. I feel as charged as if it were ten o'clock in the morning.

Mao makes a muffled guffaw.

I try to contain myself but my tears betray me.

My husband stands up, goes to the kitchen and brings back the teapot. He then pulls over a chair for me to sit down. I look at Fairlynn in disgust. There will be a day, I promise myself, that I will make her go through what she is making me go through now.

Basking in Fairlynn's admiration my husband elaborates on himself.

Deep in the landscape of my soul, I am covered with the thick fog of the yellow earth. My character carries a fatalistic culture. I have been aware of this since I was a child. I have an instinct and a craving for travel, in the meantime I have an inborn disgust of living. The ancient sages travel in order to gain distance from men. We fight in order to achieve unity. People of the Ching dynasty, before Confucius, were warlords, very strong in *yang*. They fought, possessed and expanded the land. Horseback was their life. They had passion for the sun. In fables, one sun was not enough. Nine suns have to be created so the hero Yi can have a chance to shoot eight of the nine down in order to demonstrate his strength. The goddesses were sent way up, into the Moon Palace, so the males could be challenged.

Ching period is your period, Fairlynn responds.

Yes, and I still feel that I lack the knowledge of it. I'd like to hear the shouts of the Ching soldier lunge and enter the gates of their enemy's cities. I would like to smell the blood on the tip of their swords.

You have a vision seen through the eyes of a madman.

At three o'clock in the morning Mao and Fairlynn get up to part. Jiang Ching stands behind the cave's entrance and watches them.

Our argument has not ended yet, Fairlynn says, buttoning up her gray army coat.

Next time it will be my turn to satisfy you. Mao nods a salute.

The darkness is impenetrable, Fairlynn sighs.

I'm a pearl-seeker, Mao says, looking into the night. I work on the deep and airless ocean bed. I don't come up with treasure every time. Often I come back empty-handed and purple-faced. You have an understanding of that as a writer.

But sometimes I want to be wrapped in darkness.

Well, my point is that it is not easy to live up to what's expected of Mao Tse-tung.

Surely almost everyone is drawn to deception.

The irony, as we all understand, is that magic and illusion has to take place in the dark. Mao smiles.

And certainly with distance. I am with you, Chairman.

March 1947. Mao's force has been in and out of the mountain areas of Shan-xi, Hunan and Sichuan provinces. Mao toys with Chiang Kai-shek's troops. Although Chiang has sent his best man, General Hu Zhong-nan, who commands 230,000 men while Mao has only 20,000, Chiang has not been winning.

Like a war concubine I follow my lover. I abandon everything including my favorite record player. I insist that Nah come with us. We travel with the army. It's hard to believe that we survived. Every day Nah witnesses how the dead are buried.

The village artists paint the walls with pictures of Mao. My lover still has the look of an ancient sage, even more so now. It is because the artists are trained to paint the face of Buddha. They can't paint Mao without making him look like a Buddha. Maybe it is the Buddha they see in Mao. And I'm sure it is Buddha my lover is playing.

Sleep deprivation has weakened Mao. He has caught fever. Under the blanket, he trembles uncontrollably. The guards take turns carrying him on a stretcher. In his sickness my lover continues to conduct battles. This is how I become his secretary and assistant. Now I am the one who writes down Mao's orders and drafts telegrams. I am up when he is up, and keep myself up when he sleeps.

When he is better and sees his business is going well, he wants to play. We have time. But I am not myself. My heart feels no warmth — I can't forget Fairlynn. Although I feel my love for him, I still want to make him pay for humiliating me. He seems to be accepting the punishment. The pockets under his eyes have deepened.

The troops pitch camp in a small village. Mao is asleep. Jiang Ching comes out of the hut for fresh air. She has just finished copying a long document under candlelight. Rubbing her strained eyes, she notices that Little Dragon is standing nearby. Seeing her he salutes. She nods and takes a mouthful of fresh air. In front of her there is a patch of yams and a narrow path that leads to a river. The night is quiet and chilly.

She feels lonely so she walks to the guard and greets him.

Have you heard from your family? she asks the nineteen-year-old.

The man replies that he doesn't have a family.

How so?

My uncle was an underground Communist. Chiang Kai-shek massacred my family for helping him escape.

Do you like working for the Chairman? Will you be loyal to him?

Yes, Madame. The young man lowers his head and looks at his own shadow under the bright moonlight.

Do you hear anything at night? She clears her throat.

Well, a . . . a little.

Like what?

N . . . Noises.

Suddenly she feels sorry for him. The man who has never in his life tasted the sweetness of a woman. It is not allowed. It is the rule — soldiers are the monks of Mao's temple.

What kind of noises? she asks, almost teasing. Like a noise from an owl? A field rat? Or wind?

The young man becomes tongue-tied and turns away from her.

She gently calls him by name and makes him look back at her.

I don't like myself, Little Dragon says suddenly.

She feels a strange tension rise between them. She finds herself out of words.

Little Dragon swallows a mouthful of saliva.

After a while she asks, Would you like me to ask the Chairman to transfer you?

No, please, Madame. I'd like to serve the Chairman for the rest of my life.

Of course, she murmurs. I understand. And the Chairman needs you too.

The young man stands against the wall, his breath hardens. He is confused by his own reaction toward the woman. The mysterious power clothed under his uniform. She can see sweat glistening on his forehead. He looks intimidated, fraught and defeated. He reminds her of a young gorilla in frustration, the male who is given no chance to win female trophies, the male whose semen is deposited in the dustbin of history. Little Dragon's manhood is chewed up by the bigger, more brawny, aggressive and formidable gorilla, Mao.

December 1947. Mao finally exhausts Chiang Kai-shek's troops. Before the New Year Mao launches a full-scale counterattack. The Red Army soldiers shout as they charge forward: *For Mao Tse-tung and New China!* It doesn't take long for Mao to swallow his enemy completely. As spring turns into summer, the number of Mao's forces draws even with those of Chiang Kai-shek.

Chiang's loss starts to settle in. Mao changes the title of his army from the Red Army to the People's Liberation Army.

I have become the manager of Mao's makeshift office. And have sent Nah and her siblings away to live with villagers. I will miss them terribly but the war has reached its crucial moment. My husband sets up his headquarters once again in our bedroom. I have been sleeping in mule barns. I am bitten by mosquitoes, fleas and lice. One bite under my chin swells so much that it sticks out like a second chin.

To avoid Chiang Kai-shek's air raids, my husband orders the troops to travel after sundown. Long hours of working and lack of nutrition have taken their toll on me. I become sick and can hardly walk. When we advance Mao picks me up to ride with him on the only mule the army has left. Our relationship grows in a strange direction. It has been a long time since we showed affection to one another. The more territories he wins the more I am tormented. Despite all that I have done, all that I have suffered, I have been denied recognition. My nature refuses to live an invisible life. I demand acknowledgment and respect — but I get it from no one.

One day the dog-faced journalist Old Fish comes into my office with an urgent matter. Mao is in the inner room on the phone with Vice Chairman Liu.

I am in charge of the office, I say to Old Fish. But the man pretends that he doesn't hear me. So I try again. I ask if I may help him. He gives a smile but doesn't say anything else. He doesn't let me take care of Mao's business.

It is only my most recent insult. At a Politburo meeting a few days ago Mao encouraged opinions. When I spoke up, Mao was upset. Not only did he tell me to mind my own secretarial work, he ordered me to stay out of the Politburo meetings forever.

*

The table of history has turned, Fairlynn writes in her "Red Base" column. *This time it is Chiang Kai-shek who plays an eager negotiator. From his capital city, Nan-jing, he sent Mao Tse-tung telegrams begging for a peace talk. In the meantime he has been trying to get the westerners to interfere. Britain sent a frigate,* Amethyst, *to the coast near the Yangzi River where Mao's force is in full engagement. Twenty-three Englishmen were killed and the frigate has been a dead fish for one hundred and one days. From Russia Stalin demands that Mao enter into peace talks with Chiang Kai-shek. Stalin's advisors follow Mao around attempting to stop him from sweeping through the entire South. In his war tent Mao is preparing for his final strike to take over China.*

November 18, 1948. Hundreds and thousands of boats, captained by fishermen and soldiers, sail across the Yangzi River. The People's Liberation Army lunges toward Chiang Kai-shek's capital, Nan-jing. The Chiangs flee to Taiwan.

My lover listens to the radio while he finishes a yam.

Jiang Ching looks at Mao as she washes pots and bowls. She sees the expression of an emperor who is about to mount his throne. The couple haven't discussed their future. Not long ago, Jiang Ching found a piece of Fairlynn's writing on Mao's desk. It was an essay. Jiang Ching suspected that it was a love letter in secret code.

*Chairman Mao was enlightened by the narration of the classic novel* The Dream of the Red Chamber. *The protagonist, Baoyu, couldn't be separated from a piece of jade he was born with. The jade was the root of his life. To Mao his jade was the heart of the Chinese people.* Why Baoyu the lover? Jiang Ching wonders. Is Fairlynn trying to be Taiyu, the only other soul in the mansion who understands Baoyu?

\*

I had a terrible dream last night in which my lover's dark, stained fingers play at his throat as he reads Fairlynn's article. The fingers move tenderly up and down as if struck by a sweet mood.

The People's Liberation Army takes Yenan back. While the soldiers unite with the surviving family members the headquarters packs. Mao will leave this place for good. After a celebration rally Mao is finally left alone with Jiang Ching.

The cave is dark although it is daytime. The couple haven't been intimate since the evacuation. They sit by themselves quietly. It feels strange to Jiang Ching that her body has stopped missing his.

A ray of sunlight peeks in. It slants across the corner of the desk. Mao's old chair with its back leg wrapped with bandages stands like a wounded soldier. The wall is dirty.

After an awkward silence, Mao reaches out his arms and pulls Jiang Ching toward him. Without speaking he moves his hands from her shoulders to her waist. And then down he continues. She grows rigid. Heat drains from her limbs. Silently she lies in his arms.

He undresses and positions himself. And then he pushes in. She is motionless. He tries to concentrate on the pleasure, but his mind stirs.

I liked it better when we were illegitimate, she suddenly says.

He doesn't respond, but his body withdraws. He collects himself and lies down next to her.

Her tears begin to gush and her voice trembles. I don't want to be Zi-zhen. And I am not ready to retire. To build a new China is my business too.

He is silent, shows that he is disappointed.

I have talked to Premier Zhou, she continues. I told him that I deserve a title. He gave me no straight answer. I am not sure this is not your intention.

He lies with his eyes closed.

She goes on. Describes her feelings, how she has been submerged in water, the beating of her heart making circles on the surface. Doesn't know what happened to the love she lives for. She keeps going as though to pause would mean collapse. I am a dying seed inside a fruit. Everybody is polite to me because I'm your concubine. A concubine — not a revolutionary, not a soldier, not any part of this business. Your men disrespect me. While I'm everything I'm nothing. I've been following you like a dog. What more can I offer? My body and soul have been your resting place.

Why don't we finish this business before I get too tired? the lover demands.

She protests. My mind has its own pleasure and I can force nothing.

He grips her arms with tense fingers. Against her struggles he pulls her over and forces his way inside her. She shivers, feeling that she is pushed out of her body. He moves on top of her. She watches the event with a third eye. He feels her constraint and struggles against it. After a while he gives up.

Perhaps I'm not as sympathetic to your needs as I'd like myself to be. He sits down on the edge of the bed. Or perhaps it is just one of those things that time wears out. He sticks up a finger to stop her from responding. I'd rather not go into it. No matter what's said or going to be said, it's pointless. It will be an unreasonable demand. Maybe you and I have become the past. My feet are on the breast of victory. I live more intensely in the present than I could ever in the past. I have no time for misery.

She shakes her head vigorously.

He nods to silence her.

She tries to hold back her tears.

He gets up and collects his clothes.

No! Please don't go!

Buttoning up his uniform he takes out a cigarette. The smoke eddies about his face.

She feels the way horror corners its victim.

What time is it? he asks.

She doesn't answer but gets up. Her clothes are wrinkled. Matted hair falls to her shoulders.

Reality doesn't discuss, it simply is, he says in a harsh tone and extinguishes the cigarette.

The bitter lines on her face suddenly deepen.

We will settle in Beijing. He goes to open the door. It'll be by Zhong-nan-hai in the Forbidden City. I'll occupy a compound called the Garden of Harvest. I've saved the Garden of Stillness for you.

# 13

W E HAVE WON CHINA and have moved into the Forbidden City. It is a city within a city, a vast park en-
closed by high walls and containing the government
offices and a number of splendid palaces. Our palace was designed in the Ming dynasty, built in 1368 and completed in 1644.
It has golden roof tiles, thick wooden columns and high deep-red
stone walls. The massive ornaments are on the themes of harmony and longevity. The craft is exquisite and the detail meticulous.

As his cabinet prepares for the establishment of the republic,
my husband tries to relax in his new home on an island in the
Zhong-nan-hai Lake. It takes him weeks to adjust to the spacious
living quarters. The high ceiling in the Garden of Harvest dis-
tracts him. The space makes him fearful although there are guards
behind every gate. Finally, after sleeping in different rooms, he
moves to a quiet, less solemn and more modest corner called the
Chrysanthemum-Fragrance Study.

Mao likes his door. It faces exactly south. The door panels are
wide with ceiling-high windows. Natural light pours into his new
room, which he enjoys. The sofas with extrasoft cushions, gifts
from the Russians, were sent over by Premier Zhou En-lai. Mao
has never sat on a sofa before. He doesn't feel comfortable. Can't

get used to its softness. It gives him a sinking feeling. Same thing with the toilet. He prefers to squat on his heels like a dog. He keeps the sofas for visitors and orders himself an old-fashioned rattan chair. The outer space is the drawing room, which has been converted into a library with books piled from floor to ceiling along three walls. He doesn't pay attention to the furniture but is aware that all the furniture in the imperial city is made of camphor trees. Camphor wood has the reputation of continuing to live and breathe, producing a sweet scent even after it's made into furniture.

Original hand-bound manuscripts lie on top of the long narrow stands. In the middle of the room sits an eight-by-four-foot desk. On top of the desk is a set of brush pens, an ink jar, a tea mug, an ashtray and a magnifier. The inner room serves as Mao's bedroom. It has gray-white walls and dusty wine-colored curtains. A boatlike wooden bed has many adjustable bookcases. Outside, three-hundred-year-old pine trees spread their branches to the horizon. Beyond the limestone terrace is a branch of the Zhong-nan-hai Lake, its water grass green. Dog-faced fish gather under lotus leaves. On the left side, a new vegetable garden has just been completed. At the end of the garden is an arched stone door covered with ivy. Under the ivy is a path leading to the Garden of Stillness, where Jiang Ching resides.

The Garden of Stillness is protected by the Garden of Harvest but separate from it. To the public we live together. But the path from his place to mine has been unused for so long that moss has come to cover it. After the spring the entrance is blocked by leaves. The Garden of Stillness was once the residence of Lady Xiangfei, the favorite concubine of the Ming emperor. Lady Xiangfei was known for her naturally scented skin. She was said to be poisoned by the empress. To preserve her memory the emperor ordered the residence to be permanently vacant.

I love this place, its elegant furniture and ornaments. I adore the wildness of my garden, especially the two natural waterfalls. The architect designed the place around the water course. The bamboo bushes are thick outside my window. On full-moon nights, the place looks like a magnificent frosted ground.

Yet I have never felt this bad in my life.

I am left alone with all these treasures.

I am left with my nightmares.

I have helped hatch the eggs of your revolution! she hears herself scream. She gets up at night and sits in the dark. Cold sweat drips along her neckline. Her back is wet. Her cries crawl over the floor and stick in the wall. Mao no longer informs her of his whereabouts. His staff members avoid her. When she tries to talk to them, they show impatience as if she holds them hostage.

One night she breaks through the path and enters Mao's bedroom by surprise. She reaches him and sobs on her knees. My head is filled with a storm. The mirror in my room drives me crazy with a mad skeleton! She pleads, Make the place a home for the sake of our children.

Mao puts down his book. What's wrong with where we are now? Anyin is happy at the Army School of Technology; Anqin is doing well in Moscow University. Ming and Nah are both having a good time at the Party's boarding school. What more do you want?

She keeps sobbing.

He comes and covers her with his blankets. How about I order our chefs to share the cooking space?

That night she is tranquil. She dreams that she is sleeping the last sleep, during which her heartbeat stops and her cheeks freeze against his empty chest.

I excuse myself from the dinner table. Mao pays no attention. I walk into his bedroom, turn off the light and kick off my shoes.

I lie down on his bed. Then comes the sound of his putting down his chopsticks. The sound of his striking up a match to light a cigarette. He doesn't like the modern lighters. He likes the big wooden matches. He likes to watch the match burn down to his fingers. He likes to watch the burnt end grow. It makes me sad that I have come to know his small habits.

The smoke drifts over. The garlic stinks badly tonight. I hear him walking toward his desk and pulling out his chair. I hear him turn a page of a document. In my mind's eye I see him making remarks on a document. Circles and crosses. The things we used to do together. He used to hand the pen to me and have me do the job while he enjoyed his cigarette. There has never been a discussion between us on what went wrong in our relationship. The dilemma has fed on trivial details.

He signs his name with a red brush. The new emperor. The past is still too clear. I can't forget the moment when I fell in love with the bandit! The images caress my memory's shore. I feel their tenderness.

For weeks and months I sit in my room daydreaming of the girl who carried her own sunshine. I have lost her spirit. Look at the landscape outside my window! The fabulous sunset! I remember the feeling of sitting on his lap while he conducted monumental battles. His hands were inside my shirt while the soldiers charged forward to honor his name.

A voice mimicking a fortuneteller tells me, Madame, you've got a gilded hook in your mouth.

The train plows through the thick snow. The beauty of northern ice trees and the whiteness strangely move her. She is on her way to a doctor. A Russian doctor. She had checked out her growing pain. A cyst was found in her cervix. She doesn't know why she wants to come to Russia. To escape what? Her cyst or her reality?

She is greeted by men from Moscow's Foreign Relations Bureau. Red-potato-nosed agents treat her as if she is Mao's deserted concubine. A short, rosy-cheeked translator, a Chinese woman, is with the men. She is bundled in a navy blue Lenin coat and carries herself like a big triangle. Stepping out of the station, Madame Mao is beaten by the harsh wind. The air from Siberia greets you! one red-nose says. Comrade Stalin is sorry that Comrade Mao Tse-tung's not here.

In her hotel room, holding her tea cup, she picks up a copy of *People's Daily*. The paper is sent by the embassy. The date is October 2, 1949. On the front page is a large photo of her husband. It is a wide-angle shot. He is on top of Tiananmen — the Gate of Heavenly Peace — inspecting a sea of parades. It is a good photo, she thinks. The photographer caught the elation leaping on Mao's face. He looks younger than fifty-four.

She turns the pages and suddenly sees Fairlynn's name. Fairlynn has not only survived the war, she has been active in the republic's establishment. Have they secretly kept in touch? Has she been invited to his study?

The guard at the Chrysanthemum-Fragrance Study blocks her and tells her that Mao is with a visitor and doesn't wish to be disturbed.

Hello, Chairman! I'm back! Madame Mao Jiang Ching pushes the guard to the side and invites herself in.

The room is dark. The blinds are down and the curtains are drawn. Mao is in his pajamas. He sits facing the door in his rattan chair. The visitor is a woman. She sits with her back toward Jiang Ching. She is in a navy blue Mao jacket. Seeing his wife Mao crosses his bare feet on a stool and says, The Siberian fox has come to share the spring with us.

The visitor turns around and stands up. Comrade Jiang Ching!

Comrade Fairlynn!

How have you been?

Better than ever! Madame Mao fetches herself a chair. Don't tell me that you are still single and still enjoying it.

Fairlynn supports her head with one hand and knits a crease in her trousers with the other. Her fingers nervously run back and forth along the crease. What's wrong, Comrade Jiang Ching? You are not well, are you?

Anna Karenina was stupid to kill herself for an unworthy man, Madame Mao responds. More tea!

But I was merely concerned about your health. After all you are the first lady and you have undergone surgery — it's news.

I want to tell Fairlynn that my wound has healed and the tissues have regenerated. My condition is more than perfect. I've conquered the pain. I'm nursing my heart. But there is something else I can't bear. Something, a bug, I must kill before I can go on. Fairlynn must be given this warning. She has gone too far.

My husband gets up and spits a mouthful of tea leaves into a spittoon. It's his way of shutting me up. I am humiliated. Deep within me violence begins to stir. The summons is too terrifying to measure.

Excuse me, Jiang Ching, I've promised Comrade Fairlynn a tour of the Forbidden City. It would be a shame for a writer like her not to know what's behind the great walls. Don't you agree?

I know that I am not expected to reply. But I wait. For a courtesy. I wait for my husband to invite me along, or give me a chance to refuse.

The request doesn't come.

The point of her fingernail jams into her palm, and her body holds still with extreme rigidity. When Mao and Fairlynn stride shoulder to shoulder out of the room into the sun and disappear behind the great imperial garden, she is kissed by the tongue of the beast inside her.

The draperies are down. The fragrance of gardenia in her room is strong, the ancient rug soft under her feet. A month ago, she ordered a French table with a set of matching chairs from Shanghai, but she discarded them when they arrived — her mood had changed. It is the beginning of her madness. She is not aware that it is running its course.

In the mirror she sees a backyard concubine on her way to being forgotten. Is she turning into Zi-zhen? She has never seen Zi-zhen. She has heard vivid descriptions of her: an old hag with a birdlike face, wrapped in hay hair. Once in the past she tested her husband to see if there were remains of his romance with Zi-zhen.

A soft wind breathing through the grass, was Mao's comment.

There is no one else she can talk to. In frustration she turns to Kang Sheng. She lets him know that it is an exchange. She promises to do the same for him when he needs her. He is delighted for the business. He has been promoted as the secretary of China's National Security Bureau. The apprentice of Stalin. Mao calls him "the steel teeth sunk in the republic's flesh." He comes to her rescue. Tips her off with most valuable information and guides her with advice. Ten years later he will produce a list of names, names of her enemies who he convinces her will destroy her if she doesn't destroy them first. The names will shock her. It will be two thirds of the congress. And he will encourage and hurry her to act. And she will be a soldier and will engage herself in battles out of utter fear. She will hold on to his handwritten list. The names he circled. TOP SECRET. FOR COMRADE JIANG CHING'S EYES ONLY. One hundred and five congressmen plus ninety regional representatives.

In the fifties Kang Sheng is my mentor. We are walking sticks for each other to get up, get around and get to the top. We can't do without each other. We make deals.

I am not Zi-zhen and I am not a masochist. I have tasted life and want more. Mao continues to disappoint me. He wants me to run the imperial backyard and expects me to be happy. But it was he who offered me the leading-lady role in the first place. It was our deal. It is he who breaks the promise, although he never says I don't love you or Let's get a divorce. This is worse. Because he just does it. He has taken away my identity. Ask people on the streets who the first lady is. Nine out of ten don't know. Jiang Ching doesn't sound familiar. Nobody has seen the first lady's picture in the papers. I would be fooling myself to say that it isn't Mao's wish.

*A woman's biggest wish is to be loved* — there is no deeper truth. I feel ripped from the essence of life. I come to feel for Zi-zhen. I identify with her sadness and cling to my own sanity. The Forbidden City has been the home of many who have gone mad. I wander in Mao's grounds and watch men and women act like old-time eunuchs. Like dogs, they sniff. They spend every second of their waking time trying to please the emperor. They can tell when the emperor is ready to "let go" of his concubine.

I am aware of my position. My role has no flesh. Nevertheless, illusion is available if I work to create it. I am still Mao's official wife. I have to get on the stage. Although dim, there are still lights over my head. Mao's men have tried to take away my costume. I can feel the pulling of my sleeves. But I won't let go. I am holding on to my title. I won't let the magic of my character fade away. Hope guides me and revenge motivates me.

Kang Sheng is a man of obsession. He is known for double-hand calligraphy. He also collects jade, bronze and stone carvings. He once commented that the great poet and calligrapher Guo Mou-rou's strokes were "worse than what I can write with my foot." It is not an exaggeration. When Kang Sheng speaks about art, he is a scholar of meticulous dedication. His mouth is a river from which magnificent phrases flow. At those moments, all his wrinkles spread like spring curl-grass under sunshine — it would be hard for anyone to imagine what he does for a living.

I am still learning my trade. I come regularly to Kang Sheng's house for lessons. Some lessons are tough. It is like the poison the fairy tale mermaid has to drink in order to have legs. I drink what Kang Sheng offers in order to have powerful wings that cut like saws.

His house is a museum and his tiger-faced wife, Chao Yi-ou, is his business partner. The couple live in a private palace at Dianmen, 24 Stone Bridge Lane, at the end of West Boulevard. It has an ordinary appearance, but inside it is a heaven of its own. One of the features is a manmade hill standing behind the house. It is about three stories high and is surrounded by a bamboo forest. It used to be the house of Andehai, the eunuch in chief and Empress Ci-xi's right-hand man, during the Ching dynasty. The house is guarded by a company of soldiers.

It is in Kang Sheng's house, in the basement, in the middle of his stone-carving collection that he reveals the secret. His views and his traps. He demonstrates the fire and metal in his character and shows me what I must learn and unlearn. And finally what I must endure in exchange for immortality.

I say my ears have been carefully washed — I am listening. Then Kang Sheng begins to pour. The black poison, water of terrible words, details, facts. In his unshaken voice, steady rhythms, the liquid travels, through my ear, throat, chest and down.

It is about Mao. His practice of longevity. Here is the number of virgins he penetrates. I am sorry to play the role of supplier. It's my job. You must understand this. Make no noise about the information I provide you. It is your life I am trying to protect. You must understand Mao's need for penetration. You must not compare yourself with Fairlynn and her like. You are an empress, not another vagina. Your true lover is not Mao but the emperor whose clothes he is in. Your true lover is power itself.

I wouldn't tell you this if I were not your friend, wouldn't tell you if I didn't think it best for you. I tell you this so you won't be a foolish woman; I tell you this so you will know how to gamble with very little capital. I'm trying to make sure that your status is not threatened. I am keeping an eye on whoever passes through Mao's bed. Mao sleeps with different women every day. The number is countless. Swallow that, my little Crane in the Clouds. Swallow.

Try to surface in the water that drowned Zi-zhen. It is only a prescription he takes. It is to absorb the element *yin*. He penetrates girls I bring from villages. I take care of those no-longer-virgins afterwards. Again it's my job.

You are fine, Jiang Ching. You are sailing smooth. You have crossed the ocean and are not too far from the shore.

Outside the dry leaves scratch the ground. Jiang Ching has gone back to the Garden of Stillness. She has been burying herself under the sheets and pillows. She has lost her last peace in Kang Sheng's basement. Now she can no longer sleep. She keeps hearing cracking sounds as if her skull were breaking apart. In her mind's eye, a gigantic swarm of beasts have come and filled her.

At dawn she feels her nerves burning at the tips. She wakes up and finds that she has given up understanding. She feels light and bewildered. She thinks about sending Mao concubines herself along with pots of poison mixed with ginseng soups and steamed turtles.

# 14

S HE READS FAIRLYNN'S ESSAY in *The People's Literature* on her Forbidden City tour, guided by Mao.

*Our great Savior stood next to me. The disconsolate moan of the wind over the Zhong-nan-hai Lake grew stronger. He pointed out to me the half-drowned ancient dragon boat with its tail sticking out like a monster. We discussed the history of peasant revolts. He explained heroism. I am sure my face beamed like a young school pupil. I was completely taken.*

*I opened my thoughts and told him that I had been a pessimist. In his teaching, years of ice shaped by darkness inside me melted down and drifted away. I felt light and warmth. Like a long-lost boat my heart made it to a safe harbor . . . The Chairman drew his eyes back from the shadowed walls. Our glances met. He replied when I asked his thoughts on love, We've lived in a time of chaos when it is impossible to love. War and hatred dried our soul's blood. What dissolves my despair is the memory. The memory of the sky above and the memory of the earth under — my loved ones who died for the revolution. Every day my world starts with the light they shine on me. Light, Fairlynn! The light which keeps a promising summer in my soul during the coldest winter.*

No, I am not coming to join the concubines of the Forbidden City. Jiang Ching's teeth clench as she closes the magazine. I don't belong. The abandoned souls. The names which the glittering medals, citations and stone gates honor. I don't give a damn. I hate this breath, its dampness. I have an appetite for bright, hot lights. I won't let the coldness of a funeral house seep through my skin.

It is Kang Sheng who informs me of Mao's syphilis. Again, it is Kang Sheng.

I am numbed by rage. I stare at his goat beard and his goldfish eyes.

Endurance is the key to success, he reminds me. Would you like me to make an arrangement with a doctor to give you a checkup? I mean to make sure . . .

His finger injects every vessel in my body with black ink.

Can you recall, Madame?

Yes, she does. It was after a state banquet at the People's Hall. They hadn't been intimate in years. Mao was in a good mood. Governors from all states came to report to him in Beijing, to pay him homage. The scene reminded him of emperors giving audience during the old dynasties. The revolutionary son of heaven. Business was running well. Every province orbited Beijing. The faith in him was tremendous. He has taken over the Buddha in the heart of his people. He encouraged the worship by making as few appearances as possible — the ancient trick of creating power and terror. When he did show up he kept his face hidden and his speech short and vague. He threw out a few comments during the meetings. A syllable or two. A mysterious smile and a firm handshake. It was effective. He had nothing to worry about now.

When all the guests were gone Mao took Jiang Ching and walked through the imperial kitchen. Let's go thank the cooks and the staff. On their way back to the Purple Light Pavilion, he was affectionate. She was escorted to the west wing and the two settled in the Peony Room.

She tried not to think about her feelings as she followed him.

The room seemed unnecessarily large. The light cast pink and yellow lily pads on the undulating surface of the wall. Alone with Mao she felt strange and nervous.

He sat down on the sofa and waved for her to sit down across from him. After a while, she felt awkward and asked to be excused. He acted as if surprised. He told her that he would like to chat and asked if she would sit back down. To break the silence she asked about his travels.

You have been lonely, he suddenly said.

She stood up and walked toward the door.

Stay. His word halted her.

She knew she couldn't disobey him. She went to sit back down, but on another sofa.

I am too old for guerrilla war today. He got up and came to share her seat. His hands caught her.

No, please! The words almost choked themselves out of her chest.

He was not affected. He took pleasure in her struggle. He gently forced his way. God provides food for every bird, but he doesn't throw it into its nest, she heard him say. You have to come out and pick it.

I'd rather continue my path to dust.

He didn't respond but began to pump her.

Her body shut down and her mind withdrew.

Drops of his sweat curved their way down onto the bridge of her nose, across her cheeks, down her ears and into her hair. Her rejection unnerved him. Holding her he kept lunging as if to push himself out of her.

We tryst . . . she cried suddenly, grinding the words. We tryst in the dark. Our skin once glowed, our bodies swelled in rapture, our flesh was consumed with impatience. But how would I know . . . that we were only to discover that this journey . . . the journey which gulped the fire of our youth, was . . . not worth traveling.

His right hand came to cover her mouth. His body beat her with its rhythm.

Suddenly he wound down, like a broken bicycle.

She felt herself living inside a clock, watching her own body in a strange motion. She tried to block her thoughts from shooting toward the future.

The late afternoon light continued to cut the Peony Room wall into shapes of rectangles and triangles. The burgundy carpet smelled of smoke. The ancient painting of peonies looked like spooky figures poking out of the wall. The sound of an underground pipe running mixed with the sound of a wok being scrubbed in the kitchen at the far end.

She listened for a long time. The sound of water running through the pipes tapped upon her skull. Then came the sound of steps. It was the guard on duty. The march stopped with a yell. Something fell. Some heavy bag. The guard ran. Then came the sound of two men talking. A truck driver, who was here to deliver live fish. The guard told him that he was in the wrong place. The driver asked for directions to the main kitchen entrance. The guard answered him in a strong Shan-dong dialect. The driver asked if he could use the restroom and the guard replied that he had to do it outside. Gradually the noise in the hallway died down.

She thought how strange it was that she had been married to Mao for seventeen years.

Do you know what secret it was that got us married? Mao asked as if reading her thoughts and then answered himself. It was the fascination with ourselves. We once were each other's mirror that reflected our own beauty. We sang hymns to ourselves . . . and that was all.

Getting up, he fastened his pants. *A smoker who burned his pillow with his own cigarette butt.* His tone was filled with irony.

You're wrong! she blurted out.

Come on, our life has been spent in battling the feudalists, Chiang Kai-shek, the Japanese, the imperialists, the mother earth and each other. Never mind the past. For your future's sake I advise you to remember the reason the willow blossom flies higher than a bird — it is because it has the wind's support.

Well, something you'd better remember too. You and I are two sides of one leaf — there is no way to split — your godlike picture depends on me to hold it in its place.

Play out your drama any way you like. He walked toward the door and paused. But don't assign me to any role.

The door slammed behind him.

The hall echoed.

No syphilis. The report from my doctor comes back. I let out a long breath. I was scared. Curious, I decide to telephone Mao's physician, Dr. Li. I ask if Mao has syphilis. After a nervous hesitation Dr. Li explains that he needs a letter of permission from the Politburo to reveal information on Mao's health.

Doesn't it count that I am his wife?

I was instructed not to answer any question regarding the Chairman's health, Madame.

The line is silent for a while. I press on. If I am to sleep with him tonight, will it be safe?

No reply.

I will charge you with first-degree murder if you lie, Doctor.

I let the threat sit for a while and then repeat my question.

No. The man finally cracks. It won't be safe.

So he's got syphilis.

I didn't say that, Madame! He suddenly acts hysterical. I've never said that Chairman Mao had syphilis!

*

With his medical bags in hand Dr. Li flies in on a military jet at seven-thirty in the morning. Madame Mao receives him in a cottage surrounded by the West Lake in Hang-zhou. She is in a skylighted drawing room taking photos of roses.

Dr. Li wipes his brow and begins to unpack his equipment. She stops him. I sent for you to answer me one question. What have you done to cure Mao?

The man's fingers begin to play nervously with the zipper on his equipment case.

You see, Doctor, I don't exist if Mao gets chewed up by bugs.

Dr. Li lets out a breath. Forgive me, Madame . . . The Chairman . . . he is not particularly fond of my treatment.

She laughs as she takes apart her tripod. That's typical!

Dr. Li smiles humbly. Well, the Chairman is always busy. He has a country to run.

He is an old smelly-rotten-stone from the bottom of a manure pit, she says loudly. I know how you feel, Doctor. I have been trying to change his diet for years without a single success. He loves fat pork with sugar and soy sauce. The greasier the better. But the syphilis bug is a different matter, isn't it? What will happen if he continues to be the virus carrier? Will the other parts of his body be infected? Will he die from the disease?

No, Dr. Li confirms. It does much less damage to a man than to a woman.

Are you saying that he'd be fine without taking any medication?

The doctor chooses to remain silent again.

Is it difficult to get rid of the bug?

No, not at all. All the Chairman has to do is to receive a couple of shots.

Did you explain this to him?

Yes I did, Madame.

What happened?

The man's mouth drops and he won't utter another word.

She passes him a towel to wipe his sweat. Again it's typical. My husband couldn't care less about what happens to his partners. Sit down, Doctor. You don't have to make a sound. Just correct me if I am wrong. Please believe that I know Mao inside out. Did he say that there was no way you could make him suffer the shots? I bet he said exactly that. Yes? You see. He has to continue the practice of longevity and you think what an awful human being he is, don't you?

No no no no. The man springs up from the sofa. I've never thought . . . I'd never dare . . .

She smiles as if finding the situation comical.

Dr. Li continues like a bad actor reciting his lines. I would never think of Chairman Mao in such a way. I am a one hundred percent revolutionary. I devote my life to our great leader, great teacher, great commander — our Great Helmsman.

Poor man. Putting her camera into its case she teases, Then you must think that these girls deserve the bugs, don't you? No? Why not? It's their punishment, isn't it? I understand that some of the victims of syphilis can never bear children? Am I wrong? All right, I am right. Do you sympathize with the girls? I would be surprised if you didn't. I was told that you are a decent doctor. Do you believe in the Chairman's practice? Have you encouraged him? Then you discouraged him? No? Why? Why not? You are a doctor. You are supposed to cure, to heal, to stop the virus! What? You don't know? You see, you have come to understand my situation now. Because you are experiencing what I am experiencing. It is all about how a decent person gets stripped of his dignity.

# 15

UNLIKE MAO, WHO HAS LITTLE TASTE for art and architecture, Madame Mao Jiang Ching finds herself touched by the Forbidden City, especially its Summer Palace. Her favorite spot is the Sea of Magnolia Fragrance, its forest of flowers behind the Hall of Happiness in Longevity. The plants were transplanted from southern China two centuries ago. During its blooming season Madame Mao spends hours wandering in what she calls "the pink clouds." The other spot is the Peony Terrace, built in 1903 by the old empress dowager. The flower beds are made of terraced carved rock.

In the winter, "Strolling through a picture scroll" becomes her favorite activity. She orders the guards and servants to make themselves "disappear" before she enters the "scene." The complex of buildings stands on the hillside west of the Tower of the Scent of Buddha. She loves the view: three towers, two pavilions, a gallery and an arched gateway. She listens to the wind and finds herself calmed. The third day of the snow she comes again to look at a magnificent building that has a large octagonal two-story open pavilion with a double-eave roof of green and yellow glazed tiles. It is now blanketed by snow. She weeps freely and feels understood — a great actress's disappearance.

The whiteness, the sorrow. Alone in the picture world.

*

I order servants to bring me cloth-bound picture books. I have begun studying the personalities of the Forbidden City. I share an interest in opera with the empress dowager. On splendid days I come to visit her glories. I walk directly toward the Hall of Health and Happiness. The hall stands opposite the stage at a distance of less than twenty meters. It was here that the empress enjoyed theatrical performances. I sit down on her throne. It is a gold-lacquered chair with a design of a hundred birds paying homage to the phoenix. It is comfortable. The chair is kept like new. The spirit of the woman is touchable.

I come to adjust my mood. I come to dream, and to feel what it is like to be the empress dowager and to have true power. I don't need a troupe to play for me. I see myself as the protagonist in an imagined opera. The scenes are vivid as I leaf through the empress's opera manual. They are the classic pieces I grew up with, the ones I learned from my grandfather. *The Diary of the Imperial Existence.* I can hear the tunes and arias. It was said that the empress didn't sit on the throne to watch the performances but reclined in bed in her wing and observed from the window. She had seen the opera so many times that she had memorized every detail.

I get on that bed too. I imagine her watching Emperor Guangxu sitting on the front porch to the left of the entrance accompanied by princes, dukes, ministers and other high officials, who sat along the east and west verandahs. What kind of mood was she in? A woman born to a terrible time, who lost her territories each day to foreign and domestic enemies. Was the opera her only escape?

I find it soothing when facing the Great Stage, which was constructed in 1891. The largest stage of the Ching dynasty, it is a three-story structure, twenty-one meters high and seventeen meters wide on the lowest floor. There are chambers above and below it, with trapdoors for angels to descend from the sky and devils to rise up from the earth. There is also a deep well and five square pools under the stage for water scenes. In connection with the stage is the Makeup Tower, a magnificent two-story backstage building.

I miss my role. I miss my stage.

For a while the beauty of the place occupies her. Then she becomes bored. She retreats. Visits less. Soon she stops coming. She shuts herself in the Garden of Stillness and grows depressed. She is desperate for an audience. She talks to whoever is around. The servants, the chef, the new pet — a monkey she was recently presented as a gift from the National Zoo, or the mirror, the wall, sink, chair and toilet. Gradually, it becomes an act in which she takes pleasure. It is to deal with herself, to find things to do, to forget the pressing unhappiness.

It is not that I am an expert, but Mao is definitely a science illiterate. I respect doctors, especially dentists. But Mao doesn't. He hates them. Poor Mr. Lin-po. Every time he came to clean the Chairman's teeth he would tremble. It's like he was asked to peel the skin off a dragon. The Chairman can be frightening to an ordinary person. The dentist was shaking so hard that the Chairman thought his jaw was going to fall apart. So the Chairman asked him to fix his own jaw first.

The man couldn't take the Chairman's jokes. So he was fired. The next one was recommended by Premier Zhou. He came and behaved the same way. His jaw was all right but his facial muscles twisted as if his nerves were wired with an electric cord. And there was the hairdresser too, Mr. Wei. The Chairman cracked some jokes with him and commented that his shaver was sharp. The man dropped his tool and fainted on his knees.

The Chairman calls me "Miss Bourgeois" because I refuse to eat pork. He believes that he is immortal. He believes he possesses supernatural power. No bug will attack him and no fat will clog his arteries. Well, I'd like to bet on his teeth. His periodontal disease is so severe that his teeth are green and his breath stinks. I bet he will wake up one morning and find all his teeth gone.

She forgets that her listeners are not supposed to respond, not to mention offering comments or opinions. She forgets that they are on duty. Soon she loses interest in her monologue and finds herself developing a habit of peeping and spying.

I have been following the Chairman's footprints. I want to find out what he does as the head of state. I find that he basically does two things: travel and entertain. At the beginning nobody wants to talk to me for fear of Mao. I change my strategy. I play what I call the game of confusion. I locate Mao's destination and phone the governor after his visit. I say, the Chairman asks me to send his warmest regards to you. Then I ask what the Chairman did during his stay. I learn that the Chairman was led to visit the workplaces of distinction. A steel factory in the north and a coal mill in the west, a hen farm in the south and a seafood plantation in the east. Wherever Mao goes he is told they have the greatest harvest. The governors are in competition to please Mao. They are desperate to get Mao to issue state loans. But then I ask, Why didn't you report the truth? If there has been a drought why say harvest was on its way?

Isn't the answer obvious, Madame? the governor sighs. I would rather make false reports than look foolish in front of the Chairman.

So everyone ends up raising his gun only to shoot his own foot. To such complaints my method is to change the subject. It is not that I don't care. It is my own survival I have to worry about first. My life has experienced drought after drought and flood after flood. I am sick of the bad news.

*

In her spying she has come to focus on two women. The two whom she secretly compares herself to and envies. The two who stand no chance of being her friends. One is talented and plain-looking. She is Premier Zhou En-lai's wife, Deng Yin-chao. The other is Wang Guang-mei, the wife of Vice Chairman Liu. Talented and beautiful, she disturbs Madame Mao Jiang Ching the most. The fact that both women are adored by their husbands troubles her. She finds it unbearable when Premier Zhou kisses Deng Yin-chao when leaving for trips, and when Vice Chairman Liu glues his eyes on Wang Guang-mei at parties. She takes it personally as a humiliation to herself.

The eyes of the public suck it all in, she painfully observes. The affection is caught on camera, printed in papers and deposited in the minds of the billion — she is being compared.

How do these women keep their husbands? One can almost pity Deng Yin-chao for her yam-shaped face. She has turtle eyes, a frog mouth, a hunched back, gray hair and a soy-sauce-bottle body draped in gray suits. There is no color in her speech. Nor in her expression. Yet her husband Premier Zhou is the most handsome and charming man in China.

I am pleased with Deng Yin-chao. I am pleased with her wisdom. The knowledge of knowing herself, knowing that she can't fight me, is not my rival, thus doesn't try to be one. She is a lady who knows when to shut up, when to disappear, and she treats me like a queen. She gets what she wants in the end. She understands the benefits of being humble. During my husband's twenty-seven years of ruling, the ups and downs that turn one from hero to villain and back overnight, the Zhous' boat never sinks. Deng Yin-chao doesn't come to dance parties held in the Grand Hall of the People. Once in a while she shows up to just say hello. She hunches her back and tells me that I am the best. All the nice words. I don't know what she says about me to her husband. She doesn't talk about me behind my back to anyone else, because she knows that Kang Sheng is my ear, and he is everywhere. Deng Yin-chao speaks good of me and lets her compliments travel back to me.

Wang Guang-mei is not so wise. Wang Guang-mei is the opposite of Deng Yin-chao.

Madame Mao Jiang Ching can hardly stand Wang Guang-mei. Wang Guang-mei is a New Year's lantern that shines the way to warmth. Her grace offers delight and her words bring closeness. From a prestigious and Western-influenced family, Wang Guang-mei is highly educated and self-confident. She doesn't intend to outshine Madame Mao Jiang Ching, but because Mao never publicly introduces his wife, visitors from foreign countries all regard Wang Guang-mei as the first lady of China.

Although Wang Guang-mei pays attention to Jiang Ching, mentions her name constantly, consults her on all manner of things, from dress codes to what presents to bring when accompanying her husband abroad, she is unable to please Jiang Ching. Unlike Deng Yin-chao, who makes sure that she appears as no rival to Jiang Ching, Wang Guang-mei sets limits on how much she will sacrifice her own taste. Wang Guang-mei refuses to keep Jiang Ching in her mind all the time. Furthermore, she has no guilt over her popularity.

I think of Wang Guang-mei as a thief. As a thief later on I punish her. She stole my role and I can't view her any other way. Like a bird to a worm, she is my natural enemy. Her very existence demands my sacrifice.

Wang Guang-mei tries to be a good performer, though. The problem is that she doesn't think that she's being harmful to me. She thinks the opposite. She thinks that there is nothing wrong with my not meeting foreign guests, with my not visiting the countries of my dreams. Nothing wrong that her face gets to be printed all over the papers and magazines. Nothing wrong that I am forgotten.

Because of her there is no need of me.

I can't stand looking at her waltz on the floor. The way she and her husband Liu admire each other. Their passion spills. The world is forgotten. I can't help thinking how unlucky I am. I have done everything I can to try to keep Mao. I have gathered all his children once a month to create a family environment. But it is no use. Mao is busy traveling and practicing longevity. He doesn't want me around. At those moments I am the little girl from Zhu again. In dirt and in rags, running away and begging for affection.

The history of China recognizes another great man besides Mao. It is Liu Shao-qi, the vice chairman of the republic. Vice Chairman Liu has a donkey's long face. His skin is the surface of the moon. He has bad teeth and a big garlic nose. It is his wife, Wang Guang-mei, whose beauty and elegance bring to light his quality. Vice Chairman Liu is a stubborn fellow. A man who doesn't understand politics but is a politician. In Madame Mao Jiang Ching's eyes he misjudges Mao. His tragedy is his blind faith in Mao. He is a victim of his own assumptions. Right after the establishment of the republic in 1949, Liu wants to establish law. He wants no emperor. He wants China to copy the American model and set up a voting system. Although he has never suggested that Mao copy George Washington, everyone gets the message. Later on Liu becomes number one on Mao's elimination list. He forgets that China is Mao's China. To Mao, the suggestions are equal to having him murdered under the bright sun. It is because of this that Liu and Mao become enemies. However, Liu doesn't see things this way. Liu believes that for the future of China he and Mao can achieve harmony.

*

It is not that I feel good about Vice Chairman Liu's death in 1969. But it is he who made Mao pull the trigger. Mao simply feels threatened by him. Liu has the power of a politician child. Unlike Premier Zhou, Marshal Ye Jian-ying and Deng Xiao-ping who pretend to be "innocently" making "mistakes" when Mao criticizes them, Liu stands by his belief. Like a shooting star, he fuels on his own life.

Compared to Vice Chairman Liu, Premier Zhou lives to please Mao. I don't understand why he behaves that way. He was educated in France. He doesn't like the dancing floor being spread with powder to protect Mao from slipping during movements, but he never complains. I myself hate the floor too, but Mao and the others love it. Premier Zhou is an excellent dancer, yet he forces himself to breathe the powder dust. He worships Mao. He sincerely believes that Mao's is the hand that sculpts China. He models himself after the famous Premier Zhu Ge-liang of the Han dynasty, the ancient premier who spent his life serving the family of Emperor Liu.

Premier Zhou is a man of genius, but he is incapable of saying no to Mao. He is a janitor who fixes what Mao has broken. He sends warm letters, and food coupons in Mao's name, to Mao's victims. He speaks only to provoke forgiveness. After his death in January 1976 Mao signs an order and forbids the man to be publicly mourned. Yet millions of people risk their lives to fill the streets to mourn him. Personally I admire him and feel sorry for him.

Premier Zhou has chances, but he chooses to ignore the calling of his conscience and lets them slip away. At moments of crises, he closes his eyes to Mao's problems. He fakes his emotion and follows the crowd and shouts, *Long live the proletarian dictatorship!* During the Cultural Revolution he echoes Mao. He waves Mao's little red book of quotations and praises the Red Guards' destructive behavior. He endures beyond reason. He endures at the expense of the nation. One can't help but question: Is it because he needs the job as the premier? Or is it that he lives to be another kind of immortal, the one who brings himself to the altar?

When Mao finally turns his back on him and persuades the nation to attack him, Zhou removes his services quietly. He is sent to the hospital with cancer of the pancreas in its final stage. During his last moment he begs his wife to recite Mao's new poem "No Need to Fart." It is during the reciting that he permanently shuts his eyes. Does he hope that Mao will be touched by such a performance of loyalty? Does he hope that Mao will be finally satisfied that he is now gone forever? Chinese people wonder about Premier Zhou's performance. Chinese people wonder if it was in peace that Premier Zhou left the world. Or did he realize that he had helped Mao to carry out the Cultural Revolution and buried China's chance of prosperity?

I have reached my limit. I can't stay out of my husband's affairs anymore. This isn't an option and I won't consider divorce. Kang Sheng has promised to help me. But how can I trust the double agent? He says Mao sleeps only with virgins — I am not sure if this is not the message Mao wants him to send me.

One day in February Kang Sheng comes to show his loyalty toward me. There has been a threat, he tells me. There is a unique virgin with a magnificent brain. Worse, Mao has fallen in love with her. A golden bird who sings at the emperor's window every night. Mao is so attached that he is in the mood for divorcing.

Her name is Shang-guan Yun-zhu — Pearl Born from the Clouds. She is a film actress in her early thirties. An actress! Her movies are *The Qing Family on the Water-city, In Your Voice I Sing, Lady of the Wei Kingdom, The Sisters of the Stage.*

I am talking about a woman who makes my life a joke. A joke at which I am unable to laugh.

I imagine them. My husband and Shang-guan Yun-zhu. I watch them move on my stage. The lust which I used to experience myself. I project them on the screen of my mind.

I say to Kang Sheng that it is time. It is time that I stop weeping for my misfortune. It is time I stop taking morphine to dull my senses. It is time to switch plates and bottles and make others take the drugs that have paralyzed me.

Kang Sheng says it's a good idea. I'll work with you. Let's renew our Yenan contract, let's get down to business. My advice? Start developing your own network of loyalists. Start your business of political management. Go to Shanghai and invest in people whom you know and make them your battle horses.

The secret news begins to spread. The first lady has arrived in Shanghai and invites her old friends. She throws parties in Mao's name. The gathering floor is the city hall. Special guests include the famous actor Dan, her partner in *A Doll's House,* and Junli, the most-in-demand film director. The two men in her wedding picture at the Pagoda of Six Harmonies. She thinks that they will be flattered and commit to her in no time. She is Madame Mao. She expects eagerness.

But there is no applause when the curtain descends. The parties and the reunions generate little energy. No respect and no friendship. Later on Madame Mao Jiang Ching learns from Kang Sheng that the actor and the director, the men who couldn't get over their friend Tang Nah's sadness, sent a message to Premier Zhou reporting her ambition.

I am back in Beijing, back to the life of stillness. I didn't want to come back. I was ordered back by the Politburo. I have been ridiculed in Shanghai. People gossiped about Shang-guan Yun-zhu and Mao's seriousness in taking her as a future wife. I tried to ignore the rumor. I tried to focus on what I set out to achieve. I met interesting young people, the graduates of the Music Conservatory and the School of Opera of Shanghai. I was looking for new talent and they made perfect candidates. They complained about the lack of opportunities to perform. I understand how frightening it can be for actors to grow old on the sidelines. I told them that I would love to work with them. I promised to give them a chance to shine. I am in a mood to smash chains, I said. I want to renew my dream of a truly revolutionary theater, a weapon and a form of liberation. But the young people were not enthusiastic. They were unsure of my position. They wanted to check out my power first.

This morning I asked my driver to drop me in a place where there are woods to cover me from the rest of the world. I want to stop my mind from spinning. A half-hour later I find myself in the imperial hunting ground. I ask the driver to come back in three hours.

I walk toward a hill. The air feels like warm water pouring over my face. The scene is bleak. Plants have begun to die everywhere in the heat. The grass and bushes are all yellow. Even the most heat-bearing plant — the umbrella-shaped three-leaf goya — has lost its spirit. The leaves dangle down in three different directions.

There is a rotten smell in the air. It is the dead animals. Falcons circle above my head. I suppose the rotten smell rises fast in the heat. The birds smell their food in the air. Besides falcons, there are shit-lovers, cousins of cockroaches, crawling in and out of dead plants. I didn't know that they could fly. The heat must have made them change habits, for the ground is a baking pan.

The sky is a giant rice bowl and I am walking in its bottom — unable to climb and unable to get out.

Helplessness sucks the air out of my chest.

*

You need the figurehead. You need Mao, Kang Sheng says to me. Your role is to play Mao's most trusted comrade. It is the only way to empower yourself. You have to fake it. No, you don't feel. Go and kiss the corpses of the backyard concubines. They will tell you what feeling means. Get up on the giant's shoulders. So no one can overlook you.

I suppose I have to get over Mao.

Whatever you have to do.

She dreams about Mao. Night after night. The curse — that she wishes him dead — has come to bury her. Yet there is this inborn stubbornness. The way her feeling operates. It is its own cage. It blocks her. She is at a harbor, waving behind a crowd. Turn your head away, she cries to herself.

Her heart refuses to let Mao go.

I tell him never to come to me, but I wait for him every day. I send him invitations using all kinds of excuses. When he does come, I show apathy. I either get servants to clean the room or pick up the camera and shoot roses in the garden. I long for him to stay yet I make his visits miserable.

I want him to finish us, I say to Nah. These days I have been spending more time with Nah. She is happy living in the boarding school but she makes sure to spend the weekends with me. She knows the fact that she is with me will give her father a good reason to visit. But I know it won't happen. I never look out the window and never respond to any of Nah's guesses regarding her father's arrival.

One evening my staff views a documentary film as a form of entertainment. The title is *Chairman Mao Inspects the Country*. I decline to go. When it's on, I hear the sound track from the portable projector over the kitchen. I am struck by a sudden sadness. I

can't help but walk over to the screening. When it is finished I clap
with the crowd with tears in my eyes.

Long live Chairman Mao and great health to Comrade Jiang
Ching! everyone cheers.

In my dream I hear the whistle of a steam engine from a distance. I
see wavelike crowds move in blurry dawn light. The ship begins
to slowly take off. Thousands of colorful paper ribbons break in
passengers' farewell cries. The ribbons dance in the air. It feels like
the harbor is being pushed away by the ship. Then the noise qui-
ets down. The crowd watches the ship draw away. It becomes
smaller and smaller. The ribbons stop dancing. The sound of
waves takes over. The smell of stinking fish is in the air once
again.

The vast ocean, glittering under the sunlight.

My heart's harbor vacant.

# 16

IT'S BEEN TWO YEARS since Mao instigated the movement called the Great Leap Forward. Mao has set himself to be the greatest ruler of all time — he wants to push China to the top of the world's productivity records. The strategy is to release and utilize the energy and potential of the peasants, the same peasants who prosecuted Mao's war to such a glorious conclusion. It will be an explosion of energy and innovation; thus heaven-mandated Communism will be achieved in five years. One will get to do whatever one likes and eat whatever one wants.

Inspired by the notion, the nation answers Mao's call. Every piece of private land is taken away and put under the ownership of the government. Peasants are encouraged to "experience Communism where they live" — free-food commune cafeterias begin to bloom like weeds after a rain. On the industrial front, Mao promotes "backyard steel factories." The locals are ordered to donate their woks, axes and wash basins.

The Great Leap is the perfect expression of Mao's mind and beliefs, his daring and romanticism. He waits for the results anxiously. At the beginning there is praise for his vision, but two years later come reports of violence breaking out between poor and rich. Looting for food and shelter has become a problem. Before autumn the stir becomes so serious that it begins to threaten security. Everything is consumed, including the planting seeds for next spring, while nothing is produced. The nation's last storage is empty. Mao begins to feel the pressure. He begins to realize that running a country is not like winning a guerrilla war.

1959 begins with floods and is followed by drought. A sense of desperation falls across the land. Despite Mao's call to fight the disaster — *It is man's will, not heaven, that decides* — hundreds and thousands of peasants flee their hometowns in search of food. Along the coastline many of them are forced to sell their children and some poison their entire families to end the despair. By winter, the number of deaths rises to twenty million. Reports have piled up on the desk of Premier Zhou's office.

Mao is more embarrassed than worried. He remembers how determined he was to make his plan a reality. He has issued instructions:

> "Race toward Communism"
> "Demolish family structure"
> "One rice bowl, one pair of chopsticks, one set of blankets —
>     the style of Communism"
> "One hectare, ten thousand pounds of yams, two hundred
>     thousand pounds of rice"
> "Mate rabbit with cow so the rabbit will get as big as the cow"
> "Raise chickens as big as elephants"
> "Grow beans as big as the moon and eggplants big as squashes"

In June, peasants' riots rise in Shanxi and Anhui provinces. The Politburo calls a vote to stop Mao's policy.

Mao retreats for the next six months.

My husband has fallen from the clouds. I have only seen him once in three months. He looks low and distressed. Nah tells me that he sees no one. No more actresses. The news fills me with mixed feelings. Of course, I am hopeful that he may reach out to me. But I am also surprised and even saddened — I have never imagined that he could be vulnerable.

Late one evening Kang Sheng visits my place unexpectedly. Mao is in need of you, he tells me excitedly. The Chairman's reputation has been terribly damaged. His enemies are now taking advantage of his error and are setting out to overthrow him.

I take a sip of the chrysanthemum tea. It has never tasted so wonderful as it does now.

I begin to see a way in which I can help Mao. I become so excited with the thought that I neglect Kang Sheng's presence. I see printing machines rolling, voices broadcasting and films projecting. I feel the power of the media. The way it washes and bleaches minds. I can feel the coming success. There is energy going through my body. I am about to enter an act leading to the climax of my life.

Trying to share the pleasure of finding a great role, I explain to Kang Sheng how I feel. But he has fallen asleep on the sofa.

It begins with a convention in July 1959, held on Mount Lu, a resort area where the landscape is majestic. At first Mao appears humble and modest. He admits his mistakes and encourages criticism. His sincerity moves the delegates and representatives from all over the country, among them Fairlynn. Fairlynn criticizes Mao's Great Leap as a chimpanzee experiment; Yang Xian-zhen, a theorist and the director of the School of the Communist Party, points out that Mao has romanticized Communism and has applied fantasy to reality. On July 14, Mao's claimed loyalist, Marshal Peng De-huai, the son of a peasant, a man known for his great contributions and no-nonsense character, sends a personal letter to Mao in which he reports the result of his private investigation — the shocking facts about the failure of the People's Commune — the fruit of the Great Leap Forward.

Mao smokes. Packs a day. His teeth are brown and his fingernails are tobacco yellow. He listens to what others have to say and makes no response. The cigarette travels between his lips and the ashtray. Once in a while he nods, forces a smile, shakes hands with the speaker. Good job. You have spoken for the people. I appreciate your frankness. Be proud of yourself as a Communist.

A week later, Mao claims illness and announces his temporary resignation. Vice Chairman Liu takes over the nation's business.

I do not show my face at any of the meetings although I am at Mount Lu. I read reports sent by Kang Sheng and am more than well informed about the proceedings. Mao is bruised. I have a sense that he will not take it for long. He is not the type who admits mistakes. He thinks of himself as a Communist, but by instinct he is an emperor. He lives to be a leading man, just like me, who can't see herself not being a leading lady.

Seizing the moment, I decide to make a trip to Shanghai. I make friends with fresh faces. The artists and dramatists. The young and the ambitious. I cultivate relations by attending their openings and work with them on raw material. Would you like to devote your talent to Chairman Mao? I ask. How about changing this tune to the Chairman's favorite? Yes, be creative and daring.

I educate my friends by sending reference materials, among them "Midnight Incense," a Chinese classic opera piece, and the famous Italian song "Return to Sorrento." In the beginning they are confused — they were used to the traditional linear thinking. I broaden their minds and gradually they benefit from my teaching. They thrive on my ideas. There are a few brilliant minds. One composer for violin is so quick that he turns Tchaikovsky's "Waltz of the Flowers" into a Chinese folk dance and names it "The Red Sky of Yenan."

I train what I call a "cultural troop." A troop that Mao will need to fight his ideological battles. I can hardly keep it a secret. I can see it working. I imagine Mao looking at me with the smile he shone on me thirty years ago. On the other hand I am uncertain, even a little afraid — Mao has never quite seen things my way. How can I know if he will be pleased with what I am doing?

For the first time in many years I am no longer bothered by insomnia. I throw away the sleeping pills. When I wake up I no longer feel threatened by my rivals. Even Wang Guang-mei causes me no worry. Although she and Liu, her husband, enjoy the limelight, I predict that their days are numbered.

Vice Chairman Liu never realizes that this is where Mao's grudge starts. The plot begins while Liu gets busy trying to save the nation. Liu shuts Mao's commune system down and replaces it with his own invention, the *zi-liu-de* program, which allows peasants to own their backyards and sell whatever they have planted. The locals are encouraged to operate on a family basis. In essence, it is capitalism Chinese style. It is spit on Mao's face.

Madame Mao Jiang Ching observes her husband's mood. She has just gotten back from Shanghai. She and Kang Sheng have been watching the Mao-tiger get its whiskers pulled. Every day after the convention, Kang Sheng goes to Madame Mao's hotel room and updates her with news.

Pay attention to the timing, Kang Sheng says. The dragon-tornado is coming. It is near. Mao is going to attack and it will be the end of Liu. Watch, the more enemies Mao makes the faster he will turn to you.

Without a warning Mao returns to Beijing in September. He calls up a Politburo meeting and announces the removal of the minister of defense, Marshal Peng De-huai.

There isn't a hearing on the decision. Mao makes the decision as if it is his right. Like removing a shoe from his foot. Before the members of the Politburo get a chance to react, Marshal Peng is replaced by Mao's disciple Marshal Lin Biao, a man who praises

Mao as a living god and who is trying to turn the People's Liberation Army into the "Great School of Mao Tse-tung Thoughts."

Marshal Lin Biao is a familiar character to me. I've learned from Mao that Lin Biao won key battles during the civil war and is a man of great tactics. I don't mention that I find his recent tactics rather transparent. He is the man who shouts *A long life to Chairman Mao* the loudest. But life is strange. He is also the man who orders Mao's train bombed. In the future Mao will promote him to be his successor and will also order his murder at his own residence.

Marshal Lin has always been physically weak — the opposite of his name, which means King of the Forest. He is so thin that he can be blown by wind. His wife Ye has told me that he can't stand light, sound or water. Like a thousand-year vase, he decays from the moisture in the air. He has a pair of triangle eyes and grassy eyebrows. He tries to hide his slight frame in military uniform. Still, one can tell his sickness by the bamboo-thin neck and the lopsided head as if it weighs too much for the neck.

And yet, now, she is inspired by Lin Biao. His way of getting Mao. It is so simple and childish. It works and has great effect. Lin flatters shamelessly. In the preface to the second edition of Mao's *Little Red Quotation Book* he calls Mao the greatest Marxist of all time. *Chairman Mao defends and develops internationalism, Marxism and Leninism. Chairman Mao's one sentence equals others' ten thousand sentences. Only Mao's words reflect absolute truths. Mao is the genius born from heaven.*

She has found similarities between Lin Biao and Kang Sheng when it comes to flattering Mao. Lin and Kang don't get along. She decides that for her own future she will burn incense in both of their temples.

❀

It's been a long time since Mao requested my presence. When I am finally invited I find that the Chrysanthemum-Fragrance Study has changed its face. The once wild chrysanthemums have lost their firelike energy. The plants look tamed, uniformly trimmed, straight as soldiers. He doesn't bother to greet me when I enter. He is still in his pajamas. I am facing a sixty-nine-year-old balding man who hasn't washed for days. His face is a smeared drawing — there aren't any clear lines. He reminds me of a eunuch with a face of half man and half woman. Still, my heart trips over itself.

It's noon. He seems relaxed. Sit down, he says, as if we have always been close. Comrade Kang Sheng told me that you have an important idea that I should hear about.

The lines are on the tip of my tongue. I have been preparing for this. I have rehearsed the act a hundred times. But I am nervous. Am I truly finding my way back to him?

Chairman, she begins. You have pointed out at the eighth meeting in the tenth convention that there has been a tendency to use literature as a weapon to attack the Communist Party. I can't agree more. I believe that it is our enemy's intention.

He shows no expression.

She continues as if she is once again Nora on stage. I've turned my attention to a play that has recently become popular. I think the play has been used as a weapon against you.

What is it called?

*Hairui Dismissed from Office.*

I know the story. It is about Judge Hairui from the Ming dynasty during the ruling period of Emperor Jia-jing.

Yes, exactly. The story tells how Hairui risks his post to speak out for the people and how he heroically fights the emperor and gets purged.

I see. Mao's eyes narrow. Who is the author?

The vice mayor of Beijing, professor and historian Wu Han.

Mao turns silent.

She observes a change slowly taking place in his expression. His wrinkles stretch and squish, eyes grow into a line. She feels the moment and decides to twist the knife and press his most sensitive nerve.

Have you, Chairman, ever thought of this — why Hairui? Why a tragic hero? Why the scene where hundreds of peasants get down on their knees to bid him farewell when he is escorted into exile? If it is not a cry for Marshal Peng De-huai, what is it? If it is not saying that you are the bad Emperor Jia-jing, what is it?

Mao gets up and paces. Kang Sheng has already talked to me about the play, he suddenly turns around and speaks. Why don't you go and check into it for me? Bring back to me what you find as soon as possible.

At that moment I hear a familiar aria in my head.

> Oh maiden in a palace tower
> Soothing her love-laden
> Like a glowworm golden
> In a dell of dew
> Scattering unbeholden
> Its aerial hue
> Soul in secret hour
> With wine sweet as love
> Which overflows her bower

After her report, Mao loses his composure.

I have been in power for fourteen years, he roars. And my opponents have never stopped plotting conspiracy. They wear me out. I have become the Garden of Yuanming — an empty frame. They suggest that I take vacations so they can form factions during my absence. What a fool I have been! The important posts have already been filled with their people. I can't even get through to the mayor's office.

Eagerly she responds, Yes, Chairman, that's exactly why the play *Hairui Dismissed from Office* is a hit — they have plotted the whole thing. The critics have orchestrated the play's promotion. Besides Wu Han, they include Liao Mu-sha and Deng Tuo, our country's most influential scholars.

Mao lights a cigarette and stands up from his rattan chair. His look softens for a moment. Jiang Ching, he says, many think of you as a meddler, as someone whose vision is short and feelings too strong. But you are seeing clearly now . . . It's been eight years that Vice Chairman Liu has been running the country. He has already established an extensive network. Wu Han is only a gun triggered by others.

The leading actors are yet to make their appearance, she remarks.

Let them come. This morning I read an article Kang Sheng sent me. It was written by the three men whom you have just mentioned. Did they call themselves the Village of Three?

Yes. Was one of the articles titled "The Great Empty Words"?

He nods. It is an attack!

She tells herself to be patient. She sees the hand that is working to change her fate. She leans toward him, her voice filled with tears. Chairman, your enemies are getting ready to harm you.

He turns to her and smiles.

Unable to bear his gaze she looks away.

If there is a trade that I have mastered in my life it is that I crack people-nuts, he suddenly says. The harder the better.

I am ready to fight alongside you, Chairman.

Have you some ideas?

Yes.

Let's hear them.

She begins to describe her cultural troupes, describes the plays she has been working on. All the characters are symbolic. Although the conditions for creativity are poor — for example, actors work in their backyards and use kitchenware as props —

their devotion, enthusiasm and potential are great. She tells him
that she is ready to bring the troupe to Beijing to present to him.

Stay out of Beijing, he instructs. Do it in Shanghai. Talk to my
friend Ke Qin-shi, the mayor of Shanghai, for production funds.
He is loyal. I would go out myself to support you but it would be
too obvious. Go to Ke with my message. You represent me. Get
writers you trust. Call for a national denunciation and criticism of
*Hairui Dismissed from Office.* It'll be a test balloon. If there is a
response, we shall put our worry aside. But if there isn't a response, we are in trouble.

She is unable to utter another word, so happy that she feels that
she must bid good-bye to hide her emotion.

He takes a drag on his cigarette and walks her to the door. Just
a moment, Jiang Ching, he says and waits to have her full attention. You have complained that I have caged you. You might be
right. It's been twenty-some years, hasn't it? Forgive me. I was
forced to do so. I am in a tough position. At any rate, I am putting
an end to it. You have paid enough. Now go out to the world and
break the spell.

She throws herself on his chest.

He holds her and calms her.

In her tears dawn comes to display its extraordinariness.

The secretary tells me that Mayor Ke has come two hours earlier
to wait for my arrival. It is ceremonial. It is to show his courtesy. I
tell the secretary that the mayor's hospitality is appreciated.

The noiseless car takes me to number 1245 Hua-shan Road.
Mayor Ke sits next to me and writes down every word I say. I send
him Mao's regards and tell him that I need to find writers.

Can't Madame locate good writers in Beijing? Doesn't the imperial city attract fine intellects?

I smile. A smile that demonstrates absolute secrecy. A smile

Mayor Ke reads and understands. The mayor is from peasant stock and has a head that reminds me of an onion. He is in a white cotton garment. A pair of black cotton sandals. A costume the Party cadres wear to show their revolutionary origin. Anti–leather shoes means anti-bourgeois. I am sure you'll produce results that will be to Mao's satisfaction, I say. I let him take his time, let him count his fingers and figure out his profit margin.

Mayor Ke asks me to answer one question. One question and that will be all. I nod. Are writers in Beijing no longer dependable?

I don't say a word.

He gets it. Gets that Mao regards Shanghai as his new base. Gets that Mao is ready to flatten Beijing.

The next morning Mayor Ke calls and says that he is sending a writer named Chun-qiao to my villa. Chun-qiao is the editor-in-chief of the newspaper *Shanghai Wen-hui*. He is the best I have ever known, he says.

Send Comrade Chun-qiao the Chairman's warmest hello, I say.

Two hours later Chun-qiao arrives. Welcome to Shanghai, Madame Mao. He bows to shake my hand. He is walking-stick thin and a smoker. After a few minutes of conversation I find his mind scissor-sharp.

Shanghai can do anything Madame desires. He smiles with all his teeth sprouting.

My first night in Shanghai I have difficulty sleeping. The city reminds me of how I used to eat my heart out over Tang Nah and Dan and how I longed for Junli's attention. There was not a spot of unbroken skin on my mind's body. How heroically I fought fate. My youth was a splendid bonfire with herbs of passion that smelled strongly. I have never forgotten the scent of Shanghai.

The night is bittersweet and tearful. I can't help but recall the past. My suffering. The struggle, the feeling of being entangled in my own intestines, crouching, but unable to fight back. Slowly, the dirt track of memory disappears into the flat of the horizon. I watch my sentiments burn and I scatter the ashes. I realize that if I can't live a life tending my vineyards in the sun, I have to learn to trust my own instincts. In that sense I am truly my name. *Jiang Ching. Green comes out of blue but is richer than blue.*

Chun-qiao proves himself to be a good choice. He has a clear sense of who I am. He treats me as Mao's equal. With the same regard he fights for my ideas, my thoughts and extends my strength. People say that he never smiles. But when he sees me he blooms like a rose. Behind his thick glasses, his eyes look like polliwogs. The pupils are never still. He tells me that I have given him a new life. I think he means a ladder to political heaven. He tells me that he has been waiting for a moment like this for many years. He is born to devote his life to a cause, to be a faithful premier to an emperor.

She appreciates Chun-qiao's commentary. Day after day his paper calls her "the red-flag bearer" and "the guardian force of Maoism." The articles list her deeds as a revolutionary and the closest assistant to Mao. Chun-qiao places his emphasis on Mao's growing opposition. "Without a guardian angel like Comrade Jiang Ching, China's future will shatter."

The drum beats. The actress warms up to her role. Setting out to influence others, she is unaware how susceptible she is to her own propaganda. She has never lacked for passion. She begins to sound her role in daily life. It becomes her style to open her speeches with these words: *Sometimes I feel too weak to hold the sky of Chairman Mao, but I force myself to stand up, because to sustain Mao is to sustain China; to die for Mao is to die for China.*

The more she speaks, the faster she blends into her role. Soon there is no difference. Now she can't open her mouth without mentioning that the People's Great Savior Mao is in danger. She finds the phrase binds her to the audience — the heroine risks her life for the legend. She is moved herself when she repeats the lines. Once again she is in Mao's cave; once again she feels his hands creeping up inside her shirt; and once again the passion finds its way back to her.

She grows energetic and healthy. The public's response to the media is feverish. Wherever she goes, she receives welcome and admiration. Shanghai's arts and theater circles come to embrace her. Young talents line up at her feet and beg the chance to offer their lives. Save your gift for Chairman Mao, she says. She pats their shoulders and gives them affectionate handshakes. Wasting no time, Chun-qiao develops loyalists and forms what he calls Madame Mao's Modern Red Base.

In the process of recreating herself, she studies Chun-qiao's writing and recites his lines at public rallies. In May she takes a trip back to Beijing to check on Mao.

My husband is not in. He has gone south and has disappeared in the beautiful landscape of the West Lake. When I send his secretary a telegram asking for an appointment to meet and update him with my progress, he sends me a poem about the famous lake as a reply.

> Years ago I have seen the picture of this
> I didn't believe such beauty existed under heaven
> Today I am passing through the lake
> I conclude that the picture needs work

I feel that he may finally be ready to reopen his heart to me. I can never forget the poem he sent to Fairlynn and how much it hurt me. The virgins I can forgive. Yes, I resented him, but I never hated him. Even in my worst times I never wished him overthrown. God makes strange twists. Here he is, put in front of me to be helped. I have never been superstitious until now.

We are floating on the West Lake. It is a golden autumn. Reeds are thick and the cattails are out. The dike is lined with hanging willows. Parts of the lake are covered by lotus leaves. Connected to the shore by a bridge are pavilions of various styles built throughout the dynasties. The place has intricate rocks and is surrounded with poplars, peach and apricot trees. The famous Broken Bridge is made of white marble and granite, has a thin arched beltlike body.

There is no one else but the two of us.

Mao seems absorbed by the beauty. After a while he raises his chin to feel the sun on his face.

My memories are rushing back to me. The Yenan days and earlier. I am in tears. It is not for love but for what I have endured. The way I have once again rescued myself. The triumph of my will and my refusal to give up.

Did I tell you how I first got to know the West Lake? Mao suddenly speaks, eyes focused on a faroff pavilion. It was from a painted ceramic jar of poor quality brought to me by an elderly relative who had visited the place. The print on the jar was a map of the highlights of the lake. The water, trees, pavilions, temples, bridges and galleries. They were all clearly illustrated and accompanied by elegant titles. As a country boy I had little chance to encounter pictures so I took the jar to my room and studied it. Over the years I became so familiar with the scenes that they entered my dreams. When I visited the lake later on as a grown man I felt that it was a place I knew very well. It was like reentering my old dreams.

❀

What? Does anybody dare not to listen to Chairman Mao? Chun-qiao's voice is filled with shock.

Jiang Ching rocks her chin as her tone becomes mysterious. I have Chairman Mao's full support to counterattack. She repeats the phrase as if she enjoys hearing the sound of it.

Full support! Chun-qiao exhales and claps his hands.

Here is my analysis of the situation, Jiang Ching goes on. *Hairui Dismissed from Office* is the key.

Chun-qiao sits back and combs his hair with his fingers. For you, Madame Mao, I'm willing to soak my pen with the juice of my brain.

She offers her hand for him to shake and then gently whispers into his ear: Soon the seats of the Politburo will be vacant and someone has to fill them up.

I don't drink, but today I want to show that I put my life in your hands. Come on, Chun-qiao, bottoms up.

We drink mai tais. It is past midnight. Our spirits are still high. We are finalizing the details of our plan. We are picking partners for the job.

Chun-qiao suggests his disciple Yiao Wen-yuan, who is the head of the Bureau of Propaganda in Shanghai. I have been paying attention to this man. He began to show his political talent during the antirightist movement. He is known for his criticism of Ba-jin's book *Humanity*. He is a heavy-duty weapon. People call him "the Golden Stick." His pen has put down many unshakable figures.

Good! We need golden sticks, I reply. Iron sticks and steel sticks. Our rivals are tigers with steel teeth.

Her next meeting with Mao sets history in motion.

November 10, 1965. The curtain of the epic of the Great Proletarian Cultural Revolution lifts. It is quiet in the beginning, like the changing of the tides. The sound pushes in from a distance.

After eight months of round-the-clock preparation, Jiang Ching, Chun-qiao and Yiao complete their draft entitled "On the Play *Hairui Dismissed from Office.*"

Mao reviews and revises the draft. A week later it appears in the *Shanghai Wen-hui.*

No one, from the Politburo to the congress, takes the article seriously. No one talks about it. No other paper reprints it. Like a rock thrown in a dry well, there is not a sound.

Jiang Ching enters Mao's study the nineteenth day after the publication. She tries to hide her excitement.

The resistance is obvious, she begins. Her voice is tightly controlled. It is an organized silence.

My husband turns toward the window and looks out. Zhong-nan-hai Lake is bathed in bright moonlight. The sea of trees is draped with silver rays. The shadows are velvet black. Not far in the distance, among the mists of fog, stand the pavilions of Yintai and Phoenix where every bit of grass, wood, brick and tile tells a story.

It is here Emperor Guang-xu was held hostage by the empress dowager. Mao speaks suddenly as he always does. The first vice president of the republic of China, Li Hong-yuan, was under house arrest on the same spot. Do you think they would dare?

We are all set to go, Chairman. Your health is the nation's fortune.

Have you printed the article as a handbook? Mao asks.

I have, but the bookstores in Beijing are uninterested. Only three thousand copies have been reluctantly stocked — compared to Vice Chairman Liu's *On a Communist's Self-Cultivation,* which has sold six million.

Did you relay the situation to the head of the Cultural Bureau, Lu Din-yi?

I did. His comment was "It is an academic issue."

Mao gets up and spits tea leaves from his mouth. Down with

the Cultural Bureau and the Beijing City Committee! Let's stir the country. Tell the masses to shake the enemy's boats. The revolution must be renewed.

Your order has been placed.

The first couple of China utilize their power to its full capacity. Through the media Mao launches the movement. *Let the Cultural Revolution be a soul-purifying process,* the papers quote Mao. *The old order has to be abandoned. A foot worker should be able to enter an opera hall free of charge; a sick son of a peasant should receive the same medical care as his provincial governor; an orphan should be able to obtain the highest education; and elders, the handicapped and the disabled should receive free public health care.*

In a few months, creating chaos becomes a way of life. Looting is not only encouraged, but called an act to "help one depart from evil seduction." To follow Mao's teaching becomes a ritual practice, a new religion. In Madame Mao's twenty-four-hour propaganda there is nothing left of Mao but Buddha himself.

Behind the thick walls of the Forbidden City, Mao designs slogans to inspire the masses. Like an emperor he issues edicts. Today, "Everyone is equal in front of the truth," and tomorrow, "Welcome the soldiers to take over the leadership of the schools." The governors and mayors — especially the mayor of Beijing, Peng Zhen, and the head of the Cultural Bureau, Lu Din-yi, are disoriented. Yet Mao forces them to lead in the name of the Politburo. In the meantime, Kang Sheng is assigned by Mao to monitor the mayor's performance.

Jiang Ching is sent to "go around and light fires."

You can afford to make messes, Kang Sheng tells her. If something goes wrong, Mao will always back you up. My situation is different. I have no one to back me up. I must be careful.

*

There is resistance. It comes from Vice Chairman Liu and his friend Vice Premier Deng Xiao-ping. If Mao has always considered Liu a rival, he considers Deng a valuable talent. Mao once said that Deng's "little bottle" is filled with amazing things. Educated in France Deng tasted capitalism and loved it. The man talks little but acts big. He stands by Vice Chairman Liu in supporting the capitalistic programs. On February 5, a cold day, he and Liu decide to hold a Politburo meeting to discuss the mayor of Beijing Peng Zhen's urgent paper "The Report."

The point of the paper is to clarify the confusion that Madame Mao's "On the Play *Hairui Dismissed from Office*" has caused. The goal is to narrow the criticism into an academic zone, says Peng. By the end of the meeting Peng asks Liu and Deng Xiao-ping to cosign a letter in support of "The Report." The next day both the letter and the paper are submitted to Mao.

My husband expresses no objection to "The Report." In fact, he never allows himself to get into a position where he must give a black or white answer. Mao understands that a rejection would mean rejecting ninety percent of his cabinet members. Mao lives to play the savior, not the executioner.

In the future Mao will always be remembered for his good deeds. For example, the widespread story of his attendance at Marshal Chen Yi's funeral in 1975. That he arrived in his pajamas demonstrated how he hurried to get there. The viewers were led to believe in the sincerity of Mao's sorrow. Nevertheless, the truth is that Mao could have saved the marshal's life by uttering a simple "no" to stop the Red Guards from torturing him to death.

This is not to say that I have reservations about my husband's tactics. I am with him. He is a great man, a visionary, who dreams a great dream for his nation. The goal of revolution is paradise. I have always understood that "Revolution is one class overthrowing the other by violent action" — we have all put our lives on the line.

The game continues. Mao is set to sweep his opposition. At the Party gatherings, Mao smiles and chats with Liu and Deng. He asks about their families and jokes about Deng's habit of playing poker. Mao has the ability to verbally disarm, to charm and to make his victims abandon their suspicions until they become an open door. Then he strikes.

The mayor of Beijing, Peng Zhen, is thrilled that Chairman Mao has no comments on "The Report." He assumes that he has Mao's support. The news puts Vice Chairman Liu and Deng Xiao-ping at ease.

I know my husband. He might pretend to be ill and withdrawn, but he'll come back and take his enemy by storm. It is what he is doing now. Planning the battle, rearranging his chessboard. He believes that the future of China is at stake. He believes that he is dealing with a coup d'état, that his army is rebelling. He believes that he has the allegiance of only one force from the northern provinces, led by the sickly Marshal Lin.

For years Lin has played all kinds of tricks in order to win Mao's favor. About his behavior, his colleague Marshal Luo Rei-qing is not only disgusted but criticizes him as a hypocrite.

I have come to know Lin through Kang Sheng. Kang Sheng says that Lin Biao is a bride who has been waiting for her wedding day all her life, and now she has gotten the ring.

I visit the Lin family. I mention Marshal Luo. I say Luo is now our shared enemy.

What's your story? asks Lin.

I'd like to have an official position in the Party. I thought Marshal Luo was my husband's close friend and might be willing to lend me a hand. I'd like to get the army to participate in the Cultural Revolution.

What happened?

Marshal Luo turned me down. I am too embarrassed to describe the details — he wouldn't even let me take a uniform!

You don't have to go on, Madame Mao. I know what to do about it. Why don't you come to my headquarters and open a seminar?

February 20, 1966. In a brand-new uniform, Madame Mao Jiang Ching delivers a speech against "The Report." It is the first time in her life she holds a meeting attended by the heads of state and men of the armed forces. She experiences stage fright. But she is confident. Afterwards she informs Mao of what she has done. He congratulates her.

From then on Lin Biao and Madame Mao Jiang Ching visit each other frequently. They form an alliance to help get rid of each other's enemies.

After my speech Lin's headquarters produces a booklet. It is entitled *The Summary of Discussions Held by Comrade Jiang Ching and Sponsored by Comrade Lin Biao*. It is the text of my speech. The subtitle is *On the Role of the Arts in the Army*. In short, *The Summary*.

*Comrade Jiang Ching is the model member of our Party,* Marshal Lin's hand printing reads on the cover page. *She has made tremendous contributions and sacrifices for our country. The Cultural Revolution has provided an opportunity for her to demonstrate leadership. She shines as a political talent.*

Mao is pleased with *The Summary*. I have claimed Maoism to be the greatest and only theory of the Chinese Communist Party.

In the next four weeks Mao calls me four times to personally revise *The Summary*. In April Mao issues an order to make *The Summary* the handbook of every member of the Communist Party.

*

I touch you with these hands, I put them on your burning cheeks so they will be cool.

I look in the mirror and embrace myself for what I have gone through. Taking off my glasses I see a pair of swollen eyes.

I've made you weep, I've made you love and I've made you cartwheel on the tips of knives. You were a winter fan, a summer stove — no one desired you. But now your time has come.

My new role helps me understand happiness in a different light. It is beyond lust and companionship, beyond the ordinary notion of love. I have run the earth out in wildness and know that every human being in essence is alone. I have decided to push aside silence and answer music. I have made myself an exuberant fountain.

In my heart's land the gold summer's fierce sun is thrusting through the leaves.

Can you see lily stems stand green and tall and bees collect nectar from an endless line of clover?

On March 28 Mao hosts a secret meeting in his study. The only attendants are Jiang Ching, Kang Sheng and Chun-qiao. Mao calls it a Politburo meeting although its official members, Vice Chairman Liu, Premier Zhou, Commander in Chief Zhu De, Vice Premier Chen Yun and Deng, are excluded.

The meeting lasts three full days. Mao points out that Mayor Peng's report has failed to carry out the principles of Communism. *It's time to rebel,* Mao instructs. *The old Politburo no longer works for the revolution. Down with the Cultural Bureau and the Mayor's Committee of Beijing. Let's send the devils to hell and liberate the ghosts!*

Mao turns to Chun-qiao and asks how long it will take to arrange articles of criticism against "The Report."

April 2 and 5, Chun-qiao replies.

In *People's Daily* and *The Red Flag*?

Yes, it shall serve to launch a nationwide attack.

Just as Mao used to in battle he assigns Kang Sheng as a backup force. Make sure to get rid of any dog who dares to block the way.

After the meeting they are exhausted. She observes him quietly. He sits in the rattan chair and rests his head against its back. Tears come to her eyes. She feels the leaping of time. She remembers the moment when he sat in the same pose contemplating the conquest of China. She is so in love with him that she breathes carefully, fearing to disturb his thoughts.

She quietly goes through the notes of the meeting. The silence in the room delights her. She knows that he is comfortable with her. The way they used to be with each other in Yenan. The contentment, the togetherness.

Let's take a walk in the Summer Palace, he suddenly says and gets up.

She follows him without a word. She notices that he is wearing a pair of new leather shoes. She remembers that he hates new shoes. She asks if he wants to change into cotton sandals.

They don't hurt, he explains. Little Dragon has been my walking-shoe stretcher.

The Hall of Pines used to be a large courtyard of ancient trees. There are archways on its east, west and north sides. Also exquisitely carved pillar stones. The couple walks slowly through the trees. They are now on the central imperial path running parallel to a lake. It is the path on which Emperor Hsien Feng and Empress Tzu Hsi used to stroll. The path is narrow and is shaded by tall cypresses.

She follows his footsteps. After a mile the Glazed Tile Pagoda of Many Treasures comes into view. The pagoda is a seven-story, eight-sided building more than fifty feet high. It is inlaid from top to bottom with glazed bricks of blue, green and yellow. Multiple carvings of Buddha embellish the brickwork. The pagoda rests on a white stone platform and is crowned with a gilded pinnacle.

There is a melodious sound in the wind. Mao looks up. From the top of the pagoda hang bronze bells. She comes to his side. Wiping her damp forehead she praises his good health. He makes no comment and enters the pagoda. He doesn't pause as he passes a stone tablet on which is carved ODE TO THE IMPERIALLY BUILT PAGODA OF MANY TREASURES OF LONGEVITY HILL. The characters are in Chinese, Manchu, Mongolian and Tibetan. He comes to a stop before the statues of the Buddha.

I have come here twice already this month, he suddenly says. I have come to see if I can channel an understanding between the builder of this pagoda and myself.

His voice is low and she can barely hear him. But she says nothing.

He continues. My question is, Why did the man install over nine hundred statues of Buddha on the face of this tiny temple? What motivated him? What kind of madness? Was he panic-stricken? What was chasing him? It is a dangerous spot in which to work. He could fall any time. He might have fallen just so. Why? It seems to me Buddha was his protection — the more he built the better he thought himself protected. He must have been chased by this idea. He must have been breathless in this race with himself.

She suddenly senses that Mao is speaking of himself. About his position in the Politburo. The enemies he faces. He is in fear.

Chairman! she calls. I am with you heading to heaven or hell!

He turns toward her, his eyes filled with gentleness.

She feels that she is recognized the way she used to be recognized thirty years ago in the cave of Yenan. She hears her own voice once again proclaiming love between the dropping of bombs.

In her dedication he once again recognizes himself as a hero. Slowly his gaze diffuses. His voice becomes low. I wish that it was all just in my head. An old fart, paranoid for no reason. I wish that it were just the popping of my teeth I'm upset about. You won't believe that I clapped this morning when I made a smooth shit. A stupid thing, yet it controls my mood. I am losing my sight too, Jiang Ching. Now please tell me that what I feel isn't true — that I am old and I am going down the imperial drain.

She feels for him but is not unhappy. The truth is that his fear has made him see her. She needs to have the danger continue in order to be able to stay in his view.

Lead me to the fire! she says to him. Give me a chance to demonstrate how much I can and will do for love.

He reaches for her.

Once again she feels the presence of Lady Yuji. The worship comes back and charges itself. She reenters the scene. The lovers walk around the eight sides of Buddha statues surveying the nine hundred blue, green and yellow gods. The lovers are no longer in each other's arms and their lips do not caress, but they speak and begin to hear each other. They are taking turns describing the numberless beasts around them, obscure workers of the land, terrible innocents, killers and their dreams, the gigantic swarming of bees, the way they silently mate and murder.

Oh, heaven knows how much I feel for you! she cries in a theatrical voice. The line is stylish and self-moving. Command me, Chairman, here is my sword.

No more operating solo. No more living life in splendid isolation. My body has never felt so youthful. On April 9, I am bored listening to Mayor Peng Zhen's nonsubstantial self-criticisms. I leave the matter to Kang Sheng and Chen Bo-da, a critic executioner whom I recently recruited, and who is also the director of the Institute of Marxism and Leninism in Beijing. I send a report prepared by Chen Bo-da on Peng Zheng entitled "The 5.16 Notification" to Mao. By now I sense that Mao has set his mind on bringing down Vice Chairman Liu — punishing Mayor Peng, Liu's front man, is Mao's first step.

As expected, Mao comments on the report and orders the battle to be fought publicly.

May 4. A meeting finalizing Mayor Peng's fall takes place. The host is not Mao, but Vice Chairman Liu. Liu is given no option. He is incapable of bringing himself to rebel against Mao. At the meeting Liu looks pale. He takes deep breaths when he delivers the speech denouncing his friend. He reads in the name of the Politburo. He can barely sustain his performance. Peng has been a faithful employee and an ardent supporter of his programs.

Vice Chairman Liu never dreams that he will be the next. If he had spent time reading *The Romance of the Three Kingdoms* as Mao had, he might have anticipated his leader's plans.

To please Mao, on May 8, under the pen name Gao Ju — High Torch — I published an article entitled "Toward the Anti-Communist Party Group: Fire!" It is my first publication in thirty years. The article becomes the talk of the nation. Shouts of *To guard Chairman Mao with our lives!* are heard everywhere.

It is the night of May 9. I am losing sleep to joy. I have taken fate into my own hands and am rewarded. Mao phoned this morning to congratulate me. He wanted me to have a pack of his ginseng. The phone rang again in the afternoon. It was Mao's secretary. Mao wanted me to come for dinner. Nah is home, the message said.

I have nothing to wear, I said.

The secretary was confused. Does that mean "no"?

\*

Sitting in my chair I feel my body shiver. He wants me, finally. All the years of resentment dissolve in one phone call. Am I crazy? Is he fooling me again? Or is it nothing but part of his aging? Or am I daydreaming? He has not stopped his longevity practice and continues to sleep with young girls; and yet he wants to reconnect with me. And he wants it badly.

Sometimes I feel that I know him well enough to forgive him — he is driven not by passion or lust or even his great love of country, but fear. Other times I feel that he has always been a stranger to me. An aloof, emotionally disconnected being like myself. He has never paid a single visit to his ex-wife Zi-zhen, or to his mentally disturbed second son Anqing in their hospitals. Just like me with my mother — I have never tried to find out what became of her.

Mao doesn't talk about the Korean War. It is to avoid his pain of missing Anying, his older son, who died from an American bomb. Mao has never recovered from Anying's death. Madame Mao Jiang Ching knows that Anying is always on his mind at moments of celebration, especially during Chinese New Years. Mao never accepts invitations to visit his friends or associates. It is because he can't stand the warmth of families. He says that he is an anti-tradition man. It is because everything traditional weaves around the family.

How can Mao not feel the loss or have sympathy toward pain and separation when he is such a passionate poet? One can only guess that his pain over the years has changed or, a more precise word, distorted his character. His longing for his losses gradually turns into envy of others' gain. Why does Vice Chairman Liu have all that he hasn't? Mao knows that he is by nature fragile and that to learn to be a stone-Buddha is his only way to survive. He takes tragedy in his life as his body's ulcer — he just has to live with it. Yet he is frustrated that he has no power to cure his pain. He doesn't understand that he owes himself compassion. He has taught himself to recognize no such word in his emotional dictionary.

It is after dinner. We are relaxing around the table having tea. Nah begs that we not talk about business, a request I must turn down. I count on the time I spend with Mao, because he may change his mind tomorrow. I have trained myself to always be prepared for the worst.

Nah dashes out of the room. Where are you going? I yell. Don't tell me you are going to waste time on knitting. Did you call the people I asked you to call for me? Answer me! You are sixteen years old, not six!

Leave her alone, her father says. He has had some wine and is in a good mood. He is in his usual pajamas and wears socks without sandals. The room is heated but still feels cold and empty. It doesn't seem like a home. It is more like a war headquarters with books, cigarette butts, towels and mugs lying carelessly around. He is comfortable with this on-the-move style. The walls are bare. I can't tell their original color. The color of dust. The floor is made of large gray-blue bricks. I once suggested that he install a wooden floor but he didn't want to bother. He still uses a mosquito net in the summer. His staff made one as big as a circus tent.

I have an important task for you, he says and puts down his tea.

My eyes widen and my lips tremble in excitement.

I have discussed with Kang Sheng that you will be the best candidate to take command on the ideology side of my business. What do you think?

For you, Mao Tse-tung, if your bomb misses a fuse I'll lay down my body.

May 16, after revising "The 5.16 Notification" seven times, Mao puts down his signature and entitles the document "The Man-

ual of the Cultural Revolution." As it goes to press, Mao estab-
lishes a new cabinet apart from the existing Politburo. He calls it
the Headquarters of the Cultural Revolution with himself as the
chief, Jiang Ching as his right-hand person and Kang Sheng, Chen
Bo-da and Chun-qiao as his key advisors.

From that moment on China is run by Madame Mao Jiang
Ching with Mao behind her every move.

# 17

JUNE 1966. MY BURNING SUMMER. Although the path is rough, the future looks bright. In the past my name lacked authority. The opera producers and critics showed me little respect. They rewrote my scripts. I had to fight for every line and note. The ordinary folks thought of me as Mao's house-wife. Except in Shanghai where Chun-qiao was in control, no one printed my words. Now that I have Mao's support, everyone is competing for my attention. The press, in my opinion, is like an infant — whoever offers it a nipple will be called mother. Cheap.

In Mao's name I organize a national festival — the Festival of Revolutionary Operas. I select potential operas and adapt them to serve Mao's purpose. I arrange talented artists to upgrade the pieces into high-quality extravaganzas, such as *Taking the Tiger Mountain by Wit* and *The Sha Family Pond*. I make the operas bear my signature and personally supervise every detail, from the selection of the actors to the way a singer hits the note.

There are quick learners and stubborn minds. I have to deal with them all. Not a day passes that I don't feel my enemy's shadow. When the resistance becomes strong and my projects face danger I phone Mao. This morning a couple of my play-wrights have been taken away from their work. They were put into a detention house under an order placed by my enemy. The reason was vague — "They have not served the people with their hearts and souls." I have no idea who exactly is in charge of the opposition. Everything is done through students. There is a war zone here. My enemy has many faces. The students are being manipulated.

Mao comforts me by offering substantial help. Launch a campaign, he says. Establish your own force. Go to universities and speak at public rallies on my behalf. The goal is to get the students on our side.

The thirty-seven-day festival turns out to be a great success. Three hundred thirty thousand people are received. To add excitement Mao and his new cabinet attend my closing ceremony. Standing next to Mao in a brand-new grass-green army uniform I clap. When the curtain descends I weep in happiness. With "The Manual of the Cultural Revolution" being distributed in every commune, factory, campus and street, I have established my leadership. On my order, students, workers and peasants challenge the authorities. At rallies I recite Mao's poem into the microphone:

> The brave winter plums blossom in the snow
> Only the pitiful flies cry and freeze themselves to death!

The opposition shows no sign of quitting. Vice Chairman Liu organizes his own counterattack groups. His messengers are called the Work Team. Their purpose is to put out the "wildfires" — to destroy Madame Mao.

Yet she is not worried. Mao has confirmed his desire to beat Liu. Mao is determined to set Vice Chairman Liu himself on fire.

Last night she dreamed. She fumbled her way into her lover's arms, sobbing piteously. He comforted her as if she were a child. Her tears soaked into his shirt.

This morning they have breakfast together. Being in each other's presence has become a way to show affection. She doesn't tell him about her dream. His face is calm and patient. They eat quietly. He has bread and porridge with hot pepper, and she has milk and fruit with a piece of toast. The servants stand like trees. They watch the masters eating. If it were in her residence she would send them away. Mao is not bothered. He likes to have guards and servants standing in every corner of the room while he eats. He can be perfectly at ease having bowel movements in front of his guard.

So what is going on with the students? Mao asks, drinking up his ginseng soup noisily.

I've scouted a young man from Qinghua University, a seventeen-year-old chemistry student. His name is Kuai Da-fu.

I take pleasure in describing Kuai Da-fu. I discuss him as if he were my son. He has a thin face and an intense character. He has a pair of raccoon eyes and a large nose. His lips remind me of a dry riverbed. Mao laughs at this remark.

Go on, he says. Go on.

He is shy, vulnerable and yet full of passion. His frame is not strong. He is almost delicate. But he has the charisma of a teen idol. When he speaks, his eyes sparkle and his face blushes. Although he is inexperienced, his ambition and determination will guarantee him success.

Mao pushes away his bowl and lies back in his chair. He wants to know how I came to lay my eyes on him.

It was his reaction to "The 5.16 Notification," I explain. He created a big-character poster that attacked the head of the Work Team, a man named Yelin. He called Yelin a capitalism promoter. As a result he was expelled by the school and put under house arrest for eighteen days.

But the young man has committed no crime! Mao argues loudly as if to a crowd.

Yes, Kuai Da-fu admitted no guilt, Madame Mao continues. Instead, he formed a one-person hunger demonstration.

What fine material!

I thought so too.

He must be inspiring to others.

What should I do?

Visit him!

That is exactly what I did. I sent my agent Comrade Dong — you probably don't remember him, he used to work for Kang Sheng and is loyal. He looks so ordinary and boring that he blends into the crowds without arousing any suspicion.

Yes?

I told him that he has my support and yours. I asked him to hang on and take the opportunity to set himself as an example to the nation's youth.

It is at this moment Mao leans over and puts his hand on my shoulder. Rubbing gently he whispers, I feel blessed having you by my side. Are you exhausted? I don't want to work you to death. How about a vacation? I am leaving tomorrow. Would you like to come along?

I'd love to. But you need someone to stay in Beijing. You need me to control the situation.

Mao has been avoiding Vice Chairman Liu's calls, he has gone as far as Wuhan in Hubei Province. But Liu follows him. Insisting on reporting Beijing's trouble. The student riots. The wildfires. He begs Mao to order a stop. Liu has no idea what he has gotten himself into.

No historian can understand how a brilliant man like Liu could be so ignorant. How is it possible that he doesn't see Mao's irritation? There can only be two explanations. One is that he is so humble that he never sees himself as a threat to Mao. The other is that he is so confident that he doesn't think Mao has any reason to object to his actions. In other words he has already seen himself

running China, seen the people and the Party congress voting for
him over Mao.

About Vice Chairman Liu's report Mao makes no comment.
When Liu begs him to return to Beijing, Mao refuses. Before de-
parting Liu asks for Mao's instruction. Mao drops a phrase: *Do-
what-you-see-fit.*

When Liu gets back to the capital his eagerly awaited cabinet
members greet him at the train station. Liu explains his puzzle-
ment over Mao. The cabinet tries to analyze the situation. If Liu
chooses to let it be, which means allowing Madame Mao Jiang
Ching and Kang Sheng to go on sweeping the country, Mao can
come back and fire him for not doing his job. But if he stops Jiang
Ching and Kang Sheng, Mao might take their side. After all she is
his wife.

After a nerve-racking discussion, Liu and Deng decide to send
more Work Teams to reestablish order. To assure the correctness
of his action Liu dials Mao's line. Again there is no response.

By now schools have been closed nationwide. The students
copy their hero Kuai Da-fu and crowd the streets with big-character posters. *Promote the revolution!* has become the hottest slogan. To impress each other the students begin to attack pedestri-
ans who they suspect are from the upper class. They strip clothes
made of silk, tear narrow-bottom pants and cut pointed leather
shoes. The police are under attack as "reactionary machines" and
are paralyzed. The students and workers form factions and begin
to attack each other over the control of territories. The nation's
economy comes to a halt.

At the Politburo meeting in Beijing Vice Chairman Liu's voice is
hoarse. In front of his entire cabinet he again dials Mao's line: The
chaos must be stopped at once, Chairman.

Mao's response comes cold and indifferent. I am not ready to
come back to Beijing. Why don't you go ahead with your plans?

May I have your permission?

You have been running the country, haven't you?

With this Liu gets back to work again. Hundreds more Work Teams are sent. Within two months the wildfires have been put out.

July 8, 1966. Mao writes me. The letter is sent from his hometown, Shao Shan in Hunan Province. He tells me a story of an ancient character named Zhong Kui, a hero who is known for catching evil spirits.

*Since the sixties I have become the Communist Zhong Kui.* He goes on to describe himself as an international rebel — he knows that I have an affection for rebels and bandits. *Things have their limits. What do you expect by getting to the top but that you begin to go downwards? I have been long prepared to fight until all my bones are ground into powder. There are over a hundred Communist Parties in the entire world. Most of them have quit Marxism and Leninism to embrace capitalism. We are the only Party left. We must deal with the cruelty of such reality, we must figure out what our enemies are up to, and we must act ahead to survive.*

I see my husband's perspective. I understand what is at stake and feel his determination to destroy the enemy. I see where I stand. Once again I have become a comrade in arms. During the day I am all over Beijing. I have developed hundreds of projects and they are all going on at the same time. Once in a while my body fails to catch up with me. It breaks down with fever. At those moments I send for Nah and she comes to my bedside.

Nah tries to hold me back. She doesn't understand why I have to risk my health. She doesn't see the point. I can barely express it myself. A woman like me thrives on living life to its fullest. I have cast my lot with her father. His dreams, his love and his life. I cannot bear the thought of being abandoned again. There is no logic behind the matter. Mao is simply my curse. I would never wish a love like this for my daughter. It is just too hard. I am driven by a fatal impulse. Like a bruised salmon I swim against the current to find my way back to the birth river. I worry that if I stop for only a second, Mao might turn away and my life will fall apart.

With Chun-qiao and Kang Sheng's help I alert the press to stand by. I tell the heads that the situation might change at any given moment. Chairman Mao is contemplating his final decision. On July 17, I dial Mao's line and leave a message. *The situation in Beijing has ripened.* The next day, Mao's train zips back to Beijing. It catches everyone by surprise.

The same night, Vice Chairman Liu hurries to see Mao. But Mao's bodyguard blocks him. The Chairman has retired for the evening. But Liu notices that there are other cars parked on the driveway. Obviously there are guests.

Liu begins to sense his fate. He goes back home and discusses his fear with his wife. The two have a sleepless night. At midnight they talk about whether to wake up the children to leave their will. They change their minds because they convince themselves that Mao is the leader of the Communist Party, not a feudal king. But still they are restless. They sit in the cold and wait for the day to dawn. Before daybreak Liu is suddenly scared.

I am old, he says.

The woman opens herself up to hold the man. She feels his body tremble slightly. You are doing all you can for the interest of China, she says gently. Would you pay the price if there is one?

The man says yes.

You are stubborn.

It was our marriage vow.

I haven't forgotten. She lays her head on his chest. I swore that I would proudly collect your head if you are slaughtered for your belief.

Fear gives way to courage. The next day the Lius convey their fears to Deng and the rest of their friends. The cold air is now in everyone's lungs. Some members begin to plan their escape while the rest wait.

I am alone with my husband. He sent for me and only me. To be with me is his way of rewarding me. He expects me to appreciate it and I do. Six months ago I was crying, What's the body that is empty of a soul?

I am fifty-two years old and I have a spiritual marriage with Mao.

Outside there is a symphony of crickets. Tonight it sounds magnificent. Mao and I sit facing each other. The tea is getting cold, but our feelings have just warmed up. It's past midnight and he is not tired, nor am I. He is in his robe and I am in an army uniform. It doesn't matter what I wear now. But I still come carefully dressed. I want to resemble the way I looked back in Yenan.

In the rattan chair he sits like a big ship stuck on the rocks. His belly is a carry-around table. He rests his tea mug on the "table." His face is getting puffier. His spider-web wrinkles spread out. His eyes are much smaller now. The lines on his face have become feminine. All are beautiful to me.

You have done a terrific job in keeping me informed, he says, lighting up a cigarette.

I tell him not to mention it. You have my loyalty forever.

My colleagues call me a madman. What do you think?

Stalin and Chiang Kai-shek used to call you the same thing, didn't they? It's part of the hysteria — your rivals are jealous of your dominance. But the truth is no one saves China but Mao Tse-tung.

No, no, no, listen, you've got to listen to me, something is happening. I am not the man you used to know. Come and sit by me. Yes, just like this.

We chat. He tells me of his long waking nights. How he suspects an ongoing conspiracy. He describes his horror of not being able to control the situation. It crystallized when he returned to the capital. When he saw that everything was in order — his absence of five months caused no stir — he panics. You see, Liu has proved to the Party and the citizens that he can run the country without me.

He stops talking. I need to be left alone now. Oh, wait. On second thought, don't go. Stay and finish your tea.

He sits back down. Yes, this is what I am going to do. Got to place an order . . . Are you with me, Jiang Ching? Come closer. There are voices inside my head. I can hear Liu ask what his fault is, and I can hear myself replying: I simply can't sleep when I hear your footsteps walking around my bed.

I wait until my husband finishes his monologue. What do you think? he asks again. He looks at me eagerly.

I can't come up with a response. I have lost my concentration. I begin to improvise my answer. I speak in my usual style. It is your vision that will lead China to greatness. I say that the hostility is part of the business. Conspiracy comes as a package of high power. I smile. Anyway, dear Chairman, we are here to celebrate living.

I feel rather out of place. His mood suddenly changes. I am tired, he says. You have to go now.

I bid him good-bye and walk toward the door.

Jiang Ching, he calls, getting up from the rattan chair. Do you believe that we are capable of driving people to the horizon of a great existence?

Yes, I reply. We will grow a tremendous red honeysuckle and populate the sky with it.

The next morning Vice Chairman Liu visits Mao in his study. Liu is not only anxious but nervous. Mao greets him warmly. Mao jokes about his trip. Liu is affected by Mao's humor and lightness. He begins to relax. But when they sit down, Mao's tune changes.

It was a rather sad scene when I got off the train, Mao begins. School gates were closed. There weren't any people in the streets. The mass activity used to be like bamboo shoots in spring — shooting up in good spirits. But it is out of sight now. Who has put out the wildfires? Who has repressed the students? Who is afraid of the people? It used to be the warlords, Chiang Kai-shek and the reactionaries. Mao makes a motion striking his arms and speaks loudly. Those who repress the students will end up being destroyed themselves.

Vice Chairman Liu is stunned with disbelief. Mao becomes a stranger in his eyes. Painfully Liu questions his own ability and judgment. He can't imagine Mao being the organizer of the coup d'état of his own government.

Student Kuai Da-fu from Qinghua University has become a national Maoist icon. He has proven himself a talented organizer. He has grown taller since I last saw him. When I point this out to him, he is embarrassed. It makes me like him even better. His behavior reflects my effort. Kang Sheng says Kuai Da-fu is my pet. I can't disagree. The young man needs help in building self-confidence. I tell Kuai Da-fu that he shouldn't worry about being inexperienced. Chairman Mao started his rebellion when he was the same age. I praise Kuai Da-fu and encourage his every step. You have a true understanding of Maoism. You are a natural leader.

I like to watch Kuai Da-fu when he speaks to his fellow students. Part of his attractiveness comes from his awkwardness. His face turns from pale pink to red and then blue. He doesn't know enough, but he tries hard to be taken seriously. He has turned eighteen today. To put gas in his ego tank, Kang Sheng goes out of his way to help. He follows Kuai Da-fu and shouts slogans. He shows the crowd that Kuai Da-fu has a direct connection to Mao.

The boy is near the sun. The boy is golden. The students long to be given the same power and respect as their leader, Kuai Da-fu. The eager ones have already set themselves up to get noticed. Their names are Tan Hou-lan from Beijing Teachers University, Han Ai-jin from Beijing Aviation Institute, Wang Da-bin from Beijing College of Geology and the forty-year-old little-known literary critic Nie Yuan-zi. They each lead their schools and work hard to please Madame Mao Jiang Ching. Like hundreds and thousands of bees swarming to attack an animal, they try to kick the Work Teams off the campuses. There is resistance. The Work Teams insist on setting the classes back in order. Fights break out while the tension continues to mount.

Appointed by Vice Chairman Liu, the head of the Work Teams, Yelin, stands firm. Although he has released Kuai Da-fu from house arrest, Yelin has gone to Liu and Deng and obtained permission to criticize Kuai Da-fu as a negative example. While Yelin begins his public criticism, Madame Mao Jiang Ching and Kang Sheng come to Kuai Da-fu's rescue. Without notifying Yelin, Jiang Ching and Kang Sheng call up a student rally and demand that the Work Teams disperse.

Yelin begins to understand that the fight is not just between him and the students. Higher powers are involved. Something he has refused to believe is happening. To avoid confrontation, Yelin leaves the campus and goes to hide at the headquarters of the People's Liberation Army, where he originally came from.

Kuai Da-fu is determined to live up to Madame Mao Jiang Ching's expectation. He has organized a student body into an army called the Jing-gang Mountain Group. The students proclaim themselves soldiers and sing "Unity Is Power" day in and day out from campus to campus. They are joined by thousands of other students from outer provinces. The Jing-gang Mountain Group is now a 600,000-member organization with Kuai Da-fu as its commander in chief.

To demonstrate his power Kuai Da-fu takes a group of students to the headquarters of the People's Liberation Army. He demands Yelin. When blocked by the guards the students form a sound-wall. *Down with Yelin!* they shout. The guards hold their rifles and pay no attention. No trick Kuai Da-fu plays can make the guards open the gate.

The students begin to sing Mao-quotation songs. *It's good to rebel, it's right to rebel, and it's necessary to rebel!* The guards play deaf. The students sing louder, they begin to climb onto the gate.

The soldiers line up and raise their rifles to aim.

The students turn to Kuai Da-fu.

*Catch Yelin and get respect!* the hero shouts, remembering what made his name. He climbs on top of the gate and stands erect. Forming his palms into a megaphone, he suddenly declares a hunger demonstration. He then leaps off the human wall and lands on the concrete ground. He lies down like a dead fish and closes his eyes. Behind him a thousand bodies stretch flat across the ground.

It is ten o'clock in the morning when I receive a report from my agent, Mr. Dong. I had sent him to secretly check on the students. I asked him to send my regards to Kuai Da-fu. I have ordered water from nearby hospitals to be infused with glucose and delivered to the students.

I have the operator connect me to my friend Lin Biao, whom Mao recently has appointed as the vice chairman of the Communist Party.

What's up?

I need your help, Marshal Lin.

Speak up, please.

Your employee Yelin is giving my kids from Qinghua University a hard time. The kids just want a word with him but the guards don't understand. The kids are undergoing a hunger strike.

What are you going to do with Yelin?

I'm going to criticize him as a capitalism promoter.

A capitalism promoter? I have never heard of such a title.

My dear Vice Chairman, once the kids get Yelin, they will hold a stadium-size rally to criticize him under that title. They will shout out the phrase officially.

Over the phone I hear Lin placing an order. I hear him yell, I don't care whether or not Yelin is sick. If he can't move, send him out on a stretcher!

After she puts Yelin in Kuai Da-fu's hands, she begins to plan bigger battles. On July 29, she opens a 2,000-person rally at the Grand Hall of the People to honor the Cultural Revolution activists. Invitations are sent to all high-ranking officers including Vice Chairman Liu, Deng and Premier Zhou. The rally once again denounces the Work Teams. Liu, Deng and Zhou are pressed to give criticisms, to which they reluctantly agree. Both Deng and Zhou give nonsubstantial speeches. The words are dry and copied from newspapers. But Vice Chairman Liu doesn't give in easily. In his speech he leaves questions to the crowd. How to carry out the Cultural Revolution? I have no idea. Many of you claim that you are not clear either. What's going on? I am not clear about the nature of my mistake. I have not realized the greatness of the Cultural Revolution.

Do you see how we are rejected? Madame Mao Jiang Ching says, grabbing the microphone as she gets up on the stage. The crowd's clapping becomes thunderlike. Madame Mao continues, her voice resonant. She suggests that the crowd take a look at the streamer above their heads, which reads: *Is the Cultural Revolution a spare-time activity or a full-time job?*

Do you see how our enemies use every chance to put out the revolutionary wildfires? And do you understand why Chairman Mao has to worry?

Liu responds. He emphasizes the discipline and the rules of the Communist Party. He says that no one should be above the Party.

Madame Mao is challenged.

I see people agree with Liu. Murmuring rises in the crowd. The youths start to argue among themselves. The representatives of factions get on the stage and present their views one by one. The tone of the speakers begins to change. Sentence by sentence they echo or simply take Liu's side.

My rally is backfiring! I sit on the panel's seat and start to panic. I look toward Kang Sheng, who is sitting at the end of the bench, for help. He gives me a look that says *Stay calm* and then slips from his seat. After a short while he is back. He passes me a note: "*Mao is on his way here.*"

Before I can tell Kang Sheng how relieved I am, Mao appears by the curtain. Clapping his hands, he bluntly pushes his way onto the stage. He is instantly recognized. The crowd boils: *Long live Chairman Mao!*

I hold my breath and shout with the crowd.

Mao doesn't say anything. He doesn't slow down either. He walks and claps his way from the left side of the stage to the right and disappears like a ghost.

The crowd is instantly reminded that Madame Mao Jiang Ching is backed by her man.

August 1. She and Mao meet again in his study. He tells her that he has written a letter in response to an organization called the Red Guards. I am adding new divisions to your force. He sits her down. I am giving you wings. The students are from the Middle

School of Qinghua University. They are even younger than your kids. They can't wait to do what your kids are doing.

I like the title the Red Guards. It shows guts. Red, the color of the revolution, and Guards, your defender. Have you given them any inscription?

I have. A red armband with my calligraphy, *Red Guards,* on it.

She asks him if she can join him to inspect the Red Guards' representatives. I'd like to offer my support. She is welcomed. I have it scheduled on August 18, he says. Show up with me at the Gate of Heavenly Peace in Tiananmen Square.

Dawn, August 18, 1966. Tiananmen Square is packed with one and a half million students and workers. It is an ocean of red flags. The entire Boulevard of Long Peace is blocked by youths from all over the country. Everyone wears a red armband with Mao's yellow calligraphic *Red Guards.* The crowd extends miles, from the Gate of Xin-hua to the Security Building, from the Golden Water Bridge to the Imperial Front Gate. Upon the news of Mao's inspection, hundreds and thousands of student organizations have changed their title overnight into Red Guards, including Kuai Da-fu's faction the Jing-gang Mountain Group. The green uniform and red armband on the left arm is the look. The crowd sings: *The golden sun rises in the East. A long life to our great leader and savior Chairman Mao.*

Eleven o'clock. In the midst of the melody of "The East is Red" comes stormy clapping. The million and a half shout. Tears pour. Some bite their sleeves to hold their cries. Mao appears on top of the Gate of Heavenly Peace. He moves slowly toward the bars at the edge of the platform. He wears the same identical army uniform and armband as the youths. The cap with a red star on the top sits on his big head. He walks in the middle with Madame Mao Jiang Ching on his right and Marshal Lin Biao on his left. They wear the same costumes as Mao.

*

I feel that my life is so complete that I can die in happiness. The crowd pushes us like morning tides. It is my first time being seen in public with Mao shoulder to shoulder. The king and his lady. We are wrapped by the waves of sound. *Long live Chairman Mao and salute to Comrade Jiang Ching!*

Still moving we come down the gate toward the crowd. The security guards line up to form a human path to assure our way. We pay no attention to colleagues behind. The two of us stride along the bar, looking down at the ocean of the rocking heads.

*Long live!*

*Ten thousand years of long life!*

We are descending. Suddenly, as if seized by emotion, Mao stops short and walks back up the gate. He walks quickly all the way to the right corner and leans against the bar. Taking off his cap he strikes his arms and shouts, *Long live my people!*

I am ready to climb a mountain made of knives for Chairman Mao, young Kuai Da-fu swears at a meeting where Madame Mao Jiang Ching arranges for him to meet Chun-qiao. It doesn't take long for Chun-qiao to enlighten him.

When will time mature? Kuai Da-fu asks.

Listen to your heart's call, Madame Mao answers. What does Chairman Mao teach us?

Pull up the weeds by the roots.

Here we go.

Seek the biggest root, says Chun-qiao.

We need a breakthrough, nods Madame Mao Jiang Ching.

Midnight, January 13, 1967. Mao has a warm meeting with Vice Chairman Liu at the Grand Hall of the People. The next day Liu is arrested and held overnight by the Red Guards.

It is not the end of Liu, but it is a strong punch in the stomach. In Mao's world one is put in constant confusion and terror. Throughout the Cultural Revolution Mao makes Jiang Ching believe that she is inheriting China. What's hidden from her is that Mao makes the same promise to others, including those whom she considers his enemies, Deng Xiao-ping and Marshal Ye Jian-ying. When Deng is made to believe that he has a hold on the nation's power, Mao switches and passes the power key to another man.

Madame Mao knows her husband's tactics as well as anyone. But during this season of fever she believes she is exempt. She thinks of herself as the prime mover of Mao's salvation. She plays her role with such conviction that she has lost herself. She sacrifices more than she knows.

I am concerned about Nah. I ask her to help me control the military. She has graduated from the People's University with an advanced degree in history. But Nah is a crooked seed that won't sprout. To help her I ask Marshal Lin to introduce me personally to Wu Fa-xian, the commander of the air force. I ask if Wu can offer Nah a position as a senior editor at *The Liberation Army*. The favor is granted and Nah goes to work. A few weeks later my daughter tells me that she is bored. No matter how much saliva I waste, she is not going back.

For the past two weeks my worries about Nah have kept me from sleep. I try to get help from Mao but his mood has soured. He is frustrated that he can't generate the public's hatred toward Vice Chairman Liu. Mao thinks that Liu's popularity is a conspiracy itself. Crack the nut! Mao said the last time we are together. He doesn't care about Nah's future. He has asked me to choose between helping him or helping Nah.

Today I am working on someone else's daughter. I am helping Mao. Her name is Tao, the daughter of Vice Chairman Liu from his previous marriage. Tao resents her father's divorce and doesn't get along with her stepmother. I visit Tao and take her out for lunch. I offer her the chance to be a Maoist. I listen to her patiently and direct her thoughts. I press on until she is able to express herself freely without fear.

I think my father is a capitalism promoter, the girl begins.

Yes, Tao, Madame Mao Jiang Ching nods gently. You are getting the justice you deserve. Firm your tone and trim your phrase. Take off the "I think." Say, My father is a capitalism promoter. Say it clearly. Think about how your stepmother made your father abandon your mother. Think about how she takes up your mother's spot in the bed. Recall your misery as a child. Wang Guang-mei ought to pay for your suffering. Don't cry, Tao. I feel your pain. My child, this is your aunt Jiang Ching speaking. Uncle Mao is behind you. Let me tell you, Mao has put out his own big-character poster on August 5. The title is BOMBARD THE HEADQUARTERS. I am sure you know whom he is bombarding, don't you? It is to save your father. To save him from being kicked out of history. You must help him. Uncle Mao and I know that you disagree with your father and stepmother. You are an outcast of the Liu family. Here is your chance to establish yourself as a true revolutionary. Tao, nobody else will speak for you. You must do it for yourself. Catch the light in your dark life, girl. Come on, write your thoughts down and read them at tomorrow's rally.

The girl trembles as she finishes her speech. The title is "The Devil's Soul — In Denouncing My Father Liu Shao-qi." The effect is overwhelming. The story of the Lius' corruption spreads overnight. Colored by rumor and fueled by imagination the monstrous details travel from ear to ear. Cartoons illustrating the Lius as bloodsuckers are all over China's walls and buildings. The couple are described as traitors and Western agents since their cradle days.

August 25. Kuai Da-fu leads five thousand Red Guards to spread leaflets for the upcoming event called "Trial of the Lius." Kuai Da-fu marches across Tiananmen Square and shouts through the amplifiers, *Down, smash, boil and fry Liu Shao-qi and his partner Deng Xiao-ping!*

I am sitting in the greenroom of the Beijing Worker's Stadium. It is eight o'clock in the morning. The stadium is packed with forty thousand Red Guards, students, workers, peasants and soldiers. I have come to test my power. Kuai Da-fu has been in the front cheerleading the crowds. The sound is ear-blasting.

Kuai Da-fu has been holding over fifty members of the congress and Politburo hostage. Among them the mayor of Beijing, the head of the Cultural Bureau, and Luo Rei-qing, the former minister of national defense. They are the men who believe that they needn't respect me because their loyalty toward Mao will make him back them in the event of misunderstanding. Well, we'll see.

Luo Rei-qing is in a manure basket. His leg is broken. He had resisted arrest by jumping off a building. Two Red Guards now carry him up with a shoulder-pole. He looks like an old goat being carried to market. Madame Mao Jiang Ching hears a burst of laughter from the crowd. On the makeshift stage, her enemies are lined up. Their hands are cuffed in the back. Kuai Da-fu gives each subject a dunce cap with his name written on it and crossed out by dripping black ink. In the meantime the crowd sings Mao's teaching: *Revolution is not a dinner party. Revolution is violence.*

She has told Kuai Da-fu that Mao is happy with his achievements. Although she didn't say that Mao wants the men harmed, Kuai Da-fu has figured out what Mao would like to have done.

I shout slogans with Kuai Da-fu. *Mao's teaching is thunder that splits the sky and a volcano that breaks the ocean bed! Mao's teaching is truth!*

Mao has let me see the secret of ruling. Marshal Peng De-huai was a loyalist who once played a key role in establishing the republic. However, Mao told me that it didn't mean that Peng wouldn't turn into an assassin. Mao's ability to adapt to emotional change keeps him safe all these years. I don't see him suffer regrets. He is convinced that heartlessness is the price he has to pay.

She spellbinds the audience. Five hundred thousand Red Guards all over the country are at her command. They are more powerful than the soldiers. They are free-spirited and creative. The meeting lasts for four hours. It ends with the men ridiculed and beaten up. The stubborn Luo lost both of his legs.

Don't stop until we drive the enemies off the edge! Madame Mao shouts hysterically in the greenroom. She is excited and frightened at the same time. Kang Sheng has told her that there are serious rumors going around that her enemies will "finish Mao's woman in her own bed." Kang Sheng has traced the source to the military; this panics Madame Mao even more. The "old boys" like Marshal Ye Jian-ying, Chen Yi, Xu Xiang-qian and Nie Rong-zhen are Vice Chairman Liu's close friends. They are frustrated with Mao's elusive behavior. The anger is so great that the atmosphere in Beijing smokes. The word "kill" is in the air. It is a tradition to make an unfit emperor's concubine the victim. Killing her would teach the emperor a lesson. The tragic love story between Emperor Tang and Concubine Yang is a classic. Killing the woman is a proven method for healing relationships between warlords.

I am learning to kill. I am trying not to shake. There is no middle ground, I tell myself. Kill or be killed. On February 10, 1967, a congressional meeting takes place. The string between the oppositions tightens. The focus is whether or not to acknowledge my leadership in the army; whether Kuai Da-fu and his Red Guards are allowed to open branch offices in the army, and whether the students should be permitted to organize rallies to criticize the army heads. All meetings end up with each side banging the table. Later on a secret letter of petition signed by the "old boys" is delivered to Mao by Marshal Tan Zhen-lin.

I am sure Tan has never imagined that I would get a chance to read the letter. But I do. Mao shows it to me voluntarily. In the letter I am described as a "white-boned demon," a bloodsucker and a bad cloud hanging over the sky of the Communist Party. I am demanded as a sacrifice.

You are left with no choice, Mao says, flipping himself in his indoor swimming pool. He looks like a fat otter. Too much pork with sugar and soy sauce, I think to myself.

What are you going to do? he asks, floating. Marshal Tan says that he has never cried, but now is crying for the Party.

I look around trying to find a place to sit, but there are no chairs. I haven't been to the pool since its renovation. I don't know what Tan means, I say.

Mao dives into the water and then resurfaces. Why don't we read his letter one more time, then?

He is quitting the Party's membership. And he has done three things he regrets in life.

One?

That he is living today . . .

He is ashamed.

Second, he regrets following you and that he became a revolutionary; and third . . .

He regrets ever joining the Communist Party.

Precisely, Chairman.

Mao rolls over and swims with his belly up. It makes him look like he is holding a ball. He closes his eyes and continues to float. After a while he swims toward the edge.

I watch him climb out. The water falls from him in silver streams. He has gained a tremendous amount of weight. The muscles are puffy on his chest and arms. Below his swelling belly, his legs are extremely thin. He picks up a towel and steps into gray shorts.

Call Premier Zhou to arrange a meeting. I'll talk to the old boys on the eighteenth. By the way I want you to join me. Lin Biao and his wife too.

My sky brightens — Mao is picking up the gun himself.

I call up Kang Sheng and Chun-qiao to celebrate the news.

The meeting of historical significance opens on the evening of February 18, 1967. Premier Zhou is the host. Lin's wife Ye and I come early along with Kang Sheng, Chun-qiao and his disciple Yiao Wen-yuan. We sit on the left side of a long table with Mao and Premier Zhou on each end. We are all dressed in the People's Liberation Army uniform.

I am excited and a little nervous. I worry that I don't look tough enough. Ye is better. She is a typical military wife who can bang the table louder than her husband. Since Mao wants Lin to be his successor, Ye has been acting like a second lady. She is careful with me, though. She has learned Wang Guang-mei's lesson. She compliments me on every occasion and invites me to speak at the Institute of the People's Liberation Army. She shows her appreciation.

Ye reminds me of a midwife in my village who powdered her skin with flour in order to make herself look like a city woman with pale skin. Ye never tells me about her background. She avoids the subject when I ask. She is not proud of her origin. I am sure it's low. I am glad that she doesn't speak foreign languages and I am glad that she doesn't like to read. I selfishly feel blessed that she acts a fool when speaking in front of the public. She is a lousy speaker. She once told me that every time she gets up on the stage she gets diarrhea afterwards.

I have been thinking that if I play the game right Ye can be a perfect supporting actress. Her stupidity serves as a foil to my intelligence. For that I am willing to help her. Getting to know her will also make it easier to destroy her in the future if necessary. After all I have no idea how the Lins will treat me after Mao passes away. It won't be hard for them to find an excuse and get rid of me. I am trusting nobody.

At the moment Ye is the woman I need to replace Wang Guang-mei. Ye indulges in rumors. She goes door to door to collect them. She digs up garbage and analyzes her gatherings like a back-yard rat.

Mao gives no greeting when Marshal Chen Yi, Tan Zhen-lin, Ye Jian-ying, Nie Rong-zhen, Xu Xiang-qian, Li Fu-chun and Li Xian-nian enter the room. Premier Zhou is used to Mao's unpredictable temper and he starts the meeting anyway. By making light jokes he tries to relax everyone. Suddenly he is interrupted — Mao fires.

What are you boys up to? Conducting a coup d'état? Trying to remove me? Has Liu always been your secret choice? Why the conspiracy? Why vote for the Cultural Revolution in the first place? Why don't you vote against me and live with the honesty you claim as your principle? Why act like cowards?

The old boys are speechless.

Marshal Tan glances at the opposite side of the table where Madame Mao Jiang Ching sits sandwiched by Kang Sheng and Chun-qiao.

Tan breaks the silence. I am sticking to my view. I don't get it, to be honest with you, Chairman. What is the Cultural Revolution if its goal is to abolish order? Why torture the founding fathers of the republic? What's the point in creating factions in the army? To tear down the country? Make me get it, Chairman!

The old boys nod in unison.

Mao seems to be shocked by Tan's frankness. Good Tan! Here the devil comes to show its true face! You know what? There is no way I will allow you to bring the Cultural Revolution to a miscarriage! The Red Guards have my full support! What they are doing is what China needs. A soul operation on a mass scale! We need chaos! Absolute chaos! Violence is the only choice to turn the situation. A new China can only be born upon the ashes of the old.

She praises Mao in her heart. What a performance! Chaos, absolute chaos. She smiles although her face continues to look grave. She turns to Kang Sheng, who is nodding with the same we-are-winning glance.

Let me make myself clear, Mao continues. If the Cultural Revolution fails, I will retreat. I will take Comrade Lin Biao with me. We will go back to the mountains. You can have everything. I am sure that's why you are here today, aren't you? You want Liu and you want capitalism. You want to give the people's China back to landlords and industrialists. Fine! You shall watch our children being sold, exploited and worked to death again. Have it all! Why aren't you talking? What's wrong? What is the silence and bitter expression? You have been giving my wife Comrade Jiang Ching a hard time. You never acknowledge her as my representative and a leader in her own right. What's the truth behind this? How do you pretend that this is not directed toward me? Take over the power, then! Hey, Marshal Tan and Chen, you, the loudest, the most opinionated. Why don't you arrest my wife? Take her out! Shoot her! Pull the trigger! Destroy the headquarters of the Cultural Revolution. Put Kang Sheng into exile, get rid of me once and for all. Go ahead if you have such hatred for Comrade Jiang Ching and me. Why don't you boys fart!

Like a bug who throws himself into the fire, Tan gets up and starts to swear. Shame!

Mao clenches his teeth. A cigarette breaks between his fingers. When he speaks again, his voice has a strange throaty sound as if coming up with phlegm. It's fine with me that you choose to turn yourself into a reactionary. Fine with me that you make yourself an enemy of the people. What can I do? Thirty-three years ago I saved the army because the army was ready to be saved. Am I right, Premier Zhou?

Premier Zhou and the old boys lower their heads. Mao stirs the memory of the past, of the horror without his leadership, of three fourths of the Red Army destroyed in months, of the shame of the Party's misconduct by men including Premier Zhou himself, and of how Mao single-handedly turned defeat into victory.

The seventeen-year-old Nah stands in front of her mother.

Tea or turtle broth? the mother asks.

I don't want to talk about my marriage. The daughter puts down her bag.

Do I have the right to learn the young man's name? The mother's voice is high-pitched.

Call him Comrade Tai. He's twenty-eight years old.

Are you aware that he is a low-ranking officer?

I thought that every human being created under the sky of Mao is equal.

Would you sit down?

No.

Well, have you ever questioned the reason why he gets no promotion?

He is retiring.

You mean dropping out.

Whatever.

I hope he is not going back to the village.

Well, he is and I am going with him.

The mother's breath halts. She tries to control herself. After a long pause she manages to ask where the place is.

A village in Ninxia Province.

Ninxia? The ghost place? . . . You are doing this to me . . . Why?

The daughter keeps her mouth shut.

The mother breathes deeply as if she will pass out if she stops. What . . . what did your father say?

He blessed me and said that he would be behind me even if I chose to enter a monastery.

A choke takes hold of the mother. She begins to cough.

The daughter fetches a cup of water and goes to give it to her.

Heartless! The mother pushes her away and yells, banging her chest. Heartless!

You haven't presented me with the in-laws. Who are they?

The daughter makes no reply.

Nah!

I am not going to answer your question when I know that you are going to insult me.

Well then, I will have to put up a protest at your wedding.

There will be no wedding, Mother. We have . . . The daughter turns away and looks out the window. We have already married and I can get it for you if you would like to see a copy of our registration.

Stunned, the mother gets up, goes to the wall and begins to bang her head.

We are leaving for Wunin tomorrow. The daughter watches her mother and trembles in tears. After a while the scene becomes unbearable. Without saying a word, the daughter leaves.

The mother curls into a ball at the corner of the wall. She then crawls over the floor and onto the sofa, suffocating herself with a pillow.

I am trying to close my eyes on Nah, but I am unable to. Regret is eating my heart alive. I wish I had tied her shoelaces, packed her lunches and made her skirts when she was a little girl. I wish I had given her birthday parties and invited her friends to our home. I wish I had spent more time talking to her and learning to help with her troubles. But all is too late and out of control. She must be so lonely and desperate to marry herself off as a way out. She wants to punish me. She wants me to witness how she destroys her future — my future. I used to think that being Mao's daughter was Nah's biggest fortune . . . Have I taken out my anger toward my mother on my daughter — neglecting her the way I was neglected? I've abandoned my own wish to be a good mother.

And I hear my heart's cry. I am willing to give up everything to reclaim my daughter's love. But I can't. I am running Mao's business. It is like riding on a tiger's back — I am unable to get off. I live to please Mao. I am selfish and can't escape what made me. I can't live without Mao's affection. In that sense I am pitiful, a hostage of my own emotion. I have been trying to beat this pitifulness. I am a bloody heroine.

It didn't turn out right. Now I'm missing my little girl. Her little arms around my neck. The way she tiptoed into my bed at night. I want her back and I am going crazy thinking about what I have done . . . What happened? What's wrong with me that I refused to kiss her at every departure? I have taught her to deaden her own emotions. I meant to make her strong so she could have a life that's better than mine.

It's fate, my mother would have said. There isn't much one can do to change the way it is meant for her to live. I dream of my being killed as Mao's woman. It is the role I play with passion. It is the dance I was born to finish.

# 18

THE DARKNESS OF THE THEATER, the rows of empty seats, the sound of drums and music soothe my nerves. I am back and forth between Beijing and Shanghai these days. I continue to scout talent and look for material to adapt. My goal is to create characters who are ardent Maoists. I am holding on — trying to make Mao see my importance, to make myself indispensable. Other people are also in a race with me for Mao's affection. I must move fast. With Mao's permission and with Kang Sheng and Lin Biao's help, I have succeeded in banning other forms of entertainment — I fill the stages with the women who I'd like to be.

Yesterday I viewed a piece entitled *The Harbor.* I was not only impressed by its content but in awe of its musical design. This morning I phoned the mayor of Shanghai, Chun-qiao. I asked if he knew Yu Hui-yong, the composer. I'd like to have a copy of his dossier as soon as possible.

On the night of October 4, 1969, Madame Mao turns over the pages of the dossier and is thrilled with her discovery. She learns that the thirty-seven-year-old composer has been the key creator behind some of the best operas of recent years. The next day before breakfast she tells Chun-qiao that she would like to meet Comrade Yu immediately.

Chun-qiao reports that there is an obstacle. Comrade Yu is in prison. He was arrested at the beginning of the Cultural Revolution for having been a traitor before the liberation.

Get my car and connect me with the prison head, Madame Mao orders.

The prison head tells Madame Mao that it would be difficult to release Yu. However, he immediately sends her a record of Yu's crime. The story began in 1947 when Yu was a teenager. He was a member of Mao's Liberation Army. The civil war was at its peak. Chiang Kai-shek's troops bombed the entire area of Jiao-tong and Yan-tai. Yu's division was instructed to bury their food and belongings and get ready to fight for their lives. Yu was devastated. He thought about his mother and made a decision to fulfill his wish to be a good son. Before dawn Yu found a quiet place in the village and dug a hole under a tree. He buried his food and belongings and left a note: *Dear brothers of Chiang Kai-shek's troops: I might be dead by the time you discover this note. My only regret is that I am given no chance to pay piety to my aging mother. My father died when I was eight. My mother raised me all by herself and the hardship she has gone through is beyond description. My spirit will thank and bless you if you could mail this package to my mother for me. Here is the address.*

To Yu's dismay the note was not found by the opposition but by his own comrades. It was reported to the Communist Party authorities. Yu was turned in and detained for six months. Later on in a deadly battle he was given a chance to prove his loyalty. He survived and was forgiven, but his record was kept by the secret intelligence.

When the Red Guards of the Music Conservatory of Shanghai discovered Yu's record they celebrated — they had never had a chance to handle a "real enemy" until now.

Large productions of *Taking the Tiger Mountain by Wit* and *The Harbor* are rehearsing in Beijing and their creator is not allowed to meet with me. I have put pressure behind my request and have demanded Mayor Chun-qiao's direct attention. I am sure Chun-qiao is experiencing difficulty. I am sure my enemies are doing this to me on purpose. They know Yu's talent. They are clear that once Yu and I get together we will be an invincible team. Yu can help me promote Maoism single-handedly. He writes, composes and directs. He has a background in folk melodies and a degree in classical Western music. He has deep roots in traditional opera and a strong sense of modernism. He is trained in composition and plays almost every instrument.

I give Chun-qiao ten days to present me with Yu. Finally, when I am in the middle of reviewing *Taking the Tiger Mountain by Wit* at the Hall of Mercy, Chun-qiao comes to me with the news that Yu has been escorted to Beijing.

Where is he? I ask, so excited I raise my voice. The actor on the stage thinks that I am yelling at him and swallows his lines.

Yu is in the Guest House of Beijing at the moment, Chun-qiao whispers in my ear. He is in terrible shape. He hasn't had a chance to take off the prison uniform and he smells like a chamber pot.

Send him!

A half-hour later Yu Hui-yong arrives. The moment Madame Mao Jiang Ching lays eyes on the half ghost and half man, she stands up and quickly walks up to him. She reaches out and offers both her hands. I regret not having met you earlier, Yu.

The composer/playwright begins to tremble. He is unable to utter a word. He looks like a sick old man with gray hair and messy beard. He wears a borrowed suit. How can I ever pay back your kindness, Madame? He weeps.

Let's work together, replies Madame Mao.

By now the opera has come to its end. The curtain descends and then rises. The actors line up. The audience claps. The sound becomes louder. The security people run back and forth between the stage and the audience. It is a signal for Madame Mao to get on the stage. The weeping Yu gets up and tries to make a way for his savior.

Come with me, Yu, Madame Mao says. Come with me onto the stage.

The man is shocked.

Madame Mao takes Yu's arm and pushes him, smiling.

The man follows.

On stage Madame Mao Jiang Ching centers herself with Yu standing right next to her. The two clap and pose for photos.

The romanticism in Yu's composition moves me. Being with him is like being in a dream. He is not so attractive in appearance; neither tall nor strong, he has a broad forehead and a jaw that is too square. But below the thick eyebrows is a pair of bright eyes. He inspires me as a great artist. Since he and I are from the same province, Shan-dong, we are able to reflect on our favorite childhood tunes. I invite him for tea every day. He is humble to a fault. He won't sit down without a long string of thank-yous. He won't open his mouth unless I order him to comment. He always carries a notebook and opens it when I speak. He waits on me. It makes me laugh, because he is so serious. Very silly. I tell him that I don't want to be treated like a portrait on the wall. I want him to have fun and I want myself to have fun. My life has felt too much strain already. Think of a way to relax me. Tonight we don't talk about work. Tonight we talk nonsense.

It takes him weeks to feel comfortable with me. Finally he is himself again. He starts to bring instruments to play for me at tea. Two-string violin, flute and three-string guitar. He is a gift. We chat and he hums me rice songs, drum tunes and ancient operas that imitate the sound of desert winds. Sometimes I join him. I sing arias from *The Romance of the West Chamber*. We tease each other and break into laughter. His voice is poor but his singing is charming. It has a style of its own. His soul is steeped in music.

Like a student I ask him questions. He is the most confident in those moments. He brings me books he has written — *A Collection of Drum Songs of Shan-dong, A Collection of Folk Songs of Jiao-dong, Songs of the Forest of Shan-bei* and *Classics of One-String Banjo.*

The pleasure is enormous. Yet I can't express myself fully. My status intimidates him. There is always a distance between us. To everyone in China I am Mao's woman. No man is allowed to have personal thoughts about me. Although I would like to get closer to Yu, I withhold myself. The worst part in our friendship is that he answers me like a servant. It only makes me feel lonelier as I listen to his passionate music.

The visits continue. As much as I can I try not to mention Mao. In fact, he never asks about my life after work. I can tell that he gets curious sometimes, but he won't venture himself. We would run out of words to say. He finds excuses to depart. He is sensitive and is weak in confrontation. I beg him to stay and he insists on leaving. We do what I call "saw-movement" several times a day. Sometimes in public. People get confused when hearing me raise my voice at Yu.

You never listen to me, Yu Hui-yong! she yells, almost hysterically. There will be a day you and I split. And I won't be afraid!

He hurries to the door and leaves. He never says a word when she is angry. Later, people tell her that he weeps his way back to the Opera House of Beijing. He doesn't have a home and he lives in a storage space near backstage. He has made a public oath that he lives only to serve Madame Mao Jiang Ching. He doesn't care that it costs him his relationship with his wife. He wants nothing but to impress Jiang Ching. This is how he repays her kindness, with music and his life. His health is declining. He has serious stomach problems and pain in his liver. But he never complains. He conducts rehearsals day and night. He eats irregularly and has no sense of time. Often he delays the meal time and innocently starves the actors. He makes the cafeteria people wait. It has become a habit that Yu calls lunch break at four o'clock in the afternoon.

She can't explain herself. She feels hurt and yet she waits for Yu's return. When she can't take it anymore she sends her secretary to demand from Yu a "self-criticism." He hands in no paper. But he understands that Madame Mao is calling him back. He sends her a tape of a work in progress. Usually it is a newly composed song. One of the songs is called "I Won't Be Happy If I Don't Sing."

It is a strange relationship. It carries the intensity of one between lovers. In order to have him by her side she promotes him to be the new chief of the Cultural Bureau. But he declines her offer and expresses his indifference to politics. She takes it personally, believes that he looks down on her. He argues, trying to prove his loyalty. To impress her he produces more work. He is putting his fingerprints all over her operas and ballets. He highlights the female character — his dedication to a goddess. He fights for her. To convince the troupes to try his new music construction and to replace *shao-sheng* (male lead in falsetto) by *lao-sheng* (male of natural voice), he conducts weeks of seminars to educate the actors and troupe heads. For the orchestra to play his mixture of Western and Eastern instruments, he demonstrates the harmony by taking apart and putting together the arrangements. He takes away the male character's stage time and devotes it to the females. And finally there are only heroines.

When she is presented with the new productions, she is greatly impressed and deeply touched. In many ways she feels that he is a soulmate. She feels great love for him.

The effect of the operas begins to show. The arias are broadcast throughout the nation. The masses know the words and hum the tunes. The Cultural Revolution is at its height. The operas help

Madame Mao Jiang Ching's popularity. She becomes a super-star to every household. She grows more ambitious. I want all my operas and ballets to be made into films! She doesn't wait for the proposal to go through the bureaucracy. She goes to the National Treasury and demands the funding. She takes a political approach. It will test your loyalty toward Mao.

Her wish is granted.

You have to have the guts to touch a tiger's rear or you'll never get a chance to ride it.

*Let's all promote the revolutionary operas!* I thought with Mao's pronouncement I could get my films done smoothly. But that is not the case. The problem is that the film studio has been divided into eight factions. No one wants to work with any other. The head of the lighting department tells the cinematographer at what angle to set the camera. The designer refuses the director's order on costumes. The makeup artist puts pink cream on the actress's face, the color he personally favors. And the producer issues a report on the screenwriters' "anti-Mao lines." Every day there is a fight on the set. Months have passed and not a single scene has been shot.

I can't be a fire-rescuer! I yell at the troupe heads. My main business is to run the Cultural Revolution! You seem to hear me but none of the problems get solved. I have promised Chairman Mao that the films will be ready to show by fall. How dare you disappoint Mao?

I pack the cafeteria of the Beijing Film Studio with the faction groups and I speak in my toughest tones. The chefs inside the kitchen have quieted down. It is half past two and I allow no one to eat. The dishes are getting cold.

You have to make it work, I say.

*

I need help, Mao says to me. He flies me from Beijing to Fujian in the south of the country, where his train is on the run, just to say this. I ask if he is all right. He smiles. Lately I have been reading the Tang poem "The Long Separation," and would like to share my thoughts with you.

I hold my sour words between my lips.

Remember that poem? he asks. About Tang Emperor Li, who was forced to hang his lover, Lady Yang. He was forced to satisfy his generals, who were in the middle of calling up a coup d'état. What a heartbreaking poem! Poor emperor, they might as well have hanged him.

The train keeps moving. The scene slides by. Mao stops talking and looks at me. There is vulnerability in his eyes.

"The Long Separation" is my favorite too, I say.

He begins his monologue again. It takes me a while to figure out what he is saying. He is explaining the pressure he feels. He is concerned about the obstacles facing the Cultural Revolution. Half of the nation is in doubt about his decision over Liu. Sympathy is developing. Although the population hasn't had a chance to experience Liu's idea, they are now certain that Mao's idea doesn't work. It makes him more than angry.

The opposition is trying to block me from realizing the Communist dream. His tone becomes firm and his eyes fix on the ceiling of the carriage. The intellectuals are Liu's pets. They are not interested in serving the masses. They hide in labs in white coats and abandon their motherland in pursuit of world fame. Of course Liu has their loyalty, he has been their money dad. And I worry about the old boys too. They are turning their backs on me. They have called up a military exercise. But to me they are exercising a coup d'état.

Mao doesn't tell Jiang Ching his full story. He doesn't tell her that he is negotiating with the old boys and that there are deals. He doesn't tell her that one day he will be willing to play Emperor

Li and will try out the lines of "The Long Separation." She refuses to realize that this is his game. In front of him her mind quits processing facts. She can't see that in his life he has never protected anyone but himself.

To history, this is her role. The leading lady of a great tragedy.

To keep his affection she does things that hurt her on a deep level. For example, a few weeks ago Mao had a fight with one of his favorite mistresses. The woman walked out. Mao called Jiang Ching for help — she was asked to invite the woman back in the name of the first lady. Thinking back she doesn't know how she did it. She is amazed by how she abuses herself.

You are the person I trust the most, and you are the one I truly depend on. In this warm light she gives in, gives herself. She swallows the pain and puts on her costume to play Lady Yang of "The Long Separation."

In return for her favor Mao promotes her productions. To pave her way he orders a campaign called Making the Revolutionary-Model Operas Known to Every Household.

She feels that she deserves the compensation. In an odd way her marriage with Mao has been transformed and has entered into a new season. Both of them have overcome their personal obstacles to focus on a bigger picture. For him it is the security of his empire and for her, the role of a heroine. In retrospect she not only has broken the Party's restriction, she runs the nation's psyche. She is gripped by the vision that she might eventually carry on Mao's business and rule China after his death.

She doesn't take her power for granted. She doesn't think that she now has complete control over her life. Deep down she doesn't trust Mao. She knows that Mao is capable of changing his mind. And his mind is deteriorating. When he called her to help with his mistress problem did he forget that she is his wife? She hears innocence in his voice. His pain is like that of a child being robbed of his favorite toy. Is it logical to assume that tomorrow he might turn around and not know her? His aging has enhanced his paranoia and she is balancing herself on his mind's beam. Being Madame Mao she never lacks enemies. The price for her success is that she no longer hesitates when it comes to eliminating enemies. Without a thought she now calls Kang Sheng at midnight to place a name on his execution list. She is trying hard to clip the mouths that won't shut, such as Fairlynn and Dan. She fears that when Mao passes away, her battle will be like sweeping back the ocean with a broom — she will be swallowed alive by her enemy.

She needs Chun-qiao and Yu. She needs loyalists in the military too. She remembers how Mao eliminated his enemies in Yenan. Some wrongful executions he made and later regretted. But he never lets the feeling poison him. He says, Victory doesn't come cheap. Now it is her turn. She repeats his phrase.

I am trying to make films. The operas and ballets. I have eight of them lined up and have set up the production in Beijing so I can supervise the details while conducting the Cultural Revolution at the same time. Yet things are not going as I had wished. The infighting between factions has worsened at Beijing Film Studio. Actors are made up and fully costumed. But they sit through the day without getting one shot on film. As the days drag on a rumor begins to spread: *Unless Mao sends his garrison, there won't be a film.*

I take the rumor to Mao. It is a warm day in May. He is in private meetings at the Grand Hall of the People. I can't eat, he greets me. My teeth are killing me. I am talking wills with my friends.

I look at him. His face and hands are visibly swollen.

What's up? he asks.

I worry about your health. Why don't you take a break?

How can I when my enemies are walking around my bed?

Same here. I am frustrated.

What's wrong?

I'm having a hard time getting the films off the ground. The opposition is strong.

Well, it's not our style to accept defeat.

But I don't want to add more strain to you.

Well, well, well, he laughs jokingly. Your enemies will murder you the moment I exhale my last breath.

My tears begin to well up. Truthfully, it might not be a bad solution.

He comes and sits me down gently. Looking at me he says, Calm down, Comrade Jiang Ching. You'll do fine. Just tell me how shall I help you?

Overnight, Mao's 8341 Garrison led by Commander Dee arrives at the Beijing Film Studio. The soldiers are armed and move swiftly and silently. They don't respond to greetings. The workers are sought out from their living quarters and are escorted to the cafeteria.

I am here to carry out Madame Mao Jiang Ching's order, Commander Dee, a short but strongly built man with an enormous nose, says. And I shall put up with no nonsense. Whoever disobeys my order will get a military treatment. By the way, I shall recognize no favors. Listen carefully. Platoon numbers one, three and four will find their duty spot behind all the cameras. My leaders will listen to no one else's instruction but the cinematographer's. Platoon number two goes to the lighting department and platoon five will be in charge of the makeup and props. I myself will be at the command of the film's director and I'll be reporting to Madame Mao Jiang Ching daily.

In less than two days the cameras begin to roll. Within a month, half of the film is completed. Never again is there mention of faction conflicts. People work together as if operating a big family business. At the end of the day the exposed cans are sent to the lab to be processed and the next day the cuts are roughly edited and available to view.

Thrilled, Madame Mao inspects the set. She pats the shoulder of Commander Dee and praises his efficiency. If only I could get this kind of efficiency for all my projects! She begins to think about hiring Commander Dee for more jobs.

Don't confuse yourself. Mao holds his swollen cheek and speaks with irritation. You are not who you believe you are. The truth is that no one will take your orders if they don't see my shadow! When the air force commander in chief Wu Fa-xian answers your call his eyes are on the chair where I am sitting. When the Red Guards shout at the top of their voice *A salute to Comrade Jiang Ching!* it is *I* they want to please.

I understand, Chairman. I try hard to sound humble and non-argumentative. Please don't doubt that I have committed my life to helping you. And only you. I put my faith in my ability to get things done. Let me tell you about my recent creations. Let me show you the film cuts of the operas and ballets.

The operas are all right, Mao says. He picks up a hot towel from a steaming jar and places it against the swollen cheek. I am pleased with your work. The shows sound good. But don't ride them like a magic carpet. And this is my warning.

At this point he loses me. But I dare not mention my confusion. There are a lot of things we confuse each other with lately. We don't clarify. It is to keep peace. Probably confusion is better. I tell the public that I represent Mao but I am not in his life. I have no idea what his days are like. I don't enjoy chasing his mistress and I don't like the fact that he takes pleasure in intimidating me. He has been telling me how his commanders (and he won't spell out the names) would love to suffocate me in my own bed. It's tiring just to keep up with his imagination. Especially when he plays god and devil at the same time. Besides, he hates to be figured out.

The early spring is still chilly. In the morning the frost coats the Forbidden City white. This evening outside the window the vine frames shake violently. A storm has come — the winter's unwillingness to depart. Yet who can stop the spring from coming? After midnight, heavy clouds are swept from the sky. The moon is once again bare. The branches beat my windows like the knocks of spirits.

I don't know until Kang Sheng tells me later what happened on the night of the storm. April 30, 1967. Just before the clouds left the sky, Mao invited the old boys he had attacked previously to his study for a drink. He entertained them with deep-fried bear feet. He acted as if nothing had happened since February 18.

No wonder I was surprised to see all these old sticks show up happily at the celebration party on May 1 at the National Cultural Palace. I should have known that my husband was doing the two-faced trick. I should have understood that although Mao had been promoting me, my new power unnerves him and he needs to have another force to balance the game.

# 19

SHE GOES ON, LAUNCHING HERSELF aggressively into the future. On the surface she is the manager of Mao's power-house and she imagines herself above suffering like her opera heroines. But underneath there is no coming to terms with her feelings — she is exhilarated by her role, but also exhausted and nagged by doubt. Sometimes her love for Mao seems like desperation, sometimes like hate. And her sorrow about Nah has refused to go away. If she let herself, she could slip into depression. Every day she feels her character rot a bit. Last night, as she lay in bed, a girl from an ancient love story came to mind. The girl was a disappointed lover who poisoned the only well in the village.

They take advantage of the roles they play, Mao Tse-tung and Jiang Ching. They help each other and are getting closer to bringing the Lius down. There is still difficulty in making the public buy the negative image of Liu. He has been the Communist icon beside Mao for half a century. To solve the problem and strengthen her position Jiang Ching consults Kang Sheng on Mao's behalf.

Kang Sheng sips tea slowly. Name Liu a traitor. It has always been the most effective way to arouse reaction. It doesn't matter if Liu refuses to enter the scene. You create the show for him. First, bring out Liu's acquaintances with backgrounds associated with foreign agents. Interrogate them and get them to talk the way you want them to talk. Communist or not, no stomach can stand the soaking of hot-pepper water. We have a way to crack open jaws. There will be signatures, then publish the edited version.

It's not whether or not Liu is a traitor, Madame Mao Jiang Ching says to the team of investigators. Your assignment is to get evidence and produce witnesses. You have three days.

The team works around the clock. Soon names are produced. One subject of interrogation is Zhang Chong-yi, a sixty-nine-year-old professor in the foreign language department of Normal University at Hebei Province. Before the liberation he was a head secretary at Furen University. He doesn't know Vice Chairman Liu or Wang Guang-mei personally but he knows their friends at Furen University. Zhang is now a professor of international affairs.

Work on Zhang, Madame Mao orders. Force a confession.

The man can't talk, the team reports. Professor Zhang has been diagnosed with liver cancer and is dying. The man is a breathing skull. His whole face is sunken. His eyes are yellow with jaundice. The right side of his face is paralyzed. His left eye is unable to blink. There is blood in his urine. He is in and out of consciousness.

Race with death, Madame Mao insists. We must have his confession. We must get his voice on tape before he dies. Remember, Chairman Mao is waiting for the results.

The interrogation begins. The recording tape rolls. The tapes are filled with shouts and cries.

Confession or death! Talk, Zhang Chong-yi! Tell us what you know about Wang Guang-mei the traitor.

The dying man fumbles for words. Don't, please don't pull my arm. I'll talk. I am talking. All right, I remember now. Wang Guang-mei, a woman, isn't she? She is Vice Chairman Liu's wife, isn't she?

On the tape there is a slamming sound followed by Zhang Chong-yi's cry.

Stop kicking him! an interrogator yells. He'll be dead if you give him one more blow. Then we will all be in trouble.

Don't even think of fooling us! comes the voice of the head interrogator.

But, Comrade, I am speaking the truth. I am not trying to fool anybody. You see, I . . . don't want to die.

When did you know Wang Guang-mei as a foreign agent?

Yesterday.

How do you know that she is a foreign agent?

Well, you have told me . . . You asked me what she did as a foreign agent. So I figure she must be a foreign agent. Or why otherwise would you ask this kind of question?

Watch your mouth! If you conceal the foreign agent you are a foreign agent yourself. Now is a good time to earn credit.

I understand, sir, the dying man gasps. Now that I have stated that she is a foreign agent, will you let me go? . . . Let me go, please. I beg you. I know Wang Guang-mei is a foreign agent. Not only a foreign agent, she is a Communist agent too.

On the tape the voice becomes breathless. The sound fades. By the time Jiang Ching receives the tape, Professor Zhang Chong-yi has already died. Jiang Ching shakes hands with the investigators. Chairman Mao and I are pleased with your work. Now, we need a witness for Liu.

The same method applies. A witness is produced overnight. This time, it is a friend, a longtime Party worker, Wang Shi-yin, who is suffering from lung cancer. His chest is bound by plastic tubes. But that doesn't stop the investigators. The yelling and shouting blast the tape.

I have no idea. The patient struggles to speak. I am not an inventor of truth.

The sound of banging metal objects.

You will cry when we present you with the coffin and it will be too late, the head investigator says in a low voice. You will force us to disconnect the oxygen machine and pull out the tubes. Are you sure?

Silence.

Finally a fainting voice comes. Do whatever you please. I am dying anyway. I am not afraid of anything anymore. Although the man's words are disconnected, his voice is firm. I have confessed all I know about Vice Chairman Liu. One thing you can be sure of is that he is not a traitor but a man of integrity and honesty. There is nothing more you will get from me.

Shame! Madame Mao Jiang Ching points her fingers at the investigators. You are incompetent. Go back and work until you succeed. Break his jaw if you have to.

What if the subject dies?

You go on and interrogate his spirit!

March 26, 1968. Wang Shi-yin, the lung cancer patient, the man of iron will, dies during the interrogation. Although he doesn't incriminate Vice Chairman Liu Shao-qi, at the Communist Party convention on November 24, 1968, Liu is nevertheless pronounced a "hidden traitor," and is thrown out of the Communist Party.

The news sweeps the nation.

Madame Mao Jiang Ching monitors the biggest drama from the wings. She witnesses life's fragility in its most concrete form. There is no substance when speaking of loyalty. One's downfall can come with the turning of a hand. Mao's managers bring Wang Guang-mei to be publicly criticized first. The rally opens at the stadium of Qinghua University. A crowd of three hundred thousand Red Guards shows up. The shouts are ear-blasting. Jiang Ching feels strange. It is surreal to watch Wang Guang-mei. A woman who falls because of her husband. Will the masses betray her the same way one day? Now she understands why Mao doesn't take chances when it comes to potential enemies — he can't afford to. The suspects have to die.

Mao has overcome difficulties to make the rally happen. His obstacles were Liu's loyalists, Premier Zhou En-lai included. The decision wasn't settled until Mao forced the members of the congress to choose between him and Liu.

In the National Library there is a famous image of this time. A black and white photo documents Wang Guang-mei's moment of humiliation. An ocean of heads is its background. In the left corner is a journalist who wears glasses and carries a camera. He is excited. He has a smile on his face. Wang Guang-mei is in the center of the stage. Her face is half hidden under a white, wide-brimmed straw hat — she has been forced into her foreign-tour garments. A knee-length "necklace" made of Ping-Pong balls hangs from her neck. It's Kuai Da-fu's work.

In the future Kuai Da-fu will be sentenced to seventeen years in prison for what he does now. In the future Madame Mao will also pay for this and will be shown the famous photo. And she will refuse to comment. However, what she will say is that when she was a young actress she drew a clear line between living and acting. But in truth, for Madame Mao, there is no line between living and acting. The Cultural Revolution is a breathing stage and Mao is her playwright.

History will prove that the surviving Wang Guang-mei is wise. When the world is made to believe that Madame Mao Jiang Ching is solely responsible for her husband Liu's death, Wang

Guang-mei says, Liu did not die at the hands of the Gang of Four (the name used to describe Madame Mao Jiang Ching, Chun-qiao and two of his disciples at the end of the Cultural Revolution). At my husband's death there was no such gang. Who is responsible? She doesn't provide the answer. She hopes that the population will seek it themselves.

Yes, I have a personal grudge against Wang Guang-mei. But this is not the only reason I denounce her. My desire to please Mao has become the driving force behind my every act. To stop would mean death. No one can imagine the pleasure I experience when reading Kuai Da-fu's reports — knowing that Mao will be proud of me. It brings me right back to Yenan, to the time when I was Mao's only focus.

Wang Guang-mei deserves the treatment. She who stepped on my toes by leading others to think that she was the first lady of China. She whose elation was caught by the camera and printed in papers throughout the world. Did you say with your pretty, cheery lips, *I am sorry Madame Mao is not well enough to greet you personally*? I never gave you permission to say that. You should never have gone abroad, should never have worn that priceless white pearl necklace and that pair of black high-heeled shoes — you should never have stolen my role. Now try the costume on for the last time and be an object of ridicule. Under the sun, this clear April day, take your turn across my stage of hell.

Madame Mao admits to herself that she admires Wang Guang-mei regardless. Madame Mao is almost touched by Wang Guang-mei.

I hear my husband sigh at night, Wang Guang-mei confesses to the crowd. I have never seen him so sad. I regret that he closes his eyes to reality. His love for China and Chairman Mao is blind. And I understand him. He can't go on without serving China. It is his faith, his purpose for living. As a wife I accept my husband's fate. I accept my reality.

Madame Mao Jiang Ching wishes that she could do the same with Mao. To lay herself on the altar of love. To live the opera. But she won't. It makes her feel tragic. She stares at the report, and gradually anger takes over. The more Wang Guang-mei demonstrates her will to suffer for Liu, the deeper it cuts Madame Mao inside — she is now desperate to see Wang Guang-mei destroyed.

At the back of the stage, Wang Guang-mei struggles with the Red Guards. She had been dragged here. She points at the garment she is wearing, a brown suit, and says, This is already a costume. I wore it to meet foreign guests.

We don't care. Today is a day you wear what we put on you.

I can't. The dress is not proper; besides, it is too small.

You had it on during your trip to the Philippines.

It was years ago. I have aged and lost my shape.

Sounds like you have forgotten who you are.

I am Wang Guang-mei.

No. You are the people's enemy . . . You've got to wear this.

I don't and I won't.

Wear it or we are going to make you wear it.

Let me die, then.

No deal. We are putting you back on the stage. You are going to sink in the spit of millions.

Later on Madame Mao Jiang Ching listens over and over again to a live tape brought by Kuai Da-fu. On the tape Wang Guang-mei's voice changes. She speaks like a heroine: You can force me to kneel but you can't take away my dignity.

Get down! the crowd shouts. You smelly wife of the anti-Communist! You are nothing but a spy and a traitor! To allow you freedom is to allow crime. This is the proletarian dictatorship at its best.

Strip me, then, Wang Guang-mei replies. The rest of her words disappear in the shouting of a crowd of three hundred thousand: *Down with Liu Shao-qi! Down with Wang Guang-mei! Long live Chairman Mao! A salute to our dearest Madame Mao Jiang Ching!*

The scene is grand but actress Jiang Ching suddenly breaks down sobbing.

It has been raining for three days. The drizzle is like tears leaking from the sky. This is an unusual autumn. The bare electric lights throughout the ancient city of Kai-feng in Hebei Province tremble in the wind like ghost eyes.

Vice Chairman Liu's eyes have been shut for days. He has turned seventy in prison. He has had a heart attack, suffers from high blood pressure and complications of diabetes and lung failure. He is unable to swallow. A feeding tube runs into his nose. This morning he opens his eyes. His surroundings are strange and the faces encountered are hostile. He shuts his eyes again and lies in silence. A cotton blanket is wrapped tight around his body.

The northern wind rustles through the courtyard at night. Two tall but leafless ancient trees in the quadrangle stand like madmen having an argument. What is on Liu's mind? His wife has been sentenced to death. His eldest son, Liu Yong-bing, has been beaten to death at a rally. His three daughters are either in prison or have been forced into exile. His partner and best friend, Deng Xiao-ping, has been sent away to a remote labor camp.

Liu doesn't want to believe that the republic he helped build has denounced him. He doesn't want to believe that Mao has ordered his murder. In darkness, he spends his last twenty-some days.

The morning of November 11, he opens his eyes for the last

time. He stares at the spider-webbed ceiling, at the insects trapped in the webs, sucked dry.

The last image the Chinese people have of Vice Chairman Liu Shao-qi is of him holding a book and trying to explain law to the students of Qinghua University. The students laugh and mock. They think him a foolish man. They push him around, making fun of his Book of Law.

Chairman Mao's teaching is law! the youths shout.

Liu knows that his time has come. His body decides to give up before his mind. He is not ready to exit life. Not ready without having a word with Wang Guang-mei and the children, not without embracing the ash-box of his son Yong-bing.

The sadness hardens him by minutes.

November 12, 1969, 6:45 A.M. Vice Chairman Liu's face suddenly glows. The wrinkles begin to stretch and his facial muscles relax. Eternity settles in. There is almost a smile when the great heart stops beating.

In the extreme quietness, the snow begins to descend. The wind stops wailing and the old trees stop shaking.

China lies still.

The Maos are sitting in the morning sun enjoying chrysanthemum tea while Fang, Mao's new secretary and mistress, passes him the report on Liu's death. Mao opens a page as he lights a cigarette. His eyes move through the lines.

Madame Mao leans over and takes a glance.

It's Premier Zhou's handwriting. *Ninety-four hours of nonstop interrogation . . . Separated from his family . . . severely beaten and wounded . . . His bladder infection worsened . . . Fever persisted. His body gave up control . . . bed was constantly wet. He was shut in a small room with no food or water. The medical treatment I sent was blocked . . . His weight came down to sixty-five pounds . . . died of pneumonia with complications.*

Mao exhales smoke.

Madame Mao knows that he feels safe again.

They move on to other reports. By the time Mao reaches the news of Marshal Peng De-huai's death he is tired.

What is Lin Biao doing? he suddenly asks her. Did you know that factions in Wuhan are out of control? The steel workers are manufacturing machine guns themselves. I'm sure a bloody civil war is on the way. Would you tell Lin Biao to do something about it?

I don't know what Lin Biao does as the minister of national defense. It seems that his only job is to flatter Mao. He uses military jets to fly in live lobsters for Mao's kitchen. He sends platoons into the mountains to seek the best ginseng root for Mao. Lin Biao is working toward his own future. He has illusions about Mao and himself.

Unlike Lin I don't have any illusions about Mao. I prepare for Mao's unexpected change. It is a fantasy and also a tragedy that I am Mao's wife. If I were Wang Guang-mei, I might have settled down to be a good housewife. I hate to admit that after all I envy Wang Guang-mei — she had a woman's biggest wish fulfilled. But, then again, I'm not sure I would have settled for pearls.

# 20

ONE MORNING IN THE NATIONAL PRISON, Fairlynn's name is called. She is to be taken to witness an execution as part of a torture program.

The sound of heavy boots. Guards appear. The prisoners are escorted to an open truck. Fairlynn doesn't know that she is only to be a witness. She believes that this is the last day for her on earth. She weeps uncontrollably and starts to shout Mao's name. Shouts her story with him. A guard comes and blindfolds her with a piece of cloth.

Fairlynn regrets that she ever bothered to write to Mao. Mao doesn't care about her, not anymore. Yet Fairlynn can't stop thinking of him. She has a hard time believing that Mao's affection had been insincere. She remembers the last time they departed from one another. "Let us last," he whispered in her ear. She wonders if she offended him by pointing out his mistakes in 1957. He wouldn't admit that his Great Leap Forward was in fact a great leap backward. She was only speaking her conscience as a writer. She asks herself, Was it not her truthfulness and frankness that gained his respect and adoration in Yenan in the first place? Shouldn't he know all her criticisms came from a wish to consolidate his power? She believed that they had understood each other.

It must be Jiang Ching, then, Fairlynn concludes. Her evil hand must be behind this curtain.

This is not a fantasy, I tell the leading actress of my opera. The heroine is real. She has come through hardship. I want you to treat the red paint on your chest as a real wound. Feel its burn. Feel its consuming power. You are being eaten alive and are crying without being heard. Project your voice to its fullest range.

I come to the studio and meet my chief, Yu. I work with him closely on the filming. I am pleased with the progress. The details especially. The color of a patch on the protagonist's pants. The shape of her eyebrows. I like the sound quality of the drums in the background and the orchestra. I have gathered the top artists of the nation. I enjoy every expression on my favorite actress Lily Fong's face and I like the way they light her. I have told the crew that I will allow no imperfection. I order retakes. Endless retakes. I don't pass them until the footage is flawless. At the moment three thousand cultural workers are laboring on my projects. The cafeteria is open twenty-four hours a day. Yu finds me catching myself from falling asleep during my own speech. I am too tired.

Can I stop? It is a bloody battle with invisible swords. The choice is life or death. The other day I visited Mao and witnessed the deterioration of his health — he can no longer get himself out of the rattan chair without assistance. This frightened me. A house won't stay if the center beam falls. But I hide my fear. I have to. The nation and my enemies are watching my performance. I face a scary audience.

I phone Yu. Let's discuss how to make the political message in the operas exciting to the working class. We are courting the youth — it is crucial to my survival that they identify with my heroine. The loving and caring goddess who selflessly sacrifices herself for the people.

Yu picks actresses who resemble my look to play the lead. He comforts me.

I come to the set after conducting the day's affairs. I feel at home in the studios. That has always been the case. The lights soothe me. Mao has gone south again on his train. I have no idea where he is. He keeps his schedule a secret. And changes his mind often. I am trying to mind my own business. I am trying to think of the good Mao has done for me and must remind myself constantly to be grateful.

Indeed, I should be content about how things have finally worked out for me. With Dee commandeering the set, my films are coming out. The silent bullets that lie in the chambers of his soldiers' guns speak louder than my voice ever could.

On October 1, 1969, *Taking the Tiger Mountain by Wit* is released and is a hit. Within weeks, I hear its arias being sung on the streets. To make the script available to the public, I order it published in its entirety in *People's Daily* and the *Liberation Army Daily*. It takes up the whole paper and there is no space for other news or events.

In the next few months *Story of a Red Lantern* is completed and released to theaters nationwide. It is followed by two three-hour ballet films, *The Women of the Red Detachment* and *The White-Haired Girl,* and the opera films *The Harbor, The Sha Family Pond* and *Raid the White Tiger Division.*

What a feeling! I can't go anywhere without being congratulated.

*Story of a Red Lantern* is so popular that Mao expresses his desire to view it. I take it as an honor and accompany him to his private viewing booth. He likes everything except the ending where the heroine and the hero are shot.

It's too depressing, he complains. He suggests that I make it a happy ending. I disagree but promise to consider his remarks and tell him that I shall try my best to make the change.

The fact is that I am determined to do nothing about it. I won't touch the ending. It is symbolic. It is how I feel about life. The flying bullets are in the air. It's my life. So many times I have been shot.

It is an open space. Man-high wooden poles stand three feet apart against the gray sky. Twenty of them. Weeds are waist high. The wind is harsh. The prisoners are kicked out of the truck and tied to the poles. Blinders are removed. Colorless faces, some with towels stuffed in their mouths. The chief executioner shouts an order. Some prisoners begin to lose consciousness. Their heads drop to their chests as if they have already been shot.

Fairlynn is shaking hard. She struggles to breathe. Suddenly her legs start to walk by themselves. She walks toward the wooden pole involuntarily. She wails, Chairman Mao!

The chief executioner comes and pulls Fairlynn up by the collar. He drags her to the side. Fairlynn's mind is paralyzed. She feels as if she were a cooked fish lying on a plate with its spine taken out.

The soldiers raise their guns. The sound of the wind can be heard. One female prisoner turns around. Her eyes seek Fairlynn. It is Fairlynn's cellmate, Lotus. Fairlynn rolls on the ground and then rises up on her knees. Suddenly she sees Lotus wave her hands, punching her fists toward the sky. Lotus's mouth opens, shouting *Down with Communism! Down with Mao!*

The woman stops punching her fists toward the sky — she is hit by a bullet. But her mouth keeps moving.

In terror Fairlynn lifts her head and crawls toward Lotus. Her surroundings spin. The earth is upside down. Her ears begin to buzz. Suddenly everything starts to float soundlessly in front of her eyes.

The prisoners fall, scattered in all directions. Some of them bounce off the wooden poles. Shot-broken ropes drop to the ground. Lotus runs toward Fairlynn. She wags her body with her chin toward the sky. Behind her, the clouds have fallen to the earth, rolling like giant cotton balls.

The chief executioner shouts his last order. In extreme silence, Fairlynn witnesses Lotus's face break. The splattered blood paints a blooming chrysanthemum.

Chimpanzee experiment! Fairlynn passes out.

Although Fairlynn survives the Cultural Revolution, the moment Lotus's face became a bloody chrysanthemum, an important compartment in her own conscience bursts as well, as her memoir suggests (written in 1985 and published by South Coast China Publishing in 1997).

> *True, Chairman Mao has his weaknesses. They seem more poignant during the last few years of his life. I think it is all right to write about it. But under the circumstances I refuse to reveal more than what's known. There are people who intend to deny Mao's great contributions and heroic deeds. They not only want to smear his name but also want to have him nailed as a demon, and I will not allow that. No matter how wrongful the treatment I was made to endure in the past, I will not use my pen to write any word attacking Mao.*

In later chapters the seventy-nine-year-old legend lingers on an encounter with Mao in a tone of elation:

> *It was in Yenan. I visited Mao's cave quite often. Almost every time I went he would give me a poem of his own or by others as a gift. All presented in his beautiful calligraphy on rice paper. Once Mao asked me, Do you agree that Yenan is like a small imperial court, Fairlynn?*
> *I was sure that he was joking, so I answered, No, for there*

*isn't a board of one hundred advisors. He laughed and said, That's easy. Just make a board. Let's draw up a list. He took out a pen and pulled a sheet of paper and said, Come on, you produce the candidates and I'll grant them titles.*

*I pronounced the names that came to my mind as he wrote them down. We were having such fun. He wrote ancient titles next to the names. Li-bu-shang-shu — Judge of the Supreme Court, Bing-bu-shang-shu — Minister of National Defense. There were others, like prime ministers and secretaries of state. After that he asked me, What about wives and concubines? I laughed. Come on, Fairlynn, names!*

*On that of course I retreated because I want no more trouble with Jiang Ching.*

It's New Year's Eve. The snow has turned the Forbidden City into a frozen beauty. Yet I am in no mood to visit my favorite plum flowers. On the surface I have achieved a dream — I have walked out from the shadow of an imperial concubine and have established myself as the ruler-to-be. And yet, to my discontent, I've once again lost my way to Mao's door — he has declined my invitation to spend New Year's Eve with me.

It has, I am sure, a lot to do with the success of my opera and ballet films — he believes that my popularity has diminished his name. He feels damaged. What will happen? I don't have to look far — this was the reason he removed Liu.

I feel as lonely as ever, yet I can't stop doing what I have been doing. Like a moth I am destined to chase after light. To escape depression I plan my own New Year's Eve party in the Grand Hall of the People. I invite my creative team and crew members, three hundred in all. Comrade Jiang Ching would like to honor everyone by spending New Year's Eve with you.

After a cup of wine my tears begin to spill. To beat this, I ask my bodyguards to bring out firecrackers. They are surprised at first — they all know I have an aversion to loud noise and heavy smoke. It's true my nerves have been weak. But I am desperate to hide my feelings and to get rid of the public's suspicion that I am falling from Mao's grace.

My bodyguards come back emptyhanded. There is a security rule that no fireworks are allowed in front of the Grand Hall of the People.

Well, I don't care. I am Jiang Ching! Bring firecrackers to me in twenty minutes or you're fired! Steal them if you have to!

A half-hour later, the bodyguards arrive with cases of fire-crackers.

The bullet sounds begin. The fireworks cover the sky. The crackers bounce up and down and side to side. I laugh to tears. I hate Mao. I hate myself for walking this path.

When the head of the hall's security comes and tries to stop me I throw an "earth dragon" at him. The firecrackers shoot out like magic ropes encircling him and leaving black burning dots on his clothes.

My bodyguards follow me. They "shoot" him in the chest and feet and finally he backs off.

She changes. The rhythm of her temper reflects Mao's mood and his treatment of her. In public she is more than ever a Mao zealot. She resides in Shanghai and makes all members of her opera troupes wear army uniforms. She tells them that every perfor-mance should be taken as seriously as a battle. To her it is more than true. She feels that she has to fight for the right to breathe. She becomes hysterical and nervous. Nothing lasts forever, she comments out of nowhere. When she has a good night's sleep she wakes up thinking about her past. One day she reveals a secret to her favorite opera singer. You know, this is the exact same stage where I played Nora.

She wonders where actor Dan has been. The last time she saw

him was on the screen. He had been playing emperors and heroes of all sorts. The image is still magnificent and irresistible. Since the Cultural Revolution his name has disappeared from the papers and magazines. She suddenly desires him. She now understands why the empress dowager was obsessed with actors. Fed yet feeling hungry. Breathing yet feeling buried alive. There is this need to hold on to fantasies.

She can't touch them but keeps them as possessions. She is surrounded by handsome and intelligent men. Men in whose eyes she sees herself once again as a goddess. Her favorite men are Yu Hui-yong the composer, Haoliang the opera actor, Liu Qing-tang the dancer and Zhuang Zedong the world table-tennis champion. There is only one man who won't get down on his knees before her. It is Dan. She burns for him, for she appreciates his genius — compared to the emperors he portrays, Mao is like a fake. And yet she can't stand him. In front of him she feels defeated.

They meet again when she is taking a short break at West Lake. They happen to stay in the same hotel. Dan has been doing research for *Biography of Lu Xun* — a movie he dreams of making. They run into each other in the lobby. She recognizes him but he doesn't acknowledge her. She follows him to his room and he is surprised. They shake hands. She is restless that night. A handshake is no longer enough for her. The next time they meet she hugs him. Her arms circle his neck and then her lips seek his mouth.

He freezes but doesn't remove himself. The kiss lasts long seconds. He is a good actor. Finally she lets him go.

They sit facing each other in a teahouse. He compliments her on how good she looks. *The highest place is the coldest,* she responds, quoting an ancient poem.

His face turns pale but he goes along with the performance. She convinces herself that he is just as interested. They discuss art. She tells him that his role as the Ching dynasty marshal has been her favorite. He asks if she could lift the ban. There is silence. She asks if he has ever thought of her all these years. He smiles and gives no reply at first. After a while he says, Buddha always grants me the opposite of what I pray for.

She smiles. I'll grant what you have been praying for tonight.

He pauses and says, But I have become a man of empty guts.

In my eyes, you are forever the daring Dan. Tell me what happened to you after *Doll's House*. How is Lucy?

There has been a string of bad luck, he sighs. I was imprisoned as a Communist suspect by Chiang Kai-shek. I was sent to a prison in Xin-jiang Desert for five years. Lucy was told that I was dead and she married my friend Du Xuan. I —

Dan, I'd like to share tears with you tonight. We will drink the imperial liquor I brought from Beijing. We will have a good time. Here — my key.

She waits and imagines. She counts the minutes. Half past ten and Dan still hasn't shown up — he has checked out of the hotel.

The air bites and the water poisons. She feels like she is losing her own feet while plotting to possess other people's new shoes.

For his action Dan is put away. The excuse is a typical Cultural Revolution dunce cap label: *Chiang Kai-shek's agent*. The cell reminds Dan of a movie set he once was in while playing an underground Communist. The wall is three feet thick and thirty feet into the earth. He lives in total darkness and is given two bowls of thin porridge a day. He is also given tools to end his own life.

For fifteen years Dan fights to see the light. I couldn't even manage to walk a block after I got out, Dan says when he was released after Madame Mao's downfall in 1977. My second wife tried to divorce me. My children demonstrated their resentment by joining the Red Guards. At a public rally my son took a whip and hit me.

How can I tell life from a movie?

The footage is disappointing. The direction is stiff and the performance superficial. The lighting has too much shadow and the camera frames the wrong angle. Before lunch I order the production shut down. Everyone is terrified. It makes me feel a little better. But my good time doesn't last. Someone is sticking his neck out for my bullets. What timing! He is a producer. He says we should go on filming. Chairman Mao has instructed us to promote the operas. We shouldn't stop working on the assignment of honor. The biggest idiot in China now is the one who doesn't know how to read my mind. So I order him fired on the spot. You see, I can do this effortlessly. There is no need to beg anybody.

The key actress cries and thinks that she is the reason I am upset. I fire her too. I can't stand pitiful characters! I wish I could fire myself too. This is a horrible role I'm playing. There is no way to make it shine. Nothing is working. My role is laughable. I have the power to shut the nation down but I can't achieve one individual's affection.

Her mood starts to change drastically. Half of the crew members are fired within a month. The productions have turned into a mess. Finally the cameras stop rolling. Still she looks for the enemy. Trapped deeper and deeper in her own misery she sees poison in her bowl and a murderer behind every wall.

The lady of the mansion, Shang-guan Yun-zhu, has been trying to contact her lover Mao since morning. She wants to tell him that she has been reading poems about the Great Void. She is tired of her role as a mistress and is sick of the endless waiting. She wants to tell him how she misses acting. She has been watching movies produced by the Shanghai Film Studio and has recognized roles which originally were created for her. She wants to tell him about the threatening calls from Jiang Ching's agents asking her to "count her days." But she can't reach Mao — her phone has been disconnected and her maids have disappeared.

Shadows are cast over Shang-guan's mind. She senses her own ending. She imagines Madame Mao Jiang Ching's laughter as she recites a thirteenth-century verse:

> *Flower-gathering girls have dropped out of sight*
> *Suddenly*
> *For sightseeing I feel disinclined*
> *Rover that I am*
> *I rush through all the scenes*
> *Grief deprives me of what pleasure I can find*

> *Last year*
> *Swallows flew away horizon-far*
> *Who on earth knows in whose house this year they are*
> *Stop, will you?*
> *Don't listen to the rain at night in the third moon*
> *For it cannot help blossoms to appear soon*

It's time, she murmurs, slowly closing the book.

They were in the middle of lovemaking. Mao was sitting on a sofa and Shang-guan Yun-zhu was on his lap. He was enjoying photographs of her movies, the roles she had played. You are a pearl.

She smiled and bent over. A string of fresh jasmine dangled from her ears.

He grabs her and begins to undress her.

She feels him and feels her love for him.

Don't be sad, I'll make it work someday, he says.

She shook her head. I am afraid.

Oh, heaven! How I miss you! Have mercy. Come on. Oh, you cold beauty. You're stone-hearted.

The more he caressed her the sadder she became. What about tomorrow? Yet she dared not ask. She had asked before and it had driven him away.

Shang-guan was flattered but concerned when Mao first pursued her. At first she refused to be disloyal to her husband, Mr. Woo, an associate director, a humble man at the Shanghai Film Studio. But it didn't stop Mao. Soon the problem was solved by Kang Sheng. Mr. Woo offered his wife. The next problem was Madame Mao Jiang Ching. Shang-guan was not able to overcome her fear, to which task Mao again assigned Kang Sheng. Kang Sheng kept Shang-guan a secret from Jiang Ching until he learned that Mao and Jiang Ching had reunited — Mao didn't mind sacrificing Shang-guan in order to please Jiang Ching.

It was not that Shang-guan lacked perspective. She had entered show business at a young age and had learned its nature. She knew what she was doing. She was thirty-five years old when she met Mao. She had her own plan. Her career as a screen actress had peaked and she was looking for an alternative. She took up with Mao when Kang Sheng convinced her that Jiang Ching was out of favor and was unsuitable as a political wife. Kang Sheng's analysis was thorough and inspiring. The idea of becoming Madame Mao made Shang-guan Yun-zhu abandon her husband and career.

Shang-guan left Shanghai, stepped into Mao's palace and put on the costume of Lady Xiang-fei. However, she soon discovered that she was not the only one Mao kept.

Shang-guan had wanted to get out, but Kang Sheng's private eyes were everywhere. It is a national affair you are conducting, he warned her. We must guard you twenty-four hours a day. You ought to have no reason to be bored. Making yourself available to the Chairman should be the only goal in your life.

But Mao hasn't shown up for a long time! He has lost interest and has turned away, don't you see?

It is your duty to wait, the cold voice continued.

She waited, through the long winter and summer. Mao never came. When the Cultural Revolution began and Shang-guan Yun-zhu saw the picture of Mao and Jiang Ching standing shoulder to shoulder on the Gate of Heavenly Peace, she knew she was doomed.

Shang-guan's thought pauses. In front of a long mirror, she smiles wearily. Her residence has been quiet this morning. It is a single mansion sitting in rich meadows. A suburb of Beijing. Two nights ago Shang-guan discovered that her guards had been removed. A platoon of new men came.

Tomorrow has already begun to run its course, she mutters. To-morrow will finish all my trouble. The feather of my imagination finally gets caught.

Shang-guan sits down and begins to write a letter to her husband. She resents him for giving her up. Although I understand that you were under pressure and had no option, I can't forgive you. My life is so hateful that I think it's better to stop it. But then she feels that she is not being honest. Mr. Woo was never her choice in terms of love. It was she herself who was lured by the idea of becoming Madame Mao.

She tears up the letter.

Shang-guan gets up and goes to the garden to lock the gate. She walks quickly and holds her breath as if to avoid the scent of spring. She hurries and slashes through the blooming plants. Her gown drags the petals along. She walks back into her bedroom and closes the door behind her. She looks around. Two windows facing east stand symmetrically like giant eyes without eyeballs. The dark gray rolled-up curtains look like two bushy eyebrows. A redwood ceiling-high closet stands between the windows. The floor is covered with a noodle-colored carpet. The room makes her think of Mao's face.

Shang-guan paces elegantly. She holds herself as if in front of a camera. She remembers how at ease she was with the most difficult camera movements. The sophisticated technical demands were never her trouble. She had good instincts and was always on line and on cue. The lighting and camera directors adored her. She lived up to the expectations of the audience and critics as well. The reviewers said it was her confidence that made her glamorous and her restrained performance that moved hearts.

She can feel the weight of her fake eyelashes. She has applied a rich layer of creams and powders. In the mirror, she rehearses the act. With her chin up she holds a distant expression. The breath of death hits her cheeks as she paints her lips for the last time. Afterwards, she takes a white blanket and covers the mirror with it. She stops in front of the closet. Opening the doors, her hand reaches in. She pulls a drawer and takes out an indigo-blue ceramic bowl, which is covered with brown waxed paper. A yellow string is tied around the rim. She unties the string and lifts the cover. Inside, a pack of sleeping pills.

Carefully, Shang-guan presses the edge of the paper. She folds it into a diamond shape. She then presses it flat again before she throws it into a waste bin under the table. She goes to the kitchen holding the bowl. She takes out a glass and a bottle of half-finished *shaoju* from the cupboard and mixes the liquor with the pills. She stirs and grinds, and takes time with her act. Afterwards she goes back to her bedroom and remakes her bed. She smoothes every wrinkle from the sheet. From underneath the bed she pulls out a black suitcase and takes out a set of dresses and a pair of shoes. She changes her blouse into a peach-colored dress — a gift from Mao. Then changes her mind. She takes off the dress and replaces it with a navy blue garment which she bought from a nun on location near Tai Mountain. She changes her slippers into a pair of black cotton sandals. She puts the peach dress and the slippers into the suitcase and pushes it back under the bed.

Shang-guan gulps the drink down. There is no hesitation. She washes her hands and rinses her mouth. She then goes to lie down on her bed, spreading her limbs evenly.

Her mind begins to empty itself. The people she used to know come into focus, then fade like smoke, among them Mao Tse-tung and Jiang Ching. She feels that fate is finally releasing her. She is running into the earth's wilderness where peace opens its arms. As the pain comes and her breath grows thin, she exhales a whisper, a line she favored when playing Lady Taimo:

*Can anyone reconstruct a string of jasmine from a pot of tea?*

# 21

KEEPING UP WITH MAO has exhausted me although the tactics of the game have become simpler. The struggle to get ahead has come down to three parties. Premier Zhou, Marshal Lin Biao and I have become the only rivals. In April 1968, my strategy is to ally with Lin and isolate Zhou.

It is not that I enjoy the slaughter game. Given a choice I'd rather be with Yu and spend time in film studios and theaters. But my rivals are waiting to knock me out. I smell blood in the air of Beijing.

She tries to break down Premier Zhou's system. Her first objective is to replace Zhou's National Security Bureau, run by the old boys, with her own. Mao plays a delicate role here. He encourages and backs both sides. He believes that only when the warlords are involved in constant infighting will the emperor achieve peace and control.

With Mao's silent permission she allies with Lin Biao and the two finally paralyze Zhou's National Security Bureau. Pleased, Mao asks if Jiang Ching can crack the rest of the country. Excitedly she accepts the challenge. Although Premier Zhou tries every way to derail her action, she is aggressive and powerful.

The tragedy of her life begins officially. Blinded by passion she keeps going, unaware that her role is being set up to be destroyed. She has never completely given up faith that she will one day win Mao's love back. For that she refuses reality, refuses to believe that Mao will eventually sacrifice her.

When Madame Mao's forces grow too fast and too strong, Mao bends toward Premier Zhou and the old boys. In July Mao gives permission to Zhou to publish within the Party the numbers of the dead killed in the fights among factions of the Red Guards. *It's time to beat the wild dogs before they become a threat to the nation.* Zhou's action to reestablish order follows.

I have been kept in the dark. And I have no idea why Mao is displeased with me. He won't speak to me although I have been trying to reach him. Has Premier Zhou been the evil hand behind this? Sometimes Mao can be so insecure that he senses a storm in a breeze. And Zhou's words have an effect on him. The last time he saw me he quoted a saying, *The taller the tree, the longer its shadow.* I regret that I didn't pay attention. I hope that it is only his hysteria. Once it runs its course his mind will be back on its track.

To isolate me, Mao cuts off my association with Marshal Lin. Mao orders Lin to take the army to "clear the mess left by Jiang Ching's Red Guards."

I feel crushed. I immediately write a letter to Mao claiming that I have been working only under his instruction.

Mao makes no response. It is his true character acting. A moment in which he recognizes no feelings or memory. He lets himself be taken by fear.

Once again I am betrayed and shit upon. I'm shaken, yet I don't have a place to beg.

Mao dismisses my cabinet. He sends my people away. Saws off my limbs. A national migration of youth. Two hundred million Red Guards are chased to the countryside in the name of "spread-

ing the seed of the revolution all over China." And yet I am not allowed to say a word. His purpose is to make me see how ill built
my power is. There is no foundation. I am no different than Liu.
This scares me to death. I am afraid to think about the future. If I
can be stripped like this while Mao is living, what about when he
dies?

But no, I can't get off the tiger. It is either eat or be eaten.

Lin Biao sees his chance to succeed both Premier Zhou and me.
He races on. In the Party's Ninth Convention Mao officially pronounces Lin Biao his successor.

Believe me. History is full of tricks. Real-life drama is better
than any playwright's imagination. Marshal Lin has no confidence that his own health will last. He fears that Mao will change
his mind and decides to act. He plots a coup d'état. At the same
time as he flies Mao live lobsters he sends his son to bomb Mao's
train. Well, Mao is the bigger witch in the temple of magic —
Mao has two security trains of four cars apiece run in advance.
Lin has no luck in catching him.

She is sitting next to Mao, opposite Lin Biao and his wife, Ye
Qiun. On the other side of the table sits Premier Zhou and his
wife, Deng Yin-chao. She doesn't realize what is going on until
the next morning. At the table she observes nothing unusual. Mao
begins the ceremony by opening a bottle of imperial wine sealed
in its original Ming dynasty porcelain vase 482 years earlier. He
then lights incense. Let's celebrate the Moon Festival.

The dinner is elaborate, with sea cucumbers and other land and
ocean delicacies. Mao uses his chopsticks to heap Lin's plate with
tendons of tiger shot a week ago in Manchuria. The atmosphere is
pleasant. She is not aware that her husband is starring in a live opera. She is in a sentimental mood. Mao had his secretary tell her
that she must leave the banquet by exactly ten-thirty. She took it
as an insult but nevertheless came to dinner. During the meal, she

feels her heart ache over the courtyards, flowers and bamboo tree. She used to live here with Mao. The liquor makes the animal statues on the ancient stone tablets and fountains come to life. She turns to the other side. The little vegetable patch is a picture of a harvest. Beans are green and peppers are red. Again she is reminded of their life in Yenan.

The group is dressed casually except for Mao. He is oddly formal tonight, wearing a starched jacket buttoned up to the chin. After a toast he turns to Lin. How's the army doing?

Can't be beat.

Nice job you did in Wuhan.

It's nothing to squash the rebels.

The People's Liberation Army under your command has shown itself a good model for the people, Premier Zhou says, finally inserting his comment.

Lin has been working too hard, Lin's wife cuts in. His doctor begged him to stay in bed. But we all know that he is out of himself when he hears the Chairman call. He breathes for you, Chairman.

Very kind, very kind. Mao heaps two pieces of fried pork rib on Lin's plate and then fills his own cup with more wine. Ye Qiun, you must take good care of your man. He is the only one I've got — he has to run the business after I'm gone.

Premier Zhou seems to have no appetite, but tries to eat to please his host. His wife carefully picks oily fish skin out of her husband's plate and replaces it with green vegetables. Once in a while she watches her husband with concern. He eats slowly and is paying close attention to Mao.

So, what have you been doing, Premier?

Zhou wipes his mouth and states that he has just come back from a trip to Northern Three Province. I went there to check on the Red Guards who were sent there a year ago.

Oh, looking after the kids. Mao laughs and nods. And how are they? I have been wondering myself. Have they adapted to the situation well and have they been productive? I assume they know how to run tractors better than the peasants. They are educated and can read instructions, can't they? I expect them to produce a great harvest. It is a good year in terms of the weather.

Well, the picture is not so good, Premier Zhou answers. The youths and the locals don't get along. The youths don't know much about the importance of catching the seasons. They thought the machines could do everything at any time. But it was the rainy season. Hundreds of tractors entered the field — they were like frogs with their legs chopped off. They got stuck and couldn't move an inch. And it was too late when they realized their mistake. With the help of the locals they collected as much wheat as they could with sickles and left the rest of the grain to rot in the fields. The last day I was there, the kids used their clothes and blankets to bag up the grain and lay it out on their beds to dry —

Always a price for lessons, Mao interrupts. As if no longer interested in Zhou's details he turns to Jiang Ching. You are doing well, aren't you?

She doesn't know where he is heading so she quickly answers, Yes, Chairman, the opera films are doing beautifully. The troupes are making new ones. It will be an honor if the Chairman can inspect the troupe.

He throws her a mysterious smile and then goes on to comment on the wine. She is having a hard time following him — on one hand he tries to generate a conversation, on the other, he is not listening. It is the first time she plays a role without knowing that she is even on a stage.

The group keeps drinking. *Don't expect too much. The truth is, no cripple will lend you his stick.* In between sips and toasts Mao throws comments as if drunk. *The mouse's greatest happiness is to steal away a fistful of grain.*

*

Oh look, the host exclaims, I totally forget the time. We should do this more often, right? Premier Zhou? Jiang Ching, are you full?

I look at my watch. It is ten-thirty. I get up. Mao comes over and gives me a comrade-style handshake.

What am I supposed to say? Thank you for dinner? I leave silently.

We'll leave with Comrade Jiang Ching. Premier Zhou and his wife get up.

We will too. The Lins follow.

Mao holds up his hand to Lin. No, do stay at least for another half-hour. We haven't really gotten a chance to talk yet.

When the Lins sit back down Mao chats freely. He asks about Lin's family and health and suggests places for him to vacation. He listens tentatively and recommends to Lin his own herb doctor. He then asks Ye about her dream for their son "Tiger." Ye is flattered and starts to babble about Tiger's achievement.

Your son is talented and deserves a high position in the army. Mao lights up a cigarette. The people need him. Listen, Lin Biao, have you ever thought of promoting your son as the commander in chief of the entire army? That way you can free yourself to take up my job.

Well, Tiger is only twenty-six . . .

If you are not going to do it, I will. He owes the people his gift.

At ten fifty-four the Lins bid farewell.

Allow me to walk you to the door, Mao offers. I'd like to see you off personally.

At midnight, the phone at the Garden of Stillness rings. Jiang Ching picks up the receiver half asleep. It is Kang Sheng.

The Lins are dead, he reports. The mission was completed neatly and quietly within the compound of the Forbidden City.

To hide her shock Madame Mao asks Kang Sheng for the details of the execution.

One of Mao's table servants is a transportation expert, and another an explosives expert. Aren't you glad?

She is, but she is also scared — again, will Mao do the same to her one day?

How are you going to break the news to the world? she asks, barely controlling her voice.

Here, I've just finished my draft: *September 15, 1971, from New China News Agency: People's enemy Lin Biao was caught in an action attempting to murder Chairman Mao. Lin took a small plane and flew to Russia after his evil plan was exposed. Lin's plane crashed in Mongolia when the fuel ran out.*

With Lin Biao out, Premier Zhou and I have become the only rivals for the position as Mao's successor. I must hurry. I must battle against Premier Zhou's men as well as my own husband.

I am anxious and can hardly sit still. In my dreams I hear steps. I get nervous going near closets. I fear assassins are behind the clothes. I skip meals to reduce the chances of being food-poisoned. I change my secretaries, bodyguards and servants once every two weeks. But the new faces frighten me even more. I know it's foolish but I can't help suspecting these people as Premier Zhou's spies.

The golden autumn views of the Forbidden City and Summer Palace no longer interest me. I used to love walking across the five-hundred-stone dragon bridge, but now I fear that a mysterious hand will come out of the water to pull me down.

I decide to go to Shanghai where my friend Chun-qiao has become the head Party secretary of the southern states. I have come to depend on Chun-qiao. We select my future cabinet members together. Again he recommends his faithful disciple, now the famous "Marshal of Pens," Yao Wen-yuan, and two other men of talent. One is Wang Hong-wen, a handsome thirty-eight-year-old, who very much resembles Mao's late son, Anyin. Wang is the chief of the Shanghai Workers Union. Chun-qiao points out that the union has been recently adapted into a military force and it is under my command.

Excellent. I congratulate Chun-qiao and his men. This is exactly what we need. I'd like to take all of you to Beijing. I'd like to introduce you to Mao. And of course, I shall take Composer Yu, my dearest friend, along. Mao is a fan of his work and he should be working in a much more important position than he is now. So what if Yu is an artist and a slob who often catches himself wearing two different socks? I adore him. There is no one who understands the artistic part of me more than Yu. It's all right that Yu dislikes politics. I dislike it too. The point is that you can't enjoy composing if your head and feet are going to be in different places. Anyway, Chun-qiao, I shall leave Yu to you to enlighten.

Gathering up all her courage, she brings her new political talent to Mao. The old man's movements are stiff and his hand trembles and half his front teeth are gone. Nevertheless he is once again charmed by his wife. He is particularly impressed by the handsome pine-tree-like Wang Hong-wen. As toward a son, he draws Wang to his side and invites him back to spend time. A few months later Mao names Wang the vice chairman of the Communist Party replacing Lin Biao. Mao announces the promotion at the Party's convention.

There is a condition. To my shock Wang Hong-wen tells me that Mao wants him to be his pet and not mine. In fact, Mao wants him to "stop being nursed by Jiang Ching."

This is a robbery. I speak to Wang and demand his loyalty. But

Wang is a man of no honor. He goes for the bigger breast. I ask Chun-qiao to tell Wang that if he continues to be disloyal to me, I shall "leak" the information of his true background — he is not a man of any talent. He was a high school dropout and his is a made-up story.

After that Wang repositions himself. Soon Mao finds out that it is in my voice Wang speaks. The old man begins to doubt his arrangements. He calls us "the Gang of Four," meaning Wang, Chun-qiao, his disciple Yiao and me.

January 10, 1972. At Marshal Chen Yi's funeral Mao acts senti-mental. He had originally declined to attend but changed his mind at the last minute. To the nation it is a clear sign that Mao is picking up the old boys.

By the time Mao arrives, the funeral has already begun. Getting out of the car Mao rushes toward the casket. His appearance sur-prises everyone. The detail is immediately caught by the cameras: Mao is in his black coat with the tail of his white pajamas show-ing underneath. It suggests Mao came here in such a hurry that he didn't have the time to change. It hints that Mao couldn't make himself not come. To the host, Premier Zhou, Mao's arrival has not only honored the old buddies, but also denounced Jiang Ching and her gang.

Following the ceremony Mao conducts a closed-door conversa-tion with Premier Zhou. Days later a document entitled "Putting Things Back in Order" is issued from Premier Zhou's office.

What can I do but wash my face with tears? If Mao places his trust in the old boys, I simply have no future. Although Premier Zhou has recently been diagnosed with cancer, he won't rest until he sees his comrade Deng Xiao-ping secure the premier's seat. Even on his hospital bed Zhou conducts a media show. He asks people to pass their affection for him on to Deng. It is quite a moving show. Deng is now grabbing the headlines. *Rely on Comrade Deng to revive the nation's economy* has become a household slogan.

She resists diminishment. She believes in her network and in her loyalists in the media, who in the past months have printed the manuscripts of all her operas. For a decade, she has worked to create a perfect image of herself through the operas and ballets. A heroine with a touch of masculinity. The woman who came from poverty and rises to lead the poor to victory. She believes that the minds of the Chinese have been influenced. It's time to test the water — the audience should be ready to embrace a heroine in real life.

I have it all planned out, she phones Kang Sheng. I am in the middle of a grand project. I am preparing myself to enter a real scene.

Whatever you do, Kang Sheng whispers, put poison in Zhou's rice bowl before he puts it in yours. Mao is losing his mind and you'd better hurry.

I can't breathe. My worst nightmare has come to seize me. I am stuck in a classic story of the Forbidden City. The setting is called the Forgotten Yard. The characters are limbless imperial concubines. They visit my dreams and won't leave me in the morning.

I see no chance to turn back Mao's clock.

I am going apple-picking at Coal Hill, Jiang Ching says to Mao. Would you like to join me?

I am hopping on my last leg, the seventy-nine-year-old man coughs. I can feel my bones decay by seconds.

Why don't you call your doctor?

No! Put the phone down! A cockroach can be an assassin these days.

She stares at him.

He perspires heavily and then moves slowly back to his bed.

He is more than tired, she thinks to herself. The man is fading. Although he has an appetite, he has been starving. He is toothless but refuses to install plastic teeth. He is so weak that he sank in the pool.

He calls her in for no particular reason. He did the same yesterday. When she arrived he had nothing to say. She waited patiently. But he couldn't get his point across. He mumbles about high blood pressure and minor cuts that don't heal. The doctor says that I have ulcers. They are everywhere. In my mouth, down my throat, on my stomach, intestines and anus. Look here. He opened his jaw. See the ulcer? Here, under my tongue, the sores. They come regularly and stay around the clock.

She smells death on his breath.

It's about time. The words accidentally slip out of her mouth.

He turns toward her in a quick motion.

Sorry, what I mean is that it's never too late to take good care of one's health.

I try to get up and walk nowadays, Mao gasps. I just keep walking. I am afraid that if I stop walking, I'll never walk again. I love the way my feet touch the ground. I love to feel its solidness. The smell of earth comforts me. Only while I am walking am I able to experience my day and know that I am living and my organs are functioning. Oh, how wonderful the way my lungs pump. A healthy body walking on a healthy ground! It's the connection between me and the ground. It's the only thing I can trust and depend upon. And it's what I am breathing for. You see, when I stretch out my legs, the ground receives me. It greets, supports and praises me, no matter how terrible I am. I stand, the ground lies beneath me, sincerely and silently. It extends all the way from my feet to infinity . . .

She pictures a makeup artist polishing the nails of the dying.

As if fascinated by his own thoughts Mao takes hold of her arm, then goes on. I haven't been doing much because I dream of walking all night long and I wonder if I have been sleepwalking . . . I don't remember whether there were stars last night. It was . . . as if someone had kicked me to the road. I was tired but I couldn't stop. Because I don't want to die. There have been bad signs. Another murder has been plotted against me — do you know anything about it? Do you? I have sensed it. I trust my instinct. It is by someone who calls him- or herself my comrade in arms, someone who knows my habits and secrets, someone who sees what I am doing now. Do you know that person?

He lets go of her arm and crashes back into his rattan chair.

She takes off her glasses, wipes the oozing sweat from her forehead. Then she puts the glasses back on. But they don't stay. They keep sliding down — there is moisture on her nose. She tries to hold the glasses with her fingers. Still they won't stay. Finally she decides to take them off.

You know, *Jia-zei-nan-fang — The house thief is the hardest to guard against.* I am sure you know what I am talking about, don't you?

Her eyes widen. Clearing her throat she responds, Dear Chairman, you have everyone's love in this nation. You have accomplished more than any human being on earth. You've captured and redefined our nation's rage and longing. You have given us the best example of the true spirit of a patriot. Your fellow countrymen idolize you the way they have never before —

Shut up! Mao springs up. Make sure *Huang-mu-niang-niang* — the Mother of Heaven — empties no chamber pot of her majesty's on my funeral day!

*

The night leaves smell like the breath of a child's mouth. Jiang Ching's mind goes back to the scene of the morning. She wonders if all is but a sleepwalking. As she passes the courtyard, she hears cats wail outside the deep walls and a loud sneeze comes out of a bush.

Leaning on his bed Mao doubts the safety of his pool. He calls the chief of the security force and asks if the pool is missile-proof. When the answer is uncertain, Mao orders the entire pool torn down. Turn it into an underground bomb shelter!

A team of doctors are summoned for Mao's sleeping disorder. Yet nothing they prescribe works. It worsens after the summer. Mao refuses to get out of bed, let alone brush, wash or dress. He is in his pajamas twenty-four hours a day. He grows more restless. He mistakes his secretary for an assassin and throws an ink bottle at him when he comes to deliver the news of American president Richard Nixon's visit.

Mao describes his symptom to a doctor. I hear drizzle. Day and night this ceaseless rain inside my head. It sweeps me away.

She can no longer wait. She wants to get Mao to write a will. She is sure that a stroke or a coma is on its way. She visualizes its coming. The flood that bursts the brain.

Mao doesn't want to see her. But she keeps presenting herself, making excuses to break into his bedroom.

He fires a guard who fails to stop her by the gate.

As the acting head of state she hosts and escorts the Nixons to her operas and ballets. It makes her feels proud and finally compensated. But in the meantime she feels danger approaching. She talks nervously and the translator has a hard time following her.

I don't feel my age although I am sixty years old. My strength gets exercised every day. Mao has failed to hide his ill health from the public's eye. In the hands of the best cameraman and film editor Mao's saliva drools helplessly in a documentary called *Greeting Imelda Marcos*. His eyelids drop low, his chin sags, and his mouth and jaw are out of place. Eighty-two years old. The sun can't help setting. What frustrates me is that he won't acknowledge his fate. He refuses to quit. He is not passing me the business. I tell myself that he is too old to think of me.

It's been too long a battle to give up now. A few years ago I asked Chun-qiao to draw up a proposal in the name of the Party's Committee of Shanghai and send it to Mao. Brilliantly, Chun-qiao described me as "the initiator of the Cultural Revolution" and "the key contributor of the Communist Party." *At the moment of crisis, Comrade Jiang Ching puts her personal welfare on the line. She leads the Party and the Revolution single-handedly. She fights against the toughest enemies such as Liu Shao-qi and Deng Xiao-ping. There isn't a better person than Comrade Jiang Ching to lead the nation and carry on the Mao Tse-tung flag.*

To my great disappointment, after three years of collecting dust on Mao's desk, the proposal is turned down. Not only that, Mao writes a nasty comment on its cover: *Discard*.

I am lying on the ground breathless. I don't even have the strength to kill myself. If Mao had proven to me that he was the king of Shang, I would copy Lady Yuji and knife myself gladly. And there would have been dignity. But it is too late. Everything is a mess.

Dawn is coming and I have not slept. I recall my youth. The first moment we laid eyes on each other. It still amazes me. The moment of pure magic. The happiness. The way he and I stood in front of the Yenan cave, unable to part.

Now I am a cornered and beaten-up dog. I bite in order to escape. The irony is that my character refuses to give up its idealism. My character tries to save my soul. It pushes me to live, to survive and to create light in hell. Every time I sit in the theater I see a fleeting ghost of myself. I hear my voice in the heroine. The way she conquers fear. I pray for the spirit to stay with me. And I am fine. Hope once again fills me. It keeps telling me that there will be life after Mao. When love exhales there will still be something for me to live for. It is myself. The image of Madame Mao. Mao's death will help define my role.

But the moment she walks out of the theater she is weak again. She feels strange about the way she talks and moves. The underdog is coming through her. She breathes the dirty air and smells the trash. The feeling is like discovering a rotting body with a swarm of flies on it at five o'clock in the morning by the shore of a beautiful spring river. There is nothing she can do to change the course of her fate. She is led.

The voice in which she speaks is not familiar. She presses on nevertheless. There is no map, and she doesn't know if she will ever find her way. She keeps walking. She has to tell Yu. I have survived rapids and now simply moving on has become the journey itself. She no longer makes requests to see Mao. She misses Nah, but leaves her alone. It's better not to be reminded of her failure as a mother. She is too fragile to bear any more loss. Every day she changes hotels, every day she wears the uniform and conducts battles of propaganda promoting herself. In November she launches a campaign for Chun-qiao as the premier. She waits for Mao's response. There is no move. She assumes that Mao is considering. She prays. She goes around the country and praises Chun-qiao like a cheerleader.

Personally she is not a fan of Chun-qiao. A man full of hatred. But she needs him. She needs a strong head. A man who is as powerful and determined as Mao. Chun-qiao is good at plotting. His character mirrors Kang Sheng's. Chun-qiao is an eloquent Communist theorist by trade. His works have greatly added to the flames of the Cultural Revolution. His ability to convince is incomparable. He and his disciple Yiao work well together. Like musicians, Chun-qiao sells melodies and Yiao sells arrangements. They have been working on *The Great Quotations of Comrade Jiang Ching.*

She can't say that she hasn't expected Mao's mind to change on her. But when the moment arrives, she finds herself unprepared.

July 17, 1974. Mao orders a meeting of the congress held at the Purple Light Pavilion.

Without warning he pronounces Deng Xiao-ping the new premier. Mao looks tired and uninterested. His cigarette drops from his fingers several times. He dismisses the meeting while tea is being served.

Before Jiang Ching has time to adjust to the first shock a second hits her. The day following Deng's promotion, Mao issues a public document criticizing Jiang Ching as the head of the Gang of Four. The press in Beijing immediately follows. Rumors turn into official news. Jiang Ching thought she had been in control of the media, thought that she had loyalists, but she is now proven foolish. She has no instinct for politics. She has been in it for the wrong reasons. It has always been the case. It was the way when she was with Yu Qiwei and Tang Nah. She was in it to get close to the man she loved but ended up losing herself. She doesn't know when Mao's joke about her being the head of the Gang of Four became an official criminal title.

# 22

ON OCTOBER 1, 1975, the National Independence Day, the Shanghai press led by *The Liberation News* releases a series of stories on Empress-turned-Emperor Wu of the Han dynasty, around A.D. 200. The reviews praise Wu's wisdom and strength and her success ruling China for half a century. Next to the stories are pictures of Madame Mao Jiang Ching. The pictures document her visits to factories, communes, schools and the military. She appears among the rugged-faced masses. Her expression is firm and her eyes look into the future with a glow. In Beijing the criticism of her continues. The following week the news of Premier Zhou's deteriorating condition in the hospital blankets the pages. A week later, Madame Mao Jiang Ching disappears from the papers and Deng Xiao-ping takes up the scene.

There is one important man the media has been neglecting. It is Kang Sheng. He is terminally ill and suffers from paranoia. In Mao's distance he senses Jiang Ching's downfall. He doesn't want to go down with her. He has played an ambiguous role between the Maos. Mao is not unaware that Kang Sheng has provided Jiang Ching with crucial information that helped her get where she is. To demonstrate his dismay Mao has stopped responding to Kang Sheng's letters and notes.

The man with the goat beard is scared. He has spent his life pleasing the emperor and is now facing dishonor and termination.

I have a terribly important message for you to pass on to the Chairman. From his sickbed Kang Sheng speaks to Mao's personal messengers, Mao's niece Wang Hai-rong, the vice minister of diplomacy, and Tang Wen-sheng, Mao's trusted translator. So many years I have withheld this information. I am near the end of my life and I feel that I owe the Party the truth: Jiang Ching and Chun-qiao are traitors. The record has been destroyed, but the truth remains.

The mouths of the two women hang open.

I would have visited the Chairman myself if he had wanted to hear me, Kang Sheng says in tears. It's just that there isn't much time for me to work for him anymore. He must realize my loyalty.

Kang Sheng shuts his eyes and lies back on his pillow. Now take out your notebooks and record carefully. I shall prove that I am good for the Chairman for the last time.

In a fading voice Kang Sheng produces the year, date, witnesses and the location of Madame Mao Jiang Ching's betrayal.

I disregard my opposition. Kang Sheng can't put me lower than I am. I am working to get closer to the stiffening Mao. He's got to open his jaw and spell my name to the nation. I will try everything. Whatever it takes. Thankfully I find a helper. He is Mao's nephew, Mao Yuan Xin. I let him know that his Aunt Jiang Ching is willing to adopt him as the prince of the kingdom. The man expresses his willingness, and he takes no time making himself trustworthy in his uncle's eyes. Now I don't have to fight the guards and will be able to send messages directly to Mao through Xin.

My enemies and I are racing against Mao's breath. I am no longer aware of the hours or days. I no longer have an appetite. My senses are focused on one thing: the movement of Mao's mouth.

Although I have convinced myself that his love for me is long dead, I still wish for a miracle. I've asked Xin to wait by his uncle around the clock with a tape recorder and a camera. I am waiting for Mao's sudden recollection of his prime. There he might see me again and remember to honor this love. I need this now desperately. I need his finger touch. His phrase "Jiang Ching represents me" will settle everything. *A dragon's one movement covers a sea-horse's ten years traveling.* It will save and heal me. I have been even thinking about an alternative. With Mao's words I might retire. I am over sixty. Looking into the future is no longer my biggest interest. Honor, however, I must not live without. I am Jiang Ching, the love of Mao's life.

But he won't do it for me. He will not pronounce my name again. His silence has become the permission for others to force me to vanish; to murder me in cold blood. No matter how hard I try to paint black pink, the truth speaks loudly for itself. Mao is determined to carry on his betrayal. He wants to punish me for being who I am. He wants to blame me for his mistress Shang-guan Yun-zhu's death. He has marked me his enemy.

Then why bother to order a graveyard built for both of us at Ba-bo Hill Funeral Home? Why lie next to me instead of Zi-zhen or Kai-hui? Or Shang-guan Yun-zhu? I will never want to record again the way you used to love me. My eyes hurt from crying for your warmth at night. Why don't you lie by yourself after all this hatred for me?

In the thickening snow of January 1976, Premier Zhou passes away. He had played against the political stream by appearing slow and foolish, blind and deaf. So many times he offered toasts to the demons. However, he is remembered as the people's premier. To Madame Mao's disappointment, the nation disregards

Mao's order to downplay the ceremony and mourns Zhou. White wreaths cover Tiananmen Square. To the sick Mao this shows obvious resentment. He suspects that Zhou's friend, the newly promoted Premier Deng Xiao-ping, is plotting a betrayal.

In muttered and half-swallowed words, Mao orders the removal of Deng Xiao-ping. The order is carried out immediately. The nation is confused.

Madame Mao Jiang Ching loses no time. She takes advantage of the situation and comes hopping onto the scene. In Mao's name she promotes her future cabinet members: Chun-qiao as the premier, his disciple Yiao as the vice premier, Wang as the minister of national defense and Yu as the minister of culture and arts.

Yu wants me to understand his suffering. He is withering like overheated summer grass. He is terrified by the new title. But I refuse to let him off the hook. We are standing face to face in my office having an argument. I push the window open to let in the cold air. I am frustrated and upset. The sky is a sapphire blue sheet with clawmark-like clouds pulling through it. I shall stand behind you, I promise. You can be a figurehead boss. Your assistants will sweep up the dust after you. So what if you are an artist? You are expected to do things differently. A great genius is supposed to have horns, I have already told everyone. People will understand.

He growls, mutters and begs.

My voice turns tender. A rainbow is forming in front of you, Yu. All you have to do is open your eyes.

He wipes his moist forehead with his sleeve and his lips begin to stretch. I . . . can't do it. I am —

Don't tell me about your fear. We have brought in the ship! Yu Hui-yong, the ship is in! Come on, get on deck!

She goes on, her gestures animated, arms shooting out and waving back and forth in the air. One more blow, the fruit of victory will fall into our hands!

Yu ceases struggling.

Madame Mao sits down, sinks into the sofa.

Other cabinet members stare at them.

Yu goes to the windowsill and picks up a flower pot. He gently loosens its soil with his finger. It is a wild kind, he suddenly says. The leaves drape around like a crown. The stems will bear little white flowers. He turns the plant toward the sunlight. I love to watch the way plants lift their leaves and the way they deepen their green. I really do.

Madame Mao stands erect like the statue of Lenin on Red Square in Moscow. There is no sentimentality in her voice. The bottom line is that I will allow no betrayal. You are my man. She pauses to restrain herself but tears suddenly pour. If you have to make me beg, I am on my knees now. I beg you to stop insulting me . . . I am not cold and without feeling by nature . . . I have chosen love before. But it didn't bring meaning to life. I have lost the soul of an artist . . . It is my ill fate. One can cure illness, but not fate. The battle I fight is inevitable. My heart is breaking . . . Let me remind you, all of you, that there is no way out now. We are all in it together and we are soldiers. So let's run toward where the fire is.

September 9, 1976. The history of China turns a page. At the age of eighty-three, Mao Tse-tung exhales his last breath. Upon learning the news from Xin, Jiang Ching forces her way into the Chrysanthemum-Fragrance Study. She sorts through Mao's letters and documents looking for a will. But there is none. Turning around, she orders a Politburo meeting at the Purple Light Pavilion. She wants to announce the Chairman's death personally.

No one else comes but her cabinet members. She checks with her secretary on what's going on and is told that a new figure, a man named Hua Guo-feng, a provincial secretary and Mao's hometown boy, has taken over. He is planning to speak to her — Mao has left a will appointing him as his successor.

Ridiculous! Absolutely ridiculous! She catches her own echo in the empty hall.

The palace is quiet. The day is windless. Mao's body lies at the Hunan Quarter of the Grand Hall of the People. He is straighter than when he was breathing. His ear-long hair has been combed to the back of his skull. The features look peaceful. There isn't a trace of pain. The arms are folded by the thighs. The gray jacket is starched. The body is covered from the chest down by a red flag with the yellow cross of a sickle and hammer.

Liar! Madame Mao Jiang Ching beats the table with her fists. The Chairman never left any will.

The handwriting style is definitely Mao's, the secretary mutters. It was confirmed by an archaeologist and calligrapher who specialized in *xing-shu*.

Madame Mao stares at the writing, halting her breath.

It is the funeral of the century. Tiananmen Square is flooded with white paper flowers. On top of the Gate of Heavenly Peace, Madame Mao stands behind Hua Guo-feng, who gives the nation the memorial speech. Dressed in a full black suit Madame Mao's head is covered with a black satin scarf. She can hardly bear sharing the same platform with her enemy.

The crystal casket is large. Mao's cheeks are painted thick with powder. His lips are unnaturally red. The corners of the mouth have been artificially pushed and lifted to form a smile. The body lies like a hill slope — from the chest drops a sudden curve — the emptied intestines make his belly looks like a hollow plain. The head looks enormous.

Madame Mao stands three feet from the casket shaking hands with strangers foreign and domestic. She has been doing this for two hours now. Her neck is stiff and her wrist sore. Pale and nervous she holds a white silk handkerchief and uses it to touch her cheeks now and then. She can't even fake tears. She keeps thinking of what Mao had said to her. *You will be pushed and nailed into my casket.*

Nah has been sobbing hard next to her mother.
    My sky has fallen.
    Half sky, Nah.
    No, the whole sky.
    You are truly a good-for-nothing.

The new head of China, Hua, has the face of an old lizard. His eyelids close halfway over his pupils giving him a sleepy expression. His gray suit copies Mao's. He stands stiffly, a frozen smile on his face. When Madame Mao questions the will, he takes a scroll out of his chest pocket and shows the familiar handwriting, which reads, *For Comrade Hua Guo-feng. With you in charge I am at rest.*

    She laughs hysterically, turns away and walks toward the door, shouting, I have the real version of Mao's will. Mao put it, himself personally, into my very ear. She runs into the seventy-nine-year-old Marshal Ye Jian-ying, who is on his way in to pay his respects to Mao.

    How can you witness this and do nothing, Marshal? she cries.

    The marshal walks past her and pays no attention.

    The Chairman's body has not turned cold and you are all plotting a coup d'état!

    Comrade Jiang Ching! Marshal Ye Jian-ying wails, my life will leave me no more than ten years to live. But I am willing to abandon this ten years in order to do this country right.

❀

Early morning, October 5, 1976. A strong wind beats the leaves into the air. Overnight the green in the imperial garden turns yellow. The bare trunks point toward the sky like spikes. In the Hall of Fishermen's Port Madame Mao Jiang Ching hosts a farewell party.

The torch-shaped bronze lamps flare brightly throughout the hall. The hour has passed midnight. Madame Mao entertains the guests with a lavish dinner and her opera film in progress. After the showing the lights come back and the host stands up. In a long, elegant blue dress, she toasts everyone's health and luck. There is nervousness hidden under the smiling mask. She calms herself by cracking jokes. Yet no one is laughing.

The guests are her loyalists from all fields. Among them the famous opera singers. You know what Empress Wu's birthday cake was made of? As if on a stage, Madame Mao speaks. She then answers herself. It was made of dirt, seeds and weeds. Why? It is nutritious!

A few laughs come from the audience. The monologue continues. Subjects change in a disconnected fashion. One moment, Madame Mao criticizes the relationship between the eunuch Li Lian-ying and the empress dowager. At another moment she describes a handmade loom she used in Yenan.

The threads broke for no reason, she laughs. I thought to myself, What an armchair revolutionary am I if I can't conquer a stupid loom! So I stayed up all night until I made it work. Yes, that's me. Stubborn as a mule. Well, enough jokes. I am anxious, as you all can tell. What were we talking about? Yes, we are talking about devotion, at the price of death. Yes, it is not a light subject.

After a moment of silence she carries on. It's my fate either to be the queen or the prisoner. Mao has left me to find out the ending myself. It is his way of teaching. As I have said he hated to be figured out. As an actress, I play the moment. The army is out of my hands. It's my biggest concern. When the Chairman was alive, they dared not touch me. Now they can do anything. Hua Guo-feng is no threat to me. The threat is the old boys. Ye Jian-ying and Deng Xiao-ping. I once had a conversation with Mao on the subject. I said that I might be born to play a tragic character. The Chairman responded with humor and said that it was a fascinating comment.

Is it? She looks around the room. Imagine me being caught and slaughtered tomorrow. Take a good look at me. I am standing still. What concerns me is you, your life and your family. Every one of you. They will come after you. They might not kill you but will make you suffer. There is a price to pay for being my follower. What am I going to say? What am I going to say to your children? Am I a worthy cause? . . . She lowers her head and her tears stream down. What can I do to protect you?

The audience responds with sobs. The opera singer Hao Liang, the lead in *The Legend of the Red Lantern*, comes forward. Men of courage, he shouts. Let's go to the Politburo, go to where people can hear us, the radio stations, the stages, the newsrooms. Let's voice our deepest wish and petition for Comrade Jiang Ching to be the chairman of the Communist Party and the president of China! Let's make the difference with action. I am sure people will follow us.

The room echoes in one voice. Oaths of loyalty follow. One guest takes out a white handkerchief. He bites his middle finger and writes a line with his blood: *Comrade Jiang Ching for the chairman or my brains painted on the Great Wall.*

It is a great moment in my life. October 5 in the Hall of Fishermen's Port. The grand passion demonstrated by the great actors. The magic of a stage. Reality is forgotten.

Through my hot tears I see Chun-qiao and his disciple walk into the hall. They call off the party with an emergency message — my enemy has begun their action. Despite Chun-qiao's panic, I take time to say good-bye personally to everyone. I have a feeling that this is the last time.

Hao Liang, I say to the actor, I'd like to thank you for the good work you have done for the film. In the future the films will speak for us. You have brightened my life. Days and nights we have sweated to get the excellence on film. The memory is our gift to each other. I can't offer you enough. But my heart will stay close to you through heaven or hell. The hero you played on stage died in the enemy's hands. Remember me and yourself that way.

At dawn, I call Chun-qiao to touch base. He reports that there have been frequent visits between the old boys and military heads. I ask him to come to my place immediately. Half an hour later he arrives.

Have you spoken with my friends Commander Wu and Commander Chen? I ask. I have cultivated a good relationship with them and they have promised to support me.

You are a fool to think that they will honor the promise they made when Mao was alive. I've checked with them and they don't return my calls.

I am beginning to feel the weight of the sky.

Forget about the army. Chun-qiao grinds his teeth. We have to depend on our own force.

The armed workers in Shanghai?

Yes. But we are short of time.

How long does it take to prepare a takeover? I grab Chun-qiao's hands. We must seize the old boys before they seize us.

At least a few days.

Act now, the ax is dropping! I'm going to Shanghai!

Please, Comrade Jiang Ching, for your safety and health, leave the matter to us.

I don't trust you! she screams. Your pessimistic view disturbs me! The show should be played the other way around, and the characters should be reversed! We are the ones who are holding the ax!

The advancing orders have already been placed. We must leave our faith to Buddha. We must trust . . . the people. Chun-qiao's voice suddenly loses its energy.

She wills herself on. She tells her secretary that she is going to Jing Hill Park in the afternoon. Get my photographer. Tell him that I'll be at the Quarters of the Apple Trees.

It is a cloudy day. Perfect for pictures. The sky is a natural gauze which helps to even out the light. The park was originally built for emperors of the Sung dynasty. Six hundred years ago Emperor Jing hanged himself here after he had lost his country. I climb to the top of the hill without stopping. Under my eyes is the complete view of the grand imperial city.

The photographer doesn't like the apple trees as the background for my picture. He says that the fruit-laden trees are too distracting. He thinks that I should be by the peonies. But Apple, *Ping*, used to be my name, I tell him. It connects me to my past. Eternity attracts me today because I smell death. This shot is either going to be my mug shot or the one that replaces Mao on the Gate of Heavenly Peace.

Finally the photographer settles down. He pulls my chair away from the trees as far as he can so the apples will be out of focus. Now he is having trouble with my Mao jacket. I have changed my costume during his battle with the apples. He likes me in the dress better but I insist on looking like a soldier. I'd like to be in these clothes when I die. It is to remind people that I have fought like a man.

The photographer screws his eye into the lens. He asks me to smile. He doesn't want to take pictures of death. But I can't get myself to smile. This morning I saw my face in the mirror. My jaw is shallow and my eyes are blank. I haven't been able to sleep much. The sleeping pills don't work.

The sound of clicking continues. Seven rolls. Finally there is one shot he likes. Which one? The one when you kind of drifted off. Did your mind travel far, Madame? There was this gaze, dreamlike. It brought out the young woman in you. The woman I recognize from the picture of you and the Chairman standing side by side in front of the cave in Yenan.

Oh, that was my favorite.

I studied the image when I was a photography student. I'm glad I have caught the heroine in you again. Your expression moved me. I shall develop the negatives and send you the prints in a few days. You'll know what I am talking about here. It is the best picture I have ever taken.

The negative never makes it to the positive.

October 5, 1976. The war room of the China military headquarters is packed with marshals and generals. With a picture of Mao hanging above the map, action begins. Around the table sits Commander in Chief Marshal Ye Jian-ying. Next to him is Hua Guofeng, Vice Premier Li Xian-nian, Chen Xi-lian, plus the newly promoted 8341 Garrison head, Wang Dong-xin.

A phone ring breaks the silence. Wang picks up the receiver. After a few seconds he reports. The enemy has made a move. Navy intelligence by the East China Sea has found out that the Shanghai Jiang-nan ship factory has turned two ships into armed vessels. The workers' force have built a defense around the entire bay. A moment ago they came to claim the army's Wu-song artillery base.

The members in the war room sit back in their seats. The only thing that troubles their minds is the consequence of destroying Madame Mao only twenty-seven days after Mao's death. Will the nation agree with the action? Could it backfire?

*

October 6. Hua Guo-feng calls Jiang Ching to meet at the Hall of Mercy in the evening. Jiang Ching's secretary, Little Moon, asks the reason for the meeting.

The publication of the late Chairman's fifth volume of works. The reply is smooth.

Comrade Jiang Ching will be absent. Little Moon's voice is gentle but clear. Sure, I'll get the message to her as soon as possible.

Madame Mao Jiang Ching appears by the door. She is in a suit with a sand-colored scarf around her neck. My sixty-third birthday is coming, she utters. I've never celebrated my birthdays. There hasn't been much to celebrate. But my life is changing and the people will begin to celebrate my birthday. I trust their judgment.

*Like a weed she breaks through the sidewalks.* She extends her arms far out and begins to sing like her opera heroine. *Cracks the patio pavement, and she will pierce the most desolate corner to find air and light!*

Evening wraps the room. Little Moon sits by the phone.

Still no answer from Chun-qiao's office? Madame Mao asks.

No.

What about Yao?

No answer either. By the way, Madame, we have also lost touch with Wang.

There is a sudden collision of thoughts in which fear realizes itself. Madame Mao feels the gradual stifling of her breathing. Pictures pass through her head like a movie, which later proves to match what really happened.

The first shot is the clock hanging on the wall of the Hall of Mercy. The time is seven fifty-five in the evening. At the hall's entrance Chun-qiao enters with quick steps. He is in a Mao jacket and looks small and thin as if in a wide-angle lens. Suddenly behind him two guards appear. They hop on his back and press him to the floor. His glasses are taken off. There is no struggle and he is taken away. The time is eight-fifteen.

The set changes. It is now the Hall of the East Wing. Disciple Yao enters. Two guards come out and block his way. He looks around and falls on his knees. Then comes Wang Hong-wen. When Wang sees the guards approaching he turns around to run but doesn't make it to the gate. He puts up a fight but is tied up eventually.

One guard walks toward the camera. There is elation on his face. He stretches out his arm and turns the camera off.

No one is picking up her calls for help. No one is at home. Everybody has "hospitalized" themselves in order to avoid her.

Suddenly she is attacked by a feeling of worthlessness. Her childhood memories rush back to her. The face of her father. The tears of her mother. Pain surfaces. Terror. The water rises, and now is throat deep. She hears her father's yell. Give it up!

Why is it so quiet here? Why are you, Little Moon, looking at me like a wakening soul? Was my guess right? Have the wolves finally infested my land? Stop it! Stop trembling like a coward! . . . There is . . . nothing I can do, I suppose. The military has always been my weak point. The Chairman didn't leave me enough time to manage the warlords. The warlords . . . maybe . . . I cannot say that the trap was not set by Mao himself . . . Come here, Little Moon.

Little Moon rises. Her stick-thin body is stiff and her eyes dwell freezingly.

Come, girl, and sit down by me. Let's chat. Cheer me up. Let me tell you stories of my life. Because in a few minutes it will be a different story. I will be called the White-Boned Demon. Come on, Little Moon, unzip your pursed mouth. It doesn't look attractive when you clench your jaw tight. You are a pretty girl. Why don't you let me fix your eyebrows? Bring me the little scissors. I have to do it now or never. No? What's wrong? Don't stare at me as if you have just swallowed a spoiled egg. Come on, courage!

Little Moon twists her mouth and breathes unevenly.

I'm getting bored listening to the sound of my own voice. Where are the wolves?

Quietly she eats her last meal as Madame Mao. Little Moon is ordered to join her. But the young woman can't make herself eat. She unshells clams with her chopsticks and puts the meat onto Jiang Ching's small side plate.

Thank you. I appreciate your loyalty and I wish you were Nah. It's a mother's foolishness. It seems now . . . that she was not unwise . . . Ninxia Desert she has escaped . . . The realm of laxity . . . Anyway, this is to cap my life. It's time to be a martyr, to stick a chopstick into my throat — I am preparing myself. A good actress can handle any scene . . . Where is Yu Hui-yong? I need to hear my operas. Yu is a born coward. It wouldn't surprise me if he ends up killing himself. He is too delicate and lives with feelings and fear. That is an artist's problem. We are artists. That is why Yu will kill himself. So would I, I am afraid. Why am I talking about this? Why am I talking about being an artist? Yu's music makes me cry. I already miss him. Chun-qiao is the toughest among us, and that is his luck.

> The sound of her silk skirt has stopped
> On the marble pavement dust grows
> Her empty room is cold and still
> Fallen leaves are piled against the doormat

Midnight, October 6. The Garden of Stillness. Along the deep walls come noises. The sound of steps rises behind the gates. Whispers. Someone is talking with the guard. Yes, sir, the guard answers. A tall shadow approaches. A man leaps. It is Zhang

Yiao-ci, the second in command of the 8341. The sound of the gate clashes and locks behind. Zhang Yiao-ci freezes at the entrance. After a moment he advances and enters the mansion. He pounds on the door. His fingers tremble.

It's open, the first lady's voice comes.

Zhang Yiao-ci lunges in. His right hand rests on top of the weapon behind his back.

Madame Mao Jiang Ching sits on the sofa, holding a mug of tea. Her calm freezes the man.

The man looks around. Sweat oozing.

A long-legged bird from the painting on the wall stares down.

Madame Mao speaks, then laughs shrilly. I have long anticipated this day! I have spread flowers all the way from my bedroom to the gate.

The man gasps and wills himself to push the syllables out of his mouth: Jiang Ching, the republic's enemy, the Politburo has ordered your arrest.

When the imaginary curtain comes up the actress presses herself forward. She envisions the billion-large audience cheering at the top of their lungs and waving flags. An ocean of red. The color sears her eyes. She smells the warm sun. In the music of her opera she strides. In her head, the drums and trumpets come together. She remembers once how Yu described his feelings when composing on her order: it is the sound of hundreds of train engines puffing smoke and churning their pistons. The notes tighten and twist to the point of breaking. It is as if the composer were choked by the claws of the madness and took each note separately off of his mind's hook and threw them all together into a giant bucket and began to stir.

Then there is a pause. She can hear Yu's sob. It is followed by a silence so complete that she hears the crack of time. A shooting star falls.

Once again, she sees her life as a film. And once again she is a young woman standing on top of a roof overlooking the city of Shanghai and dreaming of her future. She sees the gingko-nut boy and hears his selling drill: *Xiang-u-xiang-lai-nu-u-nu!* The boy's tone is smooth and mindless. Still clear. The midnight wind sweeps through the long dark lane. The boy squats in front of his wok holding an armful of firelight.

She sees herself in the cell of Qin-Cheng national prison where Vice Chairman Liu's wife, Wang Guang-mei, spends a dozen years before her. Madame Mao sits facing the wall. She is ordered to make dolls for export. She has to meet the daily production objective. The dolls will be sold in children's stores all over the world. She sews tiny colorful dresses onto the tiny plastic bodies. Tens, hundreds and thousands of dolls between 1976 and 1991. She embroiders spring on the dresses, draws flowers from her imagination. When guards are not watching, she secretly embroiders her name, *Jiang Ching,* onto the inner edges of the dresses. And then she is found out and is stopped. Nevertheless, it is too late to retrieve the ones that had already been shipped. Baskets of dolls, with her signature. Out of China and into the world. Where would they land? In a child's forgotten bin? Or a display window?

It is time to empty the stage. Remember, you will always come across me in the books about China. Don't be surprised to see my name smeared. There is nothing more they can do to me. And don't forget that I was an actress, a great actress. I acted with passion. For those who are fascinated by me you owe me applause, and for those who are disgusted you may spit.

I thank you all for coming.

# Acknowledgments

Thank you,

Sandra Dijkstra, my agent, for having the great strength to strike through the troubled river. Five years to reach the shore. *Madame Mao* is to you.

Anton Mueller, my editor, for having the talent, patience and skill to find out who I am as a writer and show the way to bring out the best in me.

Michele Dremmer, again, for your affection.

# References

Lin Qing-shan, *The Red Demon*, Century Literature, China 1997

Dai Jia-fang, *Time of the Revolutionary Operas,* Knowledge Publishing, China 1995

*Biography of Mao Tse-tung*, China Institute of the Communist Party, 1996

*The Myth of History,* South Sea Publishing, China 1997

*Behind the Important Decisions,* South Sea Publishing, China 1997

Peng Jin-Kui, *My Uncle Peng De-huai*, China Publishing, 1997

Zhang Yin, *Record of Jiang Ching and Roxane Witke Conversation,* Century Literature, China 1997

*The National Famous Figures,* South Sea Publishing, China 1997

*The Tendency of the High Court,* South Sea Publishing, China 1996

Jing Fu-zi, *Romance of the Zhong-nai-hai Lake,* Lian-Jing Publishing, Taiwan

Jing Fu-zi, *Mao and His Women,* Lian-Jing Publishing, Taiwan

*Lives of the True Revolutionaries,* South Sea Publishing, China 1996

Ross Terrill, *The White-Boned Demon,* William Morrow, 1984

Ross Terrill, *Mao — A Biography,* Harper and Row, 1980

Roxane Witke, *Comrade Chiang Ch'ing,* Little, Brown, 1977

Yao Ming-le, *The Conspiracy and Death of Lin Biao,* Alfred A. Knopf, 1983

Edgar Snow, *The Long Revolution,* Random House, 1972

Dr. Li Zhi-Sui, *The Private Life of Chairman Mao,* Random House, 1994

Zhao Qing, *My Father Zhao Dan,* China Publishing, 1997